Théophile Gautier, Eugène de Mirecourt

Famous French Authors

Biographical Portraits of Distinguished French Writers

Théophile Gautier, Eugène de Mirecourt

Famous French Authors
Biographical Portraits of Distinguished French Writers

ISBN/EAN: 9783744695374

Printed in Europe, USA, Canada, Australia, Japan

Cover: Foto ©Raphael Reischuk / pixelio.de

More available books at **www.hansebooks.com**

FAMOUS

FRENCH AUTHORS

BIOGRAPHICAL PORTRAITS

OF

DISTINGUISHED FRENCH WRITERS

BY

THEOPHILE GAUTIER

EUGENE DE MIRECOURT

ETC., ETC.

Illustrated

NEW YORK

R. WORTHINGTON, 750 BROADWAY

1879

CONTENTS.

THEOPHILE GAUTIER

LIFE PORTRAITS OF FAMOUS

FRENCH AUTHORS.

THÉOPHILE GAUTIER.*

I.

THÉOPHILE GAUTIER was born at Tarbes, August 31st, 1811. When three years old, he went to live in Paris, we might say he returned there, so much is he a part of Paris. He writes of himself, " I learned to read at the age of five years, and after that time, I could say with Apelles, *Nulla dies sine linea*. He took his first lessons at the college of Louis le Grand, and ended them as day-pupil at Charlemagne. His father, a very good linguist, assisted him in Latin ; but the boy's taste was not for the purely classic authors. Livy and Cicero wearied. him ; Martial, and Catullus, Apuleius and Petronius, were his delight. So dear to him were these writers of the decadence, that he sought to imitate them in all varieties of metre.

Scarce had he left school when he began to draw and

---

* Nouveaux Lundis.—Sainte-Beuve.

to write verses. His first poem was an imitation of Hero and Leander; he also undertook in heroic verse, a poem upon the abduction of Helen. He had written two and a half cantos, when his taste having in some degree ripened, he threw the verses into the fire. He then turned his attention to Brantôme, to Rabelais, and various other French authors.

In his last college year, he gave up his morning recitation to take lessons of Rioult, a painter of Prudhon's school who had won considerable reputation by two or three fine pictures.

Gautier was then living with his parents at Place Royale, No. 8. Two or three years later, Victor Hugo took up his abode at No. 6. He and Gautier met for the first time in 1830, and the ardent, impulsive student was easily induced to join the *Hernani*, that clique of robust, brilliant young men, renowned in all sorts of athletic exercises, and as romancists, waging a war against the classic school, fierce as any contest Guelph ever waged against Ghibeline. Victor Hugo was chosen leader of this band, and never was god adored with more fervor.

It was as painter and art-pupil, and not as literary man, that Gautier then figured; he was hesitating between the two careers. In July 1830, he published a small collection of verses, "Poems by Théophile Gautier" was its title, and its motto : *Oh ! si je puis un jour !* Thus in the new poetic school, he ranks in date immediately after Alfred de Musset. Gautier was then not quite nineteen years old.

This little volume has a nameless charm. Here the poet appears "under a blonde aureole of adolescence," which he did not long retain. The collection thus opens with a sigh and a regret :

Virginité du cœur, hélas si tôt ravie !
Songes riants, projets de bonheur et d'amour,
Fraîches illusions du matin de la vie,
Pourquoi ne pas durer jusqu'à la fin du jour ? *

And then come childish loves, sweet, smiling land-scapes, roads winding through sunny valleys, a path along the hedge and the brook-side, leading directly to the little park gate to which attaches a tender remembrance. There are steeples pointing to heaven as in Wordsworth, and cathedral towers, and Gothic silhou ettes, their stony lattice-work outlined against the glow of the setting sun. All is in its infancy, but even in the whiteness of this dawn, the treatment is pure, clear, and unhesitating, the verse perfect in form and rhythm.

A second edition of Gautier's poems, which appeared in 1830, bore the title, "Albertus, a Theological Legend," being named for the principal poem. Here we find that Théophile Gautier has become a master, and the question constantly recurs: why, although his poetry is equal to Musset's, was his success so long confined to a narrow circle of artists and connoisseurs? The French public, it would seem, can tolerate but one poet at a time.

Flitting between the studio and the literary *Cénacle*, Gautier for some time pursued the two arts with equal ardor, and even when he abandoned painting, the divorce did not remain entire; he still painted with his pen. His "Young France," published in 1833, is a sort of album of fashions, costumes and travesties of that day.

About this time he went to lodge with some friends in the blind-alley of Doyenné, that relic of old Paris, that lost, forgotten islet in a corner of the Place de Carrousel, which ere long become the head-quarters of

---

* Virginity of the heart so soon ravished! Laughing dreams, projects of happiness and of love, fresh illusions of life's morning, why do ye not endure to the end of the day ?

"Young France." In this world of aspiring artists and literary men, it was the fashion to put on ferocious airs, to feel it almost dishonor to be moved at anything. Its device might have been those oft-quoted words of Terence slightly varied ; " I am a man, and consequently I interest myself in nothing human."

Here politics were spit upon as vulgar and degrading ; here Fancy, muse of art, was held in highest honor, and when one of the members withdrew from this society so perfectly harmless in its furies, to enter the real outside life of violence, conspiracy and hatred, what sweet, amiable verses Théophile Gautier would address to him, calling him back to nature and its twin sister, art !

Mademoiselle de Maupin may be considered Théophile Gautier's first prose work. He devoted two years to its composition, and it appeared in 1836. It is a book striking both in plot and execution, the work of an artist and a poet, but it cannot be recommended to young lady readers. Every physician of the soul, every moralist, should keep a copy of it on a back shelf of his library.

"The Comedy of Death," which appeared in 1838, shows a deeper and truer development in our artist and poet. This poem is a series of mournful evocations after a walk to the cemetery on All Souls' Day. Raphael Faust, Don Juan, Napoleon himself, appear by turns, before the eyes of our poet, who demands from them their secret of life and death. But none of these great ones who has come back to him, knows the secret : each sends him to the other.

Faust says ; " Love, and you will do far better than to study." Don Juan says : " Interrogate science, learn, learn ! You have more opportunity on this side than on mine." Finally, the great Emperor, having pressed the globe in his hand and found it hollow, begins to envy the tattered goat-herd of his native isle. Ever in the midst of feasts, amid the intoxications of worldly pleasure, Death suddenly appears before the poet's eyes ; not the death of the ancients, crowned with flowers and bringing a surcease of care and sorrow, but Death with ghastly visage and ferocious sneer, leaving in your heart an apprehension like that of Hamlet, that the funereal night may not be a long slumber, but a dream, and that all may not end with life.

II.

The poet in Théophile Gautier was now ripened and complete ; at first, he had possessed the instrument, he had now gone to the depths of his inspiration, he had made the grand tour. His first journey to Spain, in 1840, had furnished him with new notes of rich and ardent tone, with fresh images and symbols ; henceforth, he would know how to apply all the colors of his pallet. His collection of poems given to the world in 1845, is a full, harmonious work. The poet here has realized his artistic dream. In one of his most beautiful pieces, " The Triumph of Petrarch," he gives us his secret, his method of procedure, which he religiously puts in practice. Addressing himself to the initiated, to poets, he says :—

> Sur l'autel idéal entretenez la flamme,
> Comme un vase d'albatre où l'on cache un flambeau,
> Mettez l'idée au fond de la forme sculptée
> Et d'une lampe ardente éclairez le tombeau.*

Is he in love, does he suffer? Instead of complaining,

---

* " Maintain the flame upon the ideal altar,
As an alabaster vase where we conceal a torch,
Place the idea at the depths of the sculptured form,
And light the tomb with a glowing lamp."

of bursting out into tears and sobs, which are unworthy of him and of his creed that the poet must not moan in public, he restrains himself, he has recourse to some image as to a veil, he throws a transparent and fanciful envelope over the naked sentiment; he knows how to symbolize an unhappy passion under a just and ingenious emblem.

In turning over the pages of Gautier's poems, we are more and more astonished that it is not as a poet he has won his highest renown. Is France exclusive in poetry as in religion? M. de Narbonne, conversing with Napoleon, who had proposed the formation of a national church, said, " There is not religion enough in France to create two churches." Can it be that there is not poetry enough in France to admit of more than one poet at a time?

The bard who has won his first laurels, finds it hard to remain solely a poet in these days. Prose smiles upon him from all sides, under all enticing forms, and finally he yields to her temptations. Balzac having read Mademoiselle de Maupin, hastened to engage the services of its author on the *Chronique de Paris*. To this journal Gautier contributed some romances and some critical articles. He wrote also for the evening journal, *La Charte*, and for *Figaro*, to which he contributed the " Romance of Fortunio," and other fantastic articles. In 1837, he entered *La Presse*, where he remained domiciled for many years. Here he became one of that brilliant galaxy of writers M. Emile de Girardin rallied around him, Madame de Girardin herself wielding the first and most valiant lance. Gautier's twofold career of art and dramatic critic began regularly for the *La Presse*, and was never interrupted until the close of his life. In 1855, he became one of the editorial staff of the *Moniteur*.

His first critical essays in *La Presse* were some articles on the paintings of Eugene Delacroix. Soon after he applied himself to theatrical criticism also. In Gautier, we see a poet, that is, a being accustomed to cultivate art and to cherish an ideal, suddenly thrown upon his own resources, and forced to take up the trade of critic for a livelihood. The critiques of artists and poets are no doubt animated, clairvoyant, thorough above all, but they must naturally be incisive and exclusive. In reading Théophile Gautier's criticisms on dramatic art, we can but admire his graceful acquittal of his task, his mastery of difficulties, his winning a half triumph for his tastes without always sacrificing them. He has been reproached as critic with a sovereign indulgence and indifference. He has, in fact, with years acquired an excess of leniency; the Gautier of the *Moniteur* is not quite he of *La Presse*, but though lenient he is not indifferent. He knows how to mark and make perceptible his shades of liking and disliking. When forced to praise what he loves least, he delicately lowers the tone, and places a damper on the praise. The trade of criticism has its secrets.

In an article upon Casimir Delavigne, Gautier says: " In the world of art there stands always below each genius, a man of talent, preferred to him. Genius is uncultivated, violent, tempestuous; it seeks only to satisfy itself, and cares more for the future than the present. The man of talent is spruce, well-dressed, charming, accessible to all; he takes every day the measure of the public and makes garments suited to its stature, while the poet forges gigantic armors which the Titans alone can wear. Under Delacroix you have Delaroche; under Rossini, Donizetti; under Victor Hugo, M. Casimir Delavigne!"

III.

In 1840, Gautier made his first visit to Spain. Up to this time he had travelled but little, having left France only for a tour through Belgium and Holland. The Théophile Gautier of these first poems is represented to us as a young man very sensitive to cold, and keeping closely at home, "living in the chimney corner with two or three friends and as many cats." That journey to Spain made another man of him. To quote his own words, "The soul has its native country as well as the body." Upon setting foot in Spain, he at once recognized his true country. Here his talent discovered an ample field for pictures, and from his first day in this enchanted land, he became the accomplished word-painter we know.

In word-painting lies Théophile Gautier's true literary conquest. The great trouble of the man of letters has been not knowing how to name things. Says Bernardin de Saint-Pierre, "The art of rendering nature is so new that not even the terms have been invented." In this regard Gautier has shown himself an exception to the general rule. He is never more at his ease than when placed face to face with natural scenery or art-objects to be developed and exhibited. His talent seems created expressly for describing places, cities, monuments, pictures, diverse skies and landscapes. His is not one of those talents which reserve themselves for display on two or three great occasions, which prepare themselves in advance, and which, the grand site once described, the grand piece executed, unbend and rest. He has a mood habitually picturesque, facile, continuous; he must inevitably see and depict all. In reading his book upon Spain, from the moment you enter that country with

him by the Bidassoa bridge, to that when you embark
at Valencia, all is painted, unrolled before your glance.
Henrich Heine, the railer, meeting Gautier at one of
Liszt's concerts on the eve of his departure, said to him,
"How will you manage to describe Spain when you
have been there?" Gautier's method was very simple.
Having seen Spain for himself, he made his readers see
it as he did. His recital forms a *bas relief*, a continuous
panorama where all is a picture. At the decisive
moment when Gautier enters Andalusia, he receives
that sunstroke which bronzes him; with an amorous
transport, he salutes that Spain warmed by breezes from
the near Afric shore, until now, his vague chimera and
his dream.

Most fascinating of all places to him is Granada with
its marvels, the Alhambra and the Generalife. He did
not content himself with haunting the palaces and
Moorish antiquities, which were his first and sovereign
passion; he saw the Moorish society, going almost every
night to the Tertulia, and mingling familiarly with the
beautiful young girls and laughing children. Some of
his finest sentiments he leaves out of the recital, to
enclose them in the sculptured form of verse. Such
sentiments we find in his pretty poem upon the Three
Graces of Granada, and in other stanzas worthy to be
set to music by Mozart.

Théophile Gautier owed to Granada and to its enchanted sky, hours of melancholy—a serene melancholy
very different from that of the North. The plastic poet
while thus giving a fête to his eyes, conjuring them to
seize every outline of the beautiful pictures they would
never see again, reveals a vivacity of sentiment, a depth
of emotion, which attest a peculiar organization. To a
laurel-tree he found blooming in the midst of the

Alhambra, "gay as victory, happy as love," he has addressed verses, almost a declaration such as Apollo might have made to the laurel of Daphne.

Having once formed a taste for travel, Gautier indulged it as much as his journalistic duties would allow. In 1845, he saw Africa for the first time, visiting Algeria in July and August, during the full heat of summer, it being his rule to enter each country in the utmost violence of its climate, the South in summer, the North in winter; to give himself up to the intoxication of the snow as well as to that of the sun. In 1846, he revisited Spain. In 1850, he travelled in Italy, in 1852, he first saw Constantinople and the Orient. He returned from Constantinople by the way of Athens, and received there a second sensation vivid as that he had experienced in Spain. In the presence of the Parthenon, of the Erectheum, of those immortal relics of an art, which as it were forms a part of nature, in sight of those grand but not lofty mountains, of that horizon sombre and perfect in outline, the harmony and proportion of all made a deep impression upon his mind. Athens gave him the sense of measurement ; upon his return he found that Venice had lost in this regard ; in its delightful confusion it seemed less divine to him than of old. "Too late have I known real beauty!" he wrote upon leaving this enchanted soil of Attica.

He seemed himself to become a part of every country he entered. "I have a wonderful facility," says he, "for yielding without effort to the life of different countries. I am a Russian in Russia, a Turk in Turkey, a Spaniard in Spain."

As soon as the tourist sets foot in a country delineated by Gautier, he verifies his descriptions at every step. All tourists render him full justice in this respect. He spares

work to his successors. Physically he exhausts his subject.

In his African journey of 1845, he accompanied the
expedition to Kabylie on the staff of General Bugeaud,
who gave him a tent, two horses and a servant. Of the
five civilians on the expedition, three died from fatigue
or heat. Gautier returned to Paris in an Arabic costume,
coifed with a fez and wearing a burnous. He made his
advent into the city on the top of the Chalons diligence,
a young lioness that had been confided to his care, between
his knees. He had himself a leonine appearance ; sun-
burnt, tawny, with flashing eyes, his friends recall him
as he was at this fortunate epoch, in all the strength and
pride of second youth, in all the opulence and amplitude
of perfect manhood, breathing in life with full lungs,
having his own style of dress, oriental in design and
color. Two little ponies worthy of Tom Thumb, har-
nessed to an elegant coupé whose body almost grazed
the pavement, bore a master with a deep olive complexion who majestically filled the inside, and at each halt
for a visit, was ready to mount with agile step to the
suite of apartments. At this time in the flush of health
and hope and worldly satisfaction, Gautier wrote his
verses entitled " Fatuity." This is the first stanza :—

> *Je suis jeune, la pourpre en mes veines abonde;*
> *Mes cheveux sont de jais et mes regards de feu,*
> *Et sans gravier ni toux, ma poitrine profonde*
> *Aspire a pleins poumons l'air du ciel, l'air de Dieu.*

These are magnificent verses of their kind, verses
overflowing with health and vitality. We comprehend
how one may be tempted to be a materialist when matter
is so rich and so beautiful. Never could a meagre, sickly
man write such poetry. The man is matured, the real
man has displaced the young man of dreams. Nature

in her vigor and vivacity transports him and transforms him. This is her law. In the Goethe of Weimar, in that majestic and tranquil personage at the middle and the end of life, who would recognize Werther?

There is much to be said upon Gautier the art critic and the romancer, the author of at least thirty complete volumes. In two or three well-turned phrases, one can not dispose of a man of genius who has written thirty years.

√ Art-criticism in the way he comprehended it, con stitutes one of the innovations and one of the especia¹ talents of Théophile Gautier. His description of a picture which he makes us see and almost excuses us from going to recognize, has this peculiarity; it is exclusively picturesque and not at all literary; he compels us to penetrate into the character of each painter, into the nature and intention of each work, and shows us the degree of esteem we should attach to it! We seem to see every picture in the light of his description; we see it not only in its plan, but in its effect, its coloring, its outline. Gautier's system of description is an exact equivalent reduction rather than a translation. Just as one reduces a symphony to the piano, he reduces a picture to an article. It is not ink he employs; it is outlines and colors; he has a pallet and brushes. He applies to painted pictures the same process he follows in regard to natural pictures and to climates: absolute submission to the object. He renders this object just as it is.

While Théophile Gautier, himself a painter and a poet, acquits himself so conscientiously in his humble rôle of critic, it is but just that he should, from time to time, allow himself some little satisfactions, some bits of execution. He must have some indemnities and consolations; he must show his own little talent, and attempt in his way something like what the artist has done in his. And so we find in his descriptions many an admirable little picture. His criticism is often pure poetry, the *lacryma christi,* they pour out to you from every street corner, on a counter of silver. And do you complain?

Théophile Gautier's ideas in regard to painting are peculiar. He would not have the artist copy all, or reproduce all, and in painting yield to that infinity of detail which is the triumph of the daguerreotype. "It is not nature he must render, but the semblance and the physiognomy of nature. All art lies there."

In his criticisms of pictures he has always maintained the absolute predominance of the picturesque. In an article upon Ary Scheffer, he remarks that picturesque thought has nothing in common with poetic thought; that an effect of light or shade, a rare outline, a happy contrast of color, all these, are thoughts, and so painters by temperament, born painters, find them.

In his criticisms upon painters, Théophile Gautier, neither shows the prejudices of the man of letters, nor shares the illusions of the crowd. No one can be more benevolent than he to all sorts of talent. Where others would be rude and harsh, he has the gentleness and consideration of a brother. "Why," says he, "write in the morning's journal things about an honest man which you would not say if he were present at dinner in the evening? Because the words you write will be read by fifty thousand persons is no reason for being impolite and wounding."

Never has a malicious sentiment entered the soul of this critic, sagacious as kindly. With the profound antipathies of his class, he always softens the expression of his dislike for works or persons. He has never seemed to feel envy of those engaged in like avocations with himself, and no personal feeling has ever made him attenuate his praise of authors or poets. None have written more charming or amiable things than he of Alfred de Musset, a rival poet preferred to himself.

IV.

Generally speaking, in both literature and painting, Théophile Gautier is a rebellious Frenchman, a refractory critic. He loves with a sincere love, both Rabelais and Ronsard, and some poets of the reign of Louis XIII. Among all the authors of the so-called grand age, La Bruyère alone pleases him. But he prefers the foreign to the national masterpieces, Shakespeare, Goethe, Heine, people his heaven, and are his gods. This feeling repeats itself in painting. There is a sort of grey (this is his word) in French art, which he can appreciate but which little charms him. He must have more sun or snow, more tropical or boreal clearness. He loves extremes. What we call lucidity, limpidity, has no great charm for him. He loves all that has savor or color. This preference has led him to a very high regard for English art from Reynolds to Landseer. This regard he has fully expressed in a series of articles called forth by what he saw at the great London Exposition of 1862.

Théophile Gautier's art vocabulary is inexhaustible and is the wonder of connoisseurs from the precision and distinctness of its shades. The French language will neither adopt nor retain all his art terms, but it suffices to his honor that he has introduced a goodly number that will endure, and that he has rendered impossible those dim and vague descriptions with which we were once content, but which are no longer in fashion.

In 1845, Gautier in conjunction with three others, Madame de Girardin, Méry and Jules Sandeau, wrote a society novel, each taking up the romance where the other left it. The title of the story is "The Cross of Berny." It was a wager, and it was admirably won. Gautier sent his last contribution, a letter, from the camp of Ain-el-Arba in Africa. A series of charming novelties, alluring from their oddity, appeared in quick succession from Gautier's pen. The first was *La Morte Amoureuse*. It was followed by *Une Nuit de Cléopâtre*, *Jean et Jeannette*, and *Le Roi Candaule*.

Gautier as romancer, has more than once thought proper to avail himself of his talent as traveller to render the various countries of his acquaintance or his dream. He loves to give as a foundation for his recitals, a precise place and country around which a large portion of the interest centres. Thus in " Militona" he shows us Spain anew ; in " Arria Marcella," he has resuscitated ancient Pompeii, in the " Romance of a Mummy," he transports us to Egypt. He has never seen Egypt with his own eyes, but he has thoroughly studied it in its literary monuments and pictures. This romance, entirely retrospective, contains nothing which could make real savants or the initiated frown.

In 1848, the position of Théophile Gautier, the luxurious artist and journalist, received a violent shock. He never complained on his own account, he took part in the February revolution only through his losses.

Taking sides with none, disconcerting himself as little as possible, he wrote of art and the ideal, to-morrow as yesterday, after, as before. He chose this stormy time which left him a great deal of enforced leisure, to engrave his " Emeralds and Cameos," and ere long, completed and arranged his casket. Of all his prose and

poetic works, the "Emeralds and Cameos" are the most
artistic and finished, and he must hold them closest to his
heart. Of his three volumes of verses, this has been the
most admired and praised, and no collection of poems
since the grand successes of Hugo, Lamartine and Musset has had so large a sale.

In these poems a deep sensibility often lies concealed
under the imagery or under irony, but it is not absent.
Le Vieux de la Vieille, for example, a souvenir of the
rendition of the ashes of Napoleon, is one of the pieces
where the smile lies nearest to tears. One evening,
when Mlle. J. of the Théâtre Français was reciting this
piece at a soirée in the presence of the author, he suddenly broke out into sobs. Bravo! stoic of art, sometimes
affecting more impassibility than you possess, do not
repent having for a moment obeyed nature, for having
betrayed that fountain of the heart which is within
you! That air of perfect insensibility often proves only
the extreme diffidence of a most tender sensibility,
which blushes at letting itself be seen by indifferent eyes.

"Captain Fracasse" is a romance of the age of Louis
XIII., an epoch very dear to Théophile Gautier, and to
which he had given a great deal of study. His volume of
"Grotesques" (1844) contains a series of original and
strongly marked portraits of that time. In composing
"Captain Fracasse," some twenty-five years ago, he assumed a most difficult task, that of writing a romance,
nearly imitative, which should correspond to the ancient
date wherein the scene was laid, and yet possess a sort
of freshness and novelty, an indispensable requisite in
every modern work. The principal characters of this
story are country comedians, the immediate predecessors
of Molière's youth. Owing to the great taste Gautier
has for art, and for a sort of conventional art, he has

chosen to study life in comedy rather than to seek after
comedy in life. This imposes upon him an entire language, a continuous style, a sort of gamut and harmonious ladder, where the key once given, there is no false
note or dissonance. He has acquitted himself marvel
lously well. The first part of the romance is a *chef
d'œuvre* of its kind; it is the classic of the romantic.

In "Captain Fracasse," we pass from picture to picture;
there is not a page which does not present some picture
entirely finished or begun. The whole story seems to
serve as a canvas and a pretext for them. It is a romance album for the use of artists and amateurs in en-
graving. *

Judging this romance from its true standpoint, it
must be pronounced a masterpiece in the literature of
the age of Louis XIII. Although treating of scenes
two centuries old, it has still the gloss of novelty.
When hereafter the literary history of that age shall be
written, this posthumous work must be included in the
record.

At this hour of awakening, this tidings of so unexpected an aftermath, we seem to gaze into that sort of bizarre
and Bacchic elysium, which we can easily imagine as
the abode of those free and somewhat foolhardy spirits
before Louis XIV. The shade of the jovial Saint-Amant
leaps for joy, the poet Théophile feels himself consoled
and avenged through all the future for his disgrace.
Scarron bounds with delight from his arm-chair, while
Cyrene more haughty than ever, passes and repasses
upon the populous Pont-Neuf, where a double row of
bourgeois and astonished knaves admire him.

* An elegant edition of " Captain Fracasse," beautifully illustrated by
Gustave Doré, has been issued in Paris, and has found its way to this

Saint-Beuve's portrait brings down the life of Théophile Gautier to 1864. He lived eight years longer, years fruitful in mental activity. His last work was *Tableaux du Siége*. He thus concludes a biographical sketch of himself dated 1867; "I have written three volumes of verse and without being a romancer by profession, a dozen romances. I have worked on *La Presse*, on *Figaro*, on *La Caricature*, on the *Family Museum*, the *Revue des Deux Mondes*, the *Revue de Paris*, everywhere Parisian journalists have written in my time. I have published innumerable articles on all sorts of subjects, three hundred volumes in all—and yet the world calls me an idler, and asks why I do not go to work."

Gautier's bosom friend, Ernest Feydeau, in his interesting memories of Théophile Gautier (Souvenirs Intimes, Paris, 1874), gives a full account of his literary and private life. He sets Gautier very high intellectually, indorsing the words of another who has styled him the French Goethe. Feydeau one day, repeated this phrase to his friend. "But in one respect at least, I can never resemble Goethe," said he, "I have no Duke of Weimar."

"A child of the sun, born to travel and to write verses," lack of fortune and the necessities of daily life, chained this brilliant poet and artist to the dull, mechanical routine of journalism. He was a literary drudge, he could attain no full development of his powers.

In religion he was a Pantheist, and at heart, beneath an outward joviality, he bore the deep sadness inherent in that cheerless faith. "I have never doubted immortality," he said, "but to my mind the second life is worse than the first."

No writer has had so copious a vocabulary as Gautier. In his hands the French language, seemingly designed expressly for lawyers, politicians and savants, becomes rich in color and full of imagery, lending itself to all the necessities of poetry and art. " Because the classic writers of the 18th century used only twelve hundred words, must we deprive ourselves of the thirty-thousand other words?" asks Gautier. His descriptive powers are unrivalled.

A lover of peace, with a shuddering horror of the barbarism and sacrilege of war, he lived through that last French reign of terror, but the shock mentally and physically was too great for him to bear. He never recovered from it. His last glance was doomed to rest upon France, the land of his love and pride and glory. conquered, humiliated, and at the mercy of a foreign foe. He died of hypertrophy of the heart. Neither himself nor his friends dreamed that his last hour was so near. The loving cares of his family smoothed his pathway to the grave. " He was all to us, — he was our entire universe," said his sister to Ernest Feydeau. He had his faults and weaknesses, but never was man better loved by his friends.

He had sought—too persistently his best friends thought—entrance to the Academy. Although his merit was never denied, this honor was refused him. Though influential members pressed his claims, the august Forty could never forget some early eccentricities of dress and manner, discarded in his wiser and riper years. But the death of Théophile Gautier, having occurred during the session of the five academies, President Camille Doucet waived the rule forbidding allusion being made, during the public session, to any but members, and paid an eloquent tribute to the illustrious dead. " Letters in despair," he said, " weep a true poet, a brilliant writer dear to us all. Numerous suffrages have proved that his place was among us, and so much the more do we deplore the sudden stroke beneath which he has fallen."

This appropriate homage to the candidate, who had he lived, might the next day have been one of their number, was received with great favor and sympathy by the whole Academy.

But he they thus sought to honor had no need of earthly praise. The tribute had come too late.   .

SAINTE–BEUVE.

Sᴀɪɴᴛᴇ-Bᴇᴜᴠᴇ has left no personal memoirs; his biography must be gathered from his correspondence and from occasional allusions to himself in his voluminous writings. Although he has been the frequent theme of encyclopedists and essayists, his true life remains to be written, and let us hope that some pen will ere long do full justice to the man, as well as to the critic, poet and historian.

M. Le Roy, professor in the university of Liége, having written to Sainte-Beuve requesting some biographical account, which might be inscribed on the records of the institution, received the following meagre and imperfect sketch dated June 28th 1868, only a few months before the great critic's death.

" Charles-Augustine Sainte-Beuve was born December 23d, 1804, at Boulogne-sur-Mer. His father, district comptroller and tax-commissioner of Boulogne, was married and died the same year, 1804, a few months before the birth of his son. His mother was the daughter of a Boulogne sea-captain who had married a lady of English descent. She was a woman of fine intellectual abilities, and with the aid of a sister-in-law, she superintended the education of her fatherless child.

Born in the honest *bourgeoisie,* and in the most modest of conditions, Charles-Augustine pursued his studies in his native city, learning rhetoric at the boarding-school of M. Bleriat, under a good humanist named M. Clouet. Having finished his rhetorical course while in his fourteenth year, he desired to complete his studies in Paris, and Madame Sainte-Beuve, entirely devoted to the future of her son, decided to gratify this laudable wish. In the month of September 1818, they arrived in Paris, where the young student entered the institution of M. Landry, at the same time attending the classes of the College of Charlemagne. In the competitions at the end of his first year, he won the prize for history.

In 1821, Sainte-Beuve entered Bourbon College, where he studied rhetoric, philosophy and mathematics. At the general competition in 1822, he won the first prize for Latin verse. He now devoted himself to the study of science and medicine, pursuing the latter until 1827. For a year he was day-pupil at the Saint-Louis hospital, and he received great benefit from his medical studies at this date.

Meantime in the year 1824, a new journal, *The Globe,* had been founded. It was under the direction of his former university professors, who had lost their places upon the triumph of the religious faction. The editor-in-chief, M. Dubois, had been Sainte-Beuve's rhetoric professor, and the young student's literary articles found a ready insertion. These first articles have not been collected. They have a general bearing upon historic works relative to the French Revolution, also upon poetic and purely literary works.

The French Academy having proposed as the subject

of its prize essay, "A Tableau of the Literature of the Sixteenth Century," Sainte-Beuve at the suggestion of a learned friend, set about the study of this subject. Abandoning the academic contest, he preferred to examine the picture on its purely poetic side. This led to the insertion in the Globe of a series of articles from his pen, which were collected in 1828, under the title of, " A Historic and Critical Tableau of French Poetry and of the French Drama of the Sixteenth Century," The work was issued in two octavo volumes, the second confined to selections from the works of Pierre Ronsard with notes and commentaries. This rehabilitation of Ronsard and the poetry of the sixteenth century, excited a lively controversy, and at the first onset, ranged Sainte-Beuve among the adherents of the romantic school.

In fact, an article inserted in *The Globe* of January 2d, 1827, and which was remarked and commented upon by Goethe, had led to an acquaintance between Victor Hugo and Sainte-Beuve, which ere long grew into an intimacy. This intimacy endured for many years, and hastened, indeed, gave birth to Sainte-Beuve's poetic development. In 1829 he published anonymously, a little 16mo volume, entitled, " Life, Poems and Thoughts of Joseph Delorme." This Joseph Delorme was Sainte-Beuve's exact moral image.

The following year, he published a collection of poems, entitled, " The Consolations," which had a success less contested than Joseph Delorme. To the *Revue de Paris* of 1829, he contributed articles upon Boileau, La Fontaine, Racine, Jean Baptiste Rousseau, Mathurin Regnier, and André Chénier, thus inaugurating that series of literary portraits since so fully developed.

The Revolution of July, 1830, could not fail to inter-
fere with the literary pursuits of young writers and
with the lucubrations of the romantic poets of that
day. Sainte-Beuve during the months immediately following the Revolution, wrote many anonymous articles
for *The Globe,* and the next year he attached himself to
The National. But his incursions into politics were
brief, he soon returned to purely literary pursuits. The
Revue des Deux Mondes just founded, furnished him
an ample and suitable frame for his critical studies.
His articles, contributed both to this review and the
Revue de Paris, were gathered into five octavo volumes,
which appeared under the title of " Critical and Literary
Portraits." These articles, constantly augmented, have
since been collected under the several titles: "Portraits
of Women—Literary Portraits—Contemporary Portraits
—and Last Portraits." This collection has been many
times republished with slight variations.

In 1834, Sainte-Beuve published a romance in two
volumes, entitled " Volupte,"—up to the present date
it has passed through five editions.

In 1837, another volume of Sainte-Beuve's poems appeared. " Thoughts in August " was its title. In
1840, the " Complete Poems of Sainte-Beuve " were
given to the world. In 1863, a similar collection in
two volumes was published by Michael Levy.

In the autumn of 1837, Sainte-Beuve journeyed to
Switzerland, where he was invited to give a course of
lectures to the Lausanne Academy, upon Port Royal, a
subject which had occupied his thoughts for several
years. He delivered eighty-one lectures upon this theme,
and they formed the basis of his work on Port Royal
which appeared, the first volume in 1840, the last in
1859. The long interval between the publication of

several volumes, is explained by the diverse labors and events which interrupted the literary life of its author.

Since the year 1840, Sainte-Beuve had been one of the directors of the Mazarin Library; in 1845, he became a member of the French Academy. The instability which after the revolution of 1848, marked the destinies of France, induced him to accept a call to the professorship of French literature in the university of Liége. In October 1848, he assumed the duties of that office, whose difficulties were 'far greater than he had dreamed. He gave three lectures a week. The Monday lectures designed for students and the public, were upon Charlemagne and his Epoch; the Wednesday and Friday courses, designed for the students alone, were exclusively upon French Literature. The remembrances of this year of university life, will always be precious to him. He came very near settling at Liége. Later, it was in his power to pay his public tribute of gratitude to Belgium, when in 1861, he published two volumes upon Chateaubriand, and his Literary Group under the Empire. His life and labors at Liége are summed up in these volumes.

Not married, but having a mother more than eighty years old, Sainte-Beuve returned to Paris in 1849, under the presidency of Louis Napoleon. Doctor Féron of the *Constitutional* proposed to him to begin immediately in that journal, a series of literary articles to appear every Monday. This series was a success, and decided our author to resume his literary pursuits. Sainte-Beuve continued these articles three years in the *Constitutional*, then in the *Moniteur*, which had become the official journal of the Empire. A collection of them appeared in 1851, under the title of *Causeries de Lundi* ("Monday Literary Gossip,") and was repeated during succeeding years, until the edition had reached fifteen 18mo volumes.

Appointed professor of Latin Poetry in the College of France, the course was stopped by political insubordination on the part of the students, when only two lectures had been given. But from these lectures came the volume entitled "A Study upon Virgil." Sainte-Beuve's name continued to figure as professor upon the college rolls long after he had renounced the duties of that office. Being now appointed professor in the Normal School, he for three or four years, scrupulously performed the functions demanded by that position.

The Constitutional, claimed anew his pen as critic and journalist, and he resumed his literary *Lundis*, on the 16th of September 1864. This series of articles has been collected under the title of *Nouveaux Lundis*.

In 1865, the Emperor was pleased to confer upon Sainte-Beuve the dignity of Senator. In August 1859, he had been made a Commander of the Legion of Honor.

Failing health has allowed him little opportunity to take part in the discussions of the Senate, even upon subjects in which he has felt the liveliest interest. The rôle he has assumed, and which has rendered him in a certain sense, the champion of free thought, has been less the result of a change of views than of an irresistible impulse.'   *   *   *   *

This dry meagre sketch from the hand that has so delightfully portrayed the lives of others of far less genius and renown, proves that no man is really fitted to be his own biographer.

Sainte-Beuve, whom the world called so happy and successful, lived and died a disappointed man. His dearest wish was to be a poet. In his poetical aspirations, he was one with Addison and Johnson, with Jeffrey and Professor Wilson, with Macaulay and Bulwer Lytton. Two young men of his time, Lamartine and Victor Hugo, had become famous as poets, and he counted nothing more glorious than to follow in their footsteps. But he could follow only afar off, and then it was but with halting gait and broken wing. He lacked that one supreme gift," the vision and the faculty divine," which distinguishes the poet born from the poet made. His poetic utterances are expressive but unmelodious, his verses when not wholly fantastical, are tame and colorless. Hazlitt's acrid sentence in regard to Campbell, applies to Sainte-Beuve's poetry as a whole: " A painful regard is paid to the expression, in proportion as there is little to express, and the decomposition of prose is substituted for the composition of poetry."

In extolling his merits as critic, Sainte-Beuve did not like to have the world treat lightly his claims as poet. As parents best love the child, sickly, deformed, unkindly dealt with by nature, so this author loved his poems in which the world saw so little to admire. Sainte-Beuve, the poet, was always jealous of the reputation of Sainte-Beuve, the critic. He liked to have people allude to his verses, to listen with apparent interest while he recited extracts from them. One word of praise, for " Joseph Delorme "—for the " Consolations," or the " August Thoughts " would cause him more delight than a lengthy eulogium of the *Causeries de Lundi*.

While the world in general ridiculed his poetry, some benevolent souls found in it much to praise and to admire. They justly ascribed to him great originality as a poet, perfect sincerity of sentiment, and an observation of nature minute as that we find in Crabbe or

2*

Wordsworth, or Cowper. Jules Janin says, "He was an inventor in poetry, he gave it a new and entirely modern note, and of the whole Cénacle, he was certainly the most romantic.＊＊ He struck the midst of the little lanes bordered by lowly flowerets where no one in France had passed before him. His execution, somewhat laborious and complicated, arises from the difficulty of reducing to metrical form ideas and images not yet expressed, or disdained until now, but how marvellously come the verses when the effort is not felt! What an intense and subtle charm! What an intimate penetration of the lassitudes of the soul! What divination of unavowed desires, and of secret aspirations! Sainte-Beuve, the poet, would be a fitting subject for a long and interesting study."

It was in criticism that Sainte Beuve reigned without a rival, and to be king of French critics is great as to be king of French poets. Here he is upon his native heath, here he can be praised without the serious qualifications with which we limit our estimate of him as poet, novelist and historian.

In many of his earlier criticisms he was ruled by the passion of the hour. In dealing with the works of Lamartine, Victor Hugo and Alfred de Musset, he showed all the fervor of the disciple who admires whatever falls from his master's lips. Later, he felt called upon to qualify, to lower the tone of some of his earlier utterances, "In criticism," he says, "I have long enough acted as advocate, let me now act as judge." His manner of dealing with Chateaubriand illustrates his own precepts. He showed that the pretended monarchist was a leveller at heart, that the eloquent defender of Christianity was a confirmed skeptic, and the admired preacher of morality, a libertine.

" Unlike Goethe, who says, ' We must encourage the beautiful, for the useful encourages itself,' Sainte Beuve took for his device, ' The true and the true only,' leaving the good and the beautiful to shift for themselves. To his mind appearances were always deceitful, the surface was not a mirror, but a veil. With Bruyère, he believed that man must not be judged like a statue or a picture, at a certain angle, and a first glance, that there is in him an interior and a heart which must be fathomed."

As critic, Sainte Beuve's great endeavor is to be just; he loves better to praise than to censure, and his criticism is usually kindly ; but sometimes it is scathing and merciless. He has a respect for tradition amounting to reverence, and a readiness to accept novelties akin to a passion. He seeks to introduce a charm into criticism blending poetry and anecdote with the rarest tact and often with a piquant humor. He pays to all truths, whether hallowed by time or struggling for recognition, an equally sincere worship.

In 1845, Sainte-Beuve was chosen to fill the vacancy left in the French Academy by the death of Casimir Delavigne; twenty-four years later, the chair left vacant by his death was to be filled by Jules Janin. The king of theatrical critics thus succeeded the king of book critics. In Janin's discourse upon his illustrious predecessor, he renders him full justice, attributing to him marvellous sagacity, profound intuition, subtle delicacy, patience of investigation, and that gift of comprehending, penetrating, feeling all, of entering into the most opposite natures, living their life, thinking their thoughts, and descending with a golden lamp in his hand, into the inmost recesses of their hearts. Janin declares that like the Hindoo gods, Sainte-Beuve had the gift of passing through a perpetual succession of incarnations and avatars. He pays a just tribute to that curiosity, always wide-awake, never satisfied, which thinks it knows nothing if the least detail escapes it. "*Homo duplex*, says the Latin philosopher. With Sainte-Beuve man was triple, and seeking to complete the portrait which to all others seemed finished, he demanded new sittings from his model, he inquired, he sought, he found; he did not allow the picture to go from his hands until the resemblance of the work on his easel left nothing to be desired."

Thus in death as in life, Sainte-Beuve's true fame must rest on his achievements as critic, rather than poet, that reputation so much dearer to his heart. Age did not chill his ardor for the Muse, nor lessen his aspirations. Thirty-two years after the appearance of his second volume of poems, he wrote to a brother bard; "You saw me during those six celestial months of my life which gave birth to the "Consolations." If the world had but dealt kindly with his poems, Sainte-Beuve would have done little in prose, and his critical portraits, superior in their way, to all other efforts in this direction, would never have seen the light. "The Consolations" was a book full of that Christian mysticism then so prevalent, and which in the works of Fénélon, Pascal and Madame Guyon, had produced so marked an influence upon French literature. "*Volupte*," Sainte-Beuve's only novel, has been justly characterized as "a romance of the flesh and the spirit." It was justly censured for immorality, and added little to the author's reputation. It may be set down as one of the sins of his youth.

Sainte-Beuve's style is original, as that of Carlyle. Balzac used to call it "the Sainte-Beuve dialect."

Mentally, the great critic resembled his father, a man

of superior culture and refined literary taste ; physically, he was the exact image of his mother, a woman of excellent sense and judgment and more than ordinary abilities. Very plain in youth and middle life, his features, with advancing years, must have won something of that spiritual beauty, with which mind transfigures matter, for one of his biographers speaks of " his beautiful face set in its frame of silver hair." He never married, but he was no woman-hater. He was more than once in love.

Piously reared in boyhood by his mother and a maiden aunt, who, both deeply religious, sought to make a saint of him, he became skeptical in later years, although there is no evidence that he ever went to the extreme of utter incredulity. He longed for a return of the simple, unquestioning faith of his boyhood, and was haunted by a continual regret that he could not still trust implicitly in the teachings he had received at his mother's knee.

This mother's old age, soothed by the affectionate care of her son, was tranquil, prosperous and happy; but there had been a time when her only child was to her a source of anxiety and disappointment. His abandonment of medicine for a literary career had almost broken her heart, and she never fully believed in him or in the wisdom of his choice, until he was admitted to the French Academy. Then she saw that to be a great author was really as fine a thing as to be a great physician.

Sainte-Beuve died October 13th, 1869, of a lingering and painful malady. He left the world in the full vigor of his intellectual powers. No family, no immediate relatives followed him to the final resting-place, but a whole nation were his mourners. In him French literature lost its brightest ornament.

In his last will and testament, Sainte-Beuve thus gave directions as to his funeral obsequies :—

"I wish my interment to be purely civil, without pomp, without solemnity, with no insignia, no tokens of honor.

" I request that the body and the societies to which I have the honor to belong, shall be represented at my interment by no deputation, but I shall be grateful if a few colleagues and confrères are pleased individually to accompany my remains. My resting-place is Mont Parnasse, at my mother's side.

" I desire no discourse from any of my testamentary executors, but that one of them, Lacoussade or Troubal, in a few simple words, thank the friends who shall have accompanied me to the tomb.

" September 28th, 1869."

The wish was respected. Without psalm or prayer, or priest, or pious word of trust in God or hope of immortal life, was consigned to earth, all that was earthly of the greatest of French critics.

MADAME SWETCHINE. *

SOPHIE SOYMONOFF, she who was one day to become Madame Swetchine, was born in Moscow, November 22d, 1782. Her father, the son of an ancient Muscovite family, occupied a high post in the civil administration of the empire ; her mother came from a race distinguished alike in letters and in arms. Her maternal grandfather, Major-General Boltine, adding arduous literary to military labors, had translated nineteen volumes of the French Encyclopedia into Russian.

Sophie's childhood witnessed the last voluptuous years of the reign of the Empress Catherine II., and the brief career of Paul, so soon to end in a tragic death. The scenes and associations of her every day life passed amid that strange medley of license and arbitrary power, could but produce grave reflections in this meditative and penetrating soul. Withdrawing as much as possible from society, she gave her hours to study, and reading became the joy and consolation of her life. Her father, although courtier and Confidential Secretary, found time to devote to his daughter's education, and with his fondness for her, soon blent a paternal pride in her rapid progress and attainments. In music, drawing and the languages, she showed like talent, and the brilliancy of her intellect was only

* *Causeries de Samedi.*—M. de Pontmartin.

equaled by the elevation of her moral nature and the goodness of her heart.

In 1796, when Paul I. succeeded to the throne, Sophie Soymonoff was named maid of honor to his wife, a woman of great loveliness of character, an angel of patience to her violent, capricious husband. Here the young girl learned her first lesson in the sorrows of life, the silent tears so often shed by those whose outward happiness and grandeur are the envy of the world. Under the maternal care of the good Empress Marie, she reached her seventeenth year. Life at court had not changed her love for study, and she acquired here many accomplishments. She was not beautiful. Her blue eyes were small and slightly crossed, but very lively and amiable in expression, her nose had *la pointe Kalmouk*, but her complexion was dazzling. She was of medium height, and of graceful, elegant bearing ; her voice was sweet and sympathetic ; she possessed the most exquisite refinement and delicacy of manner, and conversational powers of uncommon brilliancy.

This high-born young girl had many suitors, and among them was Count Strogonof, a young Russian nobleman of fortune and talent. Between these two there was ardent affection, but in those troublous times, policy determined marriages in high life far oftener than love. Without a rebellious word, Sophie yielded to the wish of the father she adored, and accepted for a husband, General Swetchine, who was twenty-five years her senior. He was a man of tall, commanding figure, of sterling character, and a firm, though gentle spirit. This married pair had few tastes in common, but they lived amicably together for fifty years, each having the good sense to allow the other to pursue the chosen path. Renouncing the idea of that highest happiness in marriage which results from perfect accord of tastes and sympathies, Madame Swetchine, while neglecting no domestic or wifely duty, gave her leisure hours to charity, to literature, and to the society of a few chosen friends. At her father's death, which occurred soon after her marriage, she took home her young sister, doubly orphaned, and became to her a second mother.

The appearance of the Count de Maistre at the Russian court, whither he had come as the moneyless ambassador of a crownless king, produced a marked change in Madame Swetchine's life and thought. These two souls, drawn together from the extremes of Europe, were united by a common piety and ardent love for the truth.

In her early readings, Madame Swetchine, had pillaged hap-hazard from her books, accepting Rousseau, and even Voltaire, proscribing neither La Harpe nor Madame de Genlis, lending a serious ear both to Marmontel and to Young's Night Thoughts. She had the instincts of a bee, which gathers honey even from poisonous flowers. The extracts she made from these early readings formed thirty-five manuscript volumes. When the decisive hour of her conversion from the Greek to the Catholic faith arrived, she had read, annotated and copied enough to fill the life of ten Benedictines. Once Catholic—she was already more than half French—she had only to journey to France to find her true country and her true countrymen.

Her removal to France occurred in 1816, at the dawn of the Restoration. She met again in Paris the elite, —alas! decimated by death—of that French colony twenty years before exiled from home, and thrown upon the shores of the Neva. The noble exiles had repaid Russian hospitality with brilliant lessons, useful services and fine examples. In these old friends Madame Swetchine greeted alike memories of her native land and the hopes inspired by the new country. She was warmly welcomed by the highest and noblest of Paris, and she ere long became the centre of a society, select, brilliant, intellectual, with higher, more spiritual thoughts and aims than characterized other aristocratic circles of the French capital. Her quick, acute, subtle intellect, the firmness and elevation of her character, gave her an ascendancy over all around her. She established a salon, grave in character, artificial in aspect, and the only one in Europe distinguished by a pronounced theological complexion.

"What kind of a salon is that," asks the skeptical Sainte-Beuve, "where a few steps from you, behind a door, you perceive an oratory, into which the pious hostess goes to edify and fortify herself before receiving you, and which she soon re-enters to edify herself anew? Do I say an oratory? It is a chapel, a consecrated chapel, where, in the midst of dazzling luminaries, is exposed the Holy of Holies, the Holy Sacrament, which many present go to adore at the stroke of midnight—*to adore*, is saying too little, since at certain solemnities, the sacred table is always ready for those who await it. "This is not a *salon;* it is a religious circle, a succursale of the church, give it what name you please—a house of charity for the use of people of the world, a vestibule of Paradise. Gay, brilliant, inspired, wise, witty salon of all time, where enjoyment, audacity, wisdom, folly, charm the hours, I do not recognize thee. —Madame Swetchine carried with her the tabernacle and the consecrated Host!"

But this was a salon after M. de Pontmartin's own heart—aristocratic, intellectual, dignified and pious.

He says: "In her salon Madame Swetchine diffused around her a nameless charm, and proved herself worthy of all the homage paid her. Here was benevolence without feudality, tolerance without skepticism; here was an aroma of goodness and intelligence. Here was authority so much the more obeyed because it never asserted itself; here was feminine tact, softening asperities and conciliating dissonances; here was that undefinable atmosphere where souls breathe at ease, that intellectual and spiritual communion which quickens the mind and expands the heart."

Madame Swetchine could not have chosen a more auspicious moment for her naturalization in France. If the women of the first Empire may be cited as types of plastic and sculptural beauty, those of the Restoration had other advantages more in harmony with the time in which they lived. Mind seemed to have dethroned force and form; never had more intellectual women been seen in Paris. Madame Swetchine, who was a soul rather than a body, had only to remain herself, to enter into the movement of ideas, and to accept here a leading place.

In the Paris of that day, Madame de Montcalm gathered around her the political celebrities. Mme. de Staël still lived, Mme. Récamier, always young, was still beautiful. A new poet had arisen; the Muse of Chateaubriand hovered over the world, suspended between two abysses. The Duchess de Duras and her daughter extended the hand of friendship to the Russian stranger, of whose genius they had a presentiment before sounding its depths; and others highest in social position and in letters, gave her kindly greeting.

We see Madame Swetchine in intimate relations or in correspondence with the most illustrious men and women of her time. Her letters, that grand superiority of superior women, already afford us glimpses of the natural and acquired perfections of a soul which later revealed itself in writings not given to the world until after her death.

The sky of France soon darkened anew,—the truce between the revolution and the tutelary monarchy was broken. Days of trial and anguish came again for those who, like Madame Swetchine, hoping better things of their age and country, had believed in a possible reconciliation between old prejudices and new ideas. A few months sufficed to change the aspect of Parisian society; the democratic element menaced it, the bourgeois element ruled it;—new names, new faces appeared at this crisis which but presaged others. Birth and education had made Madame Swetchine a monarchist, although she was no believer in absolute power, and in the new troubles which had come upon France, she naturally sided with the monarchical party. The revolution of July had affrighted her, that of 1848, agitated, but did not surprise her. She rendered full justice to those who were striving to do a little good by preventing a great deal of evil—to Lamartine, to General Cavaignac; but she gave full and clear written expression to her dislike of the motives and character of Louis Napoleon.

Madame Swetchine's house was kept with great care, though without luxury of any sort. She never gave soirées or dinners, but gathered a few people at a small round table, to the furnishing of which she attended with strict personal care. Her drawing-room was open to her friends morning and evening, and was always brilliantly lighted. She had brought from her Russian home a love of brilliant illumination, and her rooms sparkled with lamps and tapers. The first impression was that of a place of worldly fashion; but her guests soon perceived that a higher spirit reigned here, and that she who possessed all these advantages, was not herself possessed by them. She was a favorite alike with old and young, and she knew the secret of captivating women, so rare in one of their own sex. Her own toilette was simple, being invariably a costume of brown stuff, from which she never departed; but her taste in dress, as in all else, was correct and refined, and she liked to see young ladies in society elegantly attired. They used to come to her at night, when dressed for balls, and pass in review before her indulgent but critical eyes; and the next morning, these same young people would be at her side, telling their secrets, and asking her advice.

She was very systematic in the allotment of her time; her day was divided into three parts. She rose before sunrise, and the morning hours were exclusively her own. At eight o'clock, she had already visited the poor, and been to church; then until three in the afternoon, the time was at her own disposal. From three to six, her salon was open to her friends; from six to nine, it was closed; but at nine she again received guests, who remained until midnight. Her afternoon and evening visitors were generally distinct; some of those who came in the afternoon, had never met those who came at night.

Madame Swetchine was never a mother, but she had reared an adopted child, Nadine, who afterwards became the Countess de Ségur d' Aguesseau. She also took charge of Hélène, the daughter of a dear absent friend.

In 1834, this quiet household was convulsed by a

blow which came directly from the hand of the Emperor Nicholas, who ordered the exile of General Swetchine to any part of the Russian provinces he might choose, so it was only far enough from Moscow and St. Petersburgh. This sentence was for alleged misconduct of whic⁻ he had been guilty during the reign of the Emperor Paul. The decree of exile reached Paris in the heart of winter.

Madame Swetchine suffered more on her husband's account than her own. He was then seventy-seven years of age, and it was very hard for him to leave his delightful Parisian home in the Rue St. Dominique, with its stately houses and leafy gardens, for life-long exile in some dreary, provincial town of Russia. His wife told him of the decree of exile, and had difficulty in making him understand; he was not conscious of having committed any offence. Against his entreaties for her to remain in Paris, she insisted upon accompanying him. Meantime, influential friends in St. Petersburgh had obtained a respite, which Madame Swetchine employed in traversing Europe to plead her husband's cause in person. She left Paris in August, 1834, and it was not until the November following that her courageous efforts were crowned with success. In March, she reached her beloved home in the Rue St. Dominique, where she sank exhausted on a bed of sickness, and lay for three months hovering between life and death.

Madame Swetchine's charities were many, though unobtrusive, and were exercised alike at home and abroad. It has been said of her that she knew how to comfort the poor in their needs and the rich in their domestic troubles; how to arouse the moral energies of the unfortunate. Many came to her for consolation, and each left her with an expression of peace. Interested in all benevolent enterprises, her especial sympathies were aroused in behalf of institutions for the deaf and dumb, and the welfare of the serfs on her own estates in Russia lay very near her heart. She was one of the first to advocate the abolition of serfdom.

In 1850, General Swetchine died at the extreme age of ninety-two. From that time his widow lived in great retirement, although a circle of intimate friends still met at her salon in the Rue St. Dominique. In this latter period of her life, she made still further advances toward Christian perfection. Her charity grew broader and more active; she felt an affinity to all who, in these troublous times, sought the consolations of religion.

Her health, gradually declining, began to inspire the most anxious solicitude. She sank gently, almost imperceptibly. Her lovely, pious life wore away in the exercise of every Christian duty; never were her intellectual faculties brighter, nor her spiritual sense clearer than upon the day of her death, in the autumn of 1859. M. de Falloux, to whom for many years she had been the dearest of friends and spiritual mothers—for there are affinities of the soul more sacred than natural ties —in his memoirs, gives a touching account of her last hours.

A profound sorrow pervaded a large circle of friends —rich and poor alike,—when it was known that this soul, so long ripe for the celestial country, had ceased to dwell among men.

It had long been known among the intimate friends of Madame Swetchine that evenings, after leaving the salon, it was her habit to note down her thoughts. An almost unanimous demand arose for their publication. She had placed her papers in the hands of M. de Falloux, and upon him devolved the pious task of presenting them to the world. But would the thoughts which had seemed so marvellous and beautiful in that amiable *claire-obscure*, where they had met the eyes only of a few partial friends, bear the clear sunlight and the open air? The test was dangerous, but it has been triumphantly borne. Madame Swetchine's two volumes, "Thoughts" and "Airelles," will henceforth have a place in the front rank of our moralists, among the purest classics of spiritual Christianity. An admirable selection has also been made from her letters. The Swetchine literature, which has had a wide vogue in France, is, through admirable translations, becoming known and admired wherever the English tongue is spoken.

Excepting the "Airelles," none of Madame Swetchine's writings were designed for publication—these only were copied by her own hand. The others, jotted down at different times, without any fixed plan, and often written in pencil, were far from being finished according to the author's ideas. But to justify the partiality of Madame Swetchine's friends and admirers, in giving her writings to the public, we have only to quote from them. Opening the volume entitled *Pensées* (Thoughts), these are the first words that meet our eye:

"I love God as if He alone were the universe. I pity the human race as if there were no God. There is an abyss between these two extremes which is bridged by our Lord and Saviour Jesus Christ.

"Go always beyond designated duties, and remain within permitted pleasures.

"Upon the whole, there is in life only what we put there.

"*The solemn, wonderful,* majestic ocean! It exalts only to crush me under a sense of its grandeur—boundless, everlasting, pitiless of my insignificance. Wherein does it differ from me? In immensity of breadth and depth. What does it give me? A sense of infinity and of the abyss which divides me from it. The ocean, in its might and unresting immutability, in its proportions, which transcend the boldest flights of thought, is God —but God without his Christ.

"I love knowledge; I love intellect; I love faith;— simple faith yet more. I love God's shadow better than man's light.

"There can be no little things in this world, seeing that God mingles in all.

"My experience is, that Christianity dispels more mystery than it involves. With Christianity, it is twilight in the world; without it, night. Christianity does not finish the statue—that is heaven's work; but it 'rough-hews' all things—truth, the mind, the soul.

"The root of sanctity is sanity. A man must be healthy before he can be holy. We bathe the body first, and then we perfume.

"The depths of the soul are a labyrinth, and dark without the torch of religion. Left to ourselves, we are like subterranean waters,—we reflect only the gloomy vault of human destiny.

"The best of lessons for many good people would be to listen at a key-hole. 'Tis a pity for such that the practice is dishonorable.

"Let my terrace face the East! There is a mysterious affinity between this fancy of mine and my decided taste for the dawn of excellent things. Of all rising suns, I except only that of prosperity; but I bow like a true courtier before the earliest rays of piety, virtue and talent."

These perhaps are not the best of the "Thoughts," but they are all that space allows us to quote. We pass

3

on to the "Airelles,"—a name felicitously chosen by Madame Swetchine. The Airelle is a flower, whose fruit in Russia ripens in October, but grows sweet only by lying under the winter snow. "These thoughts, too," says their author, " have ripened under the snows, and taken their hue, like the red berry of the Airelle, from the fires of the interior sun."

"Let our lives be pure as snow-fields, where our footsteps leave a mark but not a stain.

"To reveal imprudently the spot where we are most vulnerable, is to invite a blow. The demi-God, Achilles, admitted no one to his confidence.

" It would seem that by our sorrows only we are called to a knowledge of the Infinite. Are we happy? The limits of life constrain us on every side.

" He who has ceased to enjoy his friend's superiority, has ceased to love him.

" To have ideas is to gather them into flowers. To think is to weave them into garlands.

" Since there must be chimeras, why is not perfection the chimera of all men?

"' Woman is in some sort divine,' said the ancient German. 'Woman,' says the follower of Mahomet, 'is an amiable creature, who only needs a cage.' 'Woman,' says the European, 'is a being nearly our equal in intelligence, and perhaps our superior in fidelity.' Everywhere something detracted from our dignity! It is very like the history of the dog!—a god in one country; muzzled or imprisoned in many others; and sometimes, ' the best friend of his master. '

"Parodies on things I love, either disgust me, or trouble my conscience. Nothing that has touched the heart ought ever to be profaned.

" Strength alone knows conflict. Weakness is below even defeat, and is born vanquished.

" It is only in heaven that angels have as much ability as demons.

" Travel is the serious part of frivolous lives, and the frivolous part of serious ones.

" We are rich only through what we give, and poor only through what we refuse.

" No two persons ever read the same book or saw the same picture.

" Men are always evoking justice, and it is justice which should make them tremble.

"*The Firmament.*—Is it not amid the rigors of winter that the celestial vault impresses us most deeply as the region of the immutable and the eternal? Type of the world of souls!—there is no trace of time in that kingdom of space. There is beauty without spot or wrinkle —immortal youth. Like the soul, the sky has dates, but not age. Like the soul, it has no night, but changes its lights as the soul varies in brightness. By a sublime immunity, the heaven, although created, knows neither change nor decay. The mighty immobility of its planets, or their triumphal march beneath the watchful gaze of the Most High, seem to image the impassibility of the saints, and their swift, irresistible zeal. The vault of heaven, resplendent and gloriously arranged, seems like the heart of the good man, to celebrate a perpetual feast—the feast of the PROMISED RESTORATION."

No one has written so tenderly and beautifully of Old Age as Madame Swetchine. With her, this season when the night-shadows fall and envelop the traveller, is only the presage of a never-ending and celestial day. She feels that with the good, the sunset rays may be brightest, and that at eventide it may be light.

We have read Cicero's *De Senectute*, so impregnated with Platonic philosophy, where the aging man consoles himself for growing old by growing eloquent, as it is said he consoled himself for the death of his daughter Tullia by dreaming of the beautiful phrases with which sorrow would inspire him. We recall those melancholy words of Chateaubriand, to whom old age was so full of sadness : " Infancy is happy only because it knows nothing, age is unhappy only because it knows all ; happy for it when the mysteries of life end, and those of death begin."

Eloquently as Cicero, more piously and hopefully than Chateaubriand, Madame Swetchine writes upon this subject so few know how to invest with any charm :

" The old man is the pontiff of the past ; nor does this prevent him from being the seer of the future. The clergyman represents the priesthood of eternity ; the old man that of time. The aged are 'Christ's poor: their wrinkles are their rags ; they warm themselves in the sunbeams ; they beg their daily bread.

" Misfortune discovers to youth the nothingness of life ; it reveals to age the happiness of heaven.

" Like the cross of Calvary, the old man is midway between heaven and earth,—held to the one by his duties, to the other by his hopes. He believes, because he has proved all things, and only the truth of the gospel has remained at the bottom of the crucible.

"Old age is not one of the beauties of creation, but it is one of its harmonies. Shadow gives light its worth ; sternness enhances mildness ; solemnity, splendor. Different flavors give zest to one another.

" 'In our day,' says M. de Chateaubriand, 'people are old, but they are no longer venerable.' This remark, perhaps, contains the whole secret of the slight respect of youth for age.

" Time is the shower of Danaë. Each drop is golden.

" Celebrated prose-writers preserve their superiority until the decline of life, while our poets, save in cases of extraordinary genius, fall with the winter. Thought with the former dwells constantly on the sober realities of the Christian life; with the latter, it is but a pastime. But this playfulness demands a sensuous rapture of which the old have ceased to be capable; and it is a glorious impotence for which they should not grieve. What laments over bright days gone we find in the votaries of the Muse! What contempt of youth in Bossuet! The great bishop dates life only by white hair. Yet the true poets, like the great artists, have scarcely any childhood, and no old age.

" 'If any man hear my voice, and open the door, I will come in and sup with him and he with me.' Happy old age! It is for supper, and not for a midday feast, where noise and tumult reign; it is to sup with us that our Lord will come. At the close of the dull, weary, toilsome day; at the hour of sweet, long, friendly talks, when intimacy grows deepest, and confidence flows with a full stream; at night-fall, when hearts approach and mingle and think of naught save how to bless and sanctify the sleep which is to follow. I collect myself, O my God! at the close of life, as at the close of day, and bring to thee my thoughts and my love. The last thoughts of a heart that loves thee, are like the last, deepest, ruddiest rays of the setting sun. Thou hast willed, O my God! that life should be beautiful even unto the end. Make me to grow and keep me green, and climb like the plant which lifts its head to thee for the last time before it drops its seed and dies.

" *Nunc dimittis.* Now lettest thou thy servant depart in peace, O Lord! His load is lightened. The weakest of thy angels could carry it under his wing. His swelling pride is humbled. The *Ego* has lost its substance. The world has withdrawn its stupid favor. The weight of sin has been removed by forgiveness and tears; and beneath thy light and easy yoke, all his limbs move freely."

We have lingered too long over these beauties, and new beauties invite us at every step. "Nowhere, says M. de Falloux, has that incomparable soul revealed itself more fully than in her treatise upon 'Resignation.' The finest observation of earthly things, here glows side by side with the anticipated peace of heaven, and strokes worthy of La Bruyère abound, together with flights worthy of St. Augustine."

We have space for only a few passages, and these almost the concluding ones:

" Suffering is profitable unto all things. Suffering teaches us how to suffer, to live and to die. Even if we could enter heaven by any other door than that of tribulation, our very love for God should deprive us of all thought or desire for so doing; for it is thus that our divine Master, and, after him, all the Saints, have entered, bearing the cross and treading a way strewn with thorns.

" Apart from grace, nothing save suffering and its mighty plenitude, can fill the abyss between the God-man and his imitators. It is through suffering that God is most human. It is through suffering that man comes nearest to God.

" Do you not feel " said Saint Madelaine, " the infinite sweetness that is contained in those dear words, ' THE DIVINE WILL?'

" How easy it is to understand that holy bishop, who forgetting or abdicating his own individuality, desired men to call him by no other name than this, *Quid Deus vult.* Is there in all the world, a tenderer prayer, or one more impressed with divine sympathy than this :—' My Father, thy will be done' ? A prayer which God himself has taught us, a talisman which enables us to banish his justice and summon his love. *Thy will be done!* Incessant miracle of a God who deigns to will, and a rebellious creature rising to the height of obedience! A sovereign prayer in its seeming self-annihilation. . . . Will of my God be mine, and continue till my latest breath to initiate me into the secret of thy growing delights."

We close the book reluctantly. It is a casket of gems, from which we have perhaps not chosen the brightest. Let those who would know more of this tender, yet profound moralist, open the casket anew.

MADAME DE GIRARDIN.[*]

(DELPHINE GAY.)

AMONG the beautiful, witty and intellectual women who have graced the salons of Paris, none have been better known or more admired than Madame de Girardin. By turns a Muse, a journalist, and the creatrice of a new order, this charming Delphine made her salon a sanctuary of the graces, the favorite resort of the most renowned men and women of her day.

Lamartine has related the circumstances of his first meeting with Delphine Gay. It was in 1825, at Terni, near the falls of Velino, that his eyes first rested upon that lovely apparition, destined never more to fade from his remembrance. "Standing like a sybil before the foaming cascade," writes he, " she was intoxicating herself with the thunder, the vertigo and the suicide of the waters." The poet gazed spell-bound upon the radiant vision, the tall, supple form with nymph-like bearing, the perfect features, the classic head, crowned with its aureole of golden hair. He was moved by the deep, liquid accents of the young girl's voice, and he loved her; but it was with a love such as Plato felt " for the beautiful, which is only the outward manifestation of the good."

Delphine was at this time only twenty-one years old, but her renown had already filled the salons of Paris.

---

[*] *Madame de Girardin.*—By Imbert Saint-Amand, Paris, 1875.

From earliest childhood she had been wont to think and to speak in verse. There was imagery in her eye, harmony in her ear, poetic passion swayed her heart and soul. Her strophes were like the carol of a bird pouring forth its artless joy in song. Her eulogy upon the happiness of being beautiful, refers to this time, that bright, matutinal season, to which remembrance carried her back when several years later, she wrote:—

> *Mon front était si fier de sa couronne blonde.*
> *Anneaux d'or et d'argent tant de fois caressés!*
> *Et j'avais tant d'espoir quand j'entrais dans le monde*
> *Orgueilleuse, et les yeux baissés.**

When less than twenty, Delphine began her literary career by the publication of her " Poetic Essays." She dedicated the book to Chateaubriand, and in return was honored with a most flattering letter from him. Ten years later, the great author of " The Genius of Christianity" wrote to Delphine, now become Madame de Girardin, congratulating her upon her poem " Napoline," a poem which Sainte-Beuve says has not been sufficiently understood or admired.

Delphine had a wonderful gift for recitation. This gift had been carefully cultivated, and was a source of exquisite delight to the literary and artistic circles of the Restoration. In the salons of Madame Récamier and the Duchess de Duras, at the matinées of the Duchess de Maille, at château Lormois, she entranced all ears and hearts. When in her rich, musical voice, thrilled by a deep poetic inspiration, she recited some beautiful poem, a rapt, admiring silence would attest the delight of all

---

* " My forehead was so proud of its blonde crown,
Rings of gold and silver so many times caressed!
And I had so much hope when I entered the world,
Confident and with downcast eyes."

who listened; for the moment, every political and social dissonance was hushed, and this young Muse of her country, as they loved to call her, held all under her magic sway.

"To my mind," writes Lamartine, "Delphine had but one fault; she laughed too much." Beautiful defect of youth, ignorant of the sorrows after life has in store! Sixteen years later, the great poet wrote to the once light-hearted young girl, "Gayety is amusing, but at bottom, it is only a pretty grimace. What is there gay either in heaven or on earth? Happiness itself when complete is sad, for the infinite is sublime, and the sublime is not gay."

Delphine and her mother had made a little sanctuary of their modest suite of rooms in the Rue de Choiseul. To their salon came the nobility of birth only to become more ennobled through association with the nobility of nature. This was the salon of friendship rather than of celebrity; it was distinguished by that entire freedom from useless social forms which should ever reign in the republic of talent. This mother and daughter, though poor, could surround themselves with attractions such as gold cannot buy. Intellectually, both were alike gifted, but the mother who had long reigned a queen of society, was now only too glad to place the crown she had worn so gracefully, upon the younger, fairer brow of the daughter she adored.

Théophile Gautier has described the impression the mere sight of Delphine produced upon a group of poets, sculptors and painters, when she appeared in her box at the Opéra Français, upon the evening of the first representation of Hernani, February 20th, 1830.

When they perceived that inspired head, those beaming eyes, those magnificent blonde locks, that white robe with the blue sash rendered celebrated in Hersent's portrait of Delphine, a triple salvo of cheers broke forth. This young woman's appearance at the theatres, the fêtes, the academies, was sure to be greeted by a low murmur of admiration. The young men were enraptured with her grace and beauty, the old men with her talent.

" Who will have the honor of marrying this beautiful Delphine ? " had been a question often asked, but it was not speedily answered. One evening at the salor of the Rue de Choiseul, appeared a young man, small in stature, but with the massive head and powerful features so familiar to all in busts of the first Napoleon. The resemblance even then when he who bore it was but twenty-nine years of age, excited much remark; it is still more striking to-day, and is said to be a source of pride to a certain world-renowned and veteran journalist, now in his seventy-third year.

This quiet, unassuming stranger, unknown to all, and receiving little attention from any but the ladies of the house, was M. Emile de Girardin. June 1st, 1830, he married Delphine Gay, then twenty-seven years old, and in the full lustre of her beauty and renown. It required no small merit, no small self-confidence in so young a man to unite his destiny with that of a woman so celebrated. Such merit, such self-confidence M. de Girardin possessed. A man of brilliant talent and unbounded ambition, he never, in this union, sank to the level of prince-consort ; he was never known to the world as " Delphine Gay's husband." His wife became his associate upon *La Presse*, the leading Parisian journal of that day, and the most brilliant among its staff of writers. This husband and wife gloried each in the talent of the other, and their marriage resting upon a sure foundation of mutual tastes and sympathies, and consecrated by true devotion, was one of almost unalloyed happiness. Madame de Girardin, while reigning undisputed queen of society, was also the centre of a refined, beautiful home. Exact in the performance of every wifely and domestic duty, " the heart of her husband did safely trust in her."

She felt proud of the position her own genius and accomplishments had won, and she avowed this pride with a noble frankness. In one of her Parisian Letters to *La Presse*, she writes:

" For ourself we have received only one pale beam in the unjust distribution of immortal flame; but this faint gleam, this trembling ray, we would not exchange for the splendors of the most illustrious fortune and the highest rank. At the banquet of Renown, we have won only a modest place, but we find that we have not purchased it too dear with the irony of fools and the ennuis of poverty."

Madame de Girardin's first salon, in the Rue Lafitte, was hung in sea-green reps, with sea-green velvet bands of a deeper shade, a tint admirably suited to her clear blonde complexion. Mornings, she wrote in an ample white dressing-gown, whose folds fell around her like a Greek chlamys, her lovely hair rippling in golden waves around her shoulders. Evenings, her favorite dress was a trailing black velvet robe, finely setting forth the snowy whiteness of arms and shoulders that Phidias would have loved to model.

In the literary tournaments of her day, Madame de Girardin appeared a warlike Amazon, armed and helmeted; and yet she was a woman in the best and noblest meaning of the word—a woman in goodness, in devotion, in tenderness, in the vivacity of her impressions, the sincerity of her enthusiasms, in the charm of her personal and intellectual beauty.

Her conversation, a series of dazzling surprises in which her marvellous imagination had full play, was varied as nature itself. She amused, she fascinated, she moved you to tears; she sparkled with wit, she glowed with poetic ardor; she was at the same time gay and' melancholy, sarcastic and tender. If she took it upon herself to defend the reputation of a friend, she became eloquent as Demosthenes. She had at her command inimitable accents. She was above so low a passion as envy, and it was her delight to assist true genius in its upward struggles. More than any person living, she possessed the art of making the success of a worthy literary or artistic work.

None better than she knew how to follow that precept of Boileau:

Passer du grave au doux, du plaisant au sévère.

She had the gift of irony, but underlying it was an enthusiasm for the good and true, a horror of deformity, a love for the beautiful. With the gift of criticism, she possessed a higher faculty, the gift of admiration. She loved to praise far better than to censure. A woman of so much wit must needs have possessed a most kindly nature not to resemble her own Napoline,

" Whose caustic wit avenged her suffering heart."

In 1841, Madame de Girardin was at the apogee of her beauty, her genius and her celebrity. Her writings had made the tour of France, of Europe and the world. She distributed renowns as a sovereign distributes orders and dignities. Artists and authors sought her suffrages and gloried in her words of praise. Among her intimate friends and correspondents, she numbered the most celebrated personages of her day, all of whom brought her their common tribute of admiration and respect, recognizing her as a woman of the highest elevation of soul, with a noble intellect, and a still more noble heart.

Madame de Girardin was a great lady in the best acceptation of that word. Habituated from childhood to the most aristocratic salons, received with the warmest cordiality by the high *noblesse* of Paris, educated in the school of her mother, a woman of the best society, an exquisite refinement characterized her every word and action.

Writing for her husband's journal under the signature of the Viscount de Launy, in her " Parisian Letters " and " Couriers de Paris," she essayed all sorts of topics, and was known far and near as the most able and brilliant of its contributors. Having won many laurels as poet, romancer and journalist, she at length turned her attention to the drama, her first venture being a comedy in five acts, entitled "The Journalist's School." It met a favorable reception at the Français, but the censor forbade its further representation. " What matters the censor?" wrote Lamartine. "The world is on your side, and the world is greatest."

In 1843, a tragedy in three acts appeared from her pen, but it was doomed to have only a literary success. It was Mlle. Rachel's first impersonation.

During the summer of 1846, Madame de Girardin went to pass a few days with M. and Mme. de Lamartine at Saint Point. The poet thus writes of that sojourn:

" She came to pass the latter days of summer at our solitude in the midst of the Saint Point heaths. She was then writing her beautiful tragedy of Cleopatra, whose style has the solidity and the polish of marble. I shall never forget the inspiration of her face and the emotion of her voice when she read to us by day what she had composed by night. She usually read mornings in the shadow of a mossy roof, covering an orchard wall, in a declivity, where the glance roved over a valley of the Tempé, with sombre mountains in the distance. No sound save the murmurs of nature broke the hush of this sequestered spot, and Delphine's beautiful verses lulled to silence all echoes from without."

In November, 1847, "Cleopatra" appeared, and was a double triumph for Madame de Girardin and Mlle. Rachel, her admirable interpreter.

In 1853, Madame de Girardin gave the world two comedies, "The Husband's Fault," and "Lady Tartuffe." The same year she published an exquisite romance, entitled "Marguerite, or Two Loves," and also one of her best novels, "We Must not Jest with Sorrow." Her talent had grown year by year, and many regard "Marguerite" as her best work.

In 1854 appeared her drama "Joy Brings Fear," and a very laughable farce, "The Astrologer's Hat."

Political dissensions, without detracting from the friendship of Lamartine and Madame de Girardin, had rendered their relations more distant. The great poet had cherished the illusion that he might some day become president of the Republic. He must have felt deeply aggrieved that the lady who had been his warmest admirer and most valiant champion when the darts of envy and calumny fell thickest about him, shared the ardor of her husband for Louis Napoleon. But Lamartine still remained one of the most welcome visitors at Madame de Girardin's salon. Here, despite his temporary fall, the accustomed incense was burned to him; here he burned incense to himself. The Girardins now dwelt in that house upon the Rue Chaillot which was Madame's last residence. This house, built after the model of the Erectheum of Athens, surrounded by a grassy lawn, with its flowers and fountains, its tufted chestnut trees half veiling the front facing the Champs-Elysées, well suited the refined, poetic woman her contemporaries so well loved to 'call the tenth Muse. When its presiding deity was no more, Théophile Gautier could never, without tears, pass this house with the white columns.

"How many times," writes he, " have I returned at two or three o'clock of the morning with Victor Hugo, and other friends, in moonlight or in rain, from this temple, where dwelt an Apolline no less beautiful than the antique Apollo! Free, confidential, delicious evenings, sparkling conversations, dialogues between genius and beauty, Platonian banquets—ye should be described with a pen of gold!"

And Alexander Dumas has thus written: " There we passed many pure, sweet, joyous hours, countless and evanescent. So swiftly did they fly that two o'clock of the morning would strike ere we were aware. Charming spirit that hovered over us, making these hours so beauteous and so fleet! Gentle raillery, animated recital, adorable grace, fine repartee, sainted goodness! Woman, sister, friend. Finally we would tear ourselves away to return homeward through the long, deserted avenues, saying of you, be sure, dear friend, words such as courtiers never said of any queen."

In 1855, while meditating new and greater literary works, Madame de Girardin was arrested midway in her career. Her mind still retained its youthful freshness, the splendor of her noon had far outshone the promise of her dawn ; fame, friends, fortune, all were hers, when she perceived the first insidious approaches of that malady which had proved fatal to Napoleon I.—cancer in the stomach. Théophile Gautier thus describes her as the supreme hour drew near:

"Her beauty had assumed a character of grandeur and of singular melancholy. Her idealized features, the indolent languor of her poses, did not betray the dumb ravages of a mortal disease. Half reclining upon a divan, her feet covered with a red-and-white afghan, she had more the air of a convalescent than of an invalid."

Her friends would not believe in the gravity of her disease. They were dreaming of a serene, majestic old age for her, full of days, labors and honors. Time, they thought, would surely need many years in which to blanch to silver bands the long spirals of golden hair enframing that beautiful face, so well known through the pencil and the burin.

Now and then, triumphing over her cruel sufferings, she would resume the pursuits that had so adorned her life. Méry had described one of the last dinners at which she played her once so successful rôle of hostess.

"Her noble face was somewhat emaciated, and her large blue eyes glowed with the fire of fever. She ate nothing, and she had such a transport of inspiration as none of us had ever seen or shall see or hear again. She would pass from one subject to another, leaving a luminous track upon all. She was by turns profound, brilliant and poetic, and we all listened in rapt admiration. When we rose from the table, George Sand, who had remained silent during the marvellous improvisation, exclaimed, " How beautiful and how witty she is ! " "

But after these fevered flashes of inspiration, the gifted invalid would relapse into melancholy. She felt the loss of that olden public, amorous of art, intoxicated with romance and poetry, in whose warm sympathy the first flowers of her genius had blossomed. She had little confidence in this new race,—prosaic, calculating, *blasé*,—which had neither love nor admiration nor faith

nor hope. She began to feel herself an exile in a country where literature and art had become vulgarized.
Her works were still in vogue; they laughed at her
comedies, they wept at her tragedies. But the new
times could never be to her beautiful as the old. Théophile Gautier, over whose last days a like shadow was
ere long to fall, thus describes the state of Madame de
Girardin's mind :

"Although she was tenderly devoted to her husband,
whose conflicts she had espoused, although fame, success, fortune, all that can make mortals in love with
life, had come at her desire, although admiring, stead-
fast friends were around her, she seemed to cherish a
secret longing to have done with all. The times did
not please her, she felt that the level of souls was lower-
ed, and she already sought presages from the other
world. Like Leopardo, the Italian poet, to whom Musset has addressed some beautiful verses, she dreamed of
the charm of death. When the funereal angel at length
came for her, she had long awaited him. She poured
out her sorrows, her aspirations, in delicious reveries,
and composed her "Song of the Night," so full of tenderest poetic beauty."

The opening stanza of this 'Song' is as follows :

> *Voici l'heure où tombe le voile,*
> *Qui le jour cache mes ennuis ;*
> *Mon cœur à la première étoile*
> *S'ouvre comme une fleur des nuits.**

---

*"Behold the hour when falls the veil
That hides my sorrows from the light,
My heart, when morn's first star I hail,
Opes like a flower that blooms by night."

Intellect and melancholy are sisters, and the lives of these favored ones of genius are full of sadness. With a glance deeper than that of the common throng, they gaze into the abyss of life, shuddering alike at sight of a cradle or a tomb. They realize that no finite mind can solve the problem of human destiny, that life is unsatisfying, and death mysterious as terrible. And when, seeking some consolation, plucking some flower along the route, yielding to the spell of some momentary delight, they pause suddenly, and cry out with Alfred de Musset:

Je ne puis, malgré moi, l'infini me tourmente !

It is a cry wrung from the depths of their inmost consciousness.

And she, too, was sad, this adorable Madame de Girardin, she who had enjoyed so marvellous a dawn, so magnificent a day; she who, like the goddesses of old, had walked in a luminous path, who had known all success, all splendor, all renown.

On the 29th day of June, 1855, she rendered her soul to God. Gentle and courageous with death as she had been with life, her last hours were full of holy joy and peace.

In the hey-day of his renown, when upon his still youthful brow rested the triple crown of poet, orator and historian, Lamartine had written these words to Delphine: "A quarter of an hour of love is worth more than ten centuries of glory, and one minute of virtue, of prayer, of enthusiastic aspiration of the soul toward God, is worth more than a whole century of love."

Madame de Girardin had the same deep, religious sentiment. It would appear even in her worldly chronicles of *La Presse*. In his beautiful eulogy, pronounced at her grave, the Abbe Mitrand said:—

"She was a Christian, this brave soul, who, seeing death approach from afar, calmly awaited the king of terrors and defied his power, invoking Him who is the resurrection and the life. She was a Christian, this elegant, witty, intellectual woman of the world, who, too proud to kneel to earthly powers, humbly prostrated herself at the feet of the minister of Christ she had summoned, submitting meekly to the will of God."

A few years previous, at the funeral of General Foy, Madame de Girardin had said "It is thus I would wish to die, in the midst of so many illustrious men and mourning women." Her wish was granted.

The tidings of her decease caused a marked sensation in Paris. Those who had known her only by name, wept; those who had enjoyed her love and friendship were inconsolable. That charming salon, now desolate, the courts, the garden, even that avenue of the Champs Elysées, were not vast enough for the immense concourse gathered to pay her the last honors.

In the Parisian journals there was one unanimous burst of regret and homage. The world of letters and journalism wept her who had reigned its queen. Many tributes were paid to her memory, and from the shades of his voluntary exile, Victor Hugo sent a poetical adieu, which will live as long as the language endures.

Alas! what has become of that house with the white columns, that sacred temple of beauty and friendship, of art and genius? *Tempus edax, homo edacior.* Time demolishes, but man is more destructive still. Nothing remains of that Greek temple, not even the ruins; the very street on which it stood has disappeared.

Thus all changes, all passes, thus we ourselves are

passing, few of us leaving any more trace, than the bird that sweeps the air, the bark that glides over the river's breast.

All that is mortal of Madame de Giradin rests at Montmartre. "Place above my grave a simple cross as its sole ornament," she had written in her last testament. The wish was held sacred. Beside hers is another waiting grave with a mortuary slab upon which is this inscription ·

La mort les a séparés,
La mort les a réunis.

The complete works of Madame de Girardin have been published under the auspices of her husband, in six elegant volumes. This beautiful edition is a worthy and enduring monument to the memory of her who has been so justly styled the most intellectual woman of the nineteenth century.

ARSÈNE HOUSSAYE. *

ARSÈNE HOUSSAYE was born at Bruyères, March 28th, 1815. He comes from a family of agriculturists, of noble descent. He has the right, if it seems good to him, to bear the title of Count de Valbon-Montherault, and to wear the armorial insignia of his race. From a book of Arsène Houssaye's, *Un Voyage à ma Fenêtre*, we copy some details of his childhood.

"I was very young," he says, "when I left my dear mountain, all sown with daisies and eglantine, its declivities decked with generous vines of gold and purple hue. . Study was impossible in my paternal house, a great hive of labor, a real industrial city. My father for a time confided me to the care of his father, who had another noisy house, where they worked little but amused themselves a great deal. There were every day, Homeric repasts and long night vigils, during which we told stories, and played and danced and supped. I loved better the more quiet and simple abode of my maternal grandfather, who lived at the centre of the town."

This maternal grandfather was an old · *sans culotte*, a sculptor in wood, and a distant cousin of Condorcet.

---

* Portraits et Silhouettes.—Eugene de Mirecourt.

He had been mayor of the town in the good old time of Saint-Just and Maximilien. By a strange chance, here, in the very heart of the nation, a Picardian commune, emancipated under Philip Augustus, had preserved all its privileges, all its franchises, and, '93 had found it peopled with republicans, of whom the Robespierres and Dantons had little to learn. Neither the radiant passage of the imperial meteor, nor the re-installation of the legitimate monarchy, could change the sentiments of this ex-mayor of Bruyères. He educated his grandson in principles of the broadest independence, and in the hatred of tyrants.

"He was a very honest man, esteemed by all the world, even by my paternal grandfather," continues Arsène, "from whom he had violently wrested authority in 1789; for both had succeeded to the helm of affairs in Bruyères during the flux and reflux of republican and royalist opinions."

According to his own confession, this boy Arsène was a precious good-for-nothing, always ready to laugh in the face of his masters, and giving play a decided preference to study.

"Our school," writes he, "was composed of about twenty-five young scapegraces, each more determined to hack at his neighbor's tree than at the tree of knowledge. This small army, very heroically seeking to imitate Fra Diavolo and his band, diffused itself over the town and surrounding meadows, and committed all sorts of mischief. If I was not the chief, I was one of the captains always obeyed, because my grandfather was mayor, and possessed large gardens which we took by assault. Among our lawless proceedings, there is one, I would it were in my power to expiate by some monkish penance. The old church of Bruyères, in 1825, had the most beautiful Gothic windows remaining in the country. One evening, when we did not know where else to throw our stones, we had the impiety (double impiety, since it at the same time outraged art and religion) to hurl them at the pious personages of the Passion. Would you believe that this act of vandalism was not punished? The towns-people concluded that we had done right in destroying these antiquated objects, and delighted at having new, plain glass, came very near voting us a public recompense. The Curé himself regarded this only as an inconsequential boyish frolic."

But all at once, a solemn self-absorption replaced this wild exuberance of spirits in young Arsène. He shut himself up from morning to night in his grand father's library. A very little volume, printed in 1752, with the king's approval, was the sole cause of the great change that had come over the lad. The volume was a collection of French poetry from Villon to Benserade. In his strolls over the mountains and meadows Arsène took the precious volume along with him, learning by heart many of its sonnets and ballads.

" What the deuce are you repeating?" asked the master of the Bruyères school one day, as the boy was reciting to himself one of his newly learned poems. "It cannot be your syntax lesson."

" No, it is a stanza of Saint-Amant's."

" And who is Saint-Amant?"

The admirer of the old poets shrugged his shoulders in utter disgust at such ignorance in his teacher. He declared that henceforth he would learn only verses, and the master never afterward sought to impose upon him any other exercise of the memory. This master was a man of fifty years, who sang in church and drank

huge bumpers at the inn. He dearly loved his monthly
wages, but gave himself little trouble about the instruction of his pupils. Arsène always learned what he liked
best.

"I thank you, O my first master, for what you did
not teach me," he wrote in after years. "For Geography,
which makes a botch of the world, for History which
dishonors it, for Philosophy, which doubts God! I
thank you for having withdrawn from my lips, that
bitter cup of the Danaides. There we shed all our
tears, but the cup is never full."

They feared that Arsène was ill; he was only becoming a poet. Like all young poets, he fell in love, and
wrote näive, sweet verses to the adored one. She died
in early girlhood, but he always wept her in his rhymes,
this fair Cecile.

Arsène was his mother's idol, and she, in league with
the republican grandfather, was in a fair way to spoil
the lad, by yielding to all his caprices. But Houssaye
père, was made of sterner stuff; he was a man of un-
poetic mould and of inflexible resolution. When he
learned that Arsène was given to rhyming, he fell into
a terrible rage, and ordered him to abandon all such
nonsense.

But he who has ascended Parnassus, does not so
easily make up his mind to descend. Arsène offered no
open resistance to his father's will, but he still paid
secret court to the Muse. The master of the house
one day discovered some new verses from his son's pen.
The storm broke forth with new fury. Those few
volumes of poetry so dear to our young rhymer, were
consigned to the flames. Brebœuf, Saint-Amant, Théophile, were roasted without mercy. La Fontaine himself found no favor in the eyes of this stern contemner

4

of the Muses. Never had there been witnessed such an auto-da-fé of poets.

Arsène was shut up in his chamber with a treatise on Algebraic Equations, and Condilla's "Art of Thinking," for company. Pen and ink were taken from him, so that he could yield to no temptation to rhyme. Seeing the door of his chamber closed upon him by a double lock, the lad decamped through the window. His two grandfathers opened their purses to him, and now behold our young poet *en route* for Paris, where he hoped to rhyme in perfect freedom.

When he arrived in Paris, the cholera was raging fearfully. It had already carried off eighteen hundred victims, and at the hotel Malta alone, forty-eight persons had died within a single week. Arsène coming here for lodgings, found only one tenant left, a young Hollander named Paul Van del Heyl. As he was about to flee to less dubious quarters, the Hollander smiled and said: " Remain in this house ; Death believes that no person is left here."

Van del Heyl was also engaged in literature, and he and Arsène became friends at once. The Houssaye, who has since grown so impassioned for art, had little respect for it at this time. With his new friend Paul, he composed a melodrama full of murders and all sorts of crime. The two young men also wrote verses for the street singers, which sold marvellously well, thanks to their pompous title: *"Songs after the Manner of Béranger."*

These were only boyish recreations ; the lads were really occupied in serious studies. Arsène had found a Greek master, and replunged into antiquity. As he lived opposite the Collége de France, he attended the lecture-courses. He soon met Roger de Beauvoir and Gavarni, and he had formed some acquaintance with Théophile Gautier, at the Louvre, where that intrepid admirer of form was passing entire days in contemplating a Suzanne at the bath. Gautier ere long introduced him to several poets, painters, and sculptors, all great lovers of plastic beauty, and pagans to the end of their finger-nails. This pleiad of artists, who fraternized in all sorts of ways, in age, in taste, in beliefs, and especially in want of money, resolved to lodge under the same roof, to share their property in common, and march to glory in a close phalanx.

In a sort of ravine, hollowed out between the Louvre and the Place du Carrousel, a narrow street at that time descended to the Seine, its houses, old and black, bearing the architectural seal of the sixteenth century. It was in one of these dwellings that our artist friends set up their household gods.

The proprietor unhesitatingly offered them one of his largest *appartements*, but he bitterly repented when he saw his tenants move in. They had very little in the way of furniture, but they made up for this deficiency, by cramming their lodgings with paper packages, books, cartoons and easels.

Before their windows lay a huge, uncultivated garden, adorned with trees, that had been suffered to branch out in wild luxuriance. Half a dozen horses, two cows and four donkeys grazed at will upon this green sward in the shadow of the virgin forest. Here, too, a brood of hens, led by a high-crested sultan, lived in most amicable relations with a regiment of geese, ducks and Guinea-fowl. You would have said that the antedilu-vian Ark, had rested here in the very centre of Paris, as upon another Mount Ararat, to deposit its motley array of bipeds and quadrupeds.

To-day, the ravine is filled, the street is demolished, and the Louvre majestically extends one of its stony wings over the virgin forest. Soon after the installation of our impoverished young artists in this singular abode, one of their number, Gerard de Norval, fell heir to an inheritance, and Arsène's father, somewhat reconciled to his son and to literature, sent him some five-hundred franc notes. All shared in the new riches, and abundance suddenly reigned in this phalanstery of letters.

Armed with pencils and brushes, our artists frescoed their ceilings, and covered the wood-work with masterpieces. They soon had a splendid salon, which became the scene of many a jovial reunion. Théophile Gautier laid down æsthetic laws for the band, and one of them was that no meagre woman should be admitted to their soirées.

This was a conclave of pagans, of infatuated Athenians, who seemed to believe themselves living in the age of Pericles, and to whom beauty and glory were the highest good. After having gone back twenty-three centuries in their manners and their creeds, they were one day forced to abandon their dream. One of them, Edward Ourliac, took refuge in religion, which was most wise, Esquires plunged into politics, which was most imprudent; others, in materialism, found what they believed to be the true science of living. Each clipped the white wings of his muse, and plunging into active work, became a part of the practical, prosaic days in which he lived. One alone, sought to go on dreaming. He was the simplest, the most sincere of all, a beautiful soul, cruelly wounded in his self-love, a noble intelligence, who knew not how to walk leaning on the staff of faith. This one, Gérard de Norval, awoke at last, but it was only to suicide.

This Bohemian life lasted from 1833 to1837, and Théophile Gautier and Arsène Houssaye were its leading spirits.

Upon his arrival in Paris, Arsène was only seventeen years old. A precocious youth, he belonged to a precocious epoch. When not quite twenty, he published his first book, the *Couronne de Bluets*, a paradoxical romance, more to be commended for the beauty of its style than the philosophy it preaches.

A certain publisher of Paris, pleased with Arsène's first book, proposed to purchase from the young author a second romance, entitled *La Pécheresse*, and to pay him in books.

"Much obliged," replied Arsène, "I pay my landlord in francs!"

Another publisher paid cash down for *La Pécheresse*, and two days after the appearance of this strange novel, the author received from his Majesty, the king of critics, this agreeable note:

"Come and see me, I have read a charming book of yours, which I greatly admire.   JULES JANIN."

The young romancer hastened to respond to the flattering invitation, and made the acquaintance of the great journalist of the *Débats*.

At this period, the Saint-Simonians were proclaiming the emancipation of women. They gave Arsène's romance an enthusiastic welcome, as it was supposed to be a sort of apology for their doctrines. He wrote sixteen or eighteen other romances, in a few of which he was assisted by Jules Sandeau.

His poems, published in 1852, give evidence of no

very high poetical inspiration, but they bear the impress of remarkable delicacy and grace. Without the power of Victor Hugo or the originality of Alfred de Musset, Arsène Houssaye holds his rank among the poets of our day. His poetry is blonde, dreamy and melancholy. He is not gifted with the brilliant voice of the nightingale, but he has the sweet, limpid melodies of the linnet.

More and more an enthusiast for art, he, in 1840, made an excursion upon the old Hollandais soil, to study the works of Rembrandt and Rubens. Chosen two years previous, to render accounts of the expositions of painting, he continued them up to 1843, when he took charge of *L'Artiste*. Under his direction, this art journal became an elegant review, embellished by the highest efforts of both the pen and pencil. A pleiad of young writers, some already known, others ambitious of distinction, grouped themselves around the editor-in-chief. The direction of the *Artiste* did not prevent Houssaye's still writing for the *Revue de Paris*, where, in 1838, he had begun a charming gallery of Portraits of the Eighteenth Century, which will remain models of their kind. The volume entitled " Philosophers and Comediennes " completes the collection. M. Boyer has written a very remarkable critique upon these Portraits, in which we find the following sentence:

" Arsène Houssaye is a literary Cagliostro who has danced the minuet with Madame de Pompadour, and who now waltzes with Mademoiselle Rachel."

This is painting a man with one stroke of the brush.

Doctor Veron was then throned on *The Constitutionnel*. Actresses, living or dead, always allured this personage. He found that Houssaye had admirably sketched the graceful and spirituelle figures of Sophie Arnould and

Guiniard. "Here is some one who would enliven the *Constitutionnel* and its readers," thought he.

That very day, Houssaye received, with the doctor's card, a note inviting him to call at the editorial rooms.

"What does the *Revue de Paris* pay you? But very little I imagine," said this admirer of actresses. "As for *La Presse* it is not generous. Girardin pays Théophile Gautier with what he takes from the others. If I were to accept all your Portraits, what would you wish for each?"

"A hundred francs," returned Houssaye. "I will give you one hundred and fifty. Is it a bargain? If so, let us go and dine at Véfour's."

Enchanted at the nabob's generosity, Houssaye went down with the doctor. A magnificent carriage was awaiting them. They entered it. "Have you horses?" asked Veron.

"No, certainly not; I have as much as I can do to go on foot."

"One reason the more for having an equipage. Horses, my dear fellow, are a stimulus. Those who walk, never arrive."

O, philosophy of our age, here is one of thy apostles! Arsène allowed himself to be only half seduced by these triumphant maxims. He has a carriage now, but he almost always goes on foot.

In 1846, Houssaye, received the Cross of the Legion of Honor for a History of Flemish Painting, a remarkable work, which has had a great sale, and has brought a large sum to its author. Before publishing this history, he revisited Holland, and made the tour of all the museums of Germany, Italy and France.

Arsène Houssaye is a silent soul, who has a profound

horror of garrulousness. He often repeats to himself that fine saying of Pythagoras, "Hold your tongue, or say something better than silence."

Like many well known personages, he does not, mornings, prepare *bons mots* for use during the day. His witty replies betray neither pretension nor research. They are improvisations, and pure gold.

When Emile Deschamps wished to enter the French Academy, he had at first twelve votes; then the number was reduced to four, and finally to two. "Poor Deschamps! he is dying of extinction of the voice," said Arsène.

At a dinner given to men of letters, each in turn spoke of his manner of writing.

"I work at night," said the author of 'Alonzo.' "Four hours of sleep suffices me."

"Ah, Monsieur le Ministre," replied Houssaye, "you often preside at the councils of the university!"

We might recall a score of sallies of this kind.

Married in 1847, to a charming woman, rich, happy in his domestic relations, with a well-earned and some-what extended fame, and a broad, fruitful career before him, Houssaye took one false step, which conducted him to the edge of an abyss. He plunged into politics, thinking that this way lay the road to the Chamber, to the Ministry, to all sorts of civic honors. The remembrance of his grandfather electrized the democratic fibre of his nature. He harangued the Picardian students, and as he drank champagne with them at the Château-Rouge, he reminded them that they had the honor of being from the same province as Condorcet, Camille Desmoulins and Saint-Just. In brief, he arrayed his blonde head in a Phrygian cap, and no longer went to dine with the Duke de Montpensier at Vincennes.

From the great revolutionary clock, the hour of the republic struck. Houssaye flung himself into the movement, founded a club, and straightway shrank back affrighted.

He had believed he hailed a dawn, and perceiving in the sky only an extinguished comet, he at once faced about and turned his back to the waning star whose uncertain beams could illumine only ruins. From the stage where he had thought to play a *rôle*, he leaped into the parterre, became one of the audience, and hissed that wicked parody of '93 they were trying to present as a new piece. He abandoned politics, resumed the pen, and began his "History of the Forty-first Chair of the Academy."

At this time, the Théâtre Français was given over to anarchy. They wished to place at its head a conciliatory man who could restore order, and Houssaye was chosen director. He remained seven years in this office, and his directorship gave universal satisfaction. Rival cliques were reconciled, old grievances removed, old costumes sent to Rag Fair; new scenery and new pieces wooed back the public to the deserted boxes, and Houssaye's administration proved artistically and financially a most brilliant success.

Returning to literature, some unhappy impulse moved Houssaye to write and publish his "King Voltaire," a sort of nonsensical apology for the most despicable of men and the most infamous of philosophers. In writing this bad book, Houssaye must have been deceived as to the sentiment of the present age, which has given over Voltaire to almost universal reprobation.

We should have pity for every sin, they say. Yes, if the sin is followed by repentance; but our author, after "King Voltaire," published the *Charmettes*, a sort of

4*

apotheosis of Jean Jacques Rousseau, who is no better than the Sieur Arouet.

Of all his literary confrères, Arséne Houssaye is the one it seems most painful to reproach. He is amiable, generous, obliging and unselfish. Egotism has never tarnished his soul. He has a heart magnanimous enough to confess, some day, the sins of his pen.

It would be useless to seek to present a complete list of this author's works. They have already been given to the public in ten octavo volumes. We must not forget to mention a curious weekly serial which for a long time appeared in *La Presse*, under the signature of Pierre de l'Estoile, and which he has given the title of "History in Slippers." He has also written several theatrical pieces.

After the completion of his "Forty-First Academy. Chair," a grand success, M. Houssaye tried his hand at history. "King Voltaire" was followed by "Mademoiselle de La Vallière" and "Notre Dame de Thermidor," both of which won a great, but much contested success. Even as a historian, our author still remains a fashionable romancist.

Two of his recent romances, "Mlle. Cleopatra," and "The Romance of the Duchess," have been very much read. Houssaye is *par excellence* the painter of new Paris, and of feminine manners. He has also lately written eight volumes of memoirs relating to French history.

Since his entrance into letters, Arsène Houssaye has known all the world, and none better than he can depict the men and things of his time. His official functions as inspector general of the Fine Arts have made it his mission to study the artistic wealth of France, to serve young artists while establishing ancient renowns. Every six months he pronounces orations before some statue that has been reared, or harangues the young laureates of the arts.

The journalist in him has survived. For more than twenty years he has conducted *L'Artiste*, and some years ago, he founded the "Review of the Nineteenth Century," the ark, more or less sacred, of the literary mind so compromised in our day.

Arsène Houssaye's unvaried success has passed into a proverb. He has never met a reverse of fortune. One 2d day of December he made five hundred thousand francs by operations at the Bourse, to which he then respectfully bade adieu, promising to try his luck there no more. To be just, we must say that this money honestly won by Houssaye, fell back, a plentiful rain into the hands of the less fortunate artists around him. His hotel in the Champs Elysées, is lined with the masterpieces of modern artists.

In 1855, Houssaye had the misfortune to lose his wife. She died of heart disease, leaving to console her stricken husband, the loveliest child in the world. The boy's head was like a fine pastel of La Tour; a head Greuze might choose for a model. As this boy, Henry Houssaye, has grown up, he has devoted himself to literature, to Greek literature in particular. Born in 1848, he has already published a "History of Apélles."

Arsène Houssaye still devotes himself to art and literature. A successful journalist and author, a man of wealth and social position, his life is one the world calls peculiarly happy and prosperous. He is becoming widely known in this country through his correspondence to the New York Tribune. A brilliant, fascinating volume, compiled from his letters, has been recently published, entitled "Life in Paris."

One of his late letters throws some new light on his

domestic history.   Speaking of the precocity of Parisian youth, he says:

"Children no longer play.   I have a son ten years of age.   He is something of an American, for his mother is a charming woman of Peru."   After narrating some freaks of this precocious young gentleman, M. Houssaye père adds: "I should tell you that I have two sons. If the one belongs to the New World, the other belongs a great deal to the ancient world.   He is the historian of Apelles and Alcibiades."

GEORGE SAND.*

MADAME DUDEVANT, the George Sand of our day, was born in 1804. She is a lineal descendant of Augustus II. of Poland, and her maiden name was Amantine-Lucile-Aurore Dupin. Reared by her grandmother, she passed her early years at the Château de Nohant, an estate lying in one of the loveliest valleys of Berri. This grandmother, the Countess de Horn, was a woman of uncommon wit and grace, but far more brilliant than solid. She had all the anti-religious ideas, all the paradoxical whims of her century. She set the philosophy of Jean-Jacques Rousseau above the gospel, and sought to educate the young girl committed to her care in accordance with these peculiar views.

At fifteen, Aurore was a graceful dancer, an adroit equestrienne; she also perfectly understood the arts of managing a gun and sword. She was a lively, petulant amazon, a charming, thoughtless young creature, able, like her grandmother before her, to follow the chase, to dash through the avenues of Marly; but she did not know how to make the sign of the Cross.

It was soon whispered in the grandmother's ears, that the pious Restoration had little sympathy with the doctrines of Jean-Jacques Rousseau, and desired that young

---

* Portraits et Silhouettes.—*Eugene de Mirecourt.*

persons should not be educated after the fashion of Emile. This greatly surprised the old lady, and in philo-osophical matters, gave her a very low opinion of the new régime. Nevertheless, it was decided to send Aurore to a Parisian convent to receive that religious instruction of which she had not the least tincture.

This was a painful separation for the young girl, who adored her grandmother. In later years, whenever in her books, she speaks of this dear guardian of her infancy, it is always with a profound sentiment of regret, veneration and love. About 1836, at the time of her suit for divorce, she writes:

" O grandmother, arise and come to me! Cast off the winding-sheet in which they have wrapped thy broken body, for its last sleep; let thy old bones arise. Come to succor me and to console me. If I must be forever banished from thee, follow me afar off. Ah! if thou hadst lived, all this evil would not have come upon me. I should have found in thy bosom a sacred refuge, and thy paralyzed hand would have revivified, to shield me from my enemies."

We find in the " Letters of a Voyager," certain curious details as to the life of Aurore at the Château de No-hant. Like all lively imaginations, she was extremely fond of reading. She thus speaks of her early pursuits: " Who is there of us that does not lovingly recall the first books we devoured and relished? The cover of a dusty old volume which met you on the shelves of a forgotten book-case, has it never retraced for you the graceful pictures of your early years? Have you not imagined you saw before you the broad meadows bathed in the rosy splendors of the twilight, as you read it for the first time? How quickly the night shadows fell over those divine pages! How the unpitying darkness made the characters swim upon the paling leaves! The day is over, the lambs bleat, the sheep have arrived at the fold, the chirp of the cricket is heard in the thatched cottages. You must go, for the dam is narrow and slippery, the banks are rough. You hasten, but you will arrive too late; supper will have begun. The servant, who loves you, has set back the clock as much as he dares, but it is all in vain; you will have the humiliation of entering last, and the grandmother inexorable as to etiquette, even in the seclusion of her country home, will reproach you in a sweet, sad voice, very softly, very tenderly, but you will be more sensible to her gentle chiding than to the severest chastisement. And when, asking you how you have passed the day, you confess to her that you have been reading in a meadow; when called upon to show the book, you draw trembling from your pocket—"Estelle and Némorin," Oh! then the grandmother will smile. Reassure yourself, your treasure will be restored to you, but you will have no need henceforth to forget the supper-hour. Happy season! Oh, my valley of the Noire! O Corinne! O Bernardin de Saint-Pierre! Oh, the Iliad! O Millevoye! O Atala! Oh, the willows by the river! Oh, my vanished youth!"

All these details are delicious. We find many other such where George Sand reveals to her readers charming glimpses of her own history. We see that the young girl's grandmother allowed her to read whatever suited her fancy. Corinne, and especially Atala, were to awaken singular dreams in this young head of fourteen years. The curious child read all that fell into her hands. Her ardent imagination sought food everywhere, and was inflamed at the first spark. Once at the convent, she was seduced by the poetry of Catholicism, and often yielded to transports of religious fervor. Like Saint Theresa, she passed entire hours in ecstasy at the foot of the altar. The death of her grandmother, which occurred in the mean time, only increased her ascetic disposition. She left the convent to pass a few weeks with Madame de Francueil, and returned firmly resolved to become a nun. It required all the authority of her family to induce her to marry six months after.

They gave her hand to the Baron Dudevant, an old, retired soldier, who had become a gentleman farmer, much versed in the rearing of stock, and himself overseeing the workmen. He was a man with a bald forehead, a gray mustache, and a severe eye; an exacting master, before whom all trembled, wife, servants, horses and dogs. Never were surroundings more uncongenial to the haughty and at the same time tender nature of this young woman. She possessed a fortune of nearly half a million. The agricultural husband used this dowry to enlarge his rural operations. He stocked his stables with pure-blooded animals, and doubled the number of his farming implements.

He concerned himself with everything but his wife, and did not seem to perceive that Aurore, with her seventeen years, her refined mind and her exquisite sensibility, must languish in the midst of this prosaic existence.

Madame Dudevant, at first, bore her sorrows with resignation; two beautiful children came ere long to console her with their infantile smiles and caresses. But soon, finding her heart wounded even in its maternal affections, she could bear up no longer. She fell dangerously ill; the faculty of Berri ordered her to drink the water of the Pyrénées. Baron Dudevant, bound to his merinos and his ploughshares, did not accompany his wife on the journey.

At Bordeaux, where she first went, and where she

bore letters of introduction to old friends of her family, Madame Dudevant could at last gain some knowledge of the world. She was overwhelmed with attentions, and people were pleased to extol the valuable qualities with which heaven had endowed her. Homage and admiration everywhere attended her.

Returned to her home, the young wife found her husband as coldly indifferent, and life monotonous and irksome as of old. In order to combat those ideas of revolt which had begun to assert their empire, she surrounded herself with friends and acquaintances, and she received with open arms, as so many, saviours, poetry, art and science.

A young compatriot of hers, Jules Sandeau, a law-student, was in the habit of visiting Château de Nohant during his vacations. It was he who first directed the glance of Aurore toward that literary horizon where her star was ere long to dawn, and ascend upward until lost from view. The naturalist, Neraud, dwelt upon an adjoining estate, and about this time began to come to the Château to give its young mistress lessons in botany and entomology. He was married and had two children, to whom he had wished to give the names of plants. They had allowed him without remonstrance, to name his son Olivier, but when he wanted to name his daughter *Petite Centaurée*, Madame Dudevant protested. She pursued her studies with this enthusiastic and eccentric teacher for the most part in the open air. Her little son, then four years old, was the companion of their rambles. These relations were without reproach. Neraud was a little, copper-colored man, absorbed by two passions, science and politics ; he had early enrolled himself under the flag of the republic, and had joined a club of Carbonari in Paris.

The friendship of a man for a woman seldom endures long without an admixture of love. Jules Sandeau returned to Paris, bearing in his head a profound passion which he dared not avow. And Neraud, too, soon yielded to the spell of Madame Dudevant's charms. He wrote *billets-doux* to her into which every now and then, slipped some little madrigal. The discovery of one of these led to a violent scene with the young wife's husband, in the midst of which a fancy seized the savant to quit the country and join the Moravian brethren. He stopped at the rocks of Vaucluse, resolved to live and die on the borders of that fountain, where Petrach had been wont to evoke the image of Laura from the mirror of the waters. Madame Dudevant had never returned his passion. " I was not much disquieted at this fatal resolution," writes she. "I knew him too well to believe his sorrow irreparable. So long as there were flowers and insects upon the earth, Cupid's arrows must glance from him without effect."

In fact, he returned with a herbarium full of treasures. Aurore ran to meet him, and laughing, gave him two hearty kisses. A tear coursed slowly down the cheek of the botanist. Love was submerged, but friendship survived. The suspicious husband would not believe in this sudden cure. His relations to his wife were poisoned by doubt and jealousy, and it becoming impossible for the pair to live together, a voluntary separation took place. Madame Dudevant left all her fortune in exchange for her liberty. Unhappy with her husband, deserted by Sandeau, Aurore went to Paris, where she took refuge in the same convent in which a portion of her youth had been spent. But her heart was so much agitated that she could not long enjoy the quiet of this holy retreat.

We ere long find Madame Dudevant in a little attic

of the Quay Saint Michel, where Jules Sandeau soon discovered her. She was absolutely destitute of resources. As for Sandeau, the son of a modest attorney, he received only a small allowance from his family, and was himself struggling with poverty. Mme. Dudevant having a slight knowledge of painting, Sandeau applied to the keeper of a fancy shop, who gave her some candle-stick trays and snuff-box covers to paint. But this work was both fatiguing and unremunerative. She resolved to write, stating her embarrassment, to Latouche, a native of her own province, the editor-in-chief of *Figaro*. He replied, inviting her and Sandeau to visit him at Vallée aux Loups, where he dwelt, near Châteaubriand. " Why do you not attempt journalism? " he asked. " It is less difficult than you think. Be one of our editors, Sandeau," he added—

" Ah me ! I am very indolent about writing," the young man replied naïvely.

" Oh, never mind that ! I will help you," said Aurore smiling.

" An excellent idea ! " exclaimed Latouche. " Go to work, and bring me your articles as soon as possible."

From that day Madame Dudevant abandoned the pencil for the pen. And thus began that literary partnership which attracted so much attention in the reading world of Paris. Our aspirants for money and fame set themselves to the work. At the end of six weeks, they had finished a book, entitled, "Rose and Blanche, or The Comedienne and the Nun." But they could find no publishers until Latouche at length came to their aid. He persuaded an old bookseller to pay four hundred francs for the manuscript.

" What name shall we sign ? " asked Aurore. " I cannot without scandal, write the name given me by my husband on the title-page of a book."

" If my father learns that I have engaged in literature, he will send me his malediction at the outset," said Sandeau.

" Cut Sandeau in two," returned Latouche, " and your father will no longer recognize you."

They followed this advice. The book was signed *Jules Sand*, and the young authors believed their fortune made. The law-student, very much given to the *dolce far niente*, slept more even than usual, and imagined that the four hundred francs would last forever. Aurore at this period first adopted the masculine costume, so as to visit the theatres unattended, when Sandeau was not inclined to bear her company.

Meantime the four hundred francs vanished, and destitution again threatened the young authors. Aurore was advised to journey to Berri to obtain a separation, or at least a yearly alimony from her husband. She departed, after having drawn up with Sandeau the plot of *Indiana*. They divided the proposed work into chapters ; Aurore took her share and promised Sandeau to toil diligently during her absence. Sandeau swore to do the same, but sleep got the upper hand with him, he worked only in dreams. Upon Aurore's return, he could not present her with a single line of his task.

" Ah well ! " said the young woman, laughing, " I have not been idle. See here ! Read and correct."

Aurore had placed in his hands the entire manuscript of " Indiana."

At the very first chapter, Sandeau broke out into enthusiastic expressions of delight. " There is nothing to retouch," he said. " This story is a *chef-d'œuvre*."

" So much the better ! " cried the delighted Aurore. " Let us take the two volumes to a publisher."

" But I have not worked upon this book," said the

young man hesitatingly. " You must sign it with your
own name."

" Never ! " returned Aurore. " We will continue to
use the name we have adapted for ' *Rose and Blanche.*' "

" Impossible ! " said Sandeau. " I am too honest to
steal your fame. I cannot accept your generous offer,
without descending in my own esteem.

Madame Dudevant went to Latouche, begging him to
make Sandeau reverse his decision."

" You signed your first book, Jules Sand," said Latouche. " *Sand*, then, is common property. Choose another
name than Jules. To-day is the 23d of April, Saint
George's day. Call yourself George Sand, and no one
can object."

And thus was born that pseudonym so widely celebrated. " Indiana " was sold for six hundred francs,
and its publishers prophesied for it a marvellous success.
Figaro pronounced the work passable as to style, but
mediocre in interest. Another leading critic, Alphonse
Rabbe, himself a would-be romancist, declared the
book absurd in conception, style and execution. But
Indiana became all the rage, despite these rigorous
judgments. Every journal made its commentary.
They related many anecdotes of the author, marvellous
as contradictory. Was it a man ? Who knew *her ?*
Should they say *he* or *her ?* Jules Janin, by his article
upon George Sand in the *Débats,* chose to augment both
the uncertainty and the mystery. It was given only to the
artist-world, now and then, to lift the corner of the veil.

George Sand ere long occupied a dwelling worthy of
her, where all the celebrities sued for the honor of
admittance. She here received artists as brothers,
smoked cigarettes with them, and surprised them by
her careless, witty gayety. Happy in her new name,

which had received a baptism of renown, she would be
called only George and continued to wear the masculine
costume. This costume became her marvellously. You
met her in the streets, upon the promenades, and upon
the boulevard, with a little overcoat fastened at the
waist, the loveliest black hair in the world falling over
it in curls. She carried a cane, and smoked a manilla
with the most graceful applomb.

In this first intoxication of success, she forgot the
faithful companion of her days of poverty and trial.
Sandeau, wounded to the heart, departed for Italy, on
foot, alone and penniless. He was too proud to complain, too courageous not to strive after forgetfulness or
indifference. He remained ten months in Naples, and
returned on a merchant ship, whose captain had befriend-
ed him. George Sand has more than once regretted
her friend of the Quay Saint-Michel. In 1835, she
wrote: " There hangs in my chamber the portrait of one
none here have seen. For a year, the person who left
me this portrait, sat with me every evening, at a little
table, and lived by the same work as I. We would sup
at this same little table, talking of art, of sentiment and
of the future. The future has failed in its promise to
us. Pray for me, my friend."

The author of " Indiana " soon attached other jewels
to her literary crown. The *Revue de Paris* and the
Revue des Deux Mondes, disputed for her books. *Valentine* appeared at the end of 1832. Six months after,
"*Leila* " saw the light. These three romances, like most of
those that followed, contain certain fierce attacks upon
the institution of marriage. A goodly number of critics
began to cry out at the scandal, and to accuse the author
of trying to sap the foundations of society. The editor
of " Literary Europe " could not find language strong

enough to condemn the audacious woman who sought
to overthrow the work of ages. Gustave Planche made
a cutting reply in the *Revue des Deux Mondes.* A duel
ensued, but men of letters wound only with the pen.

Wrongly or rightly, George Sand had great esteem
for the poetry of Alfred de Musset, then very young,
but nevertheless at the height of his celebrity. Buloz,
conductor of the *Revue des Deux Mondes,* brought together at a dinner the popular poet and novelist. A
few days after, Musset attended a soirée at George Sand's
and six weeks later he accompanied her on a tour to
Italy under the fallacious title of confidential secretary.

Two years after the poet's death, George Sand published that preposterous romance which has for its title,
Elle et Lui, and where each reader recognizes under the
most transparent veil, her own history and that of the
poet. This fulminating anathema, this bitter diatribe
aroused the whole world of letters. All the friends of
the deceased poet rose in energetic protest, demanding
an account of the audacious authoress for this personal
study, which she of all others, had the least right to
publish. M. Paul de Musset, the brother of Alfred,
took up the gauntlet,—he, in his turn published a personal study : *Lui et Elle,* where he presented the facts
in their true light.

On her return from Italy, Madame Sand published
five novels in rapid succession. Their titles were : " Andre," " La Marquise," " Lavinia," " Metella " and " Mat-
tea." Never has author possessed a more real and incontestable fecundity. For forty years she has known
no rest, but has heaped volume upon volume. " Leone,
Leoni," " Jacques," " Simon," " Mauprat," " La Der-
nière Aldini," " Les Maîtres Masäites," " Pauline," " A
Winter in Majorca," appeared from 1835 to 1837. Her

style has an irresistible fascination; it possesses two qualities equally precious, elegance and clearness. Her phrases, sometimes incorrect, are charming in their very incorrectness. She has very ably defended herself from the charge of immorality brought against her works. But we cannot deny that her romances have done harm, great harm. She has constituted herself the special pleader of passion insurgent against duty; of passion, ill at ease in the shackles of law, the conventionalities of society. Then as one needs replace what one has hurled down, for the unhappy ones exalted through her exaltation, led astray by her wanderings, she has conjured up the vision of a promised land where perfect freedom and happiness abide. She has created an unknown race of heroines, beautiful, noble, grand, strong, who through the elevation of their sentiments, rule the community of marriage, and who know how to rend without pity and without remorse, all the chains which restrain their inclinations.

Herself a victim of the conjugal tie, Madame Sand should have been content with claiming justice without preaching revolt; but with her, one first link of duty severed, all the rest become detached, and she made haste to proclaim herself the priestess of socialism.

In 1836, she resumed her name and title, to enter a suit against her husband, with a view to regaining possession of her fortune, and the guardianship of her children. At the different hearings which took place at the tribunal of La Châtre, and the court royal of Bourges, scandalous details enough were brought to light. The agricultural Baron Dudevant had felt a sovereign disdain for the intelligence and transcendent faculties of his young wife; "senseless, drivelling, foolish, stupid," were his frequent adjectives in addressing her. He accepted the separation most philosophically. He was very far from being all to blame. The acts of brutality of which he was accused, had a very natural excuse in the conduct of his wife, and are slight faults in comparison with conjugal infidelity.

At the time when Madame Sand gained her suit, and the custody of her children, her son Maurice was twelve, her daughter Solange was entering her nineteenth year. Soon the old manor of Nohant received her to its arms, and she wrote, " O my household gods, here you are just as I left you ! I incline before you with that respect each year of age renders more profound in the heart of man. . . Why did I ever forsake you,—you always propitious to simple hearts, you who watch over the little children while the mother sleeps, you who make chaste dreams of love hover around the couch of young girls, who give sleep and health to the aged? Do you recognize me, peaceful Penates? This pilgrim who arrives on foot, covered with the dust of the way and the mists of the night, do you not take her for a stranger?"

Madame Sand's children no more left her. They accompanied her to Paris and on her travels. Surrounded by loving hearts, her mind relieved from trouble, her soul at rest, she seemed to repudiate the desperate doctrines she had sown upon the pages of " Leila" and " Spiridion." We have seen her a Christian in her youth. Soured by misfortune, she had passed from faith to doubt, then she had given herself up to exaltation, to revolt ; now, she tried to walk in the path of repentance, but even here her old rancor against society led her astray. Like an invalid, who has long suffered, she repelled well known remedies, and resorted to quack nostrums. We now find her associated with Lamennais who had just founded the *Monde*. She wrote for this journal

5

her " Letters to Murcie," where the worthy sentiments
of the repentant Magdalene clash against a host of hete-
rodox·maxims which she shared in common with Lamennais. From this literary connection, there remained to her
a sort of asceticism alloyed with certain suspicious political tendencies. This gave birth to that series of so-
cialistic romances, which appeared one after another:
" Horace," " *La Petite Fadette*," " Consuelo," " The
Countess of Rudolstadt," " Monsieur Antoine," " *Les
Maitres Sonneurs*," etc.

"She allies herself," says Lamènie, "to those who
seek social happiness outside the eternal laws of religion
and of the family. She has become dreamy and Utopian,
but she will again become Christian."

We should never despair of the divine compassion.
But for the last twenty years, Madame Sand's works
have met with only doubtful success. Her sympathies
are with democrats and demagogues. When Madame
Sand goes to confession, she keeps nothing back. She
explains with much frankness the acrimony that is the
ruling trait in most of her works. Habituated to a
princely life, her income does not always suffice for her
expenses. Forced to earn money, she says "I have
pressed my imagination to produce, without seeking the
concurrence of my reason. Instead of coming to me
smiling and crowned with flowers, my Muse has met me
cold, reluctant, indignant, dictating to me only sombre,
bitter pages, icing over with doubt and despair all the
impulses of my soul."

Madame Sand took an active part in the political
movements of 1848, and when this new excitement was
over, she found refuge in an idyl. Her nature carries
her from one extreme to another. She has revealed
very fair dramatic qualities, and several of her pieces

lave won success before the footlights, although she
las enjoyed no brilliant theatrical triumph. Mademoiselle Rachel did not love her, and would play nothing
of hers. The great tragedienne declared laughing, that
she would read nothing of Madame Sand's for fear she
night be forced to admire her too much.

Some years ago George Sand published a "History of
my Life," in which happily, she has given herself no full-
length portrait. "The Snow-Man," "The Chateau of the
Desert," "Adriane" "Jean de la Roche" "Constance
Verrier" "The Marquis de Villemer," and "Mademoiselle de Quintine," are also among her later works. The
latter a decidedly anti-religious book, proves how far the
author is from her predicted conversion.

Madame Sand lives the greater portion of the time at
her château of Berri. Aside from the large sum earned
in literary labor she has an income of twelve thousand
francs. Always surrounded by a devoted circle of friends
and admirers, she cares for little that goes on outside
this circle, and confines within these narrow limits all
her sympathy and all her benevolence. Poor, aspiring
and talented young authors appeal to her in vain for
aid and encouragement. She makes it a rule to send
back unopened every manuscript that is offered her for
perusal. Is it right, when we have reached the summit
thus to despise those who struggle at its base? Where
would the author of "Indiana" now be if she had not
found some help at the outset? But in the domain of
letters as well as in that of the air, it is seldom that the
sparrows can count upon the eagles.

The château of Nohant is not a seignorial house. An
almost vulgar simplicity reigns within it, and the furniture attests the filial piety of the châtelaine rather than
her taste in ornamental things,

You see here needlework, drawings, sketches, all souvenirs of the happy triumphs of a pampered childhood.
The mistress of the house sleeps little, five or six hours
at most.   All the rest of her time is consecrated to literary work.   Her table is abundant and delicate, her appetite is good, her mental and physical vigor are remarkable for one of her years.   Surrounded by children
and grandchildren, her home life is cheerful and happy.
Silent and grave herself, she loves to hear conversation ;
stories and *bons mots* find in her a smiling and benevolent auditor. Occasionally she, too, indulges in jests and
witty sallies.   Her son, Maurice, is a romancer who has
written several popular books.   Although Madame Sand
is past her seventieth year, her literary activity still remains unabated, " Ma Sœur Jeanne" and " Flammarnde "
are the very latest of her works.   They have her olden
fascinations of style, and although free from the gross
immorality of her earlier works, they are still excessively French in tone and treatment.   Some of the critics
praise, others condemn.

George Sand is not read now so much as she once
was.   Take out that spice of wickedness which flavors
the ordinary French novel, and to very many readers
its charm is gone.   There are those who say that as her
moral tone has become elevated, her vigor and once
matchless style have deteriorated.

A recent Parisian letter-writer who met Madame
Sand on a flying visit to the capital where she very
seldom appears of late, describes her as having grown
fearfully ugly.   She is old, and yet above all things she
hates old age ; she cannot live long, and yet she shud-
ders at the idea of death.   She must, we think, be burdened with a consciousness of transcendent gifts un-
worthily employed ; she must feel that to the world she

is so soon to leave, she has done more harm than good. If in her, the culture of the heart had equalled that of the intellect, if the Christian graces had kept pace with the mental graces, the heavenly with the worldly aspir-rations, these declining years, so full of sadness, might have been the serene, starry evening that succeeds the heated, toilsome day, and death no angel of wrath but a messenger of love.

ALFRED DE MUSSET. *

I.

ALL records of the French *noblesse* make mention of the De Musset family, and there is no need here to record the genealogy of the poet who renders this name illustrious. Upon the list of his ancestors is a certain Calvin de Musset, who was a poet and musician, and intimate friend of Thibout, the poet-king of Navarre. But we need not go back to the time of Queen Blanche, to seek a gift for poetry and letters among the ancestors of Alfred de Musset. His maternal grandfather, a learned lawyer, in the interval of grave pursuits, paid court to the muses, and Alfred's father a soldier under the First Consul, and afterwards Minister of the Interior, found in literature a relief from the burdens of military and civic duties. He published several works, the best known being a Life of Jean Jacques Rousseau. He also wrote verses, particularly excelling in those of a burlesque character.

Alfred de Musset was born in Paris, December 11th, 1810. At the age of three years his beauty attracted the attention of all, and a Flemish painter, Van Briće, begged permission to paint his portrait. This picture is to-day in the possession of his family.

Until the age of nine years, Alfred's education had

---

been intrusted to his mother, a woman of rare virtues and accomplishments, and to private tutors ; he then entered the college of Henry IV. finding himself the youngest and most advanced of a class of sixteen. Paul Foucher, the brother-in-law of Victor Hugo, was his friend and schoolmate, and when Alfred was but seventeen, introduced him into the literary *Cénacle* of which Victor Hugo was chief. He was received by the Hugos as one of the family and often invited to dine with them. This intimacy lasted four years—years always dear to the remembrance of the younger of the two poets.

As his father did not urge his immediate choice of a career, Alfred profited by the delay, and engaged in various studies. He attended a course of lectures upon law, and one upon anatomy, and took lessons in drawing, painting, music and the English language, at the same time strengthening his mind by useful reading. At the end of a year, being questioned by his father as to his intentions, he confessed with great humility, that he had no taste for a profession, that he felt drawn only to pursuits which could lead to nothing, that is to say to the arts and poetry.

De Musset *père*, having little faith in Alfred's prospects as artist or poet, forced him to enter a bank as copyist. But this did not long endure. Soon recognizing the poetic gifts of his son, he did not seek to turn him from his true vocation.

Alfred passed all his evenings at the Cénacle. After having played for some time the rôle of auditor, he had a desire to compose and read ballads in his turn. His first lengthy effort was " Don Paez." An evening was given to its formal reading. Since leaving college the student had become transformed into the dandy. He came to the Cénacle on this all important occasion, dressed in the extreme of fashion, with dainty frills and a D'Orsay hat. The audience was ardent and enthusiastic. "Don Paez" was received with frantic applause.

The meetings of the Cénacle, which had now begun to be holden in two or three different salons, were not exclusively given to literature. Dancing was sometimes kept up until dawn, for a plenty of young girls lent the charm of their presence to these reunions. At one of these soirées, Sainte Beuve seeing the author of "Don Paez" dancing with juvenile ardor, dedicated to him his verses entitled "The Ball."

In 1829, De Musset added a new poem, "Mardoche," to the pieces already so well known to his friends, and they were published in a volume. In reading these poems, grave people frowned. "Can it be," said they, "that a young man of nineteen years, writes all this from his own experience?"—No, he did not thus write. As yet, he knew almost nothing of life. These Andelusian passions were only youthful dreams, these railing, cavalier airs were only pretence, this profligacy was only poetic license. All this existed only in his head, and women, more clairvoyant than pedants, well perceived here the very proofs of innocence and ingenuousness.

The blonde poet of the "Spanish and Italian Tales," found a most enthusiastic reception in the salons of Paris. Flattery and adulation everywhere attended him. But his happiness was not without alloy. One of his pieces was hissed at the Odeon, and from the reception given to some other dramatic efforts, he began to think that the theatres did not desire his work. He found in lyric poetry his consolation, and published many pieces in the *Revue de Paris*.

In 1851 he wrote several critical and fictitious articles for the *Temps*. By turns laborious and dissipated, he worked with incredible ardor, if nothing came to distract his thoughts. The labor once finished or interrupted, the poet again relapsed into the dandy. His friends, richer than he, too, often drew him from his books. He could not conceal his aristocratic tastes. All places consecrated to fashion exercised an irresistible attraction over him. At the Opera, the Théâtre-Italien, the Boulevard de Gand, the Café de Paris, the most distinguished men then met for play, for revels extended far into the night. To move at ease upon this dangerous ground, a fashionable coat did not suffice; one must have his pockets well garnished with money. When this indispensable requisite failed him, the young dandy was happily obliged to return to his work.

In 1832, Alfred de Musset lost his father. This event marks a turning point in his life; it changes the whole course of his ideas. He resolved to conquer a new position. His talent had ripened, and he wrote three poems very different from his " Spanish Tales." They were " The Cup and the Lip " " Of What do Young Girls Dream ? " and " Namouna." They appeared in one volume in 1833. From this moment dates his separation from the romantic school. No more triumphant evenings! No more enthusiastic cheers! But he consoled himself in thinking that he should also be relieved from sterile discussions. " I have played with words long enough," he said, " I desire now to feel, to think, to express freely, without submitting to the rule of any order, without depending upon any church."

This independence caused great wrath. Alfred de Musset was regarded as a deserter, a refugee. These were severe words to apply to a young man because he wished to arrange the metres of his own verses, and recognized some merit in the poetry of Racine.

5*

A little after the publication of these new poems, M. Buloz, of the *Revue des Deux Mondes*, came to secure the assistance of their author, and from this visit ensued relations which death alone interrupted. The first work of Alfred de Musset for this Review was "Andrea del Sarto." The comedy, "Marianne's Caprices" followed and three months later, "Rolla" appeared. Stendhal greatly admired this poem, declaring that it filled a gap in French literature, being the French equivalent for "Faust" and "Manfred" of which Germany and England are so justly proud. Its author was only twenty-two years old.

In the autumn of 1835, Alfred de Musset departed for Italy. He returned the April following, scarce recovered from a brain fever of which he had come near dying at Venice. Feeble as he was through the year 1834, he had written two of his most remarkable works "One May not Fool with Love," and "Lorenzaccio." One of his friends having remarked to him, that in the first of these two works, certain details seemed to belong to the last century, others to the present time, he answered smiling, "Can you tell me of what time man is, and under what reign woman has lived?" The latter work, dealing with events in Florence under the sway of Lorenzo de Medici, is not yet known and appreciated as it deserves to be. While this poem was going through the press, Alfred went to Baden, seeking relaxation for four months of hard work and strict seclusion in his study. From this journey he brought back the subject of his poem. "A Good Fortune," proving that the relaxation had borne excellent fruits.

The year 1835 is one of the most fruitful as well as one of the most agitated in the life of Alfred de Musset. June 1st he published "Lucia" and a fortnight after

" The Night of May." Then come " Barberina's Distaff,"
and " The Confessions of a Child of the Century."
Between these glowing pages where he traced so sombre
a picture of the evils of despair, he interrupted himself
to improvise in a few days, " The Chandelier," which is
assuredly one of his merriest comedies.

About this time, Alfred de Musset fell in love with
the pretty woman to whom he addresses the stanzas
" To Ninon." Jealousy on his part caused the ship-
wreck of this love. He was stunned by the blow, but
only for the moment. Happily it is not always true
that " The mouth keeps silence when the heart speaks ! "
The first cry torn from this new wound is the " December Night," which is no continuation of the " Night of
May," and has its source in sentiments of a very different order. This beloved one is no other than the Emmeline of the " Confessions." She occupies a considerable
place in the works of Alfred de Musset ; to her we owe two
of his most admired poems, and his best prose writings.

Musset had still one lady friend whose almost maternal affection was extremely dear to him. The Duchess
de Castries, to all the advantages of intellect united the
rare qualities of a noble character. Chained to her arm-
chair by an incurable malady of which she never spoke,
always occupied with others in the midst of incessant
sufferings, this courageous woman existed only through
the heart and the intelligence. Her life was a continual
example of patience and resignation, and this example
could not fail to exercise some influence over the most
impatient young fellow in the world. She had a very
small court composed of young women and intimate
friends, who came to divert and console her. Alfred de
Musset saw her very often. " When I have need of courage," said he, " I know where it is to be found." The

duchess read a great deal, she was conversant with all the literary novelties, which she criticized for herself with a pure, even severe taste, and with a judgment perfectly well informed. Upon the evening of the first representation of " A Caprice," she went to hear it. Despite her age and infirmities, she survived the poet she had loved as a son. None ever dared speak ill of Alfred de Musset in her presence.

Musset's writings in 1836, show that he was then enjoying great freedom of heart and mind. First comes " We Should Swear by Nothing," the " August Night," and "Stanzas on the Death of Malibran," follow. In these latter lines he had to express a general sentiment, and regrets shared by all the world. This time his poetical sensibility was moved by the sorrow of others rather than his own. In his " Letters from Two Dwellers in the Ferté sous Jouarre; " he treats several questions of literary criticism with a comic verve and a sort of wit that recalls Paul Louis Courier. These essays excited great curiosity ; their continuation was demanded, but our poet had little taste for criticism. In his opinion the best warfare to wage upon bad books is to produce good ones. He abandoned the Letters, and wrote " A Caprice." All the world knows the whimsical fortune of this comedy. In its journey from the office of the Revue des Dexu Mondes to the Rue Richelieu the " Caprice" passed through Saint-Petersburg, and was ten years on the way.

II.

Alfred de Musset was naturally confiding and even credulous.

Se défendant de croire au mal,
Comme d'un crime.

As he wrote in one of his last poems. But he could not rely upon himself to ignore what experience had taught him. From a lesson of deception came the " October Night," which may be considered a continuation of the " May Night," although written two years after.

Up to this time Musset had written no novels. He wished to attempt this species of literature which Boccaccio, Cervantes and Mérimée, have elevated to the level of poetry, comedy and tragedy. The first subject which occurred to him was " Emmeline." The success of this recital encouraged him. In the eighteen months following the first of August, 1839, he composed six novels, whose titles it is needless to repeat here. The one the author esteemed best is the " Fils de Lilien; " he had remarked the subject at the same time as that of " Andre del Sarto," in a history of Italian painting. When he had finished these six little romances, he stopped, saying he had enough of prose. But during these eighteen months he had not neglected poetry; upon three different occasions, he had returned to his first love.

One day, upon opening a volume of Spinoza, he felt greatly incensed at the demonstrative formulas of this philosopher, and in spirit engaged in a discussion with him. This redoubtable reasoner had not the power to persuade him. Once upon this ground, he set himself

to reading, night and day, with his habitual ardor, all
the books which have treated of that it is forbidden
man to know. This grand problem had often agitated
him.   Never had he lifted his eyes to heaven to contemplate the infinite, without experiencing a sort of resent-
ment at seeing and still not comprehending. At such
a moment he must have uttered his despairing cry ?

"I cannot rest; despite myself, the infinite torments
me."

But at another moment of poetic exaltation, he replied
to the great skeptical thinkers with whom he had
been mentally contending, by his poem, " Hope in God."

In 1837, Alfred de Musset received the offer of a
place as attaché to the Spanish embassy at Madrid. His
talents, his personal appearance, his perfect knowledge
of the world, rendered him peculiarly fitted for such a
post.   Some years earlier, he would have been delighted
to accept it; but now, although still very young, he
could not summon courage to break the ties of habit,
family and friendship which bound him to Parisian life.
His refusal gave no offence, and he testified his gratitude
for the good intentions of the Prince Royal, through
whom this honor had been offered him, by publishing a
poem on the birth of the Count de Paris, which did not
contain a single line of flattery.

At the close of the year 1838, two newly-risen stars
of the first lustre dawned upon Paris.   Pauline Garcia,
aged eighteen, arrived from Brussels, and began to sing
in some salons, Rachel also made her first appearance at
the Comédie Française. Alfred de Musset took an extreme interest in the success of these young artistes.
When he saw Rachel attacked by the dramatic critics,
he was stirred up to break lances in her defence. Rachel,
pleased with such championship, made the poet promise

to write her a tragedy; but ere it was finished, this inconstant woman seemed to have changed her mind, or to have forgotten all about the matter. Two or three times, guided by a vague instinct, she returned to Musset for a rôle, and he, seduced by her grace and those wonderful powers of fascination she knew so well how to exercise, when caprice or interest demanded, only too readily promised to fulfil her request. But the desired rôle was scarce begun ere she would again relapse into indifference and neglect. For this reason, these two whose accord would have been so fruitful to the world of art, became involved in a serious quarrel, and were reconciled only on the eve of Rachel's departure for America. The relations between Pauline Garcia and Musset were most friendly, the cantatrice finding in the poet a warm admirer and indulgent critic. But the public received the young singer somewhat coldly, and she resolved to seek her fortune in foreign lands. Musset's verses entitled "Adieu," seem to have been addressed to Mlle. Garcia on her departure for England or Russia.

As on one side the beautiful illusions vanished, on the other came anxieties of incontestable reality. As a result of his abandonment of prose Musset was now suffering from financial embarrassment. Though habitually lavish in his expenditures, a debt, to a nature like his, was a remorse. The debt once contracted, his most simple method of defraying it was to set about writing a goodly number of pages. But enforced composition is not well for poets, and Musset did not wish to attempt it. One day, he conceived the idea of seeking a remedy for his sufferings in writing a recital of a poet condemned by necessity to work at that which he despised. He wrote forty pages on this subject, pages of heart-rending pathos. They met no eye but that of his brother and his friend Tattet. An unforeseen event relieved our poet from embarrassment, and the work was never finished. M. Charpentier came to him with a proposal to issue an edition of his works which would bring them within the reach of persons of small fortune. The works issued in this form, made a revolution in the book trade, and passed through twenty editions.

In the midst of his financial troubles, Musset had found an obstinate pleasure in obeying the unlucrative caprices of his Muse. During these six agitated months, sonnets, songs and idyls came faster than ever from his pen, but the only one of these pieces known to the public is the "Adieu." He found a peculiar charm in these little compositions, because they did not seem work, and changed into poetry passing impressions and unforeseen circumstances.

Criticism then was no more avaricious of praises than it is to-day; it lavished them with the same profusion upon charlatanism and mediocrity, but it did not fail to deny to Alfred de Musset the rank that was his due so long as such denial was in its power. Now, chiding his modesty, it treated him as a school-boy from whom something might be hoped in the future; now it asked him when he would end his essays, and give the world the full measure of his talent. From 1838 to 1841, he had published, besides his two first volumes of poetry, thirty-five works of great diversity of character, which to-day do honor to French literature in all the countries of the earth. Musset, deeply feeling the injustice of the critics, declared that he had for years been a literary man by profession, and had performed all the duties of that office; that henceforth, he would be a poet and nothing but a poet, that he would write verses when he felt in the mood for it, but nothing more. His friends expostulated, but it was in vain.

Imaginative literature had then reached one of its climacteric epochs. The journals had instituted the serial romance. At an early age the monster gave evidence of what enormities it would be capable as it grew to maturity. "When Racine and Molière wrote for Louis XIV. and his court," said Alfred de Musset, "they had to satisfy an exacting public, too refined, perhaps, often frivolous and disdainful, but the very difficulty of pleasing kept the artist or writer wide awake, and forced him to do his best. To-day, one has only to amuse an ignorant mob. Why speak good French to it? It would not understand. As for myself, I have nothing to say to this mob."

In fine, to all arguments for breaking his silence he replied with better ones for keeping it. But when the Muse came of her own accord to seek him, he received her gladly. A public misfortune changed his ill-humor and ennui into discouragement. He had a sincere affection for the Duke of Orleans, and had built great hopes on the future reign of this young prince; hopes not for himself, but for art and letters. More than once his old schoolfellow had said to him that although there could be no new *renaissance*, they might be sure of seeing again in France a court amorous of beautiful things, and absorbed in intellectual pleasures. Suddenly, he found that these hopes were only chimeras. He felt a profound sorrow at the death of the prince royal, a sorrow which for a year he could find no words to express. Then he poured forth his love, his admiration and his regret.

He had not published a line of prose for three years, when he consented to write for an editor who had shown him great friendship, the "Merle Blanc." Designing only a *bagatelle*, he composed a little masterpiece, of subtle allegory and harmless criticism. Later, the same

editor obtained from him the little story of "Mimi
Pinson" for an illustrated publication.

Alfred de Musset had no great zeal for the service of
the National Guard. They shut up the recalcitrant poet
in prison, and he rhymed gaily on his captivity. He was
soon released. Weary of reproaches for his idleness, but
resolved to write only as the impulse seized him, in the
spring of 1845, he fled to his maternal uncle, a subprefect
in the Vosges. He visited many places, roaming
over the mountains and from town to town. Three
months away from Paris was a great deal for him; he
returned in August.

Since the death of the Duke of Orleans, a sort of
languor and palsy had stricken all. Lamartine had said
that France was ennuyéd at this time, and Musset felt
the lamentable truth of the words. He regretted having
been born in this age of transition, amid a distracted
generation with no passion but for money and stock-
jobbing, no taste but for bric-à-brac. People then spoke
less modestly than to-day of the progress of our age; the
conquests of science over matter had not consoled them
for the loss of the ideal. Our poet sought around him for
some flash of genius, and found it only in the impersona-
tions of Rachel. He did not miss one of them. Later,
when Madame Ristori came to France, he saw her thirty
times in the rôle of Mirra. Italian music remained one
of his consolations. "Without Rossini and Rachel, it
would not be worth while to live," he often said. He
did not dream of ranking himself among the brilliant
lights of poetry and genius. "I know that I am making
my furrow in this wearisome age," he said, "but they
will perceive it only after my death."

The public took his silence and his disdain for inability.
These malevolent insinuations could have upon a mind

haughty as his, no other effect than to augment his disdain and his silence. From 1845 to 1847, he published nothing but three or four sonnets; yet these were of his ·best, as if to show the world that his silence was voluntary, and that his muse had lost neither verve nor gayety.

An unexpected event somewhat changed this disdainful mood. Madame Allan-Desproux was playing the "Caprice" in Saint Petersburgh, and the manager of the Théâtre Français wished its representation in Paris. The great actress was prevailed upon to assume the principal rôle, and the success of the piece proved that the public had still a taste for Musset's refined works. Other pieces of his followed, adding greatly to his reputation.

This tardy stroke of fortune roused Musset from his contemptuous indifference, and gave him a new heart for work. He wrote several comedies, among them "Carmosine," which he considered one of his best.

Mlle. Rachel was like the Roman women she represented so well, who, according to Plutarch, ran after fortunate people. Seeing the success of Musset's late pieces, she again besieged him for a rôle. She went to see him, she several times invited him to dinner, she wrote him almost tender letters. She did better than to urge him to write her a rôle, she inspired him. He decided upon "Faustina" as his subject. But unhappily his piece "Bettina," just then being represented at the Gymnasium, was coldly received, and Rachel changed her mind. The invitations, the visits, the gracious notes, all ceased. Rachel demanded nothing more, and feigned to have forgotten *her author*, as she had been calling Musset in her letters. "Faustina" was never finished. It exists as a fragment among our author's posthumous works. The fragment is so excellent, that we know not which most to deplore, the inconstancy of the great actress or the excessive sensibility of the poet.

The Academy opened its doors to Alfred de Musset, and when he pronounced his eulogy upon M. Dupaty, whom he succeeded, all were astonished at his fine manners and his youth. But few of the members had known him before, except by name. His next work was "Augustus, Dream," a poem afterwards set to music for the stage by Gounod. The *Moniteur* demanded a novel; he wrote *La Mouche*, a fresh, graceful composition. The following year, he wrote his last work, *L'Ane et le Ruisseau.*

In childhood Alfred de Musset had been subject to palpitations of the heart of an alarming character, but at twenty, he enjoyed such robust health that fatigue was unknown to him. After 1840, he had an occasional touch of the old malady, and a severe regimen was prescribed to him, which he would not follow. When a year or two before his death, he was reproached by his brother for trifling with life and health, he answered, "I have already passed the age when I would have been glad to die." In 1855, the progress of the disease became rapid. A frequent sensation of stoppage at the heart was the certain sign of an affection of the aortic valves. But none thought death so near, when on the night of May 2d, 1857, his heart ceased to beat forever. He had died, thinking he was falling asleep, in his very last moments preoccupied with his brother's interests more than with his own, and forming projects for a distant future they were both to share.

Alfred de Musset was of medium height, elegant in form, with an exquisite ease and polish of manner. He had blonde hair, naturally curling and very abundant, a complexion of rare freshness, an aquiline nose, blue eyes, a firm glance, an expressive mouth. To his last day, "he had the May upon his cheeks" like Fantasio, and he appeared younger than he really was. In conversation he was ordinarily witty and gay, laughing without effort. He knew how to draw out others, and to place all around him at their ease. He threw a charm over even the simplest subject, and you often perceived the profundity of his thoughts only in musing upon them after his departure. With women he was an especial favorite, and young girls took great delight in his society, so diverting and yet so elevating.

His natural inclination for all the arts was so great, that if poetry had not been his imperious vocation, his genius would have found expression elsewhere. His family and friends have preserved some very remarkable drawings by his hand. Passing a month at the château of his cousin, Adolphe de Musset, he filled two albums with pictures; they are, for the most part, caricatures of very striking resemblance, and were executed from memory with a boldness and freedom of touch in which we recognize the designer and the painter.

Alfred de Musset never deserted poetry; he knew no weariness of verse, which he has called "that limpid and beautiful language, the world neither understands nor speaks." He was not a utilitarian, but he was useful in teaching men to see clearly into their own souls, in clothing in sublime, beautiful words, what they felt without the power of expressing it; in securing for them precious hours of forgetfulness, of consolation, of tenderness and of amusement.

The day following his death, the journals were unanimous in the expressions of their regret. Fame, which he had called

"That tardy plant, a lover of the tomb,"

sprang up upon his tomb, and with such splendor and

rapidity, that envy soon arose more wrathful than ever. His works, his character, his private life even, were assailed. That impious warfare still endures, but it will have an end. The assaults of his detractors already recoil upon themselves. A day will come when the life of this poet will be better understood, when none will dare insult his memory. The world will then render justice to him who no longer gives umbrage to any vanity. Alfred de Musset never did wrong, never wished wrong to any one. He was amiable, generous, and above all, sincere. He too could have spoken of himself those words of deepest meaning which he has placed in the mouth of Perdican: " It is I who have lived, and not a fictitious being, created by my pride or my ennui."

To the perhaps too partial estimate of his brother's character given by M. Paul de Musset, we append these concluding words of an essay upon the poet by Eugene de Mirecourt: .

" Alfred de Musset was an erratic poet, a victim of the corruption of others rather than of his own. It is he who has written these lines, which should make the boldest youth of our century shudder:

" ' Poisoned from youth with the writings of the encyclopædists, I early imbibed the sterile milk of impiety. Human pride, that god of insanity and egotism, closed my mouth to prayer. How miserable are those men who have ever railed at that which can save a human soul! I was born in a corrupt age. I have much to expiate. Pardon, O Christ, those who blaspheme! ' "

The poet grew grave and sad in his later years. They said that the dignities of the Academy pressed heavily upon him, little dreaming that his nature had grown deeper and more reverent. Had he lived, he would doubtless have expiated the literary sins of his youth.

VICTOR HUGO.*

WHEN France crosses the gulf of revolution, it is rare that she does not disinherit some of her noblest sons. Victor Hugo, like Alighieri driven from Florence by the Guelphs, was doomed for long years to sigh and chafe upon a foreign soil. It does not belong to us to write the history of the politician, we have to do only with that of the poet.

Of an ancient and valiant family of Lorraine, ennobled upon the battle-field, Victor Hugo was born at Besançon, in 1803. His father, a general in the service of Joseph Buonaparte, then king of Naples, was chosen to conduct the warfare against Fra Diavolo, a terrible brigand, the horror of all Italy. He succeeded in routing the band, and then accompanying Joseph Buonaparte to Spain, he won great distinction by his military science. He did not recross the Pyrenees until 1814, when Napoleon sent him to the defence of Thionville. With a handful of men, he kept back the entire armies of the Cossacks and Prussians from the ramparts confided to his protection.

In early childhood Victor Hugo travelled through Italy and Spain. The sun of the South with its most

---

* *Portraits et Silhouettes.* By Eugene de Mirecourt.

ardent rays, warmed this young, enthusiastic head, from which poetry was ere long to gush forth as from a never-failing fountain.

Before reaching his fifteenth year, the boy was contestant for an academic prize. The Academy declared that in presenting himself at this age, he had mocked at the judges. Messieurs, the Forty, could not comprehend that poetry like valor, does not depend on the number of years. The prize was divided between Saintine and Lebrun. The Academy denied Hugo a crown, but gave him the first honorable mention. Indignant at this injustice, he sent his verses to Toulouse. There were three poems, and he won three successive triumphs.

He lived at this time in the ancient abbey of the Feuillantines; here his mother, a noble and gifted woman, lavished upon him the treasures of her love. The gratitude of her son has rendered her immortal. We say the mother of Victor Hugo, as we say the mother of the Gracchi, the mother of Saint-Louis. A native of Vendée and a royalist, she was naturally the first muse of the youthful poet. Some of his finest poems seem but echoes of the maternal heart. When he lost his mother, he was nineteen years old. During his period of mourning, he wrote that book of so sombre a cast, "*Han d'Islande*," whose hero, a sort of Blue-Beard, he elevates to the sublime; a statue outside of nature, but hewn in granite. This romance was the signal for that conflict against his country so long sustained by Victor Hugo, and from which he was to emerge conqueror. From all sides, they attacked this audacious youth, who shook off the trammels of old tradition, and seemed ready to proclaim himself chief of a school. Hugo numbered his enemies, and prepared his arms.

At this time he passed most of his evenings with the father of Emile Deschamps, in the midst of a chosen circle He was very timid, but under this timidity lay a grave, almost austere dignity, which made a vivid impression upon all, and was a presage of the future. They already saluted him as the master. At these re-unions he made the acquaintance of a young girl, who awoke his heart to love. He married this Mlle. Foucher in 1823. The husband was twenty, the bride fifteen. If they were rich, it was in love, youth and hope. The adored one had all the songs of the poet and all his heart. To her he wrote :

C'est toi dont le regard éclaire ma nuit sombre,
Toi dont l'image luit sur mon sommeil joyeux !
C'est toi qui tiens ma main quand je marche dans l'ombre,
Et les rayons du ciel me vienne de tes yeux.

Hélas ! je t'aime tant qu'à ton nom seul je pleure :
Je pleure, car la vie est si pleine de maux
Dans ce morne desert tu n'as point demeure,
Et l'arbre ou l'on s'assied lève ailleurs des rameaux.

Mon Dieu ! mettez la paix et la joie auprès d'elle;
Ne troublez pas ses jours; ils sont à vous, Seigneur !
Vous devez la bénir car son âme fidèle
Demande à la vertu le secret du bonheur.

" Dear one, whose glance my sombre night enlightens,
Whose image beams o'er all my joyous days ;
My hand in thine, the deepest shadow brightens,
For from thine eyes fall heaven's serenest rays.

" I love thee so, tears from my eyes come welling;
I weep, for life is full of grief and care ;
In this drear desert thou canst find no dwelling,
The tree to shelter thee grows otherwhere.

"My God, give peace and joy to this pure spirit,
Vex not her days, her days that flow from thee ;
Sure loyal souls like hers must bliss inherit,
They ask from virtue their felicity."

These anxieties of the poet for the lot of his young household were of brief duration. The first edition of "Han d'Islande," was very soon exhausted, the second brought ease to that little dwelling, No. 42 Notre-Dame des-Champs, that poetical abode hidden like a bird's-nest amid the trees. Two lovely children had come to lend new delight to this happy home. Here the youthful wife and mother gracefully welcomed the large circle of friends the rising poet and author gathered around him. This circle which had for its leading spirits such men as Dumas, Alfred de Vigny, Méry and Sainte-Beuve, had begun to form a powerful art-coterie of which Victor Hugo was chief. They conversed, they read each other's verses, and often at sunset, they would take strolls over the hills and valleys around Paris. Sometimes they would meet on the route along the hawthorn and alder-hedges, the members of a rival. *Cénacle** installed at the inn of Mère Saget, a good woman whom Béranger has sung as Madame Grégoire. Hugo and his clique would press the hands of Thiers and his band, and there would, for the moment, be a fusion of the two Cénacles, while poetry and politics met as sisters.

Hugo had not ceased to be a royalist, but his loyalty was a matter of sentiment rather than of conviction. The patriotic feeling which inspired his odes on the death of the Duke de Berry and the birth of the Duke

---

* *Cénacle*, a Latin word meaning guest-chamber. The term was first adopted as a designation of the circle of romantic poets which met at Victor Hugo's.

de Bordeaux, dictated also that well-known ode to Napoleon. The country, decimated by war, was still haunted by that cry of despair raised by the mothers ; Rachel weeping for her children and refusing to be comforted because they were not.

In 1826, the " Odes and Ballads " appeared in two volumes, bringing their author fame and fortune. Happy in both his literary and domestic life, Hugo's lot was at this time an enviable one. In the outer world, friends, prosperity, renown smiled upon him ; at home he was blessed with the society of an adored wife and beautiful children. But he did not rest content with the laurels already won, he would not allow himself to repose amid these family joys. His life was full of effort and full of conflict. Every day some new attack annoyed him. Envious rivals dared accuse him of having appropriated the chords of Byron's lyre. When " *Bug Jargal*," his first romance, appeared, they declared that he had imitated Walter Scott. They went further. All the journals cried out that he was a barbarian ; that he persistently violated the precepts of good taste, that he despised the dictionary of the Academy, the poetics of Aristotle and the verses of Racine. They would fain clip his wings, and swathe him in the old languages of the past.

The injustice of these attacks led naturally to an exaggerated defence. The poet must either adore the public idols or burn them. He burned them.

" Cromwell " and its preface were the signal for a warfare, furious, terrible, implacable ; for another combat like that of Thermopylæ, where a handful of men led by a dauntless chief, dared fight against thousands of enemies, and were not conquered.

The Hugo family left the Rue Notre-Dame des Champs,

when they saw the architects building in the midst of their beautiful promenades, uprooting the trees, cutting off the perspective, and bringing Paris into their solitude. And besides, they had lost their first-born. In a maternal heart, souvenirs of mourning are ineffaceable enough without having all around incite them. They left this abode of so much joy and so much sorrow, but not until the poet had inscribed upon the tomb of the sweet child gone to rejoin the angels, these touching lines:

> *Oh, dans ce monde auguste où rien n'est éphémère,*
> *Dans ces flots de bonheur que ne trouble aucun fiel,*
> *Enfant! loin du sourire et des pleurs de ta mère,*
> *N'est-tu pas orphelin au ciel?* *

In the Rue Jean-Goujon at the Champs-Elysées, was reared the new tent under which Victor Hugo's family took shelter. They remained here until 1830, when they established themselves in the very heart of Paris, in the house No. 6, Place-Royale. Here it is that our literary generation has known them.

In this old hotel Louis XIII., a silent and solemn abode, for fifteen years was enthroned the king of modern poetry. He had his court like the king at the Tuilleries, an assiduous, devoted court, full of veneration for the master, always ready to defend him.

You entered Victor Hugo's house through an immense ante-chamber opening upon the Place-Royale. This ante-chamber led to a dining-hall hung with woven

---

* "Oh! in that world august, where comes nor change nor dying,
    Amid those floods of bliss where no earth-griefs arise ;
    Far from thy mother's smile and tears, art thou not sighing
    E'en for the human love, dear child, thou orphan of the skies!"

tapestry and full of ancient drawings. The stove was concealed behind a splendid panoply to which twenty centuries seemed to have paid tribute. From this room you passed into the grand salon hung with a marvellous crimson tapestry, its subject borrowed from the Romance of the Rose. At the further end of the salon was a divan, raised upon a sort of dais, whose background was a crimson banner embroidered with gold. This banner had been taken in 1830, at the siege of Algiers.

Victor Hugo was the first to restore a taste for beautiful historic furniture. His salon in the Place-Royale had a grandiose character which made one despise the narrow cells so dear to Parisian masonry. Full length portraits of the master and mistress of the house, seemed ready to descend from their Gothic frames to salute you and receive you. Not far from these hung the precious picture of Saint-Evre, presented to Victor Hugo by the Duke of Orleans. At the end of a long corridor such as we used to find in cloisters, was a sleeping-chamber, then a study, an admirable museum which the poet's fancy had peopled with all sorts of rare, curious and artistic objects. The light entered through an arched window of stained glass, throwing fantastic gleams around the chairs of sculptured oak, the lacquer-work, the stones, the statuettes, the old Sévres.

New friends thronged to this abode in the Place-Royale, to which came also all the old habitués of the rue Notre-Dâme. Victor Hugo was the acknowledged chief of the new school of literary men, and all were eager to pay him homage. Alfred de Musset, Alphonse Karr, Théophile Gautier, Arsène Houssaye, Jules Sandeau and twenty others, ranged themselves under the banner of romanticism and formed an intrepid phalanx around the master. Idolizing his talent, these young men regarded Hugo as a god.

He was at the height of literary success, but never had writer found more obstacles to conquer. Lord Byron slept, enveloped in his winding-sheet of glory, Walter Scott was read from one end of the universe to the other, and Casimir Delavigne, a cowardly romancist hidden under the classic toga, saw himself, thanks to this disguise, almost the only one in favor with the clique of the *Comédie Française*. The contest became furious, but our poet fought valiantly to the end.

His " Odes and Ballads," set his star beside that of Byron. He had still to contend against Walter Scott, and constrain M. Delavigne to yield a portion of the ground he had usurped. He published " The Last Day of a Condemned," then *Notre-Dâme de Paris*, that giant among books, before which all the works of the English story-teller pale. Then he wrote his drama, " Hernani," which in spite of the bitterest opposition, fought its way to the repertoire of the Théatre Français. " Take care how you attack Victor Hugo ! " said old Joamy, who played the rôle of Ruy-Gomez, to his fellow-actors, led on by Mademoiselle Mars, to take many exceptions to the piece ; " you are like mile-posts who insult a pyramid ! "

"Hernani " proved a triumphant success, and two years after, " Marian Delorme " had the honor of a first representation. After its eighteenth repetition, in accordance with a universally expressed desire on the part of both actors and public, that last magnificent scene was added in which Marian is pardoned. No audience can ever witness it without tears.

The romantic school of which Victor Hugo is high-priest, is accused of often exceeding proper limits. But we must exaggerate a principle in order to better establish it, and this very exaggeration has its salutary effects. "Marie Tudor," "The King Amuses Himself." "Lucretia Borgia," "Angelo," contain immense dramatic qualities, and are a forcible illustration of what can be dared in tragedy.

Victor Hugo is often reproached with loving monsters, and devoting his talent to the rehabilitation of ugliness. In the eyes of certain people, the body is all, the soul nothing. What to them avail the highest intellectual gifts, the holiest qualities of the heart, devotion, love, pity, without the material form?—To gain the good will of these individuals, one should be beautiful as the Belvidere Apollo. Hugo's enemies pretend that he has inscribed upon his banner this device; *The beautiful is the ugly!* Never was there a more impudent falsehood. That other maxim they ascribe to him, *L'art pour l'art*, is but a stupid phrase invented by themselves.

Despite these malevolent attacks, Victor Hugo, always at the breach, always fighting, always sure of victory, has not recoiled an inch from his glorious path. He has gone on, conquering and to conquer.

"Notre-Dâme" was begun in the year 1830, and when he had once set about the work our hero did not pause. This gigantic effort cost him immense research; it is at the same time, a marvel of fascination, a masterpiece of style, and a prodigy of archæological study. He devoted only six months to its composition, but they were months of persistent, unremitting labor.

On the day agreed upon with his publisher "Notre-Dâme" was in press. But even then, this most popular of authors was allowed no repose; the theatres clamored for new dramas. "The King amuses Himself," had begun to draw great crowds to the Français, when it was interdicted, and could be known only through the press. Forty thousand copies were issued. Six weeks after, at the Porte Saint-Martin, "Lucretia Borgia " won a grand success. On the evening of its first representation, the classic army had its Waterloo.

The *Revue de Paris* ere long published "Claude Gueux," and the public enthusiastically greeted a succession of new works from Victor Hugo:—"Autumn Leaves,"—"The Orientals,"—and "Twilight Songs." In this author we find the most sublime inspirations united to the most delicate sensibility and grace. He shuns monotony, that sandbank of so many poets and musicians. He knows how to descend from the Olympian heights of his genius, to extend a friendly hand to the forsaken, to weep with the sorrowing. He pleads the cause of the poor, and preaches sacred almsgiving. One of his finest poems has this opening stanza :—

Donnez, riches ! L'aumône est la sœur de la prière.

*　　*　　*　　*　　*　　*

Donnez ! afin que Dieu qui dote les familles,
Donne à vos fils la force, et la grâce a vos filles ;
Afin que votre vigne ait toujours un doux fruit,
Afin qu'un blé plus mûr fasse plier vos granges ;
Afin d'être meilleurs, afin de voir les anges
Passer dans vos rêves la nuit.*

---

*Give ye rich ! almsgiving is the sister of prayer.

*　　*　　*　　*　　*　　*

Give ! so that God, who endows families, may give strength to your sons, and grace to your daughters ; so that your vine may

Further on, as a Christian, Victor Hugo lifts up the guilty women, and to the Pharisees of our day addresses those fine lines, beginning with :

Oh ! n'insultez jamais une femme qui tombe !

Passing from the domain of charity to that of grace, we see here as everywhere, Victor Hugo reigning a master: Here is one of his purest gems :—

The flower said to the butterfly celestial
"I cannot fly,
Fate chains me down to things low and terrestrial
Thou soar'st on high !

* * * *

" The sod enchains me while the bright stars woo thee ;
Ah, cruel lot !
O, might I rise and soar aloft unto thee,
The earth forgot !

"It may not be, bright flowerets without number,
Woo thee away ;
No gross earth-bonds thine airy wings encumber;
I dwell with clay.

" Flitting from place to place, bright as the dawning,
Thy life appears ;
But every starry eve and dewy morning,
Finds me in tears.

"Oh, if thou lovest me, leave the air's dominions,
And dwell with me ;
Take root on earth, my king, or give me pinions
To soar with thee."

---

always have a sweet fruit, so that a riper grain may heap your garners. Give, that you may become better, that you may see angels passing in your nightly dreams.''

6*

"Twilight Songs" is filled with gems of rarest beauty. Victor Hugo resembles that little daughter of the fairies, who opened her mouth only for pearls, diamonds and roses to fall from it. But, suddenly, and without transition, we see him take up the lash of Juvenal, if he finds an ignominy to punish, or a traitor to scourge. Time fails us for futher quotations. As, when we open a volume of Victor Hugo's, we wish to read the whole of it, so we are in like manner enticed by the superfluity of treasures which the narrow frame of a notice like this cannot embrace.

Harel, elated at the success of "Lucretia Borgia," offered its renowned author ten thousand francs for another piece. "Marie Tudor," was soon placed in rehearsal, but rivalry between the two great actresses, Mlle. Georges and Mme. Duval, caused much trouble in the repetitions. At all times and places, the director was of Mlle. Georges' opinion, and she every day stirred up new quarrels. The poet paid no heed to the belligerent fantasies of the great tragedienne. He enveloped himself in that calm dignity, in that strength of will characteristic of him.—Despite an insolent cabal, led on by the direction itself, the drama had a wonderful success. Mlle. Georges and Harel soon made the amende honorable to our poet. But he had been too deeply wounded; he would work no longer for the Porte-Saint-Martin. Less than six weeks after, that theatre became bankrupt.

Madame Duval entered the Comédie Française, but freed from the insults of Mlle. Georges, she had to submit here to all sorts of rebuffs from Mlle. Mars. At length Mlle. Mars carried her impudence so far that Hugo demanded back her rôle.

An exclamation of horror broke from the lips of the

great actress, and was echoed from one end of the cou. lisses to the other. Take from her a rôle, from *her*, queen of the theatre, what an unheard of, preposterous idea ! Hugo, dignified and severe, would listen to no murmurs ; he persisted.

" Very well, monsieur," said " Célimène," vanquished. " I will do what you please." The lesson had proved effectual ; she became amiable and obliging, and laid aside her usual dictatorial manner. When once before the public, Mlle. Mars was sure to do her best, to intrepidly sustain what she had most attacked during the rehearsals.

Hugo often went to Bièvre, where the Bertin family received him at a magnificent country-seat. Here he frequently met Chateaubriand, his ancient and faithful admirer. Mlle. Louise Bertin would play the piano for the two poets. Recognizing her remarkable talent for execution, Hugo wrote expressly for her the libretto of " Esmeralda." It was truly a royal gift, which would have been refused to Meyerbeer himself. Those were delightful evenings they passed at Bièvre. Having written some verses in the album of Mlle. Louise Bertin, Hugo one day turned a leaf, laid aside the pen of the poet for the pencil of the artist, and began to draw delightful little fancy sketches. The public is not ignorant of the fact that this great poet is an excellent designer.

This talent is entirely original and without any known model. During the prevalence of the cholera in 1832, he filled an entire album with caricatures to divert his wife and children. At Paul Meurice's, may be seen to-day, a very large drawing, representing an old, fantastic manor, its denticulated turrets, gables and high ramparts, unfolding one by one before the sight, and losing themselves in the hazy distance. This drawing has something gigantic, strange and sombre, which takes possession of you·and transports you to the realm of dreams. It seems a powerful reflection of the character and genius of the poet. He has executed two other equally fine drawings. The·first bears the title, " One of my Castles in Spain," the second represents a ship beaten by the tempest. Bent by the violence of the winds, the masts unite and take the form of a cross. Below you read this legend :—*In mare malus fit crux.* A number of his drawings disappeared at the sale which took place in the rue *Tour d'Auvergne*, but many of them have been recovered, and placed in a special album.

In 1848, Hugo again changed his domicil. The taking down the iron-barred gate Louis XIII.which harmonized so well with the architecture of the Place-Royale, had caused him great chagrin. He has always warred against this plaster-of-paris mania, which so ruthlessly effaces the seal of a nation's history or destroys the monuments that consecrate it. France owes to him the salvation of a great number of old châteaux and Gothic capitals, vowed to ruin by governmental thoughtlessness, or menaced by the revolutionary hammer. Providence takes care that there shall arise at intervals, these powerful intelligences who unite the ages, teach descendants to know their ancestors, and make the past respected for the sake of the future.

Thanks to the taste of Victor Hugo for antique furniture, for all sorts of curiosities, the merchants of bric-à-brac constantly besiege his door, and every day persuade him to purchase new objects, so that the poet's dwelling is always a sort of antique museum. At the sale before his removal from the Place-Royale, a very valuable and miscellaneous collection was dispersed.

In changing his abode, Hugo always wishes to over-
see the upholsterers and to give them instructions foreign from their usual practice. Upon entering this last
new domicile, he said to them:

"You are going to nail this picture to the ceiling."

"But Monsieur—"

"Nail away!"

They obey reluctantly. It is a wonderfully fine picture, and its place does not seem well chosen. "Now,"
says Hugo, "fill the spaces with strips of Lyons damask
of equal length." The workmen seem to have fallen
from the clouds.

"Never," murmur they, "have we done anything of
the kind."

"So much the better! Arrange the damask upon an
inclined plane. Now fasten it all around with these
golden rods."

The upholsterers, descending from their ladders, and
gazing at their work, cry out:

"Well, truly, it is superb!"

Hugo has concealed his yellow, jagged ceiling, full .
of cracks, under a rich painting surrounded by a tapestry
frame, majestic in effect.

"Ruy Blas," Victor Hugo's next play, in which Fred-
eric Lemaitre took the principal rôle, proved a brilliant
success. The author himself says in his preface to
"Ruy Blas," "For Frederick Lemaitre, the evening
of the 8th of November (that of the first representation
of this play) was not a representation, but a trans-
figuration."

June 3d, 1841, Victor Hugo entered the Academy,
like a bullet that has made its breach, and passes in
spite of the rampart. "There are two Academies here,"

said Lamartine to him on that day, "the little and the great ; the great one is unanimous for you."

Soon after, he was elevated to the dignity of peer of France.

An incident which occurred in 1839 is well worthy of mention. The sister of Barbès, a political offender condemned to the scaffold, had come to the poet imploring him to beg her brother's pardon. A first attempt proved fruitless. The court was then in mourning for that gentle Marie of Wurtemberg, the angel of the royal family, stricken so early by the hand of death, and the Count de Paris had just been born. Hugo again sought the king. It was on the 12th July at midnight. His Majesty had just retired, and could not be seen. The poet wrote this stanza which he left upon the table :—

> Par votre ange envolée ainsi qu'une colombe,
>   Par ce royal enfant doux et frèle roseau,
> Grace encore une fois ! grace au nom de la tombe !
>   Grace au nom du berceau ! *

Upon awaking, Louis Philippe read these four lines and Barbès was saved.

In August, 1837, appeared "The Rhine," a charming volume of letters where the poet presents himself in a rôle novel as original. In May, 1840, a collection of poems, "Inner Voices" and "Lights and Shadows," was given to the world. These poems have all the inspiration, all the grace and genius of the author's most beautiful days. Victor Hugo has none of that insufferable vagueness we find in other poets : we never grow weary of reading him. All his poems bear the impress

---

* By that dove flown, that angel from you taken,
    By this dear infant, royal yet so frail,
  Pardon once more ! Your pity to awaken,
    Let both the cradle and the tomb avail.

of the heart, in them there is no dearth of ideas ; every
one has the ring of the true coin, the master-piece. Here
is one of the tenderest and sweetest ;—

La tombe dit à la rose,
" Des pleurs dont l'aube arrose,
   Que fais-tu, fleur des amours ? "
La rose dit à la tombe,
" Que fais-tu de ce qui tombe,
Dans ton gouffre ouvert toujours ? "

La rose dit :—" Tombeau sombre,
De ces pleurs je fais dans l'ombre
   Un parfum d'ambre et de miel."
La tombe dit :—" Fleur plaintive
De chaque âme qui m'arrive
   Je fais un ange du ciel!"

———

The tomb said to the rose,
" With the tears by morning shed,
What does't thou, flower of love ? "
   And the sweet rose answering said:
" What doest thou with that which falls
Within thine ever open walls ? "

The rose said : " Of these tears
   I make a perfume rare,
Honey and amber-sweet."
   The tomb said : " Floweret fair,
Of every soul unto me given
I make an angel meet for heaven."

At the Isle of Jersey, the Hugos dwelt in a pretty
English house, very simple, but comfortable. Behind
it lay a beautiful garden, ending in a terrace, bathed by
the waves. From his windows, the exile could see the
shores of France. He had tried a residence in
Belgium and in London, but could be content with
neither. The fogs and bad weather of London had
annoyed him excessively. " The good God who has

deprived us of country, will surely leave us the sun," he said.

He was banished from Jersey for having written the Queen a disrespectful letter in regard to a man sentenced to be hanged. He removed to the Isle of Guernsey.

His two sons, Charles and Victor, returned to France, where they founded a journal, the *Rappel*. From the shades of exile, Hugo counseled them to make a breach in the imperial system.

A poet friend wrote some verses to Victor Hugo asking these very rational questions :—

" Why then, O poet, you whom God sends as an emanation from his pure essence, to console, to sing, to bless, why do you seem to lose sight of your holy mission ? Why, son of heaven, do you mix yourself with the insensate broils of earth ? " Hugo replied in a poem magnificent in thought and diction, but untranslateable, like all his best poetic utterances. " The poet's mission, in these impious days," says he, " is to inaugurate better days. He is an Utopian, his feet are here, his eyes elsewhere. He is a prophet to all time, bearing in his hand a torch to illuminate the future."

These are grand thoughts, and yet we can but regret the day when Victor Hugo wore on his forehead only the radiant crown of poesy without aspiring to that of the man of party. Works inspired by hatred and revenge, dishonor not the individuals they attack, but the author who signs them.

Although crushing domestic afflictions have fallen upon this literary giant; although he is an old man, past threescore years and ten, his age is hale and hearty, his mental activity continues unabated. No longer a voluntary exile, he has returned to his dear Paris, where there is no man of greater mark than he.

He regards himself as a seer, a prophet, a sort of Moses, commissioned to lead his people out from the bondage of slavish ideas, to a promised land of prosperity and freedom. But he lacks the meekness and long-suffering of his Israelitish prototype. Many of his ideas, Utopian and visionary, could have no practical realization save at the expense of worse anarchy than has ever fallen even upon France.

His " Legend of the Ages " is a dainty poetic feast to which came as guests, the gorgons of demagogism, coifed with serpents. In " Les Misérables," this man of genius lets the thunderbolts of his wrath fall upon French society, and preaches the warfare of the poor against the rich. His " Songs of the Street and the Forests " has been redeemed neither by the prose of " The Toilers of the Sea, "—" The Man who Laughs "—nor " Ninety-Three." All these works show the wonderfully original talent and unabated powers of Victor Hugo, but they are disfigured by his most glaring faults.

This humiliated giant, not able to overthrow kings, has had the folly to set himself up for a god. Political passion and an insensate desire to take part in every attack upon Church and State, make him fall into incredible contradictions. In " Les Rayons et les Ombres," he called Voltaire " that ape of genius sent by the devil on a mission to men." .

March 12, 1867, he wrote to M. Havin:

" My dear old Colleague,

          " Subscribe for a statue to Voltaire; it is a public duty. Voltaire is a forerunner. Torch-bearer of the Eighteenth Century, he preceded and announced the French Revolution. He is the star

of that grand morning.   I send you the humble list of
the little democratic group of Guernsey.

"Your old colleague,

"VICTOR HUGO."

Alas, alas !   The contradiction yet endures. We pardon so many things to women and to poets !

Bien foi est que s'y fie !

But how melancholy is the fate of genius when it no
longer listens to aught save pride and passion !

PAUL DE KOCK.

BORN 1794—DIED 1870.

Who of the generation of to-day, would suspect the
vogue Paul de Kock enjoyed thirty or forty years ago?
Never was author more popular in the true sence
of the word. All the world read him, from the statesman
to the commercial traveller and the collegian, from the
grand lady to the grisette. He was no less celebrated
abroad than in France, and in his romances, the Russians
studied Parisian manners. The advent of the romantic
school with its grand chivalric sentiments, its lyric
enthusiasms, its love for the middle age and for local
color, its furious passions, its luxury of Shakspearean
metaphors, eclipsed this modest glory, whose rays were
extinguished before that unexpected blaze.

Paul de Kock, we may say in his praise, was a true
bourgeois, a Philistine of Marais, without a shadow of
poetry or style; he had no reading and not even any
idea of æsthetics, which he would willingly have taken,
like Pradon, for a term of chemistry. The artistic fiber
was entirely wanting in him. Do not suspect us of
irony in saying this; these seeming faults are merits,
which recommend him to the masses. Paul de Kock
had the advantage of being the absolute equal of his
readers, of sharing their ideas, their prejudices, their

sentiments ; and he possessed one especial gift, the gift
of laughter ; not of the Attic sort, but that loud, expan-
sive, irresistible animal laughter which makes you hold
your sides in its convulsive outbursts. He provoked
this merriment by comic situations, ridiculous mishaps,
grotesque attitudes, and a succession of all sorts of
blunders whose effect was irresistible. Certainly all this
is grossly designed, wanting in wit; and sketched with a
coarse pencil ; but there is in these absurdities which
crowd one upon the other, a force, a naturalness and a
truth, which must be recognized.

Paul de Kock has become a historic author. His works
contain a portrayal of manners which have disappeared
with a civilization as different from ours as that whose
vestiges we find in the ruins of Pompeii. His romances,
which were designed for recreation, will hereafter be
consulted by the learned, curious to know the life of
that old Paris, of which, ere long, no trace will remain.

Those who were born after the revolution of February,
1848, or shortly before, can little imagine what that
Paris was, where lived and moved the heroes and heroines
of Paul de Kock; so little does it resemble the actual
Paris of to-day, that sometimes, in gazing at these broad
streets, these grand boulevards, these vast squares, these
interminable lines of monumental houses, these splendid
quarters which have replaced the plats of the kitchen
gardener, we ask ourselves, can this really be the city
where we passed our childhood?

Paris, which is becoming the metropolis of the world,
was then only the capital of France. You met Frenchmen and even Parisians in the streets. Strangers doubtless came here as at all periods, in search of pleasure or
instruction, but the means of transport were difficult,
the ideal of speed did not go beyond the classic mail

coach, the locomotive had not loomed up, even as a chimera, among the mists of the future. The physiognomy of the people had not then sensibly changed.

The provincials remained at home far more than now; they came to Paris only on urgent business. You could hear French spoken on what was then called the Boulevard de Gand, and is to-day, the Boulevard des Italiens, Here you saw a type which has become rare, but which is really the pure Parisian type : — fair complexions, rosy cheeks, chestnut hair, clear gray eyes, well-made forms of medium height, and, among women, a delicate embonpoint. Olive faces and black hair were the exceptions ; the South had not yet invaded Paris with its passionately-pale complexions, its glowing eyes, its furious gesticulations. Most of the faces you met, were still blooming and smiling, and wore an air of health and good humor. The complexions we now call distinguished, would then have given the idea of illness.

The city was relatively very small, or at least, its activity was confined within certain limits, which were rarely passed. The Champs-Elysées, at night-fall, became as dangerous as the plain of Marathon ; the most adventurous stopped at the Place de la Concorde. The quarter of Notre Dame de Lorette, was only a vague space enclosed by a plank fence ; the church was not yet built, and from the boulevard, you caught a glimpse of the mound of Montmartre with wind-mills, and the telegraph extending its broad arms from the summit of the old tower. The Faubourg Saint-Germain retired early, but its slumbers were often disturbed by the tumults of the students over a new piece at the Odeon. Passing from one quarter to another was far less frequent than now ; the omnibus did not exist,—and there were marked differences of physiognomy, of costume and accent, between a native of the Rue du Temple and a denizen of the Rue Montmartre.

Paul de Kock remained master of the boulevard where he dwelt. He knew all the bourgeois who passed, as well as their spouses and sweet-hearts. He knew their thoughts, he understood their traditional jests, and laughed merrily at them. This patriarchal simplicity delighted him, and when these good people were arranging a rural party for the next Sunday, he would manage to get invited, and carry a pie or a melon under his arm. During the dinner on the grass, it was he who would say the most laughable things, and sing the merriest songs. This was gross enjoyment no doubt, inspired by blue wine and by swine's flesh, but it was honest, after all; the family was there, and the little girls in their gingham dresses, knew that the lovers who accompanied them, would, one day, be their husbands.

There existed then, all around Paris, little rural places, or places which appeared rural to the poor devils who had worked all the week in the obscurity and confinement of a shop; there were bits of forest made to order, to shade a tea-garden, fishing-huts half in the water, arbors, of hop-vines; there were Romainville, the park of Saint-Fargeau, the meadows of Saint-Gervais, with their groves of lilac, and their fountain, its water overflowing from a narrow stone basin, to which you descended by steps. This landscape sufficed for Paul de Kock, who, to say true, is neither picturesque nor gifted with those descriptive powers so much in vogue to-day. And so, he finds all charming. This bald meadow is for him the country; he paints it with a dry and meagre touch, as a background for his figures, but he understands little of what we call nature, and, in this respect, he is very French and very Parisian !

He does not always confine himself to the city precincts ; he pushes on to Montmorency, and then what delightful donkey-parties in the forest, what exclamations, what laughter, what blithesome tumblings upon the grass, what nice repasts of brown bread and cherries ! These are only clerks and grisettes to be sure, but they are quite the equals of the more artificial heroes and heroines of modern romance ; we say this with no desire to extol the past at the expense of the present, a common fault of those who have been young under another reign.

The grisettes of Paul de Kock, certainly have not the elegance of the *Mimi Pinson* of Alfred de Musset, but they are fresh, gay, amusing, good young girls, and far prettier under their percale caps or light straw hats, than the painted, artificial creatures for whom the sons of good families are ruining themselves to-day. They live by their work, poorly, but with little anxiety as the birds that nest upon their eaves : their love has no tariff, and with them the heart always plays its part. This pretty race has disappeared with many other good things of that old Paris, which now lives only in the romances, wrongly despised, of Paul de Kock. His name will survive many of the celebrities of the moment, for he represents with fidelity, with nerve and fulness, a period that has wholly vanished.

We may now regard his characters with disdainful astonishment, but they found a great deal of amusement in their simple pleasures. Our age has become more refined, and such pleasures do not suffice it. It has to pay dear for its amusements, and much good may they do it ! These rather gross, but fresh and natural enjoyments of Paul de Kock's time seem to us of *mauvais ton*. We prefer jests in a new tongue, phrases taken from the slang dictionary, and the epileptic insanities of the repertoire of the Opera Bouffe.

We render so much the more cheerfully this tardy homage to Paul de Kock, from the fact that having been one of the standard-bearers in the great romantic army, we have not perhaps, read his romances with the attention they deserve. We have looked upon the things he depicts with different eyes, and the sense has not been clear to us. And yet we feel that there is in this romancer, a sort of comic force wanting to others. At present he appears to us in a more serious, we may even say, a more melancholy light, if such a word can apply to Paul de Kock. Certain of his romances produce upon us the effect of "The Last of the Mohicans" by Fenimore Cooper. We seem to read in them the history of the last Parisians, invaded and submerged by American civilization.

ALPHONSE DE LAMARTINE.

BORN 1790—DIED 1869.

IT is not a biography of Lamartine, still less a detailed criticism of his work, which we would wish to write here; but our desire shall rather be to disengage this ground figure from the penumbra within which it has for some years veiled itself, during the retirement and the silence of these latter days, and to replace it under that ray, which henceforth will no more leave it. A humble poet, constrained to prose by the necessities of journalism, we are going to try to judge a great poet. It is a temerity upon our part. Our forehead does not reach to his feet; but it is from below that we appreciate statues. His merits to be hewn in the finest marble of Paros or Carrara, pure from every stain.

He himself has related in a style which it is given to none to imitate, his first remembrances of childhood and home; his young soul, opening to life, to dreams, to thought, gave to the world those immortal confidences of genius, and the crowd received them, each according to his pleasure; for each can cherish the illusion that this voice, so intimate and so penetrating, speaks to him only as to an unknown friend.

We shall then leave Lamartine to seek through his studies, his reveries, his passions and his travel, as in life apparently unoccupied, that path he is to follow, and which is not always easily distinguishable in the the inextricable crossways of human vocations. Doubt- less all the generous sentiments he was to express so well, love, faith, religious adorations of nature, home- sickness for Heaven, already rose within him; but he was as yet, for the world, only a handsome young man of the most aristrocratic elegance, of perfect manners, and destined to the success of the *salon*.

He had made two voyages to Italy; the impression which that pure sky must have produced upon him, those seas bluer even than the sky, those grand horizons, those trees with their shining and robust foliage, those ruins so magnificent in their decay, all this vigorous, warm, impassioned nature, where wandered like mute shades, people bending under the yoke of servitude and under the grandeur of their past: he said nothing of it all, then, but poetry was silently accumulating in his heart. The secret treasure grew each day; pearl by pearl was added to the mysterious casket, which was to be opened in the future. If he was the rival of Byron to whom he addressed an epistle equal to the most beau- tiful stanzas of Childe Harold, it was not as a dandy. Having returned to France, he allowed several years to pass in that harassing and fruitful activity, whence great works have their being, and in 1820, a modest volume appeared, which not without difficulty found a publisher; it was " The Meditations."

This volume was a rare event in the centuries. It contained an entire new world, a world of poetry more difficult perhaps to discover than an America or an At- lantis. While he had seemed to go and come indifferent- ly among other men, Lamartine had been voyaging over unknown seas, his eyes fixed upon his star, tending towards a shore which no one had reached, and he returned a conqueror, like Columbus. He had discovered the *soul !*

We cannot imagine to-day after so many revolutions, overturnings and vicissitudes in human things, after so many literary systems essayed and fallen into forgetfulness, so much excess of thought and of language, the universal transport produced by the " Meditations." It was a breath of freshness and rejuvenescence, as it were a palpitating of wings which passed over all souls. Young people, young girls, women, were enthusiastic even to adoration. The name of Lamartine was upon all lips, and the Parisians, who certainly are not a poetical race, struck with the madness of the Abderitains, who repeated incessantly the chorus of Euripides, " O love, powerful love ! " began to recite stanzas from " The Lake."— Never had success such proportions.

Lamartine in fact was not only a poet, he was poetry itself. His chaste, elegant and noble nature, seemed to be entirely ignorant of the deformities and trivialities of life. Such was the book, such was the author, and the best frontispiece one could have chosen for this volume of verse, was the portrait of the poet. The lyre in his hands and upon his shoulders the mantle lashed by the storm, did not seem ridiculous.

What a profound and novel accent ! What ethereal aspirations, what approaches toward the ideal, what pure effusions of love, what tender and melancholy notes, what sighs and supplications of the soul, which no poet had yet made vibrate !

In the pictures of Lamartine there is always a great deal of sky ; he must have celestial spaces, in order to move easily and to describe large circles around his thought. He swims, he flies, he sails ; like a swan, cradling itself in its great white wings now in the light, now amid thin vapors, anon amid stormy clouds, he rests but rarely upon the earth, and ever resumes his flight at the first breeze which lifts his wings. That fluid, transparent, aërial element, which opens before him, and closes after his passage, is his natural route; he sustains himself there without difficulty, during the long hours, and from that height he sees the vague landscapes grow azure, the waters become mirrors, and the edifice dissolve in a vaporous eclipse.

Lamartine is not one of those poets, those marvellous artists, who hammer verse like a plate of gold upon a steel anvil, contracting the grain of the metal, imprinting upon it clear and precise figures. He ignores or disdains all these questions of form, and with the negligence of a gentleman who rhymes at his leisure without confining himself more than is needful to things belonging to the trade, he composes admirable poetry traversing the woods on horseback, in a barque sailing along some shady shore, or his elbow resting on a window of one of his châteaux. His verses roll on with a melodious murmur like the waves of an Italian or Grecian sea, bearing along in their transparent scrolls, branches of laurel, golden fruit fallen from the shore, reflections of the sky, the birds, the sails, and breaking upon the flats in sparkling silver fringes. These are the unrolling and successions of undulating forms, intangible as water, but which rush on to their goal, and upon their fluidity can bear the idea as the sea bears ships, whether they be the frail skiff or the stately vessel.

There is a magic charm in these rhythmic breathings, which rise and fall like the ocean's breast; we yield ourselves up to this melody which chants its rhyming chorus like a far-off song of sailors or of syrens. Lamartine is perhaps the greatest musician of poetry.

This manner, broad and vague, is well suited to the lofty spirituality of his nature ; the soul has no need of being sculptured like a Greek marble. Gleams, melodious sounds, opal tints, rainbow gradations of color, lunar blues, diaphanous gauzes, aërial draperies lifted and swollen by the breeze, sufficed to portray it and to envelope it. For Lamartine seems to have been made that phrase of the ancients, *musa ales.*

In that immortal piece "The Lake," where passion speaks a language the most beautiful which music has not been able to equal, vaporous nature appears as it were through a silver gauze, remote, shadowy, painted in a few touches, to form a frame and serve as a background for this imperishable remembrance; and yet you see all; the light, the sky, the water, the rocks and the trees upon the shore, the mountains in the horizon, and every wave which throws its spray at the adored feet of Elvira.

We need not believe that Lamartine, because there is always in him a vibration and a resonance of the æolian harp, is only a melodious "Lakist,"—and knows but to breathe softly, melancholy and love. If he has the sigh, he has also the speech of love; he rules as easily as he charms. That angelic voice which seems to come from the heights of heaven, knows how to assume, if need be, the evil accents of man.

At Naples, a marriage, resulting from one of those admirations which attract women to the poet of their dreams, made him happy and rich. An English lady, resembling one of those charming and romantic heroines of Shakespeare, whom a glance enthralls, and who remain faithful to death, bestowed upon him her love and an almost princely fortune. France saw that very rare phenomena with her, a poet who was not poor, and whom fancy could transport in splendor to the sun. We pretend to believe that poverty, that harsh, meagre nurse, is better fitted to rear genius than riches; it is an error. The poet's nature is prodigal, improvident, generous, friendly to luxury, as the material expression of beauty; it loves to realize its caprices in its verse and in its life; to repose amid surroundings whence care is banished, as a dissonance, as something ugly, pitiful and prosaic ; mathematics repel it (Lamartine had a horror of them and regarded them as obstacles to thought), and with a hand that never reckons, it takes from the three wells of Aboul-Cassem the *dinars* it scatters around in a rain of gold. Being impeded by none of those sad obstacles which consume the better part of the strength of the greatest minds, Lamartine could give his genius full expansion, and the chills of poverty did not blight its magnificent flowers.

To the "Meditations" succeeded the "Harmonies," where the poet's wings attained the most sublime heights, seeming to blend their flight with the radiance of the stars. There are, in this volume, pieces of an ineffable beauty and a majestic melancholy. Never, since Job, has the human soul, in face of the awful mysteries of life and death, raised a plaint more dismayed, more despairing, than in the *Novissima Verba*. The success was immense, but although the work was superior, its vogue could not surpass that of the "Meditations." At the very outset, admiration had given to Lamartine all she could accord to man; she had exhausted for him her flowers and her adulation. No new ray could find place in this poet's aureole ; the splendors of his noon added nothing to the brightness of his dawn.

In the midst of this triumphal outburst, Lamartine had departed on his voyage to the Orient, not as a humble pilgrim, with staff and scallop-shell, but in royal luxury, in a ship freighted by himself, and bearing to the Emirs presents worthy of Haroun-al-Raschid. When he arrived, he travelled with caravans of Arabian horses which belonged to him, bought the houses where he lodged, and pitched in the desert tents as splendid as the gold and purple pavilions of Solomon. Lord Byron alone had made poesy travel as sumptuously. The amazed tribes followed with acclamations along the route, and nothing would have been more easy to our poet than to have himself proclaimed Caliph. Lady Esther Stanhope, that far-seeing English woman who dwelt in the Lybian desert, offered him her horse, whose back, in its folds, formed the outline of a sort of saddle, and which Hakem, the god of the Drussians, was to mount at his approaching incarnation; and as she proffered the steed, she predicted to him that one day he would hold in his gentlemanly hand, the destinies of his country.

Amid these flatteries and seductions, Lamartine went on tranquilly, almost indifferently, as a grand seignior whom nothing astonishes, and who feels himself worthy of all homage. With a benevolent smile, he received these adorations, never intoxicated by them. It was but natural that he should be handsome, elegant, rich, endowed with genius, and excite the admiration and love of all around him.

But this almost superhuman felicity was not to endure. The ancient Greeks supposed the existence of envious divinities whom they called the *Moires*, and whose jealous eyes were wounded by the spectacle of that happiness they took delight in blasting. It was to appease these Moires, that Polycrates, when too happy, flung into the sea his ring, which was recovered by a fisherman. Doubtless, one of these wicked goddesses encountered our poet in his triumphal march, and was enraged at this splendor and renown, at this concurrence of marvellous gifts. She put forth her withered hand, and Julia, the adorable child who accompanied her father into this luminous country, where life seemed endowed with new energies, bowed her head like a flower, attacked at its root by the ploughshare, and the vessel which had gone forth with white sails, returned with black sails, bringing back a coffin.

Irreparable sorrow, eternal despair, wound that nothing can close, and which must bleed forever! There is a grief which wishes no consolation; and without doubt, as an expiation of their glory, it was ordained that the two greatest poets of our time should experience it.

The Muse alone, with her rhymes, can rock and sometimes lull to rest this regret for the adored being, lost without apparent reason. Lamartine now gave to the world his "Jocelyn," a tender and pure epic of the soul, where are not recounted the brilliant adventures of a hero, but the obscure sufferings of an humble, unknown heart. It is a delicate *chef-d'œuvre*, full of emotion and of tears, of an Alpine whiteness, virginal as the snow of lofty mountain-summits, where no impure breath has come, and where the love which ignores itself is so chaste it might be contemplated by the angels. No success was more sympathetic, no book was read with more avidity, or more bathed in tears.

"The Angel's Fall" was less comprehended. Those magnificent fragments, of a splendid Oriental coloring, which seemed like leaves detached from the Bible, won only a half-favor from the strangeness of the subject, and the oddity of the pictures drawn from a world anterior to ours; from the exaggerated grandeur of personages outside of human nature, and also, it must be confessed, form a negligence, in form and execution, increasing as the work progresses.

After the publication of his " Poetic Reflections," prolonged vibrations, last echoes of the " Meditations," and the " Harmonies," our poet bade adieu to the Muse, and laid down the lyre never to take it up again. The desire for a practical, active life took possession of him. He had been attached to an embassy and body-guard; he wished to be deputy. People who believed themselves serious because they were prosaic, and ignored the fact that poesy alone acts upon the soul, and that imagination draws along the crowd, sneered, as they saw the dreamer whom they called " the singer of Elvira," approach the tribune; but they soon comprehended that he who knows how to sing, knows how to speak, and that the poet has a mouth of gold. From these melodious lips, the speeches flew winged, vibrating, having, like the bee, honey and a sting. Poetry easily transformed itself into eloquence, for poetry has passion, warmth, thought, generous sentiment, a prophetic instinct; and, whatever people may say to the contrary, that elevated and supreme reason which surveys things from a lofty height, and allows the general truth to be disturbed by no accident.

The Girondists brought about a revolution, or at least they largely contributed to it. Lamartine found himself face to face with the waves he had let loose, and which rolled at his very feet, full of foam, of uproar, whirling in their furious coils the wrecks of the submerged monarchy. He accepted the mission of haranguing this tumultuous sea, of reasoning with this tempest, of re-

taining the thunderbolt within the cloud. Dangerous
mission, which he accomplished like a gentleman and a
hero! You could then see that all poets were not cowardly like Horace, who fled from the battle-field not *bene relic-
ta parmula*. He had charmed ferocious instincts, and
amid the roar of the insurrection rising beneath his bal-
cony, the deluded mob called upon him to come out and
let himself be seen and heard. As soon as he appeared
the mob was silent; it awaited some noble words, some
austere counsels, some generous thoughts, and it withdrew satisfied, bearing away a germ of devotion, humanity and harmony.

The poet exposed himself to the ball that might be
sent from the pistol of a too advanced Utopian or a too
conservative fanatic, with that elegant disdain of a gentleman despising death as vulgar and common; a superior dandyism, difficult for the common people to imitate.
If he voluntarily threw himself into this gulf at the peril
of his life, it was not that he had any personal interests there. We saw a strange thing in modern civilization, a man in the full light of day, play in his own person the rôle of Tyrtean moderator, of an Orpheus tam-
ing ferocious beasts, *doctus lenire tigris*, urging forward
the good, putting away the evil, and making the idea of
harmony and beauty soar above disorder. Without police, without an army, without any repressive means,
through pure poetry, he kept a whole people in effer-
vescence; he said to the extreme republicans, these sublime words: " The tri-colored flag has made the tour
of the world with our glories; the red flag has made
only the tour of the Champ-de-Mars, trailing in the
blood of the people." And the three colors continued
to float victoriously in the air.

In this game, with the most generous thoughtlessness

he dissipated his genius, his health, his fortune. He made the greatest human effort which had ever been essayed; he withstood alone an unbridled mob. For several days, he saved France, giving her time to await a better destiny; and as nothing is so ungrateful as fear when the peril is past, he lost his popularity. Those who owed him their heads perhaps, their wealth and their security most certainly, found him ridiculous, when, after having thrown to the winds, for their profit, all his treasures, with the noble confidence of a poet, who believes that he may demand back a drachma for a talent from those he has charmed and saved, he seated himself upon the threshold of his ruined fortune, and extending his helmet, said; *Date obolum Belisario*. Debt was behind him jogging his elbow.

Certainly he was great gentleman enough to play with his creditor the scene between Don Juan and M. Dimanche, but he did not wish it; and France had the sad spectacle of her aging poet, bent down from morn to eve under the yoke of unremunerative literary toil. This demi-god with reminiscences of heaven, wrote romances, fragments and articles like us. Pegasus traced out his furrow, dragging the plough, when one sweep of his pinions might have borne him to the stars.

GAVARNI.

(Sulpice Paul Chevalier.)

BORN 1801—DIED 1866.

THE ancient world still rules us, as it did far back in the ages, and so arbitrary is this rule, that we scarce have a sentiment of the civilization which surrounds us. Despite the efforts of Paris and London, Athens and Rome remain the capitals of thought. Every year, thousands of young Romans and Grecians leave our colleges, knowing nothing of modern things. We yield to none in admiration of this persistent energy of the ideal, this eternal power of the beautiful, but is it not singular that art so little reflects the cotemporary epoch? Classic studies inspire a profound disdain for actual usages, manners and customs, which find so little expression in monuments, bas-reliefs, medallions and bronzes. The future Desobrys will be greatly embarrassed in reconstructing from these a Paris of the age of Napoleon III.

For instance, what idea could one form in the year 3000, of our women of fashion, of our celebrated beauties, of those we have loved, and for whose sake we have committed more or less follies, when like them, the works of most of our masters have disappeared?

Ingres was an Athenian, a scholar of Apelles and

Phidias, whose soul was evidently deceived as to its century, and entered the world, two thousand four hundred years too late ; his pictures might take their place in the pinacotheque of the Propylœa; the style of his portraits makes them antique, and deprives them of all date, to render them eternal. Delacroix seldom leaves history, the Orient or Shakspeare ; in his numerous works, we scarce find a type of our day ; without attaching himself, like Ingres, to antiquity, he goes back to the Venetians and the Flemmings, and has nothing modern but disquietude and passion. He has composed his microcosm by a sort of interior vision, and we should say that he has not even once cast his eyes around him. What we say here of these two illustrious masters, who represent, among us, the two phases of art, applies to others with equal rigor. The realistic essays of these latter times seek the deformed ideal more than the exact reproduction of nature. These few true types of *genre* pictures are almost all taken from the rustic class, and we may say in all assurance, that neither the men or women of fashionable life, nor scarce one of the thousand actors of the society of our nineteenth century, has left a trace in the serious art of our time.

Certainly, the Venus de Milo is an admirable piece of sculpture, lovingly polished by the kisses of centuries ; the supreme of the beautiful, the most successful effort of human genius to embody the ideal, and we adore this sublime marble whose divinity none can deny. But have the Parisian women not also their charms ? If sculpture wished, could it not find pure outlines in their elegant forms so charmingly arrayed ? The drapery of Polyhymnia folds itself in no more supple manner than these grand Indian shawls embrace the shoulders of our queenly, well dressed women. Heinrich Heine, the

great plastic, was not easily deceived, and he admired a
Parisian woman in her shawl, as he would have admired
a Grecian goddess in her Parian tunic. As for Balzac,
he certainly preferred to every feminine Olympian,
even to Venus, "adorably exhausted," as Goethe said,
the grand ladies he enshrines in his works. Are they,
then, unworthy of a medallion, these charming faces of
a roseate pallor, enframed in their fresh hats like the
heads of angels smiling from their ideal aureoles, with
hair wavy or in braids, Praxiteles would not wish to
disarrange, if he had to copy them in marble? Ball
coiffures, do they not offer to the intelligent artist all
imaginable resources, pearls, flowers, plumes, sprays,
network, tassels, lustrous ribbons, delicate spirals, rebellious frizzes, fluttering curls, chignons twisted like the
horn of Ammon or negligently attached? The robes,
despite the passing exaggeration of flounces and trim-
mings, with their richness of brocades, moires and satins,
the rustle and glitter of taffetas, the transparency of
laces, gauzes, tulles and tarletans, with the lustre, the
softness and the variety of tones, seem to invite the
brush of the colorist, and present to him a pallet of
seductive shades; but the colorist does not regard these
bouquets of all blossoming hues in the promenades, at
the soirees, at the boxes of the theatres. He prefers to
soak his brush in the ruddy gold of Rembrandt, the pale
silver of Paul Veronese, or the glowing purple of Rubens,
while the sculptor in the public square, disrobes some
frail nymph, utterly ashamed and disquieted at her
nudity.

Leaving the Greeks and the Romans aside, Leonardo
da Vinci, Raphael, Andre del Sarto, Titian, have given
to the beauties of their time eternal testimonials, at
which in the galleries, poets dreamily gaze, while their

hearts are moved by an irresistible retrospective desire. There is not a celebrated woman of the sixteenth century, princess, courtesan, mistress of grand-duke or painter, who has not bequeathed to us her image divinized by art. Our epoch will transmit no such legacy to future ages; the woman of to-day seems to have intimidated our artists, the fear of falling back into the false, classic ideal, has energetically pursued them, and they have occupied themselves very little with modern beauty; to find any trace of this, it will be necessary, in future, to consult the portraits executed by certain fashionable painters, whose end has been to satisfy the taste of fashionable people rather than answer the rigorous exigencies of art.

This preamble, which may seem rather long, was needed, to make the reader comprehend the whole originality of Gavarni, and the value of his scattered work in books, in albums, in series and in detached engravings. He has neither predecessors nor rivals in our day; his is not the mediocre glory of being frankly, exclusively, absolutely modern; like Balzac, to whom he has more than one resemblance, he has composed his "Human Comedy," less broad and less universal doubtless, but very complete of its kind, although lightly done. Gavarni, the grand designer and anatomist in his way, has no care for sculptured or traditional forms. He designs men, and not elaborate statues. None better than he knows the poor framework of our bodies, marred by civilization; he understands the meagreness, the defects, the baldness of Parisian dandies, the grotesque embonpoints, the flabby wrinkles, the crows' feet, the bandy knees and legs of bankers and studious men, and he clothes all these people as Chevreuil or Renard would have done; with one stroke of the pencil he transforms a paletot into a sack, and makes each vestment conform to the stature, the character, the peculiarities of the wearer.

If you would seek the Parisian of 1850 in our day, with his costume, his air, his attitude and his physiognomy, without falsehood and without caricature, and only idealized by that fine treatment which is the very soul of the artist, turn over the pages of Gavarni's work. He will soon be as instructive as the engravings of Gravelot, of Eisen, of Moreau, and as the water-colors of Baudoin during the last century. But the greatest glory of Gavarni, lies in having comprehended the Parisian disdained; as impossible by cotemporary art; he has also comprehended the Parisian woman! He has not only comprehended her, but loved her.

He has not cared much for the figures of the Parthenon, neither for the Venus de Milo, nor for the Diana of Gabies; but he has found a very sufficient ideal in the little irregular face of the Parisian woman, whose dainty ugliness is still grace; if the nose does not form a straight line with the forehead, if the cheeks are more round than oval, if the mouth turns up at the corners, if the neck is fragile, and does not offer the three folds of the neck of Aphrodite, if the form is not perfect, what matters it? It is not an antique nymph he wishes to delineate, but the woman who passes by, and whom you follow. He does not lithograph her after the deformity, but after the life.

Long before Alexander Dumas *fils*, Gavarni had crayoned the *Dame aux Camellias*, and related—drawing and legend—the chronicle of the demi-monde, with what grace, what delicate verve, what perfect propriety! The lorette, thanks to Roqueplan, who has baptized her, and to Gavarni who has fixed the fugitive description, will go down to the most remote posterity; this is neither

the Greek *hetaire*, nor the Roman courtesan, nor the
impure woman of the Regency, nor the mistress of the
Empire, nor the grisette of the Restoration; but an
especial product of our busy life, the informal mistress
of an age which has no time to be amorous, and which
is too much ennuyéd at home, They have been more
or less figurantes, actresses, pianistes; they know the
slang of the gaming table, of the studio, of the coulisses,
they dance and waltz admirably, sing a little, and make
cigarettes like Spanish smugglers—a few of them even
know how to spell—but their principal talent lies in
practising forbearance, and in success. As for their
sacred toilettes, the dancing-girls of the pagoda of Ben-
ares are not more exact in descending the white marble
staircase leading to the Ganges, and in making their
ablutions in the sacred rivers. In dress, it is only the
Parisienne by birth who distinguishes herself by some
excessive luxury or some slight negligence, from other
women of fashion; foreigners almost always fail here,
even the Russian women, who are so French. Sometimes they are not in the fashion of to-day, but in that
of to-morrow. They know how to wear everything,
moire-antique, velvet, the plumed hat, the Chantilly
lace mantle, the tight boot, the man's collar, the Amazon
wrap—all except a cashmere long-shawl; that is the
superiority of the virtuous woman; no *dame aux camellias,* no lorette can resist the temptation of drawing in
the shawl with her elbows, to display the fine contours
of her form.

Gavarni seized all shades, he expressed them with a
rapid and facile pencil, always sure of itself. With
him, we enter the silk-hung boudoirs full of china and
old Sèvres vases, where are mirrored Venetian glasses,
and gilded candelabras, and we see, inclining upon a

divan, the divinity of the place, clad in an ample dressing-gown not confined at the girdle, making her slipper dance upon the tips of her bare toes, and emitting from her rosy lips the smoke of a *papelito*, while a female friend imparts to her some droll confidence, and a gentleman, more or less wrinkled, gnaws at the head of his cane, meditating some declaration. Furniture, costumes, accessories, fashions—all is rendered with perfect propriety, with a strict modernness, which no other artist possesses in the same degree. Every gesture is true, just, actual ; this is precisely as we sit down, as we rise, as we hold our hat, as we draw on our gloves, as we salute, as we open and close the door ; under these pale-tots, talmas, and overcoats, the body always asserts itself, which does not always happen under the *pseudo antique* draperies of historical painting ; for we have said above, that Gavarni is a great anatomist.

The woman of our day, absent from painting, lives again in these historic lithographs of our artist, with her coquettish mannerism, her spiritual grace, her irregular elegance, her problematical but irresistible beauty. What eyes to catch larks ! What a nose, à la Roxalane, turned up by the finger of caprice ! What pretty dimples for nestling loves ! What delicate chins, gently rounding above a knot of ribbon ! What fresh cheeks, caressed by a curl of hair ! What delicious realities, and what adorable falsehoods, under this flood of lace, cambric and silk ! Truly it is not the most beautiful, the purest, the noblest type, neither is it the supreme expression of the feminine beauty of our epoch ; but Gavarni has none the less rendered one of the phases of modern beauty.

The carnival of Paris, to which is wanting only the Piazza, the Piazetta and the Grand Canal to eclipse the ancient Venetian carnival, has found in Gavarni its painter and its historian. Here amid the dazzling whirlwind, the smoky light of the lustres, the din of voices and of the orchestra, the artist has seized every type, every air, every physiognomy. He lends his mind to all these perhaps stupid masks; he sums up, in one expressive word, the fireside chat; he translates into a droll legend the hoarse discordant voices of the hall; he takes his characters to the Café Anglais, to the Maison d'Or, as best befits each, and intoxicates them with his poetical raptures, more exhilarating, more foamy than the wine of Champagne! ·

Who does not know his "Enfants Terribles," and especially his "Parents Terribles?" The former betray, the latter disenchant all. The whole series is so vivid in treatment, so profound in philosophy, that we are never weary of turning over the leaves. The words accompanying each plate, are sometimes a comedy, often a vaudeville, always a maxim worthy of Larochefoucauld. How much the vaudevilleists and the review-writers have borrowed from these incisive outlines! Do not imagine that because he has especially portrayed the Bohemian of pleasure, that Gavarni has no moral sense; look over his album entitled "Old Lorettes," and you will see that his lithographic pencil knows how to punish vice as well as the brush of Hogarth has done; these frayed skirts, these tartans with flabby folds, this dilapidated head-gear, these boots that let in the water, these wan faces, these hollow cheeks, these shrivelled mouths, these eyes ruined by bistre, well compensate for robes with thirty-two flounces, for cashmere shawls trailing upon the ground, for red-heeled gaiters and all the insolent luxury of the past. We can pardon them, these poor girls, for having been pretty, superb and triumphant.

"Thomas Vireloque," although a little of a misanthrope, is also a good comrade; Diogenes, Rabelais and Sancho Panza would acquiesce in more than one of his aphorisms. This creation of Gavarni's will live.

In this rapid sketch we have attempted no description of the innumerable works of this master;—in only one branch of his work we have sought to outline through its principal features, the characteristics of this artist, so original, so living, so modern, that criticism, too much occupied with pretended serious talent, has not studied him with the attention he most certainly deserves.

———

The name Gavarni has rendered illustrious is not his own; he calls himself Sulpice Paul Chevalier. In one of his first publications, he assumed this graceful pseudonym, which so well accords with his brisk, elegant and untrammelled talent. Gavarni's beginnings were pitiable, and it was only when he had rounded the cape of the thirties, that he began to emerge from the shadow, and to take his place in the sunlight. We knew him at this time. He was a handsome young man, with abundant blonde locks, in frizzed, tufted curls, very careful of his person, very fashionable in his dress, having something English in the rigid details of his toilet, and possessing in the highest degree, the sentiment of modern elegance. He worked only in a black velvet jacket, in pantaloons of the best cut, in a frilled shirt of fine cambric, in polished shoes with red heels, just as he can be seen in a picture of himself in one of the illustrated publications of Hetzel. He had rather the air of a dandy amusing himself with art, than of an

artist, in the rather extraordinary signification we usually attach to this word; and yet, what an obstinate,
what an incessant, what a fruitful worker! You could
build an immense house with the lithographic stones he
has designed.

We may say that Gavarni, although very well known,
very much in fashion and very celebrated, has not been
appreciated at his just value, neither has Raffet nor
Daumier, nor Gustave Doré, brilliant as is his reputation.
In France, we love sterile talents and have a strange
prejudice against fecundity. How believe in the merit
of those multiplied works, which come to you every
morning, under the form of the journal or the current
number of a series, especially when they are lively,
witty, taken from our very manners, full of fire, warmth
and force, original in thought and execution, owing
nothing to the antique, expressing our loves, our aver-
sions, our tastes, our caprices, our absurdities, the
garments in which we are clothed, the types of grace or
coquetry which please us, the surroundings amid which
we pass our lives? All this does not seem serious art;
and such persons as admire a nude Ajax, Theseus, and
Philoctetes, are inclined to treat Gavarni's Parisians as
very simple, mediocre productions.

No one better than Gavarni knows how to place a
black coat upon a modern form, and this is not an easy
thing. Under this coat, the artist, with three strokes
of his pencil, knows how to create a human armor with
correct articulations, and easy movements; in a word, a
living being, capable of motion, of going and coming.
Very often Delacroix might regard with a dreamy eye,
these designs apparently so frivolous, and yet of a science
so profound. He would be astonished at this perfect
aplomb, at this cohesion of the members, at these com-

posed attitudes, at this mimicry so simple and so natural. Every year rendered the drawing of Gavarni more supple, free and broad; pencil nor lithographic stone offered him further resistance, and he did with them what he would. In this nature of such peculiar originality, beside the artist, there was a philosopher, a writer, who in two lines below his plates, has written more comedies, vaudevilles and studies upon manners, than all the authors of this day together. Gavarni has been the wit of this epoch, and almost all the noted sayings of these last years have come from him. His influence, without being confessed, has been very great; he has invented a carnival more amusing, more fantastic and more picturesque, than the old carnival of Venice. His types, which we believe copies, are creations, and later, the reality imitates the design. It is he who has made live in his life of art, all the Bohemians, the student, the lorette; he has shown the deceits of women, the terrible frankness of children, what we say and what we think, not as a morose sermonizer, after the manner of Hogarth, but as an indulgent moralist who knows human frailty, and who pardons it for a great deal.

But they who believe Gavarni only graceful, witty, and elegant, greatly err. His old lorettes, with their comical yet deathly legends, reach the terrible. Thomas Vireloque, his rags torn in all the brambles, from his half-blinded eyes, throws a glance upon humanity, as clairvoyant, as profound, as cynical as Rabelais, Swift or Voltaire. From the wretched beings he saw in Saint Giles during his sojourn at London, Gavarni brought home frightful silhouettes, sinister phantoms, more hideous and more lamentable than the visions of nightmare.

His manner of composing was singular; he began to toy around the stone without a subject, without a fixed design; little by little, the figures detached themselves, assumed an existence, a physiognomy; they went and came, they gave themselves up to any action whatever. Gavarni listened to them, sought to divine what they said as when we see two unknown persons walk gesticulating, upon the boulevard. Then, when he had caught the characteristic word, he wrote his legend, or rather, he dictated it, for it was another hand that moulded the letter.

For some years, Gavarni had rather neglected drawing. His mind, at all times a lover of the exact sciences, inclined towards mathematical heights, and devoted itself to the pursuit of arduous problems, to which it found curious and new solutions. He took delight in this world of computation, where we see numbers increase to infinity, and produce the most astonishing combinations. He was not one of those chimerical persons who seek the quadrature of the circle or perpetual motion; but rather a *savant* upon whom the Institute would have set value.

He died in that villa of Auteuil, where we were his neighbor a score of years ago, and whose garden, since invaded by a railway, contained only trees of persistent foliage, cedars, pines, larches, arbor-vitæ, box, holly, evergreens, ivies, firs, and whose sombre verdure made it resemble the garden of a cemetery. It appears that this collection of trees was unrivalled, and the horticultural artist attached the greatest value to it.

CHARLES BAUDELAIRE.

BORN 1821——DIED 1867.

ALTHOUGH his existence was short—he lived scarce forty-six years—Charles Baudelaire had time to assert himself, and to write his name upon that wall of the nineteenth century, inscribed already with so many signatures, destined to endure. Do not doubt that his will remain there, for it represents an original and powerful talent, disdainful to excess of those feudal services which make popularity easy, loving only the rare, the difficult and the strange, possessed of an elevated literary conscience ; amid the necessities of life, abandoning a work only when he believed it perfect, weighing every word as misers might weigh a suspected ducat, revising a proof ten times, submitting the poèt in him to the most subtile criticism, and with unwearying effort, seeking the particular ideal he had formed for himself.

Born in India, and thoroughly acquainted with the English language, he made his début by translations from Edgar Poe, so excellent that they seemed original works, and made the thought of the author gain in passing from one idiom to the other. Baudelaire has naturalized in France that imaginative mind so wildly grotesque, and so *bizarre*, that compared with it Hoffmann is no more than a fantastic Paul de Kock. Thanks to Baudelaire, we have had the surprise of a literary flavor totally unknown. Our intellectual palate has been astonished, as when at the Universal Exposition, we drank some of those American draughts, a foaming mixture of ice, soda water, ginger and other exotic ingredients. Into what giddy intoxication we were thrown by reading the "Golden Bug," the "Usher House." "The Case of Mr. Waldemar," "King Pestilence," the "Monosuna;" and all those extraordinary histories! These fantastic tales excited public curiosity to the highest pitch, and the name of Baudelaire became, in some sort, inseparable from the name of the American author.

These translations were preceded by a most interesting study upon Edgar Poe from a biographical and metaphysical point of view. One could not in a more subtle manner analyze this genius of an eccentricity which almost seemed to border upon madness, and whose groundwork is a pitiless logic, pushing the consequences of an idea to their end. This blending of passion and coldness, of intoxication and mathematical processes, this keen raillery intermixed with lyric effusions of the highest poetry, were admirably comprehended by Baudelaire. He was seized with the most lively sympathy for this haughty and eccentric character, which so much shocked American cant—a disagreeable variety of English cant—and frequent communion with this giddy intellect exercised a great influence upon him.

Edgar Poe was not merely a recounter of extraordinary stories, a journalist whom no one surpassed in the art of launching a scientific canard, a mystifier *par excellence* of open-mouthed credulity—he was also an æsthetician of the highest power, a great poet of a very refined and very complicated sort. His poem of

8

"The Raven," through a gradation of strophes, and the disquieting persistence of the refrain, reaches an intense but melancholy effect, a terror and a fatal presentiment against which it is difficult to defend one's self. It is doing no wrong to the originality of Baudelaire to say that we find in his "Flowers of Evil," a sort of reflection of the mysterious manner of Edgar Poe, on a groundwork of romantic color.

Some years ago, as it is not our habit to wait until our friends are dead to praise them, we wrote a notice of Baudelaire, published as a preface to some extracts from his poems, inserted in a collection of French Poets, where may be found this passage upon the "Fleurs de Mal," the author's most important and most original work. This page cannot be suspected of posthumous complaisance, and what we have said of the living poet, we can report of the dead poet, so prematurely and so unhappily taken from us:

"We read in the tales of Nathaniel Hawthorne, the description of a singular garden, where a toxicologic botanist has reunited the flora of venomous plants. These plants, of strangely disheveled foliage, of a black or mineral glaucous green, as if tinged by the sulphate of copper, have a sinister and formidable beauty. We feel them dangerous, despite their charm; they have in their haughty, provoking or perfidious attitude, the consciousness of an immense power, or of an irresistible seduction. From their flowers, savagely variegated and mottled, of a purple similar to congealed blood, or of a chlorotic white, they exhale, sharp, penetrating, intoxicating odors. In their poisoned chalices, the dew changes into *aqua toffana*, and there flit around them, only cantharides cuirassed in golden green, or flies of a steel-blue, whose prick causes carbuncles (*le charbon*).

The milk-wort, the aconite, the henbane, the hemlock, mingle their cold virus with the glowing poisons of the tropics and the Indies. The manchineel here displays its small apples, deadly as those which hang from the tree of knowledge, the upas here distils its lacteous juices, more corrosive than aquafortis. Above this garden floats a sickly vapor, which benumbs the birds when they pass through it. But the doctor's daughter lives unharmed amid these mephitic effluvias. Her lungs without danger breathe this air where any other than she and her father would inhale certain death. She makes for herself bouquets of the flowers, she adorns her hair with them, she perfumes her breast with them, she nibbles at their petals as young girls nibble at roses. Slowly saturated with the venomous juices, she has herself become a living poison which neutralizes all other poisons. Her beauty, like that of the plants of her garden, has something disquieting, fatal and morbid. Her hair, of a bluish-black, contrasts in a sinister way, with her complexion, of a dull, greenish pallor, from whence her mouth gleams forth, empurpled, one might say, by some bloody berry. An insane smile reveals teeth enshrined in a sombre red, and her fixed eyes fascinate like those of serpents. You would say she was one of those Javanaise, those love-vampyres, those nocturnal demons, whose passion in a fortnight exhausts the blood, the marrow and the soul of a European. And yet, she is a virgin, this doctor's daughter, and languishes in solitude. Love tries in vain to become acclimated in this atmosphere, out of which she cannot live.

"We have never read the 'Fleurs de Mal' of Charles Baudelaire without thinking involuntarily, of this story of Hawthorne's; they have these sombre and metallic colors, these greenish-gray leaves, and these death-bringing odors. His muse resembles the doctor's daughter, whom no poison can affect, but whose complexion in its bloodless pallor betrays the surroundings amid which she dwells."

This comparison pleased Baudelaire, and he loved to recognize in it the personification of his talent. He glorified himself also with this phrase of a great poet; "You invest the heaven of art, with we know not what deadly rays; you create a new shudder."

But it would be committing a grave error to believe that amid these mandragores, these poppies, these poisonous blossoms, we may not meet here and there, a fresh rose of innoxious perfume, a large Indian flower opening its white chalice to the pure dew of heaven. When Baudelaire depicts the deformities of humanity and of civilization, it is only with a secret horror. He has no complaisance for them, he regards them as infractions of the universal rhythm. When he has been represented as *immoral*, a great word they know how to use in France as in America, he has been as astonished as if he heard them praise the virtue of the jasmine, and stigmatize the wickedness of the acrid ranunculus.

Beside the "Extraordinary Histories" of Edgar Poe, Baudelaire has translated from the same author, the "Adventures of Allen Gordon Pym," which end with that horrible ingulfment in the vortex of the South Pole. He has also rendered into French, a cosmogonic dream entitled, "Eureka," where the American author, planting himself upon the celestial mechanism of La Place, seeks to divine the secret of the universe, and believes he has found it. The difficulties encountered in the translation of such a work, may well be imagined. Under the title of "The Artificial Paradise," Baude-

laire has given us the substance of this work, blending
with his own reflections, those of DeQuincy the English opium eater; and of the whole he has made a sort of
treatise, which in many places, must run counter to
Balzac's famous theory of stimulants. It is most curious
reading, illuminated by the phantasmagoria of opium,
and a portraiture of the most brilliant, whimsical and
terrible hallucinations, produced by this seducing poison,
which, with its factitious happiness, stupefies China
and the Orient. The author blames the man who seeks
to withdraw himself from the fatality of sorrow, and
lifts himself to an artificial paradise only to soon fall
back into a deeper hell.

Baudelaire was an art-critic of perfect sagacity, and
to the appreciation of painting he brought a metaphysical subtlety and an originality of perspective, which
makes us regret that he had not devoted more time to
this sort of work. The pages he has written upon
Delacroix are among his most remarkable ones.

Toward the end of his life, he composed some short
prose poems, but in rhythmed prose, wrought and polished like the most condensed poetry; they are strange
fantasies, landscapes of the other world, unknown
figures, which it seems to you he has seen elsewhere,
spectral realities, and phantoms having a terrible
reality. These pieces have appeared at hap-hazard,
here and there, in divers reviews, and they should be
reunited in a volume, adding to them others which the
author must have preserved in his portfolio.

HONORÉ DE BALZAC.

BORN 1799—DIED 1850.

I.

THE first time I saw Balzac, he was thirty-six, a year older than the century, and his face was one of those which can never be forgotten. In his presence you thought of Shakespeare's lines upon Julius Cæsar.

> " Nature might stand up
> And say to all the world, *' This is a man !'* "

My heart beat violently, for never have I approached without trembling, a master of thought; but all the fine speeches I had prepared on the way, cleaved to my throat, allowing utterance only to some stupid phrase about the weather. Balzac, seeing my embarrassment, soon set me at my ease, and ere long my presence of mind returned, allowing me to scan him minutely.

He wore in the form of a dressing-gown, that frock of white cashmere or flannel confined at the waist by a cord, in which he was soon after painted by Louis Boulanger. It is not known why he chose this costume which he never laid aside; perhaps in his eyes, it symbolized the clauistral life to which his literary labors condemned him. A Benedictine of romance, had he not assumed the robe of his order? The frock always remained marvellously white. He boasted of this to us, showing us the sleeves, perfectly intact, and of a purity which had never been sullied by the least stain of ink. "The author should be neat when at his work," said he.

This frock, somewhat thrown back, revealed the athletic neck, round as the base of a column, without apparent muscles, and of a satiny whiteness which contrasted with the deeper hue of his face. At this time Balzac, in the flower of his age, gave evidence of a robust health, little in harmony with the romantic pallor and delicacy then in fashion. The pure ·Tourangean blood coursed rapidly through his full veins, and sent a warm color to his lips, thick, sinuous and easy to smile ; a light mustache and imperial accentuated the contours of his mouth, without concealing them. The nose, square at the end, parted into two lobes, pierced by very open nostrils of a character entirely original and peculiar. Balzac in posing for his bust, said to the sculptor, David d'Angers, "Be careful about my nose ; my nose is a world."

The forehead was immense, noble, very much whiter than the face, and with no wrinkle save a perpendicular furrow at the root of the nose. The organ of locality formed a very pronounced ridge above the arched brows; the hair, abundant, long, coarse and black, stood up behind like a lion's mane. As for the eyes, none other such ever existed. They had a life, a light, an inconceivable magnetism. Despite his long nightly vigils, their sclerotic coat pure, limpid, blueish, like that of a child or a virgin, enshrined two black diamonds, which at moments were illuminated by rich, golden reflections. They were eyes to make the eagles' pupils fall, to penetrate walls and hearts—the eyes of the sovereign, the seer, the conqueror.

Mme. Emile de Girardin in her romance entitled "M. de Balzac's Cane," thus speaks of his sparkling eyes: "Tancred then perceived on the front of this sort of club, turquoises, gold, marvellous chasings; and behind them all, two large black eyes, more brilliant than the stones."

The habitual expression of the face was a sort of energetic hilarity, a Rabelaisian and monkish jocoseness—the frock no doubt aided in producing this idea—but it was aggrandized and elevated by a mind of the first order.

At this time, Balzac's great work, the "Comédie Humaine" had not appeared, but he had written "Louis Lambert," "Seraphita," "Eugène Grandat," "The History of the Thirteen," "The Country Physician," and other works, enough, to found, in ordinary times, five or six reputations. His ascending glory, every day enhanced by new rays, beamed forth in ever-increasing splendor, and that must indeed be a bright luminary, which could shine in a sky where now glowed in their full lustre, Lamartine, Victor Hugo, Alfred de Musset, Sainte-Beuve, Alexandre Dumas, Prosper Mérimée, George Sand, and so many other lesser lights.

He lived in a narrow, little frequented street, near the Observatory, which had been christened the Cassini. Upon the garden wall, usurping nearly one side of the street, and at the end of which was the pavilion occupied by Balzac, you read 'L'Absolu; Brick-Merchant.' This odd sign which, if we mistake not, exists to-day, may have given name to Balzac's story, "The Search for the Absolute." It probably suggested to him the idea of Balthasar in pursuit of his impossible dream.

We had come to breakfast with him, myself and a few others. According to his habit, Balzac had risen at midnight, and had written until the time of our arrival. But his features betrayed no fatigue aside from a slight discoloration beneath the eyelids, and during the whole breakfast he was wildly gay. Gradually the conversation drifted toward literature, and he complain. ed of the enormous difficulties of the French language. Style very much preoccupied him, and he sincerely believed that he had none at all. It is true that he was then generally denied this quality. The school of Victor Hugo, in love with the sixteenth century and the middle age, learned in rhymes, in rhythms, in struc- ture, in periods ; rich in words, crushing prose with the gymnastics of verse, and working through a master for certain results, set value only on what was well *written*, that is to say labored and wrought up to meet the demands of a most artificial taste. This school regarded the portrayal of modern manners as useless, vulgar, and wanting in lyric art.

Balzac, notwithstanding the great popularity he had begun to attain, was not admitted among the gods of romance, and he knew it. While devouring his books, people did not pause to regard their serious side, and for a long time he remained—"the most fruitful of romancers"—and nothing more. This surprises the reading world of to-day, but we can vouch for the truth of our assertion. And so he did himself great wrong in trying to achieve a style, and in his anxious corrections, he consulted people who were a hundred times his inferiors. Before signing any production with his own name, under various pseudonyms, he wrote a hundred volumes just "to get his hand in." And yet he already possessed a style of his own, without being conscious of it.

Let us return to our breakfast. While talking, Balzac played with his knife and fork, and we remarked

8*

his hands, which were of rare beauty, the true hands of a prelate, white, with plump, slender fingers, pink and brilliant nails. He was very proud of them, and smiled as we regarded them. Such hands he considered evidence of aristocratic birth. Lord Byron, in a note, says with evident satisfaction, that Ali Pacha complimented him upon the smallness of his ears, and inferred from this that he was a true gentleman. A similar remark upon his hands would have equally flattered Balzac, even more than the praise of one his books. He had a sort of prejudice against those whose hands and feet were wanting in delicacy. The repast was dainty enough; a *pâté de foie gras* figured in it; but this was a deviation from Balzac's habitual frugality. He told us so laughing, and that for this " solemnity," he had borrowed his publisher's silver plate !

Before going farther, let us pause for a brief space, and give some details of Balzac's life anterior to our acquaintance with him. Our authorities will be Madame de Surville his sister, and himself.

Balzac was born in Tours, May 16, 1799, on the natal day of Saint Honoré. They gave him the Saint's name, which sounded well, and seemed to be of good augury. Little Honoré was not a precocious child; he did not prematurely announce that he should write the " Comédie Humaine." He was a fresh, rosy boy; fond of play, with mild, sparkling eyes, but in no way distinguished from other boys of his age. At seven, he was transferred from a school at Tours where he had been a day-pupil, to the College of Vendome, where he passed for a lad of very mediocre ability.

The first part of " Louis Lambert," contains curious information as to this period of Balzac's life. Dividing his own personality, he describes himself as an old

schoolfellow of Louis Lambert's, now speaking in his
name, and now lending his own sentiments to this personage, imaginary, and yet very real, since he is a sort
of object-glass of the writer's very soul. We quote
his own words.

"Situated in the middle of the town, upon the little
river Loire, which bathes its walls, the college forms a
vast enclosure containing the establishments necessary
to an institution of this kind: a chapel, a theatre, a
hospital, a bakery and water-works. This college is the
most noted seat of instruction the central provinces possess. Distance does not allow parents to come here
often to see their children, and the rules forbid vacations passed away from the institution. Once entered,
the pupils do not leave until the end of their studies.
With the exception of outside walks under the conduct
of the fathers, this house possesses all the advantages of
conventual discipline. In my time the corrector was a
living remembrance, and the ferule played, with honor,
its terrible rôle."

Balzac suffered prodigously in this college, where his
dreamy nature was every instant subjected to martyr-
dom from some inflexible rule. He neglected his tasks,
but favored by the tacit complicity of a tutor of mathematics, who was at the same time librarian, and occupied in some transcendental work, he did not recite
his lessons, but took away all the books he wished. He
passed his whole time in secret reading, and he soon
became the scholar of his class most often punished.
Tasks and retentions soon absorbed his hours of recreation. In certain schoolboy natures, chastisements inspire a sort of stoic rebellion, and they meet the exasperated professors with the same disdainful impassibility
which captive savage warriors oppose to the enemy who

tortures them. Neither the dungeon, starvation nor the ferule, avail to wring from them the least lament; then ensue between the master and the pupil terrible conflicts, unknown to the parents, where the arts of the tormentor are met by the constancy of martyrs. Some nervous professors cannot bear the glance of hatred, scorn and menace with which a brat of eight or ten years defies them.

Accustomed to the open air, to the independence of an education left to chance, habituated to the caresses of an old man who loved him dearly, and to thinking in the sunlight, it was very hard for Lambert to conform to the college rules, to march in the ranks, to live within the four walls of a hall where twenty-four young lads sat silent upon wooden benches, each before his desk. His senses possessed a perfection which gave them an exquisite delicacy, and they all suffered from this life in common.

This entire change of habits and discipline saddened the young lad. His head resting in his left hand, his elbows leaning on his desk, he passed the hours of study in gazing at the foliage of the trees in the yard, or at the clouds flitting across that narrow bit of sky. He seemed to be studying his lessons, but seeing his pen immovably fixed on the blank page, the professor would angrily cry out to him that he was doing nothing.

To this vivid and truthful description of the miseries of life at a boy's school, let us add an extract—where Balzac in his duality, giving himself the double soubriquet of Pythagoras and Poet, the one borne by the half of himself personified in Louis Lambert, the other, by the half confessing his own identity,—explains admirably the reason why he passed among the professors for an incapable child.

" Our independence, our illicit occupations, our apparent indolence, the torpor in which we remained, our constant punishments, our repugnance to tasks and duties, won us the reputation of being lazy, stupid and incorrigible lads; our masters despised us, and we fell into the most frightful disgrace among our comrades, from whom we concealed our contraband studies for fear of their mockeries. This double depreciation, unjust on the part of the fathers, was but a natural sentiment in our schoolfellows; we did not know how to play ball, nor to run, nor to mount stilts on these days of amnesty, when by chance we obtained a moment's freedom. We took part in none of the amusements in vogue at the college; strangers to the enjoyments of our comrades, we remained alone and melancholy, seated under some tree of the court. The Poet and Pythagoras were an exception; they led a life outside the common life. The penetrating instinct, the sensitive self-love of school-boys, gives them a presentiment in regard to minds placed higher or lower than their own; hence, on the one side, was hatred of our mute aristocracy, on the other, scorn of our incapacity. These sentiments were in us to our cost; perhaps, I have divined them only to-day. We lived then exactly like two rats, skulking in the corner of the hall behind our desks; bound there equally during the hours of study and the hours of recreation."

The result of these hidden labors, of these meditations which absorbed the time of study, was that famous *Traité de la Volonté* which is many times mentioned in " The Human Comedy." Balzac always regretted the loss of this work of which he gives a summary sketch in "Louis Lambert," and he relates with an emotion time has not diminished, the confiscation of the box which held the precious manuscript. Some jealous school fellows tried to snatch the precious casket from the two who were valiantly defending it, when suddenly attracted by the tumult of the battle, Père Haugoult roughly intervened, and quieted the dispute. "This terrible Haugoult ordered us to give the box to him; Lambert handed him the key, the tutor took the papers and glanced over them; then he said while confiscating them :—"See here, in such foolishness as this you neglect your lessons!" Great tears fell from Lambert's eyes, caused as much by a consciousness of his outraged moral superiority, as by the gratuitous insult and the treachery which overwhelmed him. Père Haugoult probably sold to a grocer of Vendome this *Traité de la Volonté* "without knowing the importance of the scientific treasures, whose germs were thus destroyed by ignorant hands."

If we open the "*Peau de Chagrin*," we find there in Raphael's confession the following sentences:

"You alone can admire my "Theory of the Will," that long work, for whose sake I learned the Oriental languages, anatomy, and physiology; to which I had consecrated the greatest portion of my time; a work which, if I do not deceive myself, would have completed the labors of Mesmer, of Lavater, of Gall, of Bichat, by opening a new route to human science. There stopped my beautiful life, this sacrifice of all my days, this toil of the silk-worm, unknown to the world, and whose sole recompense is perhaps in the labor itself. From the age of reason to the day when I ended my *Théorie*, I have observed, I have learned, I have written, I have read incessantly, and my life has been one long task. An effeminate lover of oriental idleness, amorous of my dreams, sensuous, I have always worked, denying myself the delights of Parisian life ; a gourmand, I have been temperate ; fond of travel and voyages, desiring to visit foreign countries, finding still some pleasure in making *ricochets* in the water after the manner of children, I have remained constantly seated with a pen in my hand ; a babbler, I have gone to listen in silence to the professors at the public lecture-courses of the Library and the Museum ; I have slept upon my solitary truckle-bed like a monk of the order of Saint-Benedict; and yet woman has been my sole chimera ;—a chimera I would have caressed, and which always fled from me ! "

If Balzac regretted the loss of his "Treatise on the Will," he must have been far less sensible to that of his epic poem upon the Incas, which opens thus :

O Inca, ô roi infortuné et malheureux ! an unlucky inspiration, which for all the time he remained in college, won him the derisive soubriquet of " *The Poet.*" Balzac, it must be confessed, had a gift for poetry, for versification, at least ; his thought, so complex, always remained rebellious against rhyme.

From these intense meditations, from these intellectual labors, truly prodigious for a child of twelve or fourteen years, there resulted a strange malady, a nervous fever, a sort of *coma* entirely inexplicable to the professors, who were not in the secret of the readings and the pursuits of young Honoré, apparently so idle and stupid. No one at the school suspected this precocious excess of intelligence, no one knew that in the "dungeon" where he caused himself to be put daily so as to be at liberty, this pupil, supposed to be idle, had devoured a whole library of serious books, above the usual comprehension of lads of his age.

Let us cite here some curious traits connected with the faculty for reading attributed to Louis Lambert, that is to Balzac.

"In three years, Louis had assimilated the substance of the books in his uncle's library which deserved to be read. The absorption of ideas by reading, had with him become a curious phenomenon, his eye took in seven or eight lines at a glance, and his mind appreciated the sense of them with a quickness equal to that of his glance. Often a single word of a phrase sufficed to give him its substance. His memory was prodigious. He remembered with the same fidelity, the thoughts acquired by reading and those which reflection or conversation had suggested to him. He possessed all memories; that of places, of names, of words, of things, of figures; not only did he recall objects at will, but he saw them again in himself, transfigured and colored as they were at the moment when he perceived them. This power applied equally to the most inperceptible objects of the understanding. He remembered not only the bearing of the thoughts in the book whence he had derived them, but even the disposition of his mind at remote epochs."

This marvellous gift of his youth, Balzac retained all his life, even in larger measure as the years passed on; and through this we are able to explain his immense labors—veritable labors of Hercules.

The frightened professors wrote to Honoré's parents to come for him as soon as possible. His mother hastened to him, and took him back to Tours. The astonishment of the family was great when they saw the thin, pitiful child the college had returned to them in place of the cherub it had received. Not only had he lost his fine color, his fresh embonpoint, but under the shock of a congestion of ideas, he appeared even imbecile. His manner was that of an ecstatic, of a somnambulist who sleeps with open eyes; lost in profound revery, he did not hear what was said to him; or, his mind returning from afar, arrived too late for reply. But the open air rest, the tender cares of his family, the recreations they forced him to take, and the vigorous juices of youth soon triumphed over this diseased state. The tumult caused in that young brain by the confusion of ideas, was ere long appeased.

The involved readings classified themselves, to abstractions succeeded real images. While walking for recreation, he studied the pretty landscapes of the Loire, the provincial types, the cathedral of Saint Gatien, and the characteristic physiognomy of priests and prebendaries. Many cartoons which later served for the grand frescoes of the " Comédie," were sketched during this period of fruitful inaction. Meantime, the intelligence of Balzac was no more divined or comprehended in his family than it had been in college. If anything clever escaped his lips, his mother, a very superior woman by the way, would exclaim; " Honoré, do you understand what you are saying ? " Balzac *père*, who believed at the same time with Montaigne, with Rabelais and with uncle Toby, through his philosophy, his originality and his goodness, had a better opinion of his son ; from certain systems of genesis peculiar to himself, he had made up his mind that no child of his could be a fool, and yet he had no suspicion of the great man Honoré was to become.

Balzac's family had returned to Paris ; he was placed at the boarding-school of M. Lepitre in the Rue Saint Louis, and afterwards with Messieurs Scanzer and Beuzelin in the Rue Thoringy at Marais. There as at the College of Vendôme, his genius did not reveal itself, and he remained confounded with a herd of ordinary pupils. No pious enthusiast had said to him ;—*Tu Marcellus eris !* or, *Sic itur ad astra !*

His school education ended, Balzac gave himself that second education, which is the true one ; he studied, he perfected himself, he attended the courses of the Sorbonne and read law with an attorney. This time, apparently lost, since Balzac became neither attorney nor notary, nor advocate nor judge, gave him a personal acquaintance with the lawyers' clerks of Paris, and set him to writing later, in the fashion of a man marvellously versed in that profession, what we may call the litigations of the " Comédie Humaine."

The examinations passed, the great question of a career presented itself. They wished to make a notary of Balzac ; but the future great writer, although no one believed in his genius, had a consciousness of it himself. In the most respectful manner he declined such a career, although they would have given him a commission on the most favorable terms. His father granted him an ordeal of two years, and when the family returned to the province, Madame Balzac installed Honoré in an attic, allowing him a pension scarce sufficient for his most pressing wants. She hoped that a little hardship would render him more wise.

This garret was perched in the Rue de Lesdiguières, No. 9, near the Arsenal, whose library offered its resources to the young student. To pass from an abundant and luxurious house to a miserable attic must be a great hardship for any other age than twenty-one years, Balzac's age at that time but, if the dream of every little boy is to have boots, that of every young man is to have a chamber all to himself, whose key he carries in his pocket, although he can stand upright only in its midst. A chamber is the virile robe ; it is independence, personality, delight !

Behold then master Honoré perched up near the sky,

seated before his table, and essaying a *chef-d'œuvre*, which must surely justify the indulgence of his father, and give the lie to the unfavorable horoscopes of his friends. It is a singular incident, that Balzac made his *debut* in a tragedy, in a "Cromwell!" About this time, Victor Hugo also put the last touches to his "Cromwell," whose preface was the manifesto of the young dramatic school.

II.

In attentively re-reading the "Comédie Humaine" when one has familiarly known Balzac, one finds there a dense throng of curious details in regard to his character and his life; especially in his first works, where he is not yet entirely disengaged from his own personality, and in default of *subjects* observes and dissects himself. We have said that he began his rude novitiate for the literary life, in a garret near the Arsenal. The novel "Facine Cane," published in Paris, March, 1836, and dedicated to Louise, contains some valuable indications of the life this young aspirant for glory led in his aërial nest.

"I lived then in a street which doubtless you do not know, Rue de Lesdiguières; it begins at Rue Saint-Antoine opposite a fountain, near the Place de la Bastille, and leads into the Rue de la Cérisaie. The love of science had thrown me into an attic, where I wrote all night, and passed the day in a neighboring library, that of Monsieur. I lived frugally; I had accepted all the conditions of the monastic life, so necessary to intellectual workers. Even when the weather was fine, I scarce allowed myself a walk upon the boulevard Bourdon. One sole passion enticed me from my studious

habits ; but was not this also a study ? I went to observe
the manners of the faubourg, its inhabitants and their
characters. Ill clad as the workmen, indifferent to
decorum, I did not put them on their guard against me ;
I could mingle in their groups, see them conclude their
bargains, and hear them dispute about the hours when
they quitted work. With me, observation had already
become intuitive ; it so thoroughly grasped exterior
details as to go immediately beyond them ; it gave me
the faculty of living the life of the individual in whom
I was interested, by permitting me to substitute myself
for him as the Dervish of the Thousand-and-One Nights
seized the souls of persons over whom he pronounced
certain words."

" When, between eleven o'clock and midnight, I met
a workman and his wife returning together from the
Ambigu Comique, I amused myself in following them
from the boulevard Pont aux Choux, to the boulevard
Beaumarchais. These worthy people would at first
speak of the piece they had just seen ; from this they
would descend to their family affairs ; the mother leading her child by the hand without heeding its com-
plaints or questions. The married pair would reckon up
the money that was to be paid them on the morrow.
They would expend it in twenty different ways. Now,
they would enter into household details, into lamenta-
tions over the excessive price of potatoes, or the length
of the winter and the rise in the cost of coal ; into pithy
representations as to what was due the baker, and finally into discussions where each becoming irritated, displayed his or her character in picturesque words. In
listening to these people, I could espouse their life, I
felt their rags upon my back, I walked in their dilapidated shoes ; their desires, their needs, all passed into my

soul, and my soul passed into theirs; it was the dream of an awakened man   With them, I grew exasperated at the foremen of the shops who tyrannized over them, or at the bad practices which made them go and come many times without getting their pay.   To abandon my own habitudes, to become another than myself through this transport of the moral faculties, to play this game at will, such was my recreation.   To what do I owe this gift?   To a second sight?   Is it one of those faculties whose abuse would lead to madness?   I have never sought the sources of this power; I possess it, and I avail myself of it, that is all."

These lines are doubly interesting, because they throw light upon a side of Balzac's life as yet little known, showing that he was conscious of that faculty of intuition which he possessed in so high a degree, and without which, the realization of his work would have been impossible.   Balzac, like Vishnu, the Indian god, had the gift of *avatar*, that is to say, of incarnating himself into different bodies, and of living in them as long as he wished; but the number of the *avatars* of Vishnu is fixed at ten, those of Balzac are countless, and still more, he had the power to incite them at will.

Although it may seem singular to say it in the full light of this nineteenth century, Balzac was a *seer*.   His merits as an observer, his acuteness as a physiologist, his genius as a writer, do not suffice to explain the infinite variety of the two or three thousand types which play a rôle in the " Human Comedy."   He did not copy them, he lived them ideally, he wore their clothes, he contracted their habits, he environed himself with their surroundings, he was, for the time being, their very selves.   Hence come these well-sustained, logical personages, never belying themselves, never forgetting themselves, endowed with an interior and profound ex-istence.

This faculty, Balzac possessed only for the present. He could transport his thought into a marquis, into a financier, into *bourgeois*; into a man of the people, into a woman of the world, into a courtezan, but the shadows of the past did not obey his call; he never would have known, like Goethe, to evoke from the depths of antiquity, the beautiful Helen, and make her dwell in the Gothic manor of Faust. With two or three exceptions, all his work is modern; he has assimilated the living, he has not resuscitated the dead. History even has seduced him little, as one can see from the preface to his " Comé-die Humaine : " In reading the dry and repulsive nomen-clature of facts called history, who has not perceived that writers have forgotten at all epochs, in Egypt, in Per-sia, in Greece, in Rome, in our own time, to give the history of manners ? That bit of Petronius upon the private life of the Romans, irritates, rather than satisfies our curiosity,

This void, left by the historians, of vanished societies, Balzac proposed to fill for ours, and God knows he car-ried out faithfully the programme he sketched. "Society was going to be the Historian," writes he, " and I was to be only the secretary; in drawing up an inventory of the vices and the virtues, in collecting the leading facts of the passions, in depicting characters, in choosing the principal social events, in composing types through a reunion of the traits of several homogeneous characters, perhaps I could succeed in writing the history, forgot-ten by so many historians, that of manners. By the aid of a great deal of patience and courage, I might realize that book upon the France of the nineteenth century, which we all regret that Rome, Athens, Tyre, Memphis, Persia and India, have unfortunately not left us upon their civilization.

But let us return to the garret of the Rue Lesdiguiéres. Balzac had not conceived the plan of the work that was to immortalize him; he was still seeking it, anxiously, pantingly, laboriously, trying everything and succeeding in nothing; but he already possessed that pertinacity in work, to which Minerva, however untractable she may be, must one day or other yield. He sketched comic operas, he drew up plans of comedies, Dramas and romances, whose titles Madame de Sierville has preserved for us; "Stella," "Coqsigrue," "The Two Philosophers," without counting that terrible "Cromwell," whose verses had cost him so much and yet were not worth much more than the opening line of his epic poem upon the *Incas.*

Figure to yourself our young Honoré, his legs wrapped in a ragged coachman's overcoat, the upper part of his body protected by an old shawl of his mother's, his headgear a sort of Dantesque cap, whose cut Madame de Balzac alone knew, a coffee-pot at his right, an inkstand at his left, with heaving chest and bowed forehead, laboring like an ox at the plough, the field as yet stony and uncleared of those thoughts which were later to trace for him such productive furrows. His lamp burns like a star in the depths of the sombre house, the snow descends silently upon the disjointed tiles; the wind sighs through the door and window, "Like Tulou with his Flute, but less agreeably."

If some belated passer-by had raised his eyes to that little, obstinately flickering gleam, he certainly would not have suspected that it was the dawning of one of the brightest luminaries of our age.

Would you like to see a sketch of the place, transposed, it is true, but very exact, thrown off by the author of the " *Peau de Chagrin*," that work which contains so much of himself ?

" A chamber which looks down upon the yards of the neighboring houses, from the windows of which extend long poles filled with linen; nothing could have been more horrible than that garret with those yellow, grimy walls, which exhaled misery and invited its scholar. The roof slanted regularly, and the disjointed tiles allowed glimpses of the sky; there was room for a bed, a table, some chairs, and under the sharp angle of the eaves I could lodge my piano. I lived for almost three years in this aërial sepulchre, toiling night and day, without relaxation, yet with so much pleasure that study seemed to me the most beautiful exercise, the happiest solution of human life. The calm and the silence necessary to the scholar have, like love, a sort of sweetness and intoxication. Study lends a sort of magic to one's entire surroundings. The poor desk upon which I wrote, my piano, my bed, my arm-chair, the grotesque paper-hangings, my furniture, all these things seemed to possess life and become for me humble friends, the silent accomplices of my future. How many times have I not communicated to them my soul in gazing upon them ? Often in letting my eyes wander to a warped moulding, I would encounter new developments, a striking proof of my system, or words I believed suited to render almost untranslateable thoughts."

In this same passage, he thus alludes to his labors: " I had undertaken two great works; a comedy, which in a short time was to give me renown, fortune and entrance into that society where I wished to reappear exercising the royal prerogatives of the man of genius.

You have all seen this *chef d'œuvre*, the first error of a young man just out of college, the foolery of a child! Your banterings destroyed these fruitful illusions, which since then have not again awakened.

We recognize here the unlucky "Cromwell," which read to his family and assembled friends, made a complete fiasco.

Honoré appealed from this sentence to an arbiter whom he considered fully competent, an old man formerly professor at the Polytechnic School. His judgment was that our author had better engage in anything, no matter what, except literature.

What a loss for letters, what a void in the human mind would have ensued, if the young man had bowed to the experience of the old man and had listened to his counsel, which certainly was the wisest possible; for there was not the least spark of genius nor even of talent in this rhetorical tragedy! Happily, Balzac, under the pseudonym of Louis Lambert, had not composed for nothing, while at the college of Vendôme, his last treatise on the Will.

He submitted to the sentence, but only in respect to tragedy; he understood that he must renounce trying to walk in the footsteps of Corneille and Racine, for never were geniuses more contrary to his. Romance offered him a more fitting model, and about this time he wrote a great number of volumes which he did not sign, and which he always disavowed. The Balzac whom we know and whom we admire, was still in limbo and struggling valiantly to extricate himself. Those who had judged him capable of being only a copyist, were apparently right, but perhaps even this resource would have failed him, for his beautiful handwriting had already become transformed into the rough draughts,

9

irregular, full of erasures, overloaded, almost hieroglyphical, of the writer struggling for the idea, and no longer caring for the beauty of the character.

And so nothing had resulted from this rigorous claustration, this hermit life in the Thebaid, whose budget "Raphael" draws up : " Three sous worth of bread, two sous worth of milk, three sous worth of butcher's meat, prevented me from dying of hunger and kept my mind in a state of singular lucidity. My lodgings cost me three sous a day ; I burned three sous worth of oil every night, I took care of my own room, and I wore flannel shirts so as to expend but two sous a day for washing. I warmed myself with pitcoal, whose price divided by the days of the year, never gave more than two sous for each. I had suits of clothes, linen, and shoes for three years ; I needed to dress myself in my best only to attend certain public lecture courses, and visit the libraries. These expenses all united, amounted only to eighteen sous a day; there remained two sous for unforeseen things."

Doubtless " Raphael " a little exaggerated his economy, but Balzac's correspondence with his sister shows that the romance does not differ much from the reality. " The news from my household is disastrous," writes he. " Work is inimical to neatness. That rascal *myself* neglects himself more and more ; he descends only once in three or four days, to make purchases, and then goes to the merchants nearest and most badly supplied in the whole quarter. The fellow economizes his steps, at least ; so that your brother (destined to so much celebrity) is even now nourished like a great man ; that is to say, he is absolutely dying of hunger."

Elsewhere, continuing this pleasantry, he reprimands the idler, *Myself,* who lets spiders' webs hang from the ceiling, beetles walk under the bed, and the blinding dust sift over his window-panes.

In another letter, he writes, "I have eaten two melons. I shall have to pay for them with walnuts and dry bread?"

One of the few recreations he allowed himself was to go to the Jardin or to Père La Chaise. At the summit of the funereal hill, he looked down upon all Paris. His glance sailed over this ocean of slate and tiles, which covers so much luxury, misery, intrigue and passion. Like a young eagle, he took in his prey at a glance, but he had as yet, neither wings nor beak nor talons, although his eye could already fix itself upon the sun. He said, contemplating the tombs : " There are no more beautiful epitaphs than these ; *La Fontaine—Masséna—Molière*—one single name which tells all, and which makes us dream !"

This phrase contains as it were, a vague prophetic perception which the future realized, alas! too soon. On the slope of the hill, upon a sepulchral stone, beneath a bust cast in bronze, after the marble of David, this one word "BALZAC " tells all, and makes the solitary promenader dream.

The dietetic regimen extolled by "Raphael" must have been favorable to lucidity of brain, but it was very bad for a young man habituated to the comfort of the family life. Fifteen months passed under these intellectual plummets, sadder, heavier, than those of Venice, had made our young Tourangeau with the smooth, glowing cheeks, a Parisian skeleton, wan and sallow, almost unrecognizable. Balzac then reëntered the paternal mansion, where the fatted calf was killed for the return of the child so little prodigal.

We glide lightly over the period of his life when he

tried to assure independence by speculations in the book trade, which want of capital alone prevented being fortunate. These ventures involved him in debt, mortgaged his future, and despite the aid proffered him by his family, but perhaps too late, they imposed upon him the rock of Sisyphus, which he so many times raised just to the edge of the hill, and which always fell back with more crushing weight upon the shoulders of this Atlas, burdened besides with a whole world.

This debt, which he made it a sacred duty to discharge because it represented the fortune of other beings dear to him, was the Necessity, her rod armed with sharp points, her hand full of brazen nails, who harassed him night and day, without truce or pity, making him regard every hour of repose or recreation as a theft. She ruled dolorously all his life, often rendering it inexplicable to those who did not possess its secret.

Having indicated these indispensable biographic details, we come to our personal and direct impressions of Balzac.

Balzac, that immense brain, that physiologist so penetrating, that observer so profound, that mind so intuitive, did not possess the literary gift; within, there yawned an abyss between the thought and the form. That abyss, especially in his early attempts at authorship, he despaired of passing. He threw here without filling it, volume upon volume, lucubration upon lucubration, essay upon essay: a whole library of unacknowledged books vanished here. A will less sturdy would have despaired a thousand times; but happily, Balzac had an imperturbable confidence in his genius, unacknowledged by all the world.

Unlike other writers of the romantic school, who distinguish themselves by a boldness and astonishing facility of execution, and produce their fruits at almost the same time as their flowers, Balzac, the equal in genius of them all, found his means of expression only after infinite difficulties. Victor Hugo in one of his prefaces, says with his Castilian pride : " I know not the art of soldering a beauty in the place of a defect, and I correct myself in another work." But Balzac marred a tenth proof with his erasures.

Citing himself as an example, he preached to us a strange literary hygiene. We must cloister ourselves three or four years, drink water, eat boiled peas and beans like Protogenus, go to bed at six o'clock in the evening to rise at midnight and work until morning; employ the day for revising, extending, proving, perfecting, polishing the nocturnal labor; for correcting proofs, taking notes, making the necessary studies, and we must especially live in the most absolute chastity. He insisted very much upon this last recommendation. According to him, chastity develops in the highest degree the powers of the mind, and gives to those who practise it, unknown faculties. We timidly stated that many of the greatest geniuses had not carried out his idea in this respect, and we cited illustrious names. Balzac shook his head and replied ; " They would have done far better without women."

All the concession he would grant, and this he did regretfully, was to see the beloved one half an hour each year. He allowed letters : " These form the style," said he.

It must not be believed that Balzac jested, in laying down these rules which the Trappists or Carthusian friars would have found severe. He was perfectly in earnest, and spoke with such eloquence that we conscientiously tried his method of awakening genius; we rose several times at midnight, and after having taken the inspiring coffee, proceeded according to the formula, seating ourself before a table upon which sleep did not delay to incline our head. "*La Morte Amoureuse*," published in the Paris Chronicle, was our only nocturnal work.

About this time, Balzac had written for a review, "Facino Cane," the story of a noble Venetian, who, imprisoned in the vaults of the ducal palace, in digging a tunnel for escape, had fallen upon the secret treasure of the Republic, a good part of which by the aid of the bribed jailor he carried away. Facino Cane having become blind, and a clarionet player under the name of Père Canet, had despite his blindness, preserved the second sight for gold; he divined it through walls and vaults, and he proposed to the author at a wedding in the faubourg Saint-Antoine, to guide him, if he would defray the cost of the journey, to that immense mass of riches whose location had been lost through the fall of the Venetian Republic.

Balzac, as we have said, lived his personages, and at this moment, he was Facino Cane himself, minus the blindness, for more sparkling eyes never beamed from a human face. He now saw only tons of gold, heaps of diamonds and carbuncles, and by means of magnetism, with whose practices he had been long familiar, he sought from the somnambulists the location of the hidden treasure. He pretended to have thus learned in the most precise manner the place where, near the Pointe à Pitre, Toussaint L'Ouverture had caused his booty to be buried by negroes, who were immediately shot. "The Golden Bug" of Edgar Poe does not equal in subtlety of induction, in clearness of plan, in divination of details, the absorbing recital he has given us of this expedition undertaken for the purpose of rendering himself master of that treasure, far richer than the one borne away by Tom Kidd and buried at the foot of the Talipot, at the Tête de Mort.

We implore the reader not to make too much sport of us if we confess in all humility that we soon shared the conviction of Balzac. What brain could have resisted his infatuating representations? Jules Sandeau was also soon seduced, and as two reliable friends were needed, two devoted and robust companions to make the nocturnal excavations under the direction of the seer, Balzac wished to admit us to share a quarter each of this immense fortune. A half was to revert to him by right, he having conceived and directed the enterprise.

We were to buy picks, mattocks and shovels, embark them secretly on board a vessel, and go ourselves to the designated point by different routes so as not to excite suspicion, and the blow being struck, we were to transport our riches upon a brig chartered in advance. In short, it was all a romance, which would have been admirable if Balzac had written it instead of seeking to act it.

It is needless to add that we did not unearth the treasure of Toussaint L'Ouverture. Money failed us to pay our passage; we all three had scarce enough to buy the mattocks.

The dream of a sudden fortune won by some strange and marvellous means, often haunted Balzac's brain: some years before (in 1833) he had made a voyage to Sardinia to examine the dross of the silver mines abandoned by the Romans, and which, treated by imperfect processes, must in his opinion, still contain much metal. The idea was just; and imprudently confided, made the fortune of another.

III.

WE have related the anecdote of the treasure buried
by Toussaint L'Ouverture not for the pleasure of narrating a whimsical story, but because it is connected with
a dominant idea of Balzac's—money. Certainly, no person was less avaricious than he, but his genius made him
foresee the immense rôle this metallic hero would play
in art; a rôle more interesting for modern society than
that of the Grandisons, Oswalds, Werthers, Malek-Ad-
hels, Renés, Laras, Waverleys, Quentin Durwards, etc

Until then, romance had been confined to the portrayal of one only passion, *love;* but it was love in an
ideal sphere, and beyond the miseries and necessities of
life. The personages of these recitals, entirely psycho-
logical, neither ate nor drank nor lodged, nor had an
account with their tailor. They moved amid abstract
surroundings like the characters of tragedy. Did they
wish to travel without obtaining a passport, they put
some handfuls of diamonds in their pockets, and with
this coin paid the postilions who did not fail at each
relay to have killed their horses by fatigue. Chateaux
of vague architecture, received them at the end of their
route, and with their blood they wrote to their fair ones
interminable epistles, dated on the Tour to the North.
The heroines, no less immaterial, resembled an *aqua*

tinta of Angelica Kaufmann's ; each wore a huge straw hat, hair frizzed in the English fashion, a long robe of white muslin confined at the waist by an azure sash.

With his profound instinct of reality, Balzac comprehended that the modern life he wished to paint, was ruled by one grand fact—*money* ; and in the " *Peau de Chagrin*," he had the courage to present a lover not only anxious to know if he had touched the heart of her he loved, but also, if she had enough money to pay for the cab in which he was attending her. This audacity is perhaps one of the greatest that would be allowed an author, and it alone sufficed to immortalize Balzac. The consternation was profound, and the purists were indignant at this infraction of the laws of *genre ;* but all the young people, who going out in the evening to the house of some lady, their white gloves cleansed with gum elastic, had traversed Paris on the tips of their dancing-pumps, dreading a speck of mud more than a pistol-shot,—found compensation for their trials in the anxieties of Valentine, and were vividly interested in that hat which he was obliged to renovate and preserve with cares so minute. At moments of supreme misery, the finding of one of those pieces of a hundred sous slipped between the papers of the drawer by the modest commiseration of Pauline, produced the effect of the most romantic theatrical strokes, or the intervention of a Peri in the Arabian tales.

Balzac excels in the portrayal of youth, poor as it almost always is, entering upon its first struggles with life, a prey to temptation, pleasure and luxury, and bearing profound miseries through the aid of high hopes. Many of his heroes have endured great hardships. He does not lodge them all, these fine young people without a sou, in the conventional attic with chintz hangings

and looking out upon gardens; he does not give them
to eat "simple viands furnished by the hand of nature;"
he does not clothe them in garments without luxury, but
neat and suitable; he puts them in the vulgar boarding-
house with Mamma Vauquer, or coops them up in the
sharp angle of a roof, crowds them at the coarse tables
of cheap eating-houses, muffles them up in black garments with gray seams, and does not fear to send them
to the *Mont-de-Piété*, if they still possess,—a rare cir-
cumstance,—their father's watch.

O Corinne! thou who upon Cape Misena, lettest thy
snowy arm hang upon thine ivory lyre, while the son
of Albian, draped in a superb new mantle, and shod in
exquisitely fitting, highly polished boots, gazes upon
thee, and listens in an elegant attitude;—Corinne, what
would'st *thou* have said to such heroes? And yet they
possess one little quality which was wanting to thee,
Oswald;—they *live*, and it is a life so robust that it
seems as if we had met them a thousand times, as well
as the heroines with whom they are madly in love.

At the period when the first romances signed by Balzac appeared, people had not in the same degree as to-
day, the anxiety, or we might rather say, the fever for
gold.

California was not discovered; there existed only a few
leagues of railways of whose future no one dreamed.
The public, we might say, ignored that which we call
"business," to-day, and the bankers alone gambled upon
the bourse. This movement of capital, this sudden out-
pouring of gold, these calculations, these ciphers, this
importance given to money in works still taken as simple romantic fictions and not serious portraitures of life,
singularly astonished the subscribers to the circulating
libraries, and criticism reckoned up the sum total ex-

pended or staked by our author. The millions of Père Grandet gave place to arithmetical discussions, and grave people, startled by the enormousness of the entire sum, doubted the financial capacity of Balzac, a capacity very great notwithstanding, and recognized at a later day.

Stendhal said, with a sort of contemptuous fatuity of style: "Before writing, I always read three or four pages of the Civil Code to give me *tone*." Balzac, who had so well comprehended money, also discovered poems and dramas in the Code. "The Marriage Contract," where, under the figures of Matthias and Solonnet, he introduces the ancient and the modern notary, has all the interest of the most eventful comedy of the cloak and sword. The story of the bankrupt in "The Grandeur and Decline of Cæsar Birotteau," makes your heart beat like the history of an empire's fall; the struggle of the château and the thatched cottage in "The Peasants," presents as many sudden turns of fortune as the siege of Troy. Balzac knows how to give life to a soil, to a house, to an inheritance, to a capital; and from these he creates heroes and heroines whose adventures are devoured with an eager avidity.

These new elements introduced into romance did not please at the first; these philosophical analyses, these descriptions of a minuteness which seemed to have the future in view, were regarded as tediously prolix, and were oftenest omitted to hasten on to the story. Later, we recognized that the aim of our author was not to weave intrigues with more or less felicities of plot, but to paint society in its entireness from summit to base, with its personages and its motive power; and we admire the immense variety of his types. Is it not Alexandre Dumas who says of Shakspeare: "Shakspeare, the man who has created the most after God?" The words might be still more justly applied to Balzac; never in fact did so many living creatures issue from one human brain.

At this time (1836), Balzac had conceived the plan of his "Comédie Humaine," and possessed a full consciousness of his genius. He adroitly connected the works which had already appeared to his general idea, and found them a place in the philosophical categories marked out. Some purely imaginative novels did not fit on very well, notwithstanding the clasps added for that purpose; but they are there, mere details which lose themselves in the immensity of the whole, like ornaments of another style in a majestic edifice.

We have said that Balzac wrought laboriously, and an obstinate caster, ten or a dozen times, expelled from his crucible the metal which had not exactly filled the mould. Like Bernard Palissy, he would have burned his furniture, his floor, and even the beams of his house to keep up the fire of his furnace, so as not to fail in his experiment; the most rigid necessities never made him deliver a work to his publisher, upon which he had not expended his utmost effort, and he gave admirable examples of literary conscientiousness. His corrections, so numerous that they were almost equivalent to different editions of the same idea, were charged to his account by the publishers, and his compensation, often moderate for the value of the work and the trouble it had cost him, was diminished in proportion. The promised sums did not always arrive when due, and to sustain what he laughingly called his floating debt, Balzac displayed prodigious resources of mind, and an activity which would have completely absorbed the life of an ordinary man.

But, when seated before his table in his friar's frock, in the midst of the nocturnal silence, he found himself face to face with blank sheets, upon which was projected the light of his luminary of seven candles concentrated by a shade, taking pen in hand, he forgot all. And then commenced a conflict more terrible than the conflict of Jacob with the angel, that between the form and the idea. From those battles of each night at morn he issued broken, but victorious, the fire having gone out, and the atmosphere of his room being chilled, his head smoked, and his body exhaled a mist visible as that from the bodies of horses in the winter season. Sometimes a single phrase would occupy him for an entire sitting; it was appraised and reappraised, twisted, kneaded, hammered, lengthened, abbreviated; written in a hundred different fashions, and, strangest thing of all! the necessary, absolute form presented itself only after the exhaustion of all the approximate forms. Doubtless the metal often cooled in a fuller and thicker cast, but there are very few pages in Balzac which have remained identical with the first draught.

His manner of procedure was this: when he had for a long time borne and lived a subject, in a hand-writing, rapid, involved, illegible, almost hieroglyphical, he traced a sort of *scenario* of a few pages, which he sent to the printers, who returned them in isolated columns in the midst of large sheets. He read carefully these columns, which already gave to the embryo of his work that impersonal character which manuscript does not have, and he applied to this rough sketch that critical faculty he possessed in so eminent a degree, treating his own work as if it were the work of another. He approved or he disapproved, he confirmed or he corrected, but he always added lines issuing from the beginning, the

middle or the end of phrases, and directed toward the
margins, to the right, the left, the top, the bottom, lines
leading to new developments, to insertions, to incidental
phrases, to epithets, to adverbs. At the end of some
hours of work one would have called his proof-sheet a
bouquet of fireworks designed by a child. From the primitive text, shot forth rockets of style which blazed on all
sides. Then there were simple crosses, and crosses re-
crossed like those of heraldry, stars, suns, figures, Arabic
or Roman, letters Greek or French, all imaginable signs
of reference. Strips of paper fastened on with wafers
or pins, added to the insufficient margins, and these
were striped with lines in fine characters for want of
space, and full themselves of erasures; for the correc-
tion scarce made, was at once corrected. The printed
column was almost lost in the midst of this conjuring-
book of cabalistic appearance, which the compositors
passed from hand to hand, each willing to work only an
hour upon Balzac.

The next day they sent back the proofs with the cor-·
rections made, and augmented by half.

Balzac would·again set to.work, amplifying always,
adding a feature, a detail, a description, an observation
upon manners, a characteristic word, a phrase for effect,
uniting the idea more closely with the form, always
approaching nearer his interior design, choosing, like a
painter, the definite outline from three or four contours. Often this terrible work having been accomplished with that intensity of application of which he
alone was capable, he would perceive that the thought
had been awkwardly expressed, that an episode pre-
dominated, that a figure he wished secondary for the general effect, did not accord with his plan,—and with one
dash of the pen, he would courageously demolish the

result of four or five night's work. He was heroic in these circumstances.

Six, seven, and sometimes ten proofs were sent back, with erasures and retouches, without satisfying this author's desire for perfection. We have seen at the *Jardies*, upon the shelves of a library composed of his works alone, the different proofs of the same work, from the first sketch, to the published book, each volume bound separately. The comparison of Balzac's thought at its different stages, offers a very curious study, and must contain profitable literary lessons. Near these volumes, an old book of sinister aspect, bound in black morocco without clasps or gilding, drew our glance. "Take it" said Balzac to us, "it is an unpublished work which may well have its value." The title was *Comptes Mélancoliques*, it contained lists of debts, notices of the falling due of bills-payable, memoranda of shop-keepers and all that menacing old waste-paper the stamp-office legalizes. This volume, by a sort of jeering contrast, was placed beside the *Contes Drolatiques* " of which it is not a continuation,"—added laughing, the author of " The Human Comedy."

Despite this laborious method of execution, Balzac produced a great deal, thanks to his superhuman will, supplemented by an athletic temperament and a monkish seclusion. For two or three months in succession when he had some important work in progress, he would apply himself sixteen or eighteen hours out of the twenty-four. He granted to his physical system only six hours of a heavy, feverish, convulsive sleep, induced by torpid digestion after a hastily taken meal. He would at such times disappear completely, his best friends losing all trace of him; but he would ere long descend to our lower earth brandishing a *chef-d'œuvre* above his head, laughing his hearty laugh, applauding himself with a perfect simplicity, and giving himself those praises he asked from no one. No author was less anxious than he in regard to favorable criticisms of his books; he let his reputation make itself unaided, and he never courted the journalists. He had indeed no time. He simply delivered up his copy, took his money, and fled to distribute it among his creditors who often waited in the newspaper court.

Sometimes he came to us in the morning. Out of breath, exhausted, giddy from encountering the fresh air,—like Vulcan escaping from his forge, he would throw himself upon a divan. His long vigils had almost famished him, and he would mix sardines with butter making a sort of pomade which reminded him of the *rillettes* of Tours, and which he spread upon his bread. This was his favorite food. He had no sooner eaten, than he fell asleep, begging us to waken him at the end of an hour. Without regarding this injunction, we would respect the sleep so well earned, and silence all the noises about our lodgings. When Balzac awoke of his own accord, and saw that the evening twilight was diffusing its gray tints over the sky, he would bound from his sofa, and load us with abuse, calling us traitor, thief, assassin, and declaring that we had made him lose ten thousand francs; for, if awakened, he should have formed the idea of a romance which would have brought him that sum (without the rë-impressions). We had caused the gravest catastrophes, and unimaginable disorders. We had made him miss a rendezvous with bankers, editors, duchesses; he should not be in time to meet the expiration of his notes; this fatal sleep would cost millions. But we were already habituated to these prodigious martingales of Balzac's and easily consoled ourself in seeing the beautiful color of his boyhood reappear on his rejuvenated cheeks.

Balzac then dwelt at Chaillot, Rue de Batailles, a house which afforded an admirable prospect of the windings of the Seine, the Champ de Mars, the Military Schools, the dome of the Invalides, a great portion of Paris and the hills of Meudon beyond. He had arranged here an interior luxurious enough, for he knew that in Paris they believe little in impoverished talent, and that to *seem* here often leads one *to be*. With this period are connected his inclinations toward elegance and dandyism; that famous blue coat with buttons of massive gold, that walking-stick with a turquoise head, those apparitions at the comic theatres and the opera, and those more frequent visits into society, where his sparkling animation made him much sought; these were useful visits to him besides, for he met there more than one model.

It was not easy to penetrate into this abode of Balzac's, which was better guarded than the garden of the Hesperides. Two or three passwords were required. Balzac, for fear they might get bruited abroad, changed them often. We remember these: You said to the porter. "The season of prunes has arrived," and he let you pass the threshold. To the servant who ran to the stair-case at the sound of the bell, you must whisper: "I bring laces from Belgium," and if you could assure the valet de chambre that Madame Bertrand was in good health, you were at last introduced.

These puerilities very much amused Balzac. They were necessary to send away troublesome people and other visitors still more disagreeable.

In the "Fille aux Yeux d'Or," we find a description of this salon in the Rue des Batailles. It is of the most scrupulous fidelity, and our reader will perhaps not be sorry to see the lion's lair painted by himself. There is not a detail added or omitted.

" Half of the boudoir described a delicately graceful, circular outline, opposite which lay the other half perfectly square, and having in its centre an elegant fire place of white marble and gold. You entered through a side door concealed by a rich tapestry *portière*, which faced a window. The back of the room was adorned with a real Turkish divan, that is to say with a mattrass placed upon the floor, but a mattrass as large as a bed, a divan fifty feet in circumference, covered with white cashmere, relieved by knots of black and flame-colored silk arranged in lozenges; the back of this immense bed rose several inches above the numerous cushions which enriched it still more by the taste of their adornings. This boudoir was hung with a red stuff over which was disposed an India muslin, fluted like a Corinthian column, by pipes alternately hollow and round, confined at the top and bottom by a band of flame-colored stuff upon which were drawn black arabesques. Under the muslin, the flame-color became rose, an amorous color repeated in the window-curtains which were of India muslin looped with rose-colored tafettas. Six silver-gilt arms, each bearing two wax candles, were attached, at equal distances apart, to the hangings, and lighted the divan. The ceiling, from the centre of which depended a lustre of pale vermillion, glittered with whiteness, and the cornice was gilded. The carpet resembled an Oriental shawl; it presented the designs and recalled the poetry of Persia where the hands of slaves had wrought it. The furniture was covered with white cashmere, set off by black and flame-color ornaments. The clock, the candelabras, were all of white marble and gold. The only table in the room had a cashmere cover; there were also elegant flower-stands, containing roses of all kinds, and white or red flowers."

We may add that upon the table was placed a magnificent writing-desk, in gold and malachite, the gift, doubtless, of some foreign admirer.

It was with a childlike satisfaction that Balzac showed us this boudoir, arranged in the midst of a square salon, and necessarily leaving empty spaces at the angles of the circular half. When we had sufficiently admired these coquettish splendors, whose luxury would seem less to-day, Balzac opened a secret door and made us penetrate into an obscure passage which led around the semi-circle; at one of the angles was placed a narrow iron bedstead, a kind of camp bed; in the other, there was a table with all sorts of writing materials. It was here that Balzac took refuge to labor shielded from all intrusion and investigation.

He gave us in the same boudoir a splendid dinner, in honor of which he lighted with his own hand all the wax candles in the silver-gilded arms as well as those of the lustre and the candelabras. The guests were the Marquis de B. and the painter L. B. Although very sober and abstemious from habit, Balzac from time to time did not fear to drain a beaker to the lees. He ate with that jovial gourmandism which appetite inspires, and he drank in a Pantagruelic fashion. Four bottles of the white wine of Vouvray, one of the most capital wines in the world, did not in the least affect his strong brain, and only gave a more lively sparkle to his gayety. What good stories he told us at dessert! Rabelais, Bervalde de Verville, Eutrappel, Le Pogge, Straparole, the Queen of Navarre and all the doctors of the *gaie science*, would have recognized in him a disciple and a master!

IV.

ONE of the dreams of Balzac was heroic and devoted friendship, two souls, two valors, two intelligences molten into the same will. Pierre and Jaffier of Otway's " Venice Preserved " had impressed him greatly, and he spoke of them upon several occasions. His " History of the Thirteen " is only this idea enlarged and complicated : one powerful unit composed of multiple beings, all acting blindly for an accepted and suitable end. We know what striking, mysterious and terrible effects he has drawn from this starting-point in " Ferragus," " The Duchess of Longeaîs " and " The Girl with the Golden Eyes." But the real life and the intellectual life did not clearly separate themselves in Balzac as in certain authors, and his creations followed him outside his study. He wished to form an association upon the principle of that which united Ferragus, Montriveau, Rouquerolles and their companions. A certain number of persons were to lend each other aid and succor on all occasions, and to labor according to their strength, for the success or the fortune of the individual requiring aid—upon condition of a future return which was to be well understood.

Very much infatuated with his project, Balzac recruited some associates, whom he placed in communication with each other, taking precautions as if he had to do with a political society or a gang of carbonari. This mystery, very useless indeed, amused him vastly, and he was very much in earnest in his proceedings. When the number was complete, he assembled the adepts and made known the aims of the society. We need not say that each expressed his opinions warmly, and that the statutes were voted with enthusiasm. No person in a higher degree than Balzac possessed the gift of exciting, stirring up and intoxicating the coldest brains, the most sedate reasons. He had an eloquence, overflowing, impetuous, enticing, which bore you onward at his will; no objection was possible with him; he would at once drown you in such a deluge of words that you were compelled to be silent. And besides, he had a response for all; when he cast upon you those glances so flashing, so illuminated, so charged with electricity, he infused you with his own desire.

The association, which included among its members several aspiring literary men, was called the *Cheval Rouge*. Why the *Cheval Rouge*, rather than the "Golden Lion" or the "Maltese Cross?" The first reunion of the members took place at a restaurant upon the quay Entrepôt at the end of the Tournelle bridge, whose sign was a quadruped, *rubrica pictus*, and this gave Balzac the idea of that designation, which was odd, unintelligible and cabalistic enough.

When some project is to be concerted, certain proceedings are in order. Balzac, elected by acclamation grand master of the order, sent by a trusty person to each *horse* (this was the slang name the members took among themselves) a billet upon which was the picture of a little red horse, with these words: "Stable, such a day, such a place." The place changed every time for fear of awakening curiosity or suspicion. In society, although for the most part we were very intimately acquainted, we were to avoid speaking or approaching each other save in the most distant manner, so as to prevent any idea of connivance. Often, in the middle of a salon, Balzac would pretend to have met me for the first time, and through twinklings of the eye, and gestures such as actors make in their asides, he would call my attention to his artifice, and seem to say to me: "See how well I am playing my part!"

What was the aim of the Cheval Rouge? Did it wish to change the government, to impose a new religion, to found a philosophical school, to rule men, to seduce women? Far less than that. It sought to take possession of the journals, to invade the theatres, to seat its members in the chairs of the Academy, to provide them with decorations, and to end modestly, by making them all peers of any one in France, minister or millionaire.

All this was easy according to Balzac; we had only to understand each other, and by such mediocre ambitions we should well prove the moderation of our characters. This devil of a man had such a powerful vision that he described to each of us in the minutest details, the splendid and glorious life this association would procure for us. In listening to him, we believed ourselves already established in an elegant hotel, leaning against the white marble mantel, the red cordon around our neck, a diamond order upon our breast, receiving with an affable air, political dignitaries, artists and men of letters, astonished at our mysterious and rapid fortune. For Balzac, the future did not exist, all was in the present; the future evoked by him, cleared itself of mists and assumed the lucidity of palpable things; the idea was so vivid that it became real in some sort. Did he speak of a dinner, he ate it in recounting it; of a carriage, he felt underneath him the soft cushions, and the swift, steady traction; a perfect satisfaction, a profound delight was at such times depicted upon his face, although he often fasted and walked over the sharp pavement with shoes run down at the heels.

The whole band would signalize, extol and glorify by articles, notices and conversations, the one of its members who had just put forth a book or enacted a drama. Whoever showed himself hostile to one of the horses, drew upon himself the kicks of the whole stable; the *Cheval Rouge* would not pardon; the culprit became liable to knocks, to punches, to pin-pricks, to sly thrusts, to all those means of vengeance which can drive men as well as small journals to despair.

We smile in betraying after so many years, the innocent secrets of this literary free-masonry, which had no other result than some catch-words for a book whose success had no need of them. But at the moment, we took the thing seriously; we imagined ourselves to be the *thirteen* themselves in person, and we were surprised at not passing within those walls; but the world is such a wretched machine! What an important and mysterious air we had, in jostling other men, poor *bourgeois*, who doubted nothing of our power.

After four or five reunions, the *Cheval Rouge* ceased to exist. Most of the horses had not money to pay for their oats in this symbolic manger, and the association which was going to make itself master of everything, was dissolved because its members often failed to have the fifteen francs, the price of the reckoning. Each one now replunged alone into the melée of life, fighting his way with his own arms; and this it is which explains why Balzac was not a member of the Academy, and died a simple Chevalier of the Legion of Honor.

Yet, after all, the idea was good, for Balzac, as he said of Nucingen, could not have a bad idea. Others who have succeeded, have set to the work without surrounding themselves with the same romantic phantasmagoria.

Coming down from one chimera, Balzac very quickly mounted a new one, and he set out for another voyage in the blue, with that childlike simplicity which in him, was allied to the profoundest sagacity and the shrewdest intellect.

How many whimsical projects he has unrolled to us, how many strange paradoxes we have heard him uphold, always with the same good faith! Now, he would argue that one could live upon nine sous a day; now, he would exact a hundred thousand francs for comfort even in the strictest sense. Once, summoned by us to prove his reckoning by figures, he replied to our objection that thirty thousand francs still remained unappropriated! " Ah, well! that is for the butter and radishes. Where is there a well-conducted household that does not consume thirty thousand francs worth of radishes and butter a year?" We wish we had power to portray the glance of sovereign disdain he cast upon us as he gave this triumphal reason ; that glance said ; " Decidedly this Theo is but a poor ignoramus, a ragamuffin, a paltry soul ; he understands nothing of a grand existence ; he has all his life eaten only the stale butter of Brittany!"

The *Jardies* was occupying a great deal of public attention, when Balzac bought the place with the honorable intention of making an investment for his mother. Passing over the railway leading past *Ville d'Avary* every one gazed curiously at this little house, half cottage, half châlet, which rose in the midst of a sloping and apparently loamy plot of ground.

This piece of land, in Balzac's opinion, was the best in the world : he pretended that formerly a certain celebrated vineyard had flourished here, and that the grapes, thanks to the unparalleled exposure, had dried in the sun like Tokay grapes upon the hills of Bohemia. The sun, it is true, had entire liberty to ripen the vintage in this place, where there existed only one tree. Balzac tried to enclose his piece of property within walls, which became famous for their obstinacy in crumbling away, or rolling in whole pieces down the too abrupt declivity. He dreamed of the most fabulous and exotic improvements for this place so favored of heaven

Here, naturally comes in that anecdote of the ananas, which has been so often repeated that we would not tell it again except to add one more very characteristic trait to our sketch of Balzac. The project was this ; a hundred thousand feet of ananas were planted within the precincts of the Jardies, metamorphosed into hot-house beds which from the torridity of the situation required only moderate heating. The ananas were to be sold for five francs in place of the louis they ordinarily cost, or for a total of five hundred thousand francs. From this sum one hundred thousand francs must be deducted for the cost of culture, window sashes and coal; four hundred thousand francs clear profit would remain, making a splendid income for the fortunate proprietor. "Without a single proof sheet," added he.—This was nothing : Balzac had a thousand projects of the same kind; but the finest thing of all is that we sought together, upon the boulevard Montmartre, a shop for the sale of the ananas yet in germ. The shop was to be painted black, set off with fillets of gold, and was to bear upon its sign in enormous letters, this legend : " ANANAS DES JARDIES."

For Balzac, the hundred thousand ananas reared already their crest of veined leaves above their huge golden cones arranged in quadrilles under immense crystal arches; he saw them, he expanded in the high temperature of his hothouses, he breathed the tropical perfume into his eagerly distended nostrils; and when, re-entering his house, he saw, resting his elbows on the window-sill, the snows silently descending upon his dismantled hill-side, he could scarce dispossess himself of his illusion.

Meantime, he followed our advice, which was to defer hiring the shop until the next year so as to avoid useless expense.

We write our reminiscences as they recur to us, without trying to arrange in order things which can have no natural sequence.—Besides, as Boileau says, transitions are the great difficulty of poetry—and of newspaper essays too, let us add;—but modern journalists have not so much conscience, nor above all so much leisure as the legislator of Parnassus.

Madame de Girardin professed for Balzac a lively admiration to which he was sensible, and for which he showed his gratitude by frequent visits; a costly return for him who was, with good right, so avaricious of his time and of his working hours. Never did woman possess to so high a degree as Delphine,—we were allowed to call her by this familiar name among ourselves—the gift of drawing out the wit of her guests. With her, we always found ourselves in poetical raptures, and each left her salon amazed at himself. There was no flint so rough that she could not cause it to emit one spark; and with Balzac, as you may well believe, there was no need of trying long to strike fire; he flashed and kindled at once.

Balzac was not precisely what we call a talker, quick in repartee, throwing a subtle and decisive word into a discussion. Changing the thread of the discourse at will, touching everything lightly, he had an irresistible enthusiasm, eloquence and wit; and as every one became silent to listen to him, to the general satisfaction, the conversation on his part, would soon fall into soliloquy. The starting-point was soon forgotten, and he would pass from an anecdote to a philosophical reflection, from an observation upon manners to a local description; and as he spoke, his face glowed, his eyes assumed a peculiar lustre, his voice took different inflections, and sometimes he would burst into peals of laughter, diverted by comic apparitions, which he *saw* before describing them. Thus, by a sort of flourish of trumpets, he would announce the entree of his caricatures and pleasantries, and his hilarity was soon shared by all around him.

Although this was the epoch of dishevelled dreamers, of weeping willows, of sorrowing Werthers, of Byronic disillusions, Balzac had that robust and powerful merriment we ascribe to Rabelais, and which Molière shows only in his comedies. That loud laugh expanding upon his sensuous lips, was the laugh of a god, a good fellow, who enjoys the theatrical exhibitions of human puppets, and who is troubled at nothing because he comprehends all, and grasps the two sides of a question at the same time. Neither the anxieties of an often precarious existence; nor the want of money, nor the fatigues of excessive labor, nor the solitude of study, nor a renunciation of the pleasures of life, nor sickness itself, could repress that Herculean joviality, in our opinion, one of the most striking characteristics of Balzac. By laughing, he slew hydras; by merriment, he tore lions in pieces, and, as if it had been a hare, he carried the wild boar of Erymanthus upon his gigantic muscular shoulders.

At the least provocation, the merriment broke forth from his sturdy breast. It took some fastidious individuals by surprise, but they were forced to join in it, despite every effort at gravity. But do not believe that Balzac sought merely to divert his listeners! He obeyed a sort of inward intoxication, and with a facetious talent beyond compare, dressed up the odd phantasmagoria dancing in the shadowy chamber of his brain. The impression produced by certain of his conversations was like that we experience in turning over the whimsical illustrations of the "Contes Drôlatiques" by Master Alcofribas Nasier. These are monstrous personages composed of the most hybrid elements, but an intense life animates these chimerical beings, and in their grimacing faces we recognize the vices, the follies and the passions of man. A few, although absurd beyond the utmost limits of the possible, strike you as portraits. You could give them a name.

When you listened to Balzac, a whole carnival of extravagant puppets danced before your eyes, taking you by the lappel of your coat, breathing secrets into your ear in a disguised and nasal tone, pirouetting, whirling around you in the midst of a scintillation of lights and spangles. Nothing was more calculated to make you giddy, and, at the end of half an hour, like the student after the discourse of Mephistopheles, you felt a millstone turning in your brain.

One of his favorite jests was to counterfeit the German jargon of Nucingen or Schmuke, or better yet, to speak after the fashion of the bourgeois boarding-house of Madame Vauquer. When composing "A Beginning in Life," he sought, far and near, proverbs for his "Mistigris' whom he made so witty that he afterwards gave him a fine position in the "Comédie Humaine" under the name of the great landscape-painter, *Léon de Lora*. Mme. de Girardin was also in quest of sayings for one of her characters in the "Courier of Paris." They sometimes sought the aid of the writer of this sketch, and, if a stranger had entered Mme. de Girardin's parlor some of these evenings, he would have seen the beautiful Delphine, with a profoundly dreamy air, twining the spirals of her golden hair around her white fingers, while Balzac would be seated upon one of the arms of the great cushioned easy-chair, where M. de. Girardin slept as usual, his arms crossed over his ample breast, the muscles of his face contracted, as if by some extroardinary disturbance of mind. For ourself, we crouched amid the cushions of the divan, like a hallucinated *thieriaki*. This stranger doubtless would have supposed Balzac thinking of a new Firmiani, Madame de Girardin of a new rôle for Mademoiselle Rachel, and ourself of some sonnet. But it was nothing of the kind.

What beautiful evenings were these that can return no more! We were then far from foreseeing that this grand and superb woman, sculptured as it were from the perfect antique marble, that this man, thickset, robust, vivacious, vigorous, half Hercules, half satyr, made to live more than a hundred years, would so soon go from us, to sleep, the one at Montmartre, the other at Père La Chaise; and that of the three, we should alone remain, to fix these remembrances, already distant and nearly lost.

Like his father, who died accidentally at more than eighty years of age, and who had flattered himself that he should live much longer, Balzac believed in his longevity. He often formed projects for the future. He

was going to finish the " Human Comedy," to write the
" Theory of Application," to compose the " Monography
of Virtue" and fifty dramas ; to attain to a great fortune,
to marry, and have two children, but no more ; " Two
children look well," said he, " in the front of a calèche."
All this was not to require so very long a time, but we
begged him to take note that these designs accomplished
he would be almost eighty years old.   " Eighty ! " cried
he, "bah ! that is the flower of man's age."

Balzac had in him the materials for a great actor.
He possessed a full, sonorous metallic voice with a rich
and powerful ring, which he knew how to moderate and
make soft at will ; and he read in an admirable manner,
a talent which most actors lack.   Whatever he related,
he acted with intonations, grimaces and gestures, which
no comedian could surpass.

We find in the *Marguerite* of Madame de Girardin,
this souvenir of Balzac.   It is a personage of the book
who speaks :

" He related that Balzac had dined with him yesterday, and that he had been more brilliant, more sparkling than ever.   He very much amused us with the recital of his travels in Austria.   What fire !   What poetical raptures !   What powers of imitation !   It was
marvellous.   His manner of paying the postillions is an
invention that a romancer of genius alone could achieve.
' I was very much embarrassed at each relay,' said he,
' as to how I should make my payments. I did not know
a word of German.   I did not know the money of
the country.   It was very difficult.   This was the
plan I formed.   I had a sack filled with small pieces
of money, with kreutzers.   Arrived at a relay, I
took my sack ; the postillion came to the carriage door.
I gazed attentively into his two eyes, and I put into his

hand one kreutzer—two kreutzers,—then three, then four, and so on until I saw him smile. As soon as he smiled, I understood that I had given him a kreutzer too many.—I quickly took back my piece, and my man was paid.'"

At the *Jardies* he read to us—" Mercadet," the primitive " Mercadet," but ample, complicated, elaborated like a piece arranged with skill and tact for the stage. Balzac, who read like Tieck, without indicating either acts or scenes or names, affected a peculiar and perfectly recognizable voice for each personage ; the organs with which he endowed the different species of creditors, were of a comic distinctness and clearness. They were by turns, harsh, luscious, hasty, drawling, menacing, plaintive. This yelped, that mewed, this grumbled, that growled, this barked in all tones possible and impossible. Debt sang at first a solo which ere long an immense chorus accompanied. It came from the creditors, from everywhere, from behind the stove, from under the bed, from out the drawers of the commode ; the chimney-pipe vomited it forth ; it filtered through the key-hole. Some scaled the window like lovers, others darted from the depths of a trunk like those infernal toys which take you by surprise ; others passed through the walls as through an English trap-door. It was a tumultuous crowd, a racket, an invasion, a real incoming tide. Mercadet might shake them off, still others returned to the assault, and even in the horizon, you divined a dusky swarm of creditors on the march, hasting on like legions of white ants to devour their prey. We know not if the piece was better thus, but never did representation produce such an effect upon us.

Balzac, during this reading of Mercadet, sat half reclining upon a divan in the *salon* of the Jardies, for he had sprained his ancle, in gliding, like his walls, over the surface of his estate, Some bit of hair penetrating the stuff pricked Balzac's leg and discommoded him. "The chintz is too thin: the *hay* comes through it; we must put on a thicker cover," he said, plucking out the obstrusive point.

François, the Caleb of this Ravenswood, would hear no raillery upon the splendors of the manor.—He looked reproachfully at his master and said: "the *horse hair*."— "Has the upholsterer then deceived me?" replied Balzac. "They are all alike. I ordered him to put in *hay*. Confound the thief!"

The magnificence of the *Jardies* had slight existence save in dreams. All the friends of Balzac remember having written upon the bare walls or gray paper hangings," "Palissandrian Wainscoting—Gobelins Tapestry—Venetian Glass—Pictures by Raphael."—Gerard de Nerval had already decorated an *appartement* in such a manner, and this did not astonish us. As for Balzac, he believed literally in the gold, the marble and the tapestry; but he did not complete the *Jardies*, and if he gives occasion for laughter at his chimeras, he at least knew how to build an eternal domain, a monument more durable than brass, an immense city peopled with his creations, and gilded with the rays of his glory.

V.

By an odd freak of nature, common alike to him and several of the most poetic writers of the century, such as Chateaubriand, Madame de Staël, George Sand, Mérimée, Janin,—Balzac possessed neither the gift nor the love for verse, whatever effort he made to attain it. Upon this point, his judgment, so subtle, so profound, so sagacious, was at fault; he admired a little at random, and in some sort according to public notoriety. We do not believe, although he professed a great respect for Victor Hugo, that he was ever very sensible to the lyric qualities of the poet, whose prose at the same time sculptured and colored, amazed him. This author, so laborious, who re-constructed a phrase as many times as a versifier can put back an alexandrine upon his anvil, deemed metrical labor puerile, finical, and useless. Verse, with its fixed, pure form, with its elliptical language so little suited to multiplicity of detail, seemed to him an obstacle designedly invented, a superfluous difficulty or a mnemonic usage of primitive times. His doctrine was nearly the same as that of Stendhal; "The idea that a work has been made to go hopping and skipping along, can that add to the pleasure it produces?"

The romantic school contains within its bosom some

adepts, partisans of absolute truth, who reject verse as petty or unnatural. If Talma said: "No fine verses!" Bayle said: "No verses at all!" This was really the sentiment of Balzac, although to appear liberal, comprehensive, universal, he sometimes in society pretended to admire poetry, as the vulgar feign a great enthusiasm for music, which profoundly wearies them. All the writers, young then, who attached themselves to the literary movement represented by Victor Hugo, used like the master, both the lyre and the pen. Alfred de Vigny, Sainte-Beuve, Alfred de Musset, spoke equally well the language of the gods and the language of men. It is always easy for poets to descend to prose. The bird can walk if need be, but the lion does not fly. The born prose-writers never rise to poetry, however poetical they may be elsewhere. It is a peculiar gift, that of rhythmed speech, and one may possess it without being a great genius, while it is often refused to superior minds. Among the most haughty of those who apparently disdain it, more than one even unknown to himself, cherishes a secret rancor for not possessing it.

Among the two thousand personages of the "Comédie Humaine," there are two poets. Balzac represents them both under traits little favorable. The one, Canalis, is a cold and sterile soul, full of littleness, an adroit arranger of words, a jeweler, who sets paste in gilded silver, and makes necklaces of glass pearls. His volumes have multifold blanks, wide margins, broad intervals; they contain only a melodious nothingness, a monotonous music, fitted to lull young boarding-school misses to sleep or to make them dream. Balzac, who usually warmly espouses the interests of his personages, seems to take a secret pleasure in ridiculing this one, and placing him in all sorts of embarrassing situations. He riddles his vanity with a thousand ironies and a thousand sarcasms, and ends by taking from him Modeste Mignon with her great fortune, to give her to Ernest de la Brière. This *dénouement*, so opposed to the opening of the story, betrays a half-veiled malice and a subtle mockery. One would say that Balzac is personally happy at any ill turn he plays upon Canalis. He avenges himself in his fashion, for the angels, the sylphs, the lakes, the swans, the willows, the barques, the stars and the prodigal lyres of his poet.

If in " Canalis," we have the false poet, economizing his meagre vein and paying toll to it that it may run, foam and rave a few minutes so as to simulate a cascade, the skilful man, making his laboriously-earned literary successes subserve his political ambitions, the positive being, loving money, crosses, pensions and honors notwithstanding his elegiac attitudes and his poses of an angel regretting heaven—Lucien de Rubempre, shows us the idle, frivolous, thoughtless poet, fanciful and nervous as a woman, incapable of sustained effort, without moral force, living on the hooks of commédiennes and courtesans; a puppet, whose wires designing persons draw at will. Notwithstanding all his vices, it is true, Lucien fascinates us. Balzac has dowered him with wit, beauty and elegance. The women adore him, but he ends by hanging himself at the Conciergerie.

Here we have a little bit of information to impart, which may amuse the curious. The few sonnets which Lucien de Rubempre displays as samples of his volume of verses, to the publisher Douriat, are not by Balzac. who made no verses, but demanded those he required from his friends. The sonnet upon the Daisy is by

Madame de Girardin, that upon the Camélia by Lassailly, that upon the Tulip, by your humble servant.

Modeste Mignon also contains a piece of verse, but we do not know its author.

As we have said, Balzac was an admirable reader. Like all prose-writers he read for the sense, and tried to disguise the rhyme, which the poets when they declaim their verses, accentuate in a manner insupportable to people in general, and ravishing to them alone.

The great literary man of the " Comédie Humaine " is Daniel d'Arthez, a serious writer, a hard worker, and for a long time before arriving at fame, immersed in vast philosophical, historical and linguistic studies. Balzac was afraid of facility, and did not believe that a hasty work could be good. For this reason journalism singularly repelled him, and he regarded the time and talent consecrated to it as lost. He did not love journalists much better, and he, a great critic himself, despised criticism.

Balzac never worked from a journalistic point of view. He took his romances to the reviews and the daily papers just as they came, without preparing leaving-off-places and interesting traps at the end of each instalment, to make the continuation desired. The story was cut up into slices of nearly equal length, and sometimes the description of an arm-chair begun one day, ended the next. He did not wish to divide his work into the little pictures of the drama or the vaudeville ; he thought only of the book. This method of procedure was often prejudicial to that immediate success which journalists demand from the authors they employ. Eugène Sue and Alexandre Dumas often won the advantage over Balzac in those daily morning contests, which then excited the public. His stories did

not obtain the immense vogue of the Mⱼstcries of Paris,
The Wandering Jew, and the Monte-Christo. That
chef-d'œuvre, "The Peasants," even caused a great loss
of subscribers to *La Presse*, in which its first part appeared. The editors were forced to stop its publication;
every day, letters came demanding its close. People
found Balzac tedious!

The world has not yet fully comprehended the grand
idea of the author of the "Comédie Humaine"—to take
modern society, and to make upon Paris and our epoch
that book which unhappily, no ancient civilization has left
us. The complete edition of the "Comédie Humaine,"
by collecting all his scattered works, places in relief,
the philosophical intention of the writer. From this
date, Balzac rose considerably in public estimation, and
they at last ceased to find him "The most fruitful of
our romancers," a stereotyped phrase which irritated
him as much as that other, "The author of Eugénie
Grandet."

There were numerous criticisms made upon Balzac;
he was spoken of in many fashions, but no one insisted
upon what in our opinion, is a very characteristic point;
—that point is the absolute modernness of his genius.
Balzac owes nothing to antiquity; for him, there are
neither Greeks nor Romans, and he has no need to cry
for deliverance from them. We discover in his talent
no trace of Homer, or Virgil or Horace, not even of
the *Viris Illustribus*;—no author has ever been less
classic.

In art, the supreme difficulty is to paint what you
have before your eyes; one can easily pass over his own
time without perceiving it, and it is in this respect that
so many eminent intellects have been at fault.

To behold one's contemporaries as they are, to be of

one's time,—nothing appears more simple, and nothing
is more difficult! To wear no spectacles, neither blue
nor green, to think with one's own brain, to speak in
one's real tongue, not to stitch together in centos, the
phrases of one's predecessors! Balzac possessed this
rare merit. The centuries have their perspective and
their recoil; at that distance, great masses disengage
themselves; outlines cease, trifling details disappear;
by the aid of classic souvenirs, of harmonious names of
antiquity, a very indifferent rhetorician may compose a
tragedy, a poem, a historic study. But to find one's
self in the crowd, jostled along by it, to grasp it in its
varied aspects, to understand its currents, to disentangle
its individualities, to sketch the physiognomies of so
many diverse beings, to show the motive-power of their
actions—this demands an entirely special genius, and this
genius, the author of the " Comédie Humaine," possessed
to a degree no one has equalled, or probably ever
will equal.

This profound comprehension of modern things, we
must say, rendered Balzac little sensible to plastic beauty.
He read with a negligent eye, the white marble strophes
where Greek art sang the perfection of the human form.
In the Museum of Antiquities, he regarded the Venus
de Milo without great ecstasy; but the Parisian woman
pausing before the immortal statue, draped in her long
cashmere shawl falling without a wrinkle from neck to
heel, with her elegant hat and its veil of Chantilly lace,
her perfectly fitting Jouvin gloves, the dainty foot with
its laced boot just visible beneath the hem of the flowing
robe, made his eyes sparkle with pleasure. He would
analyze these coquettish allurements while slowly dis-
cussing the classic graces, and would find, like the living
woman near him, that the goddess had a heavy form,

and could not make a good appearance by the side of Mesdames de Beauséant, de Listomière or d'Espard. The ideal beauty with its serene and pure outlines was too simple, too cold, too harmonious, for this complicated, exuberant, and diverse genius. He has said somewhere: " One must be Raphael in order to create many Virgins." *Character* pleased him more than *style*, and he preferred physiognomy to beauty. In his portraits of women, he never fails to add a mark, a fold, a wrinkle, a red patch, a pitiful weary angle, a vein too apparent, some detail indicating the bruises of life, which a poet, tracing the same image, would most certainly suppress, but wrongly, without doubt.

We have no intention of criticising Balzac for this *defect* which is his principal good *quality*. He accepts nothing from the mythologies and traditions of the past; he does not know, happily for us, that ideal created by the verses of the poets, the marbles of Greece and Rome, the pictures of the Renaissance, which intrudes itself between the eyes of the artist and the reality. He loves the woman of our day as she is, and not a pale statue; he loves her in her virtues, in her faults, in her fantasies, in her shawls, in her robes, in her hats; and he follows her through life far beyond that point in the route where love leaves her. He prolongs her youth by many seasons, he creates her springs from the summers of Saint-Martin, and he gilds their setting with the most gorgeous rays.

We are so classic in France, that after two thousand years we have failed to perceive that in our climate roses do not flourish in April, as in the descriptions of the ancient poets, but in June; and that our women begin to be beautiful at an age when those of Greece, the most precocious of all, ceased to be so. How many charming types Balzac has imagined or reproduced,—

grand ladies a plenty, not to count the *bourgeoises*, the grisettes and the *Dames aux Camélias* of his demi-monde.

And how he loved and knew this modern Paris, whose beauties in that time the amateurs of local and pictur-esque color so little appreciated! He wandered over it in every sense, by night and by day; there was not a dilapidated alley, an infected passage, a narrow street, muddy and dark, which under his pen did not become an etching worthy of Rembrandt, full of thronging and mysterious shadows, where glows one palpitating ray of light. Riches and misery, pleasure and suffering, shame and glory, grace and deformity,—he knew all of his cherished city. It was to him a monster, enormous, hy-brid, formidable, a polypus with a hundred thousand arms, which he heard, saw, and regarded as living, and which formed, as it were, in his eyes, an immense individuality. Apropos of this, see the wonderful pages placed at the beginning of " The Girl with the Golden Eyes," in which Balzac, encroaching upon the art of the musician, has sought, as in a symphony to a grand orchestra, to make sound in unison all the voices, all the sobbings, all the cries, all the rumors, all the gnashings of the teeth, of Paris in travail.

From this modernness upon which we dwell design-edly, although Balzac did not suspect it, proceeded the difficulty which he experienced in the accomplishment of his work; the French language, refined by the classics of the sixteenth century, is not suited to the rendering of general ideas or to the depicting of conventional figures amid vague surroundings. To express that multiplicity of details, of characters, of types, of archi-tectures, of furnitures, Balzac was obliged to coin an especial language, composed of all the technologies, of all the slang of the terms of science, of the jargon of the shop, the coulisses, of even the amphitheatre. Whatever word expressed anything was welcome, and the phrase, in order to receive it, opened an incision, a parenthesis, and complaisantly elongated itself. It is this which has made superficial critics say that Balzac did not know how to write. He had, although he did not believe it, a style, and a very fine style—the necessary, inevitable and mathematical style of his idea!

VI.

It is impossible to write a complete biography of Balzac; intercourse with him was necessarily interrupted by chasms, absences, disappearances. Work absolutely commanded the life of this man, and if, as he said himself with an accent of touching sensibility in a letter to his sister, he had sacrificed without pain, to that jealous god, the joys and recreations of life, it had cost him dear to renounce the delights of its friendship. He was the slave of his work, and the voluntary slave. With a very good and a very tender heart, he had the egotism of great workers. And who would have dreamed of chiding his apparent negligence and forgetfulness, when beholding the result of his flights and his seclusions? When, the work finished, he appeared, you would have said that he had quitted you yesterday; he would resume the conversation, as if, sometimes, six months or more had not fled since its interruption.

He made journeys in France to study the localities of his provincial scenes, and he withdrew from his friends into Tourraine or into the Charente, finding there a repose that his creditors did not always allow him in Paris. After some great work, he would occasionally allow himself a broader excursion in Germany, in upper Italy or Switzerland; but these tours, made rapidly, with anxieties in regard to the falling due of bills payable, of agreements to fulfil, and with a viaticum narrow enough, perhaps fatigued more than rested him.

His clairvoyant eye drank in the skies, the horizons, the mountains, the landscapes, the monuments, the houses, the interiors, to confide them to that universal and minute memory which never failed him. Superior in this to the descriptive poets, Balzac saw men and nature at the very same time; he studied the physiognomies, the manners, the characters, the passions, with the same glance as the sites, the costumes and the furniture. A detail satisfied him as the least fragment of bone suffices Cuvier to imagine and reconstitute a visible and tangible personality.

He had often observed in himself the numerous types that live in his books. It is for this reason they are so complete. But no one can absolutely follow the life of an author; he has motives which remain obscure, unknown, details of actions whose trace you lose. In even the most faithful portrait, a part must be pure creation. Balzac has created far more than he has seen. His rare faculties as physiologist and anatomist have only ministered to the poet within him.

The truth of art is not the truth of nature; every object reproduced by art, must needs be in part conventional; though this part be made small as possible, it still exists, in painting as in perspective, in literature as in language. Balzac doubtless is true, but it is with the augmentations and the sacrifices of art. He prepares sombre depths and bituminous paths for his luminous figures, he places light backgrounds against his dusky figures. Like Rembrandt, he sets its appropriate spangle of light on the brow or nose of his personage; sometimes without mentioning it, he places a microscope under the reader's eye. Where a writer of less genius would have created a portrait, Balzac has created a real form. Men have not so many muscles as Michael Angelo endows them with, to give an idea of force. Balzac is full of these useful exaggerations, these dusky outlines which sustain and accentuate the contour. While he copies, he imagines after the manner of the masters, imprinting his own touch upon everything. Balzac, whom the realistic school seems to wish to claim as a master, has no connection with it, no inclination for it.

Unlike certain illustrious literary men who nourish themselves upon their own genius, Balzac read a great deal, and with prodigious rapidity. He loved books, and he had collected a fine library. In a few days, he absorbed the voluminous works of Swedenborg, which were owned by Madame Balzac *mère*, who was a great deal pre-occupied with mysticism at that time; and to this reading we owe the " Séraphita-Séraphitus," one of the most astonishing productions of modern literature. Never did Balzac so nearly approach or grasp the ideal beauty as in this book, that mountain ascension to something ethereal, supernatural, luminous, which lifts us above this earth. The two only colors employed are celestial blue and snow-white, with some nacreous tints for shadows. We know of nothing more transporting than this effort. The panorama of Norway detached from its borders and seen from that height, dazzles and infatuates us.

" Louis Lambert " is also influenced by this reading of Swedenborg; but soon Balzac, who had borrowed these eagle pinions of the mystics to sail into the infinite, redescended to our earth, although his vigorous lungs could respire for any length of time, that subtile air fatal to feebler mortals. Perhaps his fine genius would all too soon have passed beyond our sight, had he continued to soar toward those unfathomed immensities of metaphysics, and we ought to consider it a fortunate thing, that he contented himself with "Louis Lambert" and the "Séraphita-Séraphitus," which in the "Human Comedy" sufficiently represent the supernatural side, and open a gate, as wide as we could desire, into the invisible world.

Let us pass now to some particular details. The great Goethe held three things in horror,—one of these things was tobacco-smoke; we refrain from telling the two others. Balzac, like the German Jupiter Olympus, could not endure tobacco in any form whatever; he anathematized the pipe, and proscribed the cigar. He would not even allow the light Spanish *papelito ;* the Asiatic *narguilhé* alone found grace in his eyes. In his philippics against the Nicotian weed, he did not imitate that doctor who, during a dissertation upon the absurdity of using tobacco, kept taking ample pinches from a large snuff-box placed near him. He never smoked. His " Theory of Stimulants " contains a formal plea against tobacco, and no doubt, if he had been sultan, like Amurath, he would have cut off the heads of wicked and obstinate smokers. He reserved all his predilections for coffee, which did him great harm, and perhaps killed him, although he was organized to live a century.

Was Balzac right or wrong? Is tobacco, as he pretended, a deadly poison, and does it intoxicate those it does not stupify? Is it the opium of the Occident, the cajoler of the will and the intelligence? This is a question we know not how to answer; but we may cite here the names of some celebrated personages of this century, some of whom smoked while others did not; Goethe and Heinrich Heine, singularly abstemious for Germans, did not smoke; Byron smoked; Victor Hugo does not smoke, neither did Alexandre Dumas *père*. On the other hand, Alfred de Musset, Eugene Sue, George Sand, Prosper, Mérimée, Paul de Saint Victor, Emile Agier, have smoked and do smoke; and yet without being exactly imbecile.

Nevertheless, this aversion is common to almost all the men born with the century or a little before it. Sailors and soldiers only smoked at that time; at the odor of the pipe or the cigar, women would faint away; they have become very well used to it since then, and more than one rosy lip presses lovingly the gilded end of a *puro*, in the boudoir transformed into a smoking-room. Dowagers and turbaned mothers alone have preserved their old antipathy, and stoically see their contumacious salons deserted by the young.

Whenever Balzac is obliged for the truth of the recital to allow one of his personages to addict himself to this horrible habit, his brief and disdainful phrase betrays the guilty secret: " As for de Marsay," he says " he was engaged in smoking his cigar." And to allow him to smoke at all in his work, is a concession Balzac must needs make to dandyism.

A woman, delicate and fastidious, had no doubt impressed Balzac with this aversion. This is a point we know not how to solve. Here we cannot gain a sou for our pains. Balzac must have known women, in order to paint them so well. In one of the letters he wrote to his sister, Madame de Surville, Balzac, then young and entirely ignorant, states the ideal of his life in two words; " To be celebrated and to be loved." The first part of this programme, marked out by all artists, was realized beyond his dreams. Did the second receive its fulfilment? The opinion of the most intimate friends of Balzac, is that he cherished only Platonic loves; but Madame de Surville smiles at this idea; it is a smile full of feminine *finesse* and modest reticence. She pretends that her brother possessed a discretion which was proof against anything, and that if he had wished to speak, he would have had a great many things to say. This may be, and no doubt Balzac's casket contained more notes in irregular, delicate writing, than the gilded box of his " Canalis."

There is, as it were, in his works an *odor di femina;* when you enter them, you hear through the secret doors behind the staircase, the rustle of silk and the creaking of little boots. In the course of our intimacy, which endured from 1836 to his death, Balzac only once alluded in the most respectful and tender terms, to an attachment of his early youth; and still, he would confide to us only the first name of the person, whose remembrance after so many years, made his eyes grow moist. If he had told us more, we certainly should not abuse his confidence,—the genius of a great writer belongs to all the world, but his heart is his own. We touch lightly in passing this tender and delicate side of Balzac's life, because we have nothing to say which does not do him honor. This reserve and this mystery, are those of a gallant man. If he was loved as he wished to be in the dreams of his youth, the world knows nothing of it.

Do not imagine from this that Balzac was austere and prudish in his speech. The author of the "Fantastic Tales " was too much nourished by Rabelais, too much of a Pantagruelist, not to know how to laugh. He knew good stories and he invented them; his funny recitals interlarded with Gallic crudities, would have made fastidious cant cry " *shocking!* " but his laughing, babbling lips were sealed like the tomb, when others jested upon a serious sentiment. Scarce did he let his dearest friends divine his love for a foreign lady of distinction, a love of which we may speak, since it was crowned by marriage. It is to this passion, cherished for a long time, to which we may impute those distant excursions, whose motive to the last remained a mystery to his friends.

Absorbed in his work, Balzac did not decide until rather late, to turn his attention to the drama, for which common opinion, wrongly we think, judged that he was not fitted. True, some chance essays early made, had not proved successful; but he who had created so many types, analyzed so many characters, set in motion so many personages, must have succeeded in dramatic composition. As we have said, Balzac could not perfect his work at once, and one cannot correct the proofs of a play. If he had lived, at the end of a dozen pieces, he would assuredly have found his form, and have attained success. Although the " Cruel Step-Mother," played at the Théâtre-Historique, was not a *chef-d'œuvre* his " *Mercadet,*" slightly clipped by an intelligent arranger, obtained a long posthumous vogue at the Gymnasium.

Nevertheless, his impelling motive in these attempts was a large reward which at a single stroke might free him from financial enbarrassment, rather than a real vocation. The play, we know, yields far more than the book; the continuity of the representations, upon which a large enough claim is levied, speedily produces considerable sums. If the labor of combination is greater, the material work is less. It requires several dramas to

fill a volume, and while you are taking a walk, or resting nonchalantly with your feet in your slippers, the
balustrades are lighted, the decorations descend from
the friezes, the actors declaim and gesticulate, and you
find that you have gained more money than in scrawling
a whole week painfully bent over your desk. Such a
melo-drama has been worth more to its author than the
" Notre Dame de Paris " of Victor Hugo, and " The
Poor Relations " of Balzac.

It is a singular fact that Balzac, who meditated,
elaborated and corrected his romances with such obstinate and scrupulous care, seemed, when a play was in
question, to be possessed of some demon of haste,
almost grudging the time bestowed upon such work, or
perhaps impatient for the remuneration.

11

VII.

At the beginning of this study, we recounted the inclinations toward dandyism manifested by Balzac; we
have told of his blue coat with buttons of solid gold, of
his monstrous cane surmounted by a head of turquoises,
of his apparitions into society and into that infernal club
of ours; but this magnificence was only temporary, and
Balzac recognized the fact that he was not fitted to play
the rôle of Alcibiades or Beau Brummel. Each of his
friends can recount, how he would run, usually of a
morning, to his publishers with copy and for proofs,
in an infinitely less splendid costume. We recall the
green hunting-vest with copper buttons, representing
foxes' heads, the black-and-gray checked pantaloons,
extending to the feet and thrust into the huge tied
shoes, the red silk handkerchief twisted in a cord
around the neck, and the hat, at the same time shaggy
and smooth, its blue lining faded by perspiration, which
covered rather than clothed the most "fruitful of our
romancers." But despite the poverty and disorder of
his garb, no one would have dreamed of taking him for
one of the unknown, vulgar throng, this great man with
the eyes of flame, the mobile nostrils, the cheeks impressed with violent colors, the whole face illumined by
genius,—this man who passed, borne onward by his

tream as by a whirlwind! At sight of him, raillery died
away from the lips of the *gamin*, and the serious man
did not yield to his first impulse to smile. All divined
that this was one of the kings of thought.

Sometimes, on the contrary, we saw him walking very
slowly, his nose in the air, his eyes in quest of something.
passing down one side of the street, then examining the
other, and not gaping into the air, but at the signs. He
was seeking for names with which to baptize his characters. He pretended, and with right, that a name does
not create itself any more than a word. According to
him, names are formed by themselves like languages;
real names possess besides, a life, a significance, a vitality,
a cabalistic power, and we cannot attach too much importance to their choice. Léon Gozlan, in his "Balzac
in Slippers," has related in a charming fashion, how he
found the famous "Z. Marcas" of the *Revue Parisienne.*
The sign of a chimney-doctor, furnished the name for a
long time sought from Gubetta to Victor Hugo, who is
no less careful than Balzac, in the appellations of his
characters.

This rough life of nocturnal labor, had, notwithstanding his vigorous constitution, imprinted its traces upon
Balzac's face, and we find in "Albert Savarus" a portrait, drawn by himself, which represents him as he
was at this time (1842) with but slight deviation:

"A superb head; black hair already mixed with a
few white threads; such hair as Saint Peter and Saint
Paul have in pictures, with thick and glossy curls,—hair
coarse as horse hair; a neck white and round, a magnificent forehead, parted by that deep furrow which grand
projects, high thoughts, deep meditations, inscribe upon
the foreheads of great men; an olive complexion marbled
with red spots, a flat nose, eyes of fire, thin, hollow

cheeks, marked by two long furrows full of suffering, a mouth inclined to smile, and a small chin, delicate and too short; crows'-feet at the temples, hollow eyes revolving under arched brows like two burning globes ;— but, despite all these indications of violent passion, an air placid and deeply resigned, a voice penetrating in its sweetness, and surprising you by its facility; the true voice of the orator, now pure and subtle, now insinuating, thundering when needful, now sarcastic, then incisive, M. Albert Savarus is of middle height, neither fat nor lean; he has the hands of a prelate."

In this portrait, otherwise very faithful, Balzac idealizes himself a little for the exigencies of the romance, and divests himself of some kilogrammes of embonpoint, a license well permitted to a hero loved by the Duchess d'Argalio, and by Mademoiselle de Watteville. This romance of " Albert Savarus," one of the least known and the least quoted of Balzac, contains many transposed details upon his habits of life and labor; we might even see here, if we were permitted to lift the veil, confidences of another kind.

Balzac had left the Rue de Batailles for the Jardies; he then went to live in Passy. The house where he dwelt, situated upon an abrupt declivity, presented an architectural arrangement singular enough. We entered here

Un peu comme le vin entre dans les bouteilles.

You had to descend three stories in order to arrive at the first. The main door from the side of the street, opened almost into the roof, as into a garret. We dined here once with L. G. It was a strange dinner, composed after economical recipes invented by Balzac. At our express entreaty, the famous soup of lentilles and onions, endowed with so many hygienic and symbolic

virtues, and of which Lessailly had been obliged to eat
to repletion, did not appear. But the wines were
marvellous! Each bottle had its history, and Balzac
recounted it with an eloquence, a poetic fire, a conviction, never before equalled. This Bordeaux wine had
three times made the circuit of the globe; this *Chateau-
neuf* of the Pope dated back to fabulous epochs; this
rum had come from a cask more than a century ago
cast up by the sea, and it had been necessary to break
it open with blows of the axe, so thick a crust had
been formed around it by shell fish, madrepores and sea-
weed. We, pale, surprised, aghast at these acid flavors,
protested in vain against such illustrious origins. Balzac
retained the gravity of a soothsayer; and despite the
proverb, although we kept our eyes fixed upon him, we
did not make him laugh!

At the dessert figured pears of a maturity, a size, a
lusciousness and a rarity, that might have done honor
to a royal table. Balzac devoured five or six of them;
he believed that these fruits were healthful to him, and
he ate them in such quantity as much for hygiene as
for their luscious flavor. He was already suffering
from the first attacks of the malady that was to carry
him off. Death, with his bony fingers was groping at
that robust body so as to learn where to attack it, and
finding no other weakness, it was going to kill him with
plethora and hypertrophy. Balzac's cheeks were always marked with those red spots which simulate health
to inattentive eyes; to the close observer, sallow, hepatic
tints, with their golden aureole, surrounded the weary
eyelids; but the glance, enlivened by this warm bistre
tone, appeared only the more vivacious, the more
sparkling, and deceived the anxious.

At this moment, Balzac was very much interested in

the occult sciences, in chiromancy and cartomancy. They had told him of a sibyl even more astonishing than Mademoiselle Lenormand, and he resolved that Madame de Girardin, Méry and ourself should go to consult her. The pythoness abode at Anteuil, we do not recollect in what street, that is of little import to our story, for the address given was false. We fell into the midst of a family of honest citizens sojourning there for the summer; the husband, the wife, and an old mother, in whom Balzac obstinately insisted there was a cabalistic air. The good, ancient dame little flattered in being taken for a sorceress, began to be angry; the husband took us for swindlers or pickpockets; the young wife burst into peals of laughter, and the maid-servant prudently hastened to lock up the silver plate. We had to beat an ignominious retreat, but Balzac insisted that this really was the place, and he re-entered the carriage, muttering maledictions upon the old woman in all the odd, whimsical terms his acquaintance with the litanies of Rabelais could suggest.

We said: "If she is a sorceress, she conceals well her game." We attempted some other researches, always fruitless, and Delphine pretended that Balzac had fabricated all this for the sake of a carriage drive to Anteuil, and to procure agreeable travelling companions. But we must believe that Balzac did have a solitary interview with this Madame Fontaine whom we sought together. Did he consult her seriously? Did he go as a simple observer? Several passages of the "Comédie Humaine" seem to imply in Balzac a sort of faith in the occult sciences upon which official science had not as yet pronounced its decisive verdict.

About this time Balzac began to manifest some taste for old furniture, chests, pottery; the least bit of worm-aten wood that he bought in the Rue de Lappe, had always an illustrious lineage, and he created genealogies suited to his least purchases. He hid them here and there, always by reason of those fantastic creditors whose existence we began to doubt. We even amused ourselves in spreading a report that Balzac was a millionaire, that like Aboul-Casem he had three cisterns filled to the brim with carbuncles, dinars and bmars. " They will cut my throat with this nonsense," said Balzac, protesting, and yet charmed.

What gave some sort of probability to our banterings, was the new abode in which Balzac · dwelt, Rue Fortunée, in the Beaujou quarter, less populous then than it is to-day. Here he occupied a small, mysterious house, which would have suited the fancy of an ostentatious financier. Outside, you perceived above the wall a sort of cupola, relieved by the arched ceiling of a boudoir, and the refreshing picture of closed shutters.

When you penetrated into this retreat, which was not easy, for the master of the lodge concealed himself with extreme care, you discovered a thousand details of comfort and luxury in contradiction to the poverty he affected. He nevertheless received us one day, and we saw a dining-hall finished in old oak, with a table, a fire-place, buffets, cupboards and chairs of carved wood, all of which would have delighted the heart of an antiquarian. There was also a salon of damask and gold, with doors, cornices, plinths and embrasures of ebony; a library arranged with book-cases incrusted by tortoise-shell and copper ; a bathing-hall in yellow breccia with stucco bas-reliefs; a boudoir whose ancient paintings had been restored by Edmund Hedouin; a gallery lighted from above, where later we recognized the collection of *Cousin Pous*. There were upon the étagères all sorts of curiosities, porcelains of Saxony and Sèvres, ink-horns of sea-green malachite, and upon the staircase covered by a carpet, great china vases and a magnificent chandelier suspended by a red silk cord.

"Have you then exhausted one of the pits of Aboul-Casem?" said we laughing, to Balzac, as we gazed upon these splendors. "We well see that you were right in pretending to be a millionaire."

"I am poorer than ever," replied he assuming a meek and hypocritical air; "nothing of all this is mine. I have furnished the house for a friend whom I expect.— I am only the guardian and doorkeeper of the hotel."

We quote his exact words. He made this reply to several other persons, all of whom were astonished as ourself. The mystery was soon explained by the marriage of Balzac to the woman he had long loved. On the 18th of August, 1850, Balzac married a charming woman, the Countess Eve de Hanska. He died four months after.

There is a Turkish proverb which says; "When the house is finished, death enters." It is for this reason that the sultans always have a palace in process of construction, which they take care shall not be finished. Life seems to wish nothing complete—but misfortune. Nothing is so much to be dreaded as a wish realized.

The haunting debts had at last been paid, the dreamed of union accomplished, the nest for happiness built and lined with down. As if they had a presentiment of his approaching end, those who had envied Balzac began to praise him. "The Poor Relatives" and "Cousin Pos," where the genius of the author glows in its full splendor, rallied the suffrages of all. Life was too beautiful, and nothing remained but to die.

His malady made rapid progress, but no one apprebended a fatal dénouement; all had so much confidence in the athletic organization of Balzac. We firmly believed that he would live to bury us all.

We were going to travel in Italy, and before leaving, we wished to bid adieu to our illustrious friend. He had driven out in a calèche, to bring some foreign curiosity from the custom-house, so a servant told us. We left reassured, but at the moment we were stepping into the carriage, a note was handed us from Madame de Balzac, which explained to us obligingly, and with polite regrets, the reason why we had not found her husband at home. At the end of the letter, Balzac had traced these words;

"I can no longer read or write.

"BALZAC."

We have preserved as a relic this ominous line, the last probably written by the author of the "Comédie Humaine." This was, although we did not at first comprehend it, the supreme cry: *Eloi, Eloi, lama, sabbacthani!* of the thinker and the worker. The idea that Balzac could die had not even occurred to us.

Some days after this, we were taking an ice at Café Florian, upon the place Santo-Marco. The *Journal des Débats*, one of the few French newspapers which penetrate to Venice, chanced to come into our hands, and here we saw announced the death of Balzac. We fell powerless into our chair upon the flag-stones of the place at this overwhelming news, and with our sorrow soon blent a most unchristian movement of indignation and revolt; for all souls in the sight of God are of equal value. We had just returned from a visit to the idiot asylum, upon the island of San-Servolo, and had seen there decrepit idiots, octogenarian wrecks, human hobgoblins guided not even by animal instinct, and we asked ourselves why this luminous brain had been extinguished like a torch we snuff out, while life remained tenacious in these darkened heads, vaguely traversed by deceptive rays of intelligence.

Years have flown since that fatal hour. Posterity has begun for Balzac; he seems greater every day. When he was among his contemporaries, they little appreciated him they saw; him only in fragments, and sometimes, under unfavorable aspects; now the edifice he builded towers upward as we recede from it, like the cathedral of a town hidden by the neighboring houses, and which in the horizon is outlined immense above the flattened roofs. The monument is not finished, but such as it is, it awes us by its hugeness, and the surprised generations will ask each other, "what manner of man is the giant who alone has heaved up these formidable blocks, and reared so high this Babel where are heard the murmurings of all social orders!"

Although dead, Balzac has still his detractors; they hurl upon his memory the vulgar reproach of immorality, the last insult of impotent and jealous mediocrity, or of stupidity. The author of the "Comédie Humaine" is pure, not immoral; he is even an austere moralist. A Monarchist and a Catholic, he defends authority, exalts religion, preaches duty, reprimands passion, and admits happiness only in marriage and the family.

"Man," says he, "is neither good nor bad; he is born with instincts and aptitudes; society, far from depraving him, as Rousseau has pretended, perfects him; but interest also develops his evil inclinations. Christianity, and especially Catholicism, being as I have said in the 'Country Physician,' a complete system of the repression of the depraved tendencies of man, is the greatest element of social order."

Anticipating the reproach of immorality which some ill-constituted minds would cast upon him, with the ingenuity of a great man, Balzac enumerates as one of his chief merits, the many irreproachable characters to be found in the "Comédie Humaine." Those who have read that master-piece know them well; those who have not, should hasten to make their acquaintance.

Figures of villains are not wanting in this "Comédie Humaine;" but is Paris peopled exclusively by angels?

BÉRANGER.

Born 1780—Died 1857.

WE met him in the promenades, and we greeted him with a respectful glance, but he was no longer a contemporary, although he lived among us. One need not in this hurrying epoch live many years, ere he withdraws from the mêlée, to be present at his renown as if he were his own descendant. A long time before he descended to the tomb, Béranger had the satisfaction of knowing what posterity thought of him, and he could sleep tranquilly upon his immortality, if ever such ambition enticed his heart. Men born with the century or a little before it, formed the immediate public of Béranger. The young generation best knew him from having heard him sung by their fathers, and from having sung his songs itself. It admired him a little from hearsay and from vague childish remembrances. This is a favorable condition for the poet's glory. His titles are admitted, they are no longer discussed, and the general signification of his work is more clearly revealed.

Béranger consoled humiliated France, he preserved and revived noble remembrances, and in this sense, he truly merits the title of national poet. His refrains have flitted, winged and sonorous, over the lips of men, and many know them who have never read them. No

vous écrive du [...?] May

Beranger

one was more popular, and in this respect he won that which was refused to higher and greater poets than he.

His talent was to enclose in a narrow frame, a clear, well-defined idea, easily comprehensible, and to express it by simple forms. He thought of the unlettered whom French poets too much forget, and are punished for the disdain, by a circumscribed reputation. The uneducated, women and the common people, rarely open a volume of verses. They comprehend nothing of these lyric digressions, these complicated rhymes, these far-fetched words. They must have a legend, a little drama, an action, a sentiment, something human, and suited to their capacity. Béranger possesses the sense of composition. His songs, even the least successful, have a plan, a connection, an end; they begin, develop, and close logically. In short, they contain a skeleton, like a vaudeville, a romance, or a drama. They are not mere effusions, poetic caprices, unconscious harmonies.

His design being arrested and traced by the pen, like certain painters who would not lose their outlines, Béranger filled it and colored it, laboriously sometimes, with a firm, free, exact touch, without great warmth of tone, but with that gray shade which is, as it were, the pallet of French genius. He was an enemy to all arts, transports, violences and audacities. Although he voluntarily restrained himself (and often the restraint cost him dear) to a manner which he made elevated, but which even in him, we consider inferior, he was always careful, like a true artist, of the rythm and the ryhme, without letting them predominate, as some have said. With him the consonance comes full and round, and the rhyme is almost always perfect. He has often in this way, rarities and felicities which surprise while

they content the ear.   His verse, sometimes pitiful in
structure, and almost spoiled by lack of space,—the
song not admitting more than six or eight couplets, and
not going beyond the verse of ten feet—the cæsuras
long and badly arranged for songs—is, in general, full
well constructed and well divided, infinitely superior
to all contemporary verses up to the advent of the young,
romantic school, which wrought so marvellously in
rythm.   But the execution, although he worked at it
with an amorous patience, taking and retaking the file
to erase all defects, was still only secondary in his eyes;
he subordinated all to the first intention, to the wished-
for end, to the desired effect.   As a dramatic author
who preoccupied himself less with style than a writer
properly so called, he must, we may well suppose, have
discarded many charming things which were too dis-
cursive or too lengthy for his poems.   Few poets have
this courage or this good sense.

He was born of the people, notwithstanding the
aristocratic particle which preceded his name; and he
was, in all his instincts, with the people.   He naturally
comprehended and felt their joys, their sorrows, their
regrets, their hopes;   he was also entirely modern.   He
did not go to antiquity for his subjects; he ignored
antiquity at the beginning, and feigned to ignore it to
the end.   Not having learned Latin, he ingeniously
availed himself of his pretext for not producing the centos of Horace or Virgil.   In a time of imitation he was
original rather through thought than form, and as the
critics then did not attach great importance to songs, he
did not have to submit to those violent attacks which
greeted other geniuses at their first public appearance.

The France, the Revolution of 1830, proved him well,
he who always felt the rancor of 1815 to the Restora-

tion. The success of Béranger's political songs was immense ; with rare felicity, he expressed a general sentiment, and sang aloud that which all others murmured low. He sang of the man of destiny, of the tricolor, of the old sergeant, and he gave besides to France means of mocking at its conquerors, a service which this brave, proud and intellectual people has never forgotten ; content with all, if it could only render its enemy ridiculous.

In one way, Béranger resembles Charlet, who, after his manner, has also written the familiar epic of the grand army, and has represented Napoleon as the people saw him with his little chapeau and his gray overcoat,—a difficult task in a full civilization, when the poet and the painter must find the legend in history, and with some ineffaceable traits design a silhouette at the acknowledged instant.

Here doubtless are the reasons for the great, undying popularity which is attached to the name of Béranger, but they are not the only ones ; his mind was really French, Gallic even, with no admixture of a foreign element ; that is to say, he possessed a mind, temperate, mirthful, waggish ; he had a facile wisdom, a Socratic good nature between that of Montaigne and Rabelais ; he laughed more willingly than he wept, and yet, he knew how to mingle a smile and a tear. His is not precisely a poetic spirit such as Goethe, Schiller, Byron, Lamartine, Victor Hugo and Alfred de Musset have revealed ; but the genius of France is not lyrical.

Béranger, despite his political bias, pleases a great many people, by that ingenuous lucidity, that rather homely sobriety, that proverbial good sense, which, for us, approaches too near to prose. We consent to accept what the Muse brings us on its feet, especially when those feet are shod in delicate buskins, but we would prefer that she should soar on grand pinions, even though she be lost in the clouds!

There are in Béranger's works a host of types which he has thrown off in a few couplets, and which will live forever that vigorous life of art so much more enduring than the real life:—among these are the " King of Yvetot," " Roger Bontemps, the Marquis of Carabas," " Madame Grégoire," " Frétillon," " Lisette," brilliant etchings, graceful sketches, pastels made with the end of the finger and which are equal in value to the most finished pictures. It seems as if we had met them as real personages in our every-day life; that we have spoken to them and they have answered us.

BRIZEUX.

BORN 1806—DIED 1858.

THE author of "Marie," as he was called at the time when people still occupied themselves with poets, was one of those men, common yesterday, rare now, who live only for art. The bees of Hymettus had flitted above his cradle, and had alighted on his lips. When very young, the Muse had touched him with her wing, and he respected the sacred contact. Never was he willing to descend to vulgar labors, to those pursuits which bring bread from day to day; he preferred the narrowest mediocrity of fortune—and why should he not say so?—*misery*, to what he considered a derogation to poetry. All he could take upon himself was to ask alms for Dante, whom he religiously translated, and his author gave him the obolus necessary for the day of supreme need. Brizeux was a Breton, and he loved with a jealous love

La terre de granit recouverte de chênes.

He personified Brittany under the figure of "Marie," a sweet symbol of the absent and regretted country. In this lovely poem, we respire the odor of the broom and the genista, the sharp and salubrious freshness of the neighboring ocean; and amid the sounds of the *biniou*, we hear as it were, the modulations of the antique flute. " The Bretons " " Pomel and Nola " are pictures of a local coloring, very just and very fine, painted lovingly by a hand long familiar with the sites and the men they represent. The " *Ternaires,*" have a more mystic tendency, and seem inspired by communion with Dante. The author, impressed with the importance of the number *three*, discovered it everywhere, and under a ternary rhythm, formulated Doric sentences which would not have been disowned by Pythagoras.

All these poems are constructed with extreme care, clearness and delicacy; we see that the author in his long, laborious leisure, weighed every line, every word, every syllable in balances of gold; disquieting himself in regard to an assonance, an alliteration, a light shade of thought,—all things for which the vulgar little care, charmed as they are with complicated apologues and romantic adventures. As if it were not enough for beautiful French verses to be unknown, Brizeux wrote in the dialect of Breton, and many of his Gallic ballads are popular down there in the country.

And so he lived, now in Brittany, now in Florence, melancholy, savage and proud; ignored enough, but not having been false to his poetic dream, and leaving a master-piece, " Marie." His ambition, if he had any, was to belong to the Academy. The Academy will suffer the chagrin that he died too soon for the fulfilment of this perfectly literary desire.

HENRI MONNIER.

BORN IN PARIS, 1799.

HENRI MONNIER is one of the most decided originals of our time. Long before the daguerreotopic and realistic schools, he had pursued the art of absolute truth and attained it.

" Nothing is beautiful but the true, the true alone is amiable,"

is a device he might have engraven upon his seal, for he has always conformed to it. An artist must have rare powers to conform rigorously to such a principle from one end to the other of a career which is beginning to be long, and which has led him into the triple paths of painter, author and actor.

He began by making sketches of the types of character which impressed him, and with a few strokes of the pencil he arrested their gestures, their habits, their angles of incidence and reflection, their eccentricities, their fractures, which the common throng did not perceive, and which, to the observant eye, are revelations of character. Afterward, not content with these mute reproductions, he gave voice to his delineations in those burlesques which have become celebrated ; we say burlesques, in order to avail ourselves of a consecrated word, for nothing less resembles burlesque than these mouldings upon nature, executed by a process of which Monnier alone has the secret.

It was at first like a sort of legendary caricature,—then the artist, reuniting many types, has formed from them scenes irresistibly comic, where he imitates the voices of different actors. Then he has written them, amplifying and perfecting them; for speech is winged, and the impression remains. Not content with this, he has played them at the theatre with a cool, incisive perfection which recalls Perlet, the physiologist among actors. Can we not place Monnier by the side of Potier, of Vernet, of Bouffé and other illustrious ones of this class? No; for he does not represent a dramatic action, but particular idiosyncrasies, observed types of special natures, of self-existent origin, and which demand a separate frame; he also has succeeded better than any one else in his pieces of the second rank; there he is at his ease; he squares, develops and transforms himself, abandoning the boots and the short pipe of the cattle-merchant, for shoes with marcasite buckles, and the golden snuff-box of the old epicurean.

Henry Monnier is himself the blank canvas on which he paints his personages. His own individuality disappears entirely under the colors from which he recovers it. He metamorphoses himself from head to foot; he has the shoes and the coiffure, the linen and the coat, the figure and the eyes, the voice and the accent of the type he seeks to reproduce. The resemblance is exterior and interior; it is the man himself. La Bruyère and Larochefoucauld, those pitiless anatomists, do not plunge the scalpel more deeply into nature. Such a wadded dressing-gown of Henri Monnier's is worth a page of the " Caractères ; " such a fashion of pinching the snuff between the thumb and the index finger is a new paragraph of the " Maximes."

If this be so, why is it that Henri Monnier is not the great painter, the great writer, the great actor of our epoch? Nature is not the end of art, it is at most the means; the daguerreotype reproduces objects without their colors, and the mirror reverses them, which is an inexactness, a fantasy, say the realists. In everything expressed, there must be an incidence of light, a sentiment, a touch, which betrays the soul of the artist. Henri Monnier does not select, he does not mitigate, he does not exaggerate, he makes no sacrifice; he takes care not to augment the intensity of the shadows, to throw the day into bolder relief. His porters are porters, nothing more; he does not give them fantastic ugliness, richly-sordid tatters, complexions of yellow varnish, such as the Flemmings lend to their ugly fellows; he does not, like Rembrandt, make them cook at their lodgings, sour herrings whose smoke colors the warm blonde complexions, the dirty windows, the rancid linen and the bituminous walls. Behind the stove where the stew is cooking, upon the beams where the bird-cage hangs, he does not throw doubtful and reddish shadows which look like bats or gnomes' seated upon their bended joints. His portresses are purely ignoble: he does not make them ferocious by placing a wild boar's snout over a callous lip as in the old woman of " The Temptation of Saint Anthony," by Téniers; his *bourgeois*,—and no one has painted them more justly, not even Balzac,— weary you like the real *bourgeois*, by their inexhaustible flow of commonplace and solemn stupidity. It is no longer comedy; it is stenography. But of all his silhouettes cut from life, majestically detaches itself the figure of Joseph Prudhomme, that synthesis of bourgeois stupidity; it seems as if you had known him, and as if he had just left you, shaking your hand and laughing

his loud, satisfied laugh.   What a magnificent imbecile !
Never has the flower of human stupidity more luxuriant-
ly blossomed ! It is happy ; it is radiant ! How he lets
fall from his thick lips those leaden aphorisms so hor-
rifying to common sense!   Joseph Prudhomme is the
vengeance of Henri Monnier, who indemnifies him for the
ennuis, the contradictions, the humiliations and all the
petty sufferings commonplace individuals cause artists
often unintentionally.   For this time only, he has departed from his glacial impartiality ; he has grown angry
and excited ; he has exaggerated the trait, he has over-
wrought the effect ; in fact, he has invented it.

Prudhomme, despite his extreme realness, is no longer
a copy, he is a creation.   Balzac, who made a great deal
of Monnier, has tried to introduce Prudhomme into his
" Human Comedy," under the name of Phellion.   Phellion is no doubt very fine, with his ram's head and his
face marked with small-pox, his white, starched cravat,
his vest, his black coat, and his shoes with dabbled ties ;
but his phrases will not do.

Whenever Monnier played, he attracted to the theatre
a special public of artist and connoisseurs ; but his playing was too fine, too true, too natural, to greatly amuse the
crowd.   The Prudhommes of the hall are astonished to
see him laughed at in the representation ; they have the
same ideas, they express them in the same way, and are
surprised that any one can think these fashions ridiculous.
Prudhomme himself from living with his kind has
adopted their conduct, their manner, their tones of voice,
their phraseology, and often into the most intellectual
conversation, a period *à la* Joseph Prudhomme seriously
intrudes.

Who has not read the " Popular Scenes," the " Pleasures
of the Country," " The Romance at the Gate ? " Madame

Desjardins is immortal as Madame Gibou and Madame Pochet. That cap, its loose borders fluttering like elephantine ears, floats in all memories ; and no one has forgotten the Lyonnaise woman so anxious as to the fate of little birds during the winter. The " Pleasures of the Country" is an antiphrase whose truth you may well question. Henri Monnier's peasants are not the peasants of the pastoral poem ; they are thieves like magpies, misers like griffins, rogues like foxes, diplomats who would foil Talleyrand. And what a country ! A country of city precincts, a paved expanse, dusty, without shade, without privacy and without leisure, which gives you a desire to inhabit a suite of rooms in the Rue de la Chausée d'Antin, or a garret upon the Montmartre boulevard !

ALEXANDRE DUMAS.

(1802–1870.)

ONE of the most remarkable characters that the nineteenth century has produced was the son of General Dumas and of Marie Labouret, an innkeeper's daughter. His father was an officer of remarkable gallantry, who, for his dashing exploits, had obtained the odd title of the "Horatius Cocles of the Tyrol." He was a creole, the illegitimate son of the Marquis Davy de la Pailleterie and of Louise Dumas, a black woman of St. Domingo. Long after, his grandson was to excite the laughter of Paris by claiming this title and assuming the family arms. The general had an insubordinate temper, and excited the dislike and suspicion of Napoleon, who sent him back from Egypt to languish in obscurity and die of disappointment at Villers-Cotterets, in the year 1806.

Alexandre Dumas was born on July 4, 1802, at Villers-Cotterets, where he was brought up under the care of an affectionate and pious mother.

Some of the most graceful passages of autobiography are to be found in those pages of his memoirs which are devoted to an account of his boyhood, and which present an excellent picture of French country-town life. He seems to have been an idle and a troublesome youth, and, though places were found for him with notaries and other functionaries, he

could not settle to business. The family means were slender. They were soon almost reduced to poverty; and in the year 1823 Alexandre set off for Paris to seek his fortune, where he was to make such good use of his slender opportunities, that within five years his name became famous. Within a few days of his arrival, an old friend of his father's, General Foy, obtained a clerk's place for him in the Duke of Orleans's establishment, worth only £50 a year, but it seemed a fortune. A friend, De Leuven, and he now joined their talents in a light farce, called "Le Chasse et l'Amour" (produced September 22, 1825). This was succeeded by a dramatic piece, written with the assistance of one of his friends, and called "La Noce et l'Enterrement" (November 21, 1826), known in England as the amusing "Illustrious Stranger." Meanwhile the visit of Macready and other English players to Paris had introduced him to Shakespeare, and had set him to work on a grand romantic and historical drama, which he called "Christine." The young clerk had the boldness to look forward to having it presented on the boards of the first theatre in France, and, with an energy and spirit that should encourage every friendless aspirant, set every resource he could command at work. Charles Nodier introduced him to Baron Taylor, the literary director of the theatre, who, if we are to credit Dumas, was so enchanted with the work that he accepted it and submitted it to the company at once. It is more probable that, from the corrupt fashion which then regulated such matters, the privilege was secured by the influence of the Duke of Orleans. But it happened that another "Christine" was supported by even greater influence, and Dumas's had to be withdrawn. In a short time he had written "Henri III.," which was produced (February 11, 1829) with the most extraordinary results. This piece was important as being the first

12

success of the well-known "Romantic School." "Henri III.," it is said, brought its author about £2,000. But the revolution of July now broke out and interrupted every literary scheme.

It was, however, welcomed by the creole's son, who flung himself with ardor into the struggle. And here begins that double interest in his life, which was as adventurous as that of some of his own heroes, and suggests the career of Benvenuto Cellini. He has, of course, made his own share in the exciting scenes of the Three Days as conspicuous as possible; and his expedition to Soissons, and almost single-handed capture of a powder magazine, a general, and officer, were heartily laughed at and wholly disbelieved. Allowing, however, for embellishment, it is due to him to say that his narrative seems to be true in the main. He was, however, unlucky enough to have cast his lot with the more violent party, which found itself opposed to the Orleans family, and never recovered their favor, and King Louis Philippe always treated him with good-humored contempt. He now returned to his dramatic labors, and produced "Antony" (1831), one of the earliest of those gross outrages on public morality which have helped to make conjugal infidelity the favorite theme of the French drama. But by this time he had found that the slow production of dramas scarcely offered a profitable field for his talents. The successful founding of the "Revue des Deux Mondes" tempted him into trying his skill on historical romances, professedly in imitation of Sir Walter Scott. And this would seem to be the first opening of that seam which was to be worked later with such extraordinary profit. Here he introduced that daring system of working up the ideas of others, which he had already carried out in his dramatic labors, his successful pieces of "Henri III." and "Christine" proving to consist of whole scenes stolen from Schiller and other writers almost without changing a word, though the arrangement of the plot and situations are masterly and original.

A piece of his, called the "Tour de Nesle" (produced in 1832), which caused a perfect furore in Paris, led, however, to a more serious charge of plagiarism. In consequence of a duel he was directed to leave France for a time, and set off—in July, 1832—on a tour through Switzerland, which suggested to him a series of those odd books of travels made up of long extracts from old memoirs, guide-books, imaginary dialogues, and adventures.

In 1842 he married an actress named Ida Ferrier, who had performed in his plays; but the union was not a happy one, and, after a rather extravagant career, the lady retired to Florence, where she died in the year 1859. Hitherto his success, though remarkable, could not be called European, and he was not to be distinguished from the crowd of French professional *littérateurs*. But in 1844 the famous "Monte Christo" appeared, which may be said to have excited more universal interest than any romance since "Robinson Crusoe" or "Waverley." The extraordinary color, the never-flagging spirit, the endless surprises, and the air of nature which was cast over even the most extravagant situations, make this work worthy of the popularity it enjoyed in almost every country of the world. It was followed by the no less famous "Three Musketeers." These productions were the more remarkable as they were written from day to day for the readers of a newspaper, and thus firmly established the *feuilleton* as a necessary element of French literature. In this, as in other departments where he was successful, Dumas was not original, and only took up the idea of a successful predecessor, Eugène Sue, whose "Juif Errant" had enjoyed much popularity in this shape.

This triumph made him, as it were, irresponsible in the literary world, and suggested to him a series of wholesale operations for supplying the public with books, the history of which makes an extraordinary chapter in literature. He contracted for innumerable stories, each of great length, and to be published at the same time, almost any one of which would be beyond the powers of a single writer. In a single year, 1844, he issued some forty volumes, and later on he engaged himself even more deeply to meet these heavy demands. He began by employing one or two assistants, with whose aid he furnished his two great stories; and it may be said that, with his constant supervision and inspiration, his daily direction, suggestion of incidents, manipulation of the ideas of others, consultations, etc., he might almost fairly claim the credit of having written "Monte Christo" and the "Three Musketeers." His most valuable assistant was Maquet. Indeed, the chief credit of Dumas's most important stories has been claimed for him; but as he afterwards often tried his powers alone, and with but poor success, it seems probable that his share in Dumas's works was no more than what has been described. But presently the popular writer found that even this form of partnership was too great a tax upon his time, and he began to proceed upon the simpler process of ordering works from clever young writers, to whom he suggested a subject, and perhaps a simple outline of treatment—and then issuing their work with his name. Some care in the selection was at first exercised, but later he accepted any stuff that was brought to him—travels, essays, stories—and indorsed them with his name. Indeed, a volume could be filled with the odd details and complicated ramifications of this system, which was exposed in the most unsparing fashion by Granier de Cassagnac, Jacquet, alias "De Mirecourt," and Quérard. Dumas justified his system of appropriating from dead and living authors by a theory of what he called "conquests." "All human phenomena," he says, "are public property. The man of genius does not steal, he only conquers. Every one arrives in his turn and at his hour, seizes what his ancestors have left, and puts it into new shapes and combinations."

In the meantime he was earning vast sums. Leaving the work of composition to his journeymen, he now entered on a new and reckless course, with a view of dazzling his countrymen and gratifying his own Eastern taste. In this view he built a vast theatre for the production of his own works, and a gorgeous castle at St. Germain, on the model of a palace in a fairy tale, on which he lavished every adornment.

While these follies were in progress, he succeeded in getting himself attached to the suite of the young Duke of Montpensier, then (1846) setting out for Madrid to be married, and received, besides, a sort of commission from the Government to visit Algeria, with a view to making it popular by a lively account from his pen. He was granted a passage to Oran on board one of the Government mail-boats, but, through an awkward misconception, was allowed to divert this vessel from her regular service, and used her for visiting Carthage, Tunis, and other places. On his return there was much scandal, and the ministry was very severely interrogated as to the irregularity of allowing "a contractor for stories" to make so free with public property. It was explained that this was entirely owing to a misrepresentation of the popular writer's. Another rebuff, too, was waiting him; for, having completely neglected his engagements to the various newspapers while making this agreeable tour, he found himself engaged in heavy law-suits with no less than seven journals, including the "Constitutionnel" and the "Presse." After defending himself in person, a performance that was the entertainment of all Paris, he was cast in damages. This was the beginning of his disasters. His theatre, after opening with one of his pieces, which took two nights to perform, fell on evil days, and the revolution of 1848 plunged it into difficulties. In these new scenes he was by no means popular, being suspected, from his assiduous attendance on the Orleans family. By this time all his best works had been written, and he was now only to attract attention by some extravagant literary somersault or impudent attempt at "humbugging" the public. He attempted newspapers like the "Mousquetaire," of which he would grow tired after a few numbers, but to every article in which he was ready to attach his name. His next escapade was joining Garibaldi (1860), whose messenger and lieutenant he constituted himself, and, in reward for some trifling service, he claimed the appointment of "Director of the Museum and Explorations" at Naples, an office he was presently forced to resign. After this he was reduced to all manner of devices to maintain himself, always borrowing and obtaining money by shifts and pretences, which in another could not be called honest. It becomes, indeed, painful to follow the stages in this rapid decay—to find him reduced to writing "puffs" for tradesmen, to exhibiting himself in shop windows, and to introducing grand schemes to the public, which it is impossible to read without hearty laughter. A scandalous infatuation, too, was to be associated with his old age, which last excited the contempt and pity of all who knew him. To the last he was full of schemes, devised with the fertility and roseate imagination of a Micawber; and to the last, unfortunately, he was devoted to pleasure. The result was a breaking-up of his health, and even a decay of his faculties. When the war of 1870 broke out, he was removed from Paris to Puys, near Dieppe, and there affectionately attended by his son and daughter. He died on the 5th of December in the same year. He was even poorer than when he began the world; and the brilliant novelist, who had earned more than £10,000 a year, had hardly a sou left. On the 16th of April, 1872, when the war was over, his remains were removed to Villers-Cotterets, and interred in presence of the leading *littérateurs* of Paris.

The works that bear Dumas's name are said to amount to some 1,200 volumes. His dialogue is entirely his own, full of spirit and dramatic propriety, and this, too, in spite of the temptation, to a man paid by the line, to "spin out" his matter to the utmost extent. He left about sixty dramas, of which not more than three or four will be remembered; but two, the "Mariage sous Louis XV." and "Mdlle. de Belle Isle," belong to the repertoire of the Comédie Française. These will always be listened to with delight. His most popular stories have been mentioned, but even now their undue expansion and interminable development, owing to the necessities of the *feuilleton* system, are found to be serious obstacles to their popularity.

He left a daughter, Madame Petel, who has written a few romances, and a son, the well-known "Alexandre Fils," who, unlike his father, has been distinguished by slow and careful work. He is best known by his romance, "La Dame aux Camélias," which has been translated in every language in which romances are written, and by a number of dramas which deal satirically with the characters, follies, and manners of society under the Second Empire.

MAURICE DE GUÉRIN.

I WILL not presume to say that I now know the French language well; but at a time when I knew it even less well than at present—some fifteen years ago—I remember pestering those about me with this sentence, the rhythm of which had lodged itself in my head, and which, with the strangest pronunciation possible, I kept perpetually declaiming: "Les dieux jaloux ont enfoui quelque part les témoignages de la descendance des choses; mais au bord de quel Océan ont ils roulé la pierre qui les couvre, ô Macarée!"

These words come from a short composition called the "Centaur," of which the author, Georges-Maurice de Guérin, died in the year 1839, at the age of twenty-eight, without having published anything. In 1840 Madame Sand brought out the "Centaur" in the "Revue des Deux Mondes," with a short notice of its author, and a few extracts from his letters. A year or two afterwards she reprinted these at the end of a volume of her novels; and there it was that I fell in with them. I was so much struck with the "Centaur" that I waited anxiously to hear something more of its author, and of what he had left; but it was not till the other day—twenty years after the first publication of the "Centaur" in the "Revue des Deux Mondes"—that my anxiety was satisfied. At the end of 1860 appeared two volumes with the title, "Maurice de Guérin, Reliquiæ," containing the "Centaur," several poems of Guérin, his journals, and a number of his letters, collected and edited by a devoted friend, M. Trebutien, and preceded by a notice of Guérin by the first of living critics, M. Sainte-Beuve.

The grand power of poetry is its interpretative power; by which I mean, not a power of drawing out in black and white an explanation of the mystery of the universe, but the power of so dealing with things as to awaken in us a wonderfully full, new, and intimate sense of them, and of our relations with them. When this sense is awakened in us, as to objects without us, we feel ourselves to be in contact with the essential nature of those objects, to be no longer bewildered and oppressed by them, but to have their secret, and to be in harmony with them; and this feeling calms and satisfies us as no other can. Poetry, indeed, interprets in another way besides this; but one of its two ways of interpreting, of exercising its highest power, is by awakening this sense in us. I will not now inquire whether this sense is illusive, whether it can be proved not to be illusive, whether it does absolutely make us possess the real nature of things; all I say is, that poetry can awaken it in us, and that to awaken it is one of the highest powers of poetry. The interpretations of science do not give us this intimate sense of objects as the interpretations of poetry give it; they appeal to a limited faculty, and not to the whole man. It is not Linnæus, or Cavendish, or Cuvier who gives us the true sense of animals, or water, or plants, who seizes their secret for us, who makes us participate in their life; it is Shakespeare, with his

"daffodils
That come before the swallow dares, and take
The winds of March with beauty;"
12*

it is Wordsworth, with his

> " voice. . . . heard
> In spring-time from the cuckoo-bird,
> Breaking the silence of the seas
> Among the farthest Hebrides ; "

it is Keats, with his

> " moving waters at their priestlike task
> Of cold ablution round Earth's human shores ; "

it is Chateaubriand, with his " *cîme indéterminée des forêts ;* " it is Senancour, with his mountain birch-tree : "*Cette écorce blanche, lisse et crevassée ; cette tige agreste ; ces branches qui s'inclinent vers la terre ; la mobilité des feuilles, et tout cet abandon, simplicité de la nature, attitude des déserts.*"

Eminent manifestations of this magical power of poetry are very rare and very precious: the compositions of Guérin manifest it, I think, in singular eminence. Not his poems, strictly so called—his verse—so much as his prose; his poems in general take for their vehicle that favorite metre of French poetry, the Alexandrine; and, in my judgment, I confess they have thus, as compared with his prose, a great disadvantage to start with. In prose, the character of the vehicle for the composer's thoughts is not determined beforehand; every composer has to make his own vehicle; and who has ever done this more admirably than the great prose-writers of France—Pascal, Bossuet, Fénélon, Voltaire? But in verse the composer has (with comparatively narrow liberty of modification) to accept his vehicle ready-made; it is therefore of vital importance to him that he should find at his disposal a vehicle adequate to convey the highest matters of poetry. We may even get a decisive test of the poetical power of a language and nation by ascertaining how far the principal poetical vehicle which they have employed, how far (in plainer words) the established national metre for high poetry, is adequate or inadequate.   It seems to me that the established metre of this kind in France—the Alexandrine—is inadequate; that as a vehicle for high poetry it is greatly inferior to the hexameter or to the iambics of Greece (for example), or to the blank verse of England.   Therefore the man of genius who uses it is at a disadvantage as compared with the man of genius who has for conveying his thoughts a more adequate vehicle, metrical or not.   Racine is at a disadvantage as compared with Sophocles or Shakespeare, and he is likewise at a disadvantage as compared with Bossuet.   The same may be said of our own poets of the eighteenth century, a century which gave them as the main vehicle for their high poetry a metre inadequate (as much as the French Alexandrine, and nearly in the same way) for this poetry—the ten-syllable couplet.   It is worth remarking, that the English poet of the eighteenth century whose compositions wear best and give one the most entire satisfaction—Gray—does not use that couplet at all; this abstinence, however, limits Gray's productions to a few short compositions, and (exquisite as these are) he is a poetical nature repressed and without free issue.   For English poetical production on a great scale, for an English poet deploying all the forces of his genius, the ten-syllable couplet was, in the eighteenth century, the established, one may almost say the inevitable, channel.   Now this couplet, admirable (as Chaucer uses it) for story-telling not of the epic pitch, and often admirable for a few lines even in poetry of a very high pitch, is for continuous use in poetry of this latter kind inadequate.   Pope, in his "Essay on Man," is thus at a disadvantage compared with Lucretius in his poem on Nature: Lucretius has an adequate vehicle, Pope has not. Nay, though Pope's genius for didactic poetry was not less than that of Horace, while his satirical power was certainly greater, still one's taste receives, I cannot but think, a certain satisfaction when one reads the Epistles and Satires of Horace, which it fails to receive when one reads the Satires and Epistles of Pope. Of such avail is the superior adequacy of the vehicle used to compensate even an inferiority of genius in the user! In the same way Pope is at a disadvantage as compared with Addison : the best of Addison's composition (the "Coverley Papers" in the "Spectator," for instance) wears better than the best of Pope's, because Addison has in his prose an intrinsically better vehicle for his genius than Pope in his couplet. But Bacon has no such advantage over Shakespeare ; nor has Milton, writing prose (for no contemporary English prose-writer must be matched with Milton except Milton himself), any such advantage over Milton writing verse: indeed, the advantage here is all the other way.

It is in the prose remains of Guérin—his journals, his letters, and the striking composition which I have already mentioned, the "Centaur"—that his extraordinary gift manifests itself. He has a truly interpretative faculty; the most profound and delicate sense of the life of Nature, and the most exquisite felicity in finding expressions to render that sense. To all who love poetry, Guérin deserves to be something more than a name; and I shall try, in spite of the impossibility of doing justice to such a master of expression by translations, to make my English readers see for themselves how gifted an organization his was, and how few artists have received from Nature a more magical faculty of interpreting her.

In the winter of the year 1832 there was collected in Brittany, around the well-known Abbé Lamennais, a singular gathering. At a lonely place, La Chênaie, he had founded a religious retreat, to which disciples, attracted by his powers or by his reputation, repaired. Some came with the intention of preparing themselves for the ecclesiastical profession; others merely to profit by the society and discourse of so distinguished a master. Among the inmates were men whose names have since become known to all Europe—Lacordaire and M. de Montalembert; there were others, who have acquired a reputation, not European, indeed, but considerable—the Abbé Gerbet, the Abbé Rohrbacher; others, who have never quitted the shade of private life. The winter of 1832 was a period of crisis in the religious world of France: Lamennais's rupture with Rome, the condemnation of his opinions by the Pope, and his revolt against that condemnation, were imminent. Some of his followers, like Lacordaire, had already resolved not to cross the Rubicon with their leader, not to go into rebellion against Rome; they were preparing to separate from him. The society of La Chênaie was soon to dissolve; but, such as it is shown to us for a moment, with its voluntary character, its simple and severe life in common, its mixture of lay and clerical members, the genius of its chiefs, the sincerity of its disciples— above all, its paramount fervent interest in matters of spiritual and religious concernment—it offers a most instructive spectacle. It is not the spectacle we most of us think to find in France, the France we have imagined from common English notions, from the streets of Paris, from novels: it shows us how, wherever there is greatness like that of France, there are, as its foundation, treasures of fervor, pure-mindedness, and spirituality somewhere, whether we know of them or not;—a store of that which Goethe calls *Halt ;*—since greatness can never be founded upon frivolity and corruption.

On the evening of the 18th of December in this year

1832, M. de Lamennais was talking to those assembled in the sitting-room of La Chênaie of his recent journey to Italy. He talked with all his usual animation; "but," writes one of his hearers, a Breton gentleman, M. de Marzan, "I soon became inattentive and absent, being struck with the reserved attitude of a young stranger some twenty-two years old, pale in face, his black hair already thin over his temples, with a southern eye, in which brightness and melancholy were mingled. He kept himself somewhat aloof, seeming to avoid notice rather than to court it. All the old faces of friends which I found about me at this my re-entry into the circle of La Chênaie, failed to occupy me so much as the sight of this stranger, looking on, listening, observing, and saying nothing."

The unknown was Maurice de Guérin. Of a noble but poor family, having lost his mother at six years old, he had been brought up by his father, a man saddened by his wife's death, and austerely religious, at the château of Le Cayla, in Languedoc. His childhood was not gay; he had not the society of other boys; and solitude, the sight of his father's gloom, and the habit of accompanying the curé of the parish on his rounds among the sick and dying, made him prematurely grave and familiar with sorrow. He went to school first at Toulouse, then at the Collège Stanislas at Paris, with a temperament almost as unfit as Shelley's for common school life. His youth was ardent, sensitive, agitated, and unhappy. In 1832 he procured admission to La Chênaie to brace his spirit by the teaching of Lamennais, and to decide whether his religious feelings would determine themselves into a distinct religious vocation. Strong and deep religious feelings he had, implanted in him by nature, developed in him by the circumstances of his childhood; but he had also (and here is the key to his character) that temperament which opposes itself to the fixedness of a religious vocation, or of any vocation of which fixedness is an essential attribute; a temperament mobile, inconstant, eager, thirsting for new impressions, abhorring rules, aspiring to a "renovation without end;" a temperament common enough among artists, but with which few artists, who have it to the same degree as Guérin, unite a seriousness and a sad intensity like his. After leaving school, and before going to La Chênaie, he had been at home at Le Cayla with his sister Eugénie (a wonderfully gifted person, whose genius so competent a judge as M. Sainte-Beuve is inclined to pronounce even superior to her brother's) and his sister Eugénie's friends. With one of these friends he had fallen in love—a slight and transient fancy, but which had already called his poetical powers into exercise; and his poems and fragments, in a certain green note-book (*le Cahier Vert*) which he long continued to make the depository of his thoughts, and which became famous among his friends, he brought with him to La Chênaie. There he found among the younger members of the Society several who, like himself, had a secret passion for poetry and literature; with these he became intimate, and in his letters and journal we find him occupied, now with a literary commerce established with these friends, now with the fortunes, fast coming to a crisis, of the Society, and now with that for the sake of which he came to La Chênaie—his religious progress and the state of his soul.

On Christmas Day, 1832, having then been three weeks at La Chênaie, he writes thus of it to a friend of his family, M. de Bayne:

"La Chênaie is a sort of oasis in the midst of the steppes of Brittany. In front of the château stretches a very large garden, cut in two by a terrace with a lime avenue, at the end of which is a tiny chapel. I am extremely fond of this little oratory, where one breathes a twofold peace—the peace of solitude and the peace of the Lord. When spring comes we shall walk to prayers between two borders of flowers. On the east side, and only a few yards from the château, sleeps a small mere between two woods, where the birds in warm weather sing all day long; and then—right, left, or all sides—woods, woods, everywhere woods. It looks desolate just now that all is bare and the woods are rust-color, and under this Brittany sky, which is always clouded and so low that it seems as if it were going to fall on your head; but as soon as spring comes the sky raises itself up, the woods come to life again, and everything will be full of charm."

Of what La Chênaie will be when spring comes he has a foretaste on the 3d of March.

"To-day" (he writes in his journal) "has enchanted me. For the first time for a long while the sun has shown himself in all his beauty. He has made the buds of the leaves and flowers swell, and he has waked up in me a thousand happy thoughts. The clouds assume more and more their light and graceful shapes, and are sketching, over the blue sky, the most charming fancies. The woods have not yet got their leaves, but they are taking an indescribable air of life and gayety, which gives them quite a new physiognomy. Everything is getting ready for the great festival of Nature."

Storm and snow adjourn this festival a little longer. On the 11th of March he writes:

"It has snowed all night. I have been to look at our primroses; each of them had its small load of snow, and was bowing its head under its burden. These pretty flowers, with their rich yellow color, had a charming effect under their white hoods. I saw whole tufts of them roofed over by a single block of snow; all these laughing flowers thus shrouded and leaning one upon another, made one think of a group of young girls surprised by a wave, and sheltering under a white cloth."

The burst of spring comes at last, though late. On the 5th of April we find Guérin "sitting in the sun to penetrate himself to the very marrow with the divine spring." On the 3d of May, "one can actually *see* the progress of the green; it has made a start from the garden to the shrubberies, it is getting the upper hand all along the mere; it leaps, one may say, from tree to tree, from thicket to thicket, in the fields and on the hillsides; and I can see it already arrived at the forest edge and beginning to spread itself over the broad back of the forest. Soon it will have overrun everything as far as the eye can reach, and all those wide spaces between here and the horizon will be moving and sounding like one vast sea, a sea of emerald."

Finally, on the 16th of May, he writes to M. de Bayne that "the gloomy and bad days—bad because they bring temptation by their gloom—are, thanks to God and the spring, over; and I see approaching a long file of shining and happy days, to do me all the good in the world. This Brittany of ours," he continues, "gives one the idea of the grayest and most wrinkled old woman possible suddenly changed back by the touch of a fairy's wand into a girl of twenty, and one of the loveliest in the world; the fine weather has so decked and beautified the dear old country." He felt, however, the cloudiness and cold of the "dear old country" with all the sensitiveness of a child of the South. "What a difference," he cries, "between the sky of Brittany, even on the finest day, and the sky of our South! Here the summer has, even on its highdays and holidays, something mournful, overcast, and stinted about it. It is like a miser who is making a show; there is a niggardliness in his magnificence. Give me our Languedoc sky, so bountiful of light, so blue, so largely vaulted!"

And somewhat later, complaining of the short and dim sunlight of a February day in Paris, "What a sunshine," he exclaims, " to gladden eyes accustomed to all the wealth of light of the South!—*aux larges et libérales effusions de lumière du ciel du Midi.*"

In the long winter of La Chênaie his great resource was literature. One has often heard that an educated Frenchman's reading seldom goes much beyond French and Latin, and that he makes the authors in these two languages his sole literary standard. This may or may not be true of Frenchmen in general, but there can be no question as to the width of the reading of Guérin and his friends, and as to the range of their literary sympathies. One of the circle, Hippolyte la Morvonnais—a poet who published a volume of verse, and died in the prime of life—had a passionate admiration for Wordsworth, and had even, it is said, made a pilgrimage to Rydal Mount to visit him; and in Guérin's own reading I find, besides the French names of Bernardin de St. Pierre, Chateaubriand, Lamartine, and Victor Hugo, the names of Homer, Dante, Shakespeare, Milton, and Goethe; and he quotes both from Greek and from English authors in the original. His literary tact is beautifully fine and true. "Every poet," he writes to his sister, "has his own art of poetry written on the ground of his own soul; there is no other. Be constantly observing Nature in her smallest details, and then write as the current of your thoughts guides you—that is all." But with all this freedom from the bondage of forms and rules, Guérin marks with perfect precision the faults of the *free* French literature of his time—the *littérature facile*—and judges the romantic school and its prospects like a master: "that youthful literature which has put forth all its blossom prematurely, and has left itself a helpless prey to the returning frost, stimulated as it has been by the burning

sun of our century, by this atmosphere charged with a peri-
lous heat, which has over-hastened every sort of development, and will most likely reduce to a handful of grains
the harvest of our age." And the popular authors—those
" whose name appears once and disappears forever, whose
books, unwelcome to all serious people, welcome to the rest
of the world, to novelty-hunters and novel-readers, fill with
vanity these vain souls, and then, falling from hands heavy
with the languor of satiety, drop forever into the gulf of
oblivion ;" and those, more noteworthy, "the writers of
books celebrated, and, as works of art, deserving celebrity,
but which have in them not one grain of that hidden
manna, not one of those sweet and wholesome thoughts
which nourish the human soul and refresh it when it is
weary," these he treats with such severity that he may in
some sense be described, as he describes himself, as "invoking with his whole heart a classical restoration." He
is best described, however, not as a partisan of any school,
but as an ardent seeker for that mode of expression which
is the most natural, happy, and true. He writes to his
sister Eugénie:

" I want you to reform your system of composition ; it is
too loose, too vague, too Lamartinian. Your verse is too
sing-song; it does not *talk* enough. Form for yourself a
style of your own, which shall be your real expression.
Study the French language by attentive reading, making
it your care to remark constructions, turns of expression,
delicacies of style, but without ever adopting the manner
of any master. In the works of these masters we must
learn our language, but we must use it each in our own
fashion." *

---

* Part of these extracts date from a time a little after Guérin's residence at La Chênaie ; but already, amidst the readings and conversations of La Chénaie, his literary judgment was perfectly formed.

It was not, however, to perfect his literary judgment that Guérin came to La Chênaie. The religious feeling, which was as much a part of his essence as the passion for Nature and the literary instinct, shows itself at moments jealous of these its rivals, and alarmed at their predominance. Like all powerful feelings, it wants to exclude every other feeling and to be absolute. One Friday in April, after he has been delighting himself with the shapes of the clouds and the progress of the spring, he suddenly bethinks himself that the day is Good Friday, and exclaims in his diary:

"My God, what is my soul about that it can thus go running after such fugitive delights on Good Friday, on this day all filled with thy death and our redemption? There is in me I know not what damnable spirit, that awakens in me strong discontents, and is forever prompting me to rebel against the holy exercises and the devout collectedness of soul which are the meet preparation for these great solemnities of our faith. O how well can I trace here the old leaven, from which I have not yet perfectly cleared my soul!"

And again, in a letter to M. de Marzan: "Of what, my God, are we made," he cries, "that a little verdure and a few trees should be enough to rob us of our tranquillity and to distract us from thy love?" And writing, three days after Easter Sunday, in his journal, he records the reception at La Chênaie of a fervent neophyte, in words which seem to convey a covert blame of his own want of fervency:

"Three days have passed over our heads since the great festival. One anniversary the less for us yet to spend of the death and resurrection of our Saviour! Every year thus bears away with it its solemn festivals; when will the everlasting festival be here? I have been witness of a

most touching sight; François has brought us one of his
friends whom he has gained to the faith. This neophyte
joined us in our exercises during the Holy week, and on
Easter day he received the communion with us. François
was in raptures. It is a truly good work which he has thus
done. François is quite young, hardly twenty years old;
M. de la M. is thirty, and is married. There is something
most touching and beautifully simple in M. de la M. letting
himself thus be brought to God by quite a young man;
and to see friendship, on François's side, thus doing the
work of an Apostle, is not less beautiful and touching."

Admiration for Lamennais worked in the same direction
with this feeling. Lamennais never appreciated Guérin;
his combative, rigid, despotic nature, of which the characteristic was energy, had no affinity with Guérin's elusive,
undulating, impalpable nature, of which the characteristic
was delicacy. He set little store by his new disciple, and
could hardly bring himself to understand what others
found so remarkable in him, his own genuine feeling
towards him being one of indulgent compassion. But the
intuition of Guérin, more discerning than the logic of his
master, instinctively felt what there was commanding and
tragic in Lamennais's character, different as this was from
his own; and some of his notes are among the most interesting records of Lamennais which remain.

" 'Do you know what it is,' M. Féli * said to us on the
evening of the day before yesterday, 'which makes man
the most suffering of all creatures? It is that he has one
foot in the finite and the other in the infinite, and that he
is torn asunder, not by four horses, as in the horrible old
times, but between two worlds.' Again he said to us as

---

* The familiar name given to M. de Lamennais by his followers at
La Chénaie.

we heard the clock strike : 'If that clock knew that it was
to be destroyed the next instant, it would still keep striking
its hour until that instant arrived.   My children, be as the
clock; whatever may be going to happen to you, strike
always your hour.'"

Another time Guérin writes,

"To-day M. Féli startled us.   He was sitting behind the
chapel, under the two Scotch firs; he took his stick and
marked out a grave on the turf, and said to Elie, 'It is
there I wish to be buried, but no tombstone! only a simple hillock of grass.   O, how well I shall be there!'   Elie
thought he had a presentiment that his end was near.
This is not the first time he has been visited by such a presentiment; when he was setting out for Rome, he said to
those here: 'I do not expect ever to come back to you;
you must do the good which I have failed to do.'   He is
impatient for death."

Overpowered by the ascendancy of Lamennais, Guérin,
in spite of his hesitations, in spite of his confession to himself that "after a three weeks' close scrutiny of his soul, in
the hope of finding the pearl of a religious vocation hidden
in some corner of it," he had failed to find what he sought,
took, at the end of August, 1833, a decisive step.   He
joined the religious order which Lamennais had founded.
But at this very moment the deepening displeasure of
Rome with Lamennais determined the Bishop of Rennes
to break up, in so far as it was a religious congregation,
the Society of La Chênaie, to transfer the novices to
Ploërmel, and to place them under other superintendence.
In September, Lamennais, "who had not yet ceased,"
writes M. de Marzan, a fervent Catholic, "to be a Christian and a priest, took leave of his beloved colony of La
Chênaie, with the anguish of a general who disbands his
army down to the last recruit, and withdraws annihilated

from the field of battle." Guérin went to Ploërmel. But here, in the seclusion of a real religious house, he instantly perceived how alien to a spirit like his—a spirit which, as he himself says somewhere, "had need of the open air, wanted to see the sun and the flowers"—was the constraint and monotony of a monastic life, when Lamennais's genius was no longer present to enliven this life for him. On the 7th of October he renounced the novitiate, believing himself a partisan of Lamennais in his quarrel with Rome, reproaching the life he had left with demanding passive obedience instead of trying "to put in practice the admirable alliance of order with liberty, and of variety with unity," and declaring that, for his part, he preferred taking the chances of a life of adventure to submitting himself to be "*garotté par un réglement*—tied hand and foot by a set of rules." In real truth, a life of adventure, or rather a life free to wander at its own will, was that to which his nature irresistibly impelled him.

For a career of adventure, the inevitable field was Paris. But before this career began, there came a stage, the smoothest, perhaps, and the most happy in the short life of Guérin. M. la Morvonnais, one of his La Chênaie friends—some years older than Guérin, and married to a wife of singular sweetness and charm—had a house by the seaside at the mouth of one of the beautiful rivers of Brittany, the Arguenon. He asked Guérin, when he left Ploërmel, to come and stay with him at this place, called Le Val de l'Arguenon, and Guérin spent the winter of 1833-4 there. I grudge every word about Le Val and its inmates which is not Guérin's own, so charming is the picture he draws of them, so truly does his talent find itself in its best vein as he draws it.

"How full of goodness" (he writes in his journal on the 7th of December) "is Providence to me! For fear the

sudden passage from the mild and temperate air of a religious life to the torrid clime of the world should be too
trying for my soul, it has conducted me, after I have left
my sacred shelter, to a house planted on the frontier between the two regions, where, without being in solitude,
one is not yet in the world; a house whose windows look
on the one side towards the plain where the tumult of men
is rocking, on the other towards the wilderness where the
servants of God are chanting. I intend to write down the
record of my sojourn here, for the days here spent are full
of happiness, and I know that in the time to come I shall
often turn back to the story of these past felicities. A
man, pious, and a poet; a woman, whose spirit is in such
perfect sympathy with his that you would say they had
but one being between them; a child, called Marie like
her mother, and who sends, like a star, the first rays of her
love and thought through the white cloud of infancy; a
simple life in an old-fashioned house; the ocean, which
comes morning and evening to bring us its harmonies; and
lastly, a wanderer who descends from Carmel and is going
on to Babylon, and who has laid down at this threshold
his staff and his sandals, to take his seat at the hospitable
table;—here is matter to make a biblical poem of, if I could
only describe things as I can feel them.

Every line written by Guérin during this stay at Le Val
is worth quoting, but I have only room for one extract
more:

"Never" (he writes, a fortnight later, on the 20th of
December), "never have I tasted so inwardly and deeply
the happiness of home-life. All the little details of this
life which in their succession make up the day, are to me
so many stages of a continuous charm carried from one end
of the day to the other. The morning greeting, which in
some sort renews the pleasure of the first arrival, for the

words with which one meets are almost the same, and the separation at night, through the hours of darkness and uncertainty, does not ill represent longer separations; then breakfast, during which you have the fresh enjoyment of having met together again; the stroll afterwards, when we go out and bid Nature good-morning; the return, and setting to work in an old panelled chamber looking out on the sea, inaccessible to all the stir of the house, a perfect sanctuary of labor; dinner, to which we are called, not by a bell which reminds one too much of school or a great house, but by a pleasant voice; the gayety, the merriment, the talk flitting from one subject to another and never dropping so long as the meal lasts; the crackling fire of dry branches to which we draw our chairs directly afterwards, the kind words that are spoken round the warm flame which sings while we talk; and then, if it is fine, the walk by the seaside, when the sea has for its visitors a mother with her child in her arms, this child's father and a stranger, each of these two last with a stick in his hand; the rosy lips of the little girl, which keep talking at the same time with the waves—now and then tears shed by her and cries of childish fright at the edge of the sea; our thoughts, the father's and mine, as we stand and look at the mother and child smiling at one another, or at the child in tears and the mother trying to comfort it by her caresses and exhortations; the Ocean, going on all the while rolling up his waves and noises; the dead boughs which we go and cut, here and there, out of the copse-wood, to make a quick and bright fire when we get home—this little taste of the woodman's calling which brings us closer to Nature and makes us think of M. Féli's eager fondness for the same work; the hours of study and poetical flow which carry us to supper-time; this meal, which summons us by the same gentle voice as its predecessor, and which is passed amid the same joys, only less loud, because evening sobers everything, tones everything down ; then our evening, ushered in by the blaze of a cheerful fire, and which with its alternations of reading and talking brings us at last to bedtime ;—to all the charms of a day so spent add the dreams which follow it, and your imagination will still fall far short of these home-joys in their delightful reality."

I said the foregoing should be my last extract, but who could resist this picture of a January evening on the coast of Brittany ?

"All the sky is covered over with gray clouds, just silvered at the edges. The sun, who departed a few minutes ago, has left behind him enough light to temper for awhile the black shadows, and to soften down, as it were, the approach of night. The winds are hushed, and the tranquil ocean sends up to me, when I go out on the doorstep to listen, only a melodious murmur, which dies away in the soul like a beautiful wave on the beach. The birds, the first to obey the nocturnal influence, make their way towards the woods, and you hear the rustle of their wings in the clouds. The copses which cover the whole hillside of Le Val, which all the day-time are alive with the chirp of the wren, the laughing whistle of the woodpecker,* and the different notes of a multitude of birds, have no longer any sound in their paths and thickets, unless it be the prolonged high call of the blackbirds at play with one another and chasing one another, after all the other birds have their heads safe under their wings. The noise of man, always the last to be silent, dies gradually out over the face of the fields. The general murmur fades away, and one hears

---

* "The woodpecker *laughs*," says White of Selborne : and here is Guérin, in Brittany, confirming his testimony.

hardly a sound except what comes from the villages and hamlets, in which, up till far into the night, there are cries of children and barking of dogs. Silence wraps me round; everything seeks repose except this pen of mine, which perhaps disturbs the rest of some living atom asleep in a crease of my notebook, for it makes its light scratching as it puts down these idle thoughts. Let it stop, then! for all I write, have written, or shall write, will never be worth setting against the sleep of an atom."

On the first of February we find him in a lodging at Paris. "I enter the world" (such are the last words written in his journal at Le Val) "with a secret horror." His outward history for the next five years is soon told. He found himself in Paris, poor, fastidious, and with health which already, no doubt, felt the obscure presence of the malady of which he died—consumption. One of his Brittany acquaintances introduced him to editors, tried to engage him in the periodical literature of Paris; and so unmistakable was Guérin's talent, that even his first essays were immediately accepted. But Guérin's genius was of a kind which unfitted him to get his bread in this manner. At first he was pleased with the notion of living by his pen: "*je n'ai qu'à écrire*," he says to his sister—"I have only got to write." But to a nature like his, endued with the passion for perfection, the necessity to produce, to produce constantly, to produce whether in the vein or out of the vein, to produce something good or bad or middling, as it may happen, but at all events *something*—is the most intolerable of tortures. To escape from it he betook himself to that common but most perfidious refuge of men of letters, that refuge to which Goldsmith and poor Hartley Coleridge had betaken themselves before him—the profession of teaching. In September, 1834, he procured an engagement at the Collège Stanislas, where he had himself been educated. It was vacation-time, and all he had to do was to teach a small class composed of boys who did not go home for the holidays—in his own words, " scholars left like sick sheep in the fold, while the rest of the flock are frisking in the fields." After the vacation he was kept on at the College as a supernumerary. "The master of the fifth class has asked for a month's leave of absence; I am taking his place, and by this work I get one hundred francs (£4). I have been looking about for pupils to give private lessons to, and I have found three or four. Schoolwork and private lessons together fill my day from half-past seven in the morning till half-past nine at night. The college dinner serves me for breakfast, and I go and dine in the evening at twenty-four *sous*, as a young man beginning life should." To better his position in the hierarchy of public teachers, it was necessary that he should take the degree of *agrégé-ès-lettres*, corresponding to our degree of Master of Arts; and to his heavy work in teaching there was thus added that of preparing for a severe examination. The drudgery of this life was very irksome to him, although less insupportable than the drudgery of the profession of letters; inasmuch as to a sensitive man, like Guérin, to silence his genius is more tolerable than to hackney it. Still the yoke wore him deeply, and he had moments of bitter revolt : he continued, however, to bear it with resolution, and on the whole with patience, for four years. On the 15th of November, 1838, he married a young Creole lady of some fortune, Mademoiselle Caroline de Gervain, " whom," to use his own words, " Destiny, who loves these surprises, has wafted from the farthest Indies into my arms." The marriage was happy, and it ensured to Guérin liberty and leisure ; but now "the blind Fury with the abhorred shears," was hard at hand. Consumption declared itself in him: "I pass my life," he writes, with his old playfulness and calm, to his sister, on the 8th of April, 1839, "within my bed-curtains, and wait patiently enough, thanks to Caro's * goodness, books, and dreams, for the recovery which the sunshine is to bring with it." In search of this sunshine he was taken to his native country, Languedoc, but in vain. He died at Le Cayla on the 19th of July, 1839.

The vicissitudes of his inward life during these five years were more considerable. His opinions and tastes underwent great, or what seemed to be great, changes. He came to Paris the ardent partisan of Lamennais: even in April, 1834, after Rome had finally condemned Lamennais—"To-night there will go forth from Paris," he writes, "with his face set to the west, a man whose every step I would fain follow, and who returns to the desert for which I sigh. M. Féli departs this evening for La Chênaie." But in October, 1835—"I assure you," he writes to his sister, "I am at last weaned from M. de Lamennais; one does not remain a babe and suckling forever; I am perfectly freed from his influence." There was a greater change than this. In 1834 the main cause of Guérin's aversion to the literature of the French romantic school, was that this literature, having had a religious origin had ceased to be religious: "it has forgotten," he says, "the house and the admonitions of its Father." But his friend, M. de Marzan, tells us of a "deplorable revolution" which, by 1836, had taken place in him. Guérin had become intimate with the chiefs of this very literature; he no longer went to church; "the bond of a common faith, in which our friendship had its birth, existed between us no longer." Then, again, "this interregnum was not destined to last." Reconverted to his

---

His wife.

old faith by suffering and by the pious efforts of his sister
Eugénie, Guérin died a Catholic. His feelings about society underwent a like change. After "entering the world
with a secret horror," after congratulating himself when he
had been some months at Paris on being "disengaged from
the social tumult, out of the reach of those blows which,
when I live in the thick of the world, bruise me, irritate
me, or utterly crush me," M. Sainte-Beuve tells us of
him, two years afterwards, appearing in society "a man
of the world, elegant, even fashionable; a talker who
could hold his own against the most brilliant talkers of
Paris."

In few natures, however, is there really such essential
consistency as in Guérin's. He says of himself, in the very
beginning of his journal: "I owe everything to poetry, for
.there is no other name to give to the sum total of my
thoughts; I owe to it whatever I now have pure, lofty,
and solid in my soul; I owe to it all my consolations in the
past; I shall probably owe to it my future." Poetry, the
poetical instinct, was indeed the basis of his nature; but
to say so thus absolutely is not quite enough. One aspect
of poetry fascinated Guérin's imagination and held it pris-
oner. Poetry is the interpretress of the natural world,
and she is the interpretress of the moral world; it was as
the interpretress of the natural world that she had Guérin
for her mouthpiece. To make magically near and real the
life of Nature, and man's life only so far as it is a part of
that Nature, was his faculty; a faculty of naturalistic, not
of moral interpretation. This faculty always has for its
basis a peculiar temperament, an extraordinary delicacy of
organization and susceptibility to impressions; in exercising
it the poet is in a great degree passive (Wordsworth thus
speaks of a *wise passiveness*): he aspires to be a sort of
human Æolian-harp, catching and rendering every rustle

of Nature. To assist at the evolution of the whole life of the world is his craving, and intimately to feel it all:

> " the glow, the thrill of life,
> Where, where do these abound?"

is what he asks: he resists being riveted and held stationary by any single impression, but would be borne on forever down an enchanted stream. He goes into religion and out of religion, into society and out of society, not from the motives which impel men in general, but to feel what it is all like; he is thus hardly a moral agent, and, like the passive and ineffectual Uranus of Keats's poem, he may say:

> " I am but a voice;
> My life is but the life of winds and tides;
> No more than winds and tides can I avail."

He hovers over the tumult of life, but does not really put his hand to it.

No one has expressed the aspirations of this temperament better than Guérin himself. In the last year of his life he writes:

"I return, as you see, to my old brooding over the world of Nature, that line which my thoughts irresistibly take; a sort of passion which gives me enthusiasm, tears, bursts of joy, and an eternal food for musing; and yet I am neither philosopher, nor naturalist, nor anything learned whatsoever. There is one word which is the God of my imagination, the tyrant, I ought rather to say, that fascinates it, lures it onward, gives it work to do without ceasing, and will finally carry it I know not where; the word *life*."

And in one place in his journal he says:

"My imagination welcomes every dream, every impression, without attaching itself to any, and goes on forever seeking something new."

And again, in another:

"The longer I · live, and the clearer I discern between true and false in society, the more does the inclination to live, not as a savage or a misanthrope, but as a solitary man on the frontiers of society, on the outskirts of the world, gain strength and grow in me. The birds come and go and make nests around our habitations, they are fellow-citizens of our farms and hamlets with us; but they take their flight in a heaven which is boundless, but the hand of God alone gives and measures to them their daily food, but they build their nests in the heart of the thick bushes, or hang them in the height of the trees. So would I, too, live, hovering round society, and having always at my back a field of liberty vast as the sky."

In the same spirit he longed for travel. "When one is a wanderer," he writes to his sister, "one feels that one fulfils the true condition of humanity." And the last entry in his journal is—"The stream of travel is full of delight. O, who will set me adrift on this Nile!"

Assuredly it is not in this temperament that the active virtues have their rise. On the contrary, this temperament, considered in itself alone, indisposes for the discharge of them. Something morbid and excessive, as manifested in Guérin, it undoubtedly has. In him, as in Keats, and as in another youth of genius, whose name, but the other day unheard of, Lord Houghton has so gracefully written in the history of English poetry—David Gray—the temperament, the talent itself, is deeply influenced by their mysterious malady; the temperament is *devouring;* it uses vital power too hard and too fast, paying the penalty in long hours of unutterable exhaustion and in premature death. The intensity of Guérin's depression is described to us by Guérin himself with the same incomparable touch with which he describes happier feelings; far oftener than any pleasurable sense of his gift he has "the sense profound, near, immense, of my misery, of my inward poverty." And again: "My inward misery gains upon me; I no longer dare look within." And on another day of gloom he does look within, and here is the terrible analysis:

"Craving, unquiet, seeing only by glimpses, my spirit is stricken by all those ills which are the sure fruit of a youth doomed never to ripen into manhood. I grow old and wear myself out in the most futile mental strainings, and make no progress. My head seems dying, and when the wind blows I fancy I feel it, as if I were a tree, blowing through a number of withered branches in my top. Study is intolerable to me, or rather it is quite out of my power. Mental work brings on, not drowsiness, but an irritable and nervous disgust which drives me out, I know not where, into the streets and public places. The Spring, whose delights used to come every year stealthily and mysteriously to charm me in my retreat, crushes me this year under a weight of sudden hotness. I should be glad of any event which delivered me from the situation in which I am. If I were free I would embark for some distant country where I could begin life anew."

. Such is this temperament in the frequent hours when the sense of its own weakness and isolation crushes it to the ground. Certainly it was not for Guérin's happiness, or for Keats's, as men count happiness, to be as they were. Still the very excess and predominance of their temperament has given to the fruits of their genius an unique brilliancy and flavor. I have said that poetry interprets in two ways; it interprets by expressing with magical felicity the physiognomy and movement of the outward

13*

world, and it interprets by expressing, with inspired conviction, the ideas and laws of the inward world of man's moral and spiritual nature. In other words, poetry is interpretative both by having *natural magic* in it, and by having *moral profundity*. In both ways it illuminates man; it gives him a satisfying sense of reality; it reconciles him with himself and the universe. Thus Æschylus's "δράσαντι παθεῖν" and his "ἀνήριθμον γέλασμα" are alike interpretative. Shakespeare interprets both when he says,

> "Full many a glorious morning have I seen,
> Flatter the mountain-tops with sovran eye;"

and when he says,

> "There's a divinity that shapes our ends,
> Rough-hew them as we will."

These great poets unite in themselves the faculty of both kinds of interpretation, the naturalistic and the moral. But it is observable that in the poets who unite both kinds, the latter (the moral) usually ends by making itself the master. In Shakespeare the two kinds seem wonderfully to balance one another; but even in him the balance leans; his expression tends to become too little sensuous and simple, too much intellectualized. The same thing may be yet more strongly affirmed of Lucretius and of Wordsworth. In Shelley there is not a balance of the two gifts, nor even a co-existence of them, but there is a passionate straining after them both, and this is what makes Shelley, as a man, so interesting. I will not now inquire how much Shelley achieves as a poet, but whatever he achieves, he in general fails to achieve natural magic in his expression; in Mr. Palgrave's charming "Treasury" may be seen a gallery of his failures.* But in Keats and Guérin, in whom the faculty of naturalistic interpretation is overpoweringly predominant, the natural magic is perfect; when they speak of the world they speak like Adam naming by divine inspiration the creatures; their expression corresponds with the thing's essential reality. Even between Keats and Guérin, however, there is a distinction to be drawn. Keats has, above all, a sense of what is pleasurable and open in the life of Nature; for him she is the *Alma Parens:* his expression has, therefore, more than Guérin's, something genial, outward, and sensuous. Guérin has above all a sense of what there is adorable and secret in the life of Nature; for him she is the *Magna Parens:* his expression has, therefore, more than Keats's, something mystic, inward, and profound.

So he lived like a man possessed; with his eye not on his own career, not on the public, not on fame, but on the Isis whose veil he had uplifted. He published nothing: "There is more power and beauty," he writes, "in the well-kept secret of one's self and one's thoughts, than in the display of a whole heaven that one may have inside one." "My spirit," he answers the friends who urge him to write, "is of the home-keeping order, and has no fancy for adventure; literary adventure is above all distasteful to it; for this, indeed (let me say so without the least self-sufficiency), it has a contempt. The literary career seems

---

* Compare, for example, his "Lines Written in the Euganean Hills," with Keats's "Ode to Autumn" ("Golden Treasury," pp. 256, 284). The latter piece *renders* Nature; the former *tries to render* her. I will not deny, however, that Shelley has natural magic in his rhythm; what I deny is, that he has it in his language. It always seems to me that the right sphere for Shelley's genius was the sphere of music, not of poetry; the medium of sounds he can master. but to master the more difficult medium of words he has neither intellectual force enough nor sanity enough.

to me unreal, both in its own essence and in the rewards which one seeks from it, and therefore fatally marred by a secret absurdity." His acquaintances, and among them distinguished men of letters, full of admiration for the originality and delicacy of his talent, laughed at his self-depreciation, warmly assured him of his powers. He received their assurances with a mournful incredulity, which contrasts curiously with the self-assertion of poor David Gray, whom I just now mentioned. "It seems to me intolerable," he writes, "to appear to men other than one appears to God. My worst torture at this moment is the over-estimate which generous friends form of me. We are told that at the last judgment the secret of all consciences will be laid bare to the universe; would that mine were so this day, and that every passer-by could see me as I am!" "High above my head," he says at another time, "far, far away, I seem to hear the murmur of that world of thought and feeling to which I aspire so often, but where I can never attain. I think of those of my own age who have wings strong enough to reach it, but I think of them without jealousy, and as men on earth contemplate the elect and their felicity." And, criticising his own composition, "When I begin a subject, my self-conceit" (says this exquisite artist) "imagines I am doing wonders; and when I have finished, I see nothing but a wretched made-up imitation, composed of odds and ends of color stolen from other people's palates, and tastelessly mixed together on mine." Such was his *passion for perfection*, his disdain for all poetical work not perfectly adequate and felicitous. The magic of expression to which by the force of this passion he won his way, will make the name of Maurice de Guérin remembered in literature.

I have already mentioned the "Centaur," a sort of prose poem by Guérin, which Madame Sand published after his death. The idea of this composition came to him, M. Sainte-Beuve says, in the course of some visits which he made with his friend, M. Trebutien, a learned antiquarian, to the Museum of Antiquities in the Louvre. The free and wild life which the Greeks expressed by such creations as the Centaur had, as we might well expect, a strong charm for him; under the same inspiration he composed a " Bacchante," which was meant by him to form part of a prose poem on the adventures of Bacchus in India. Real as was the affinity which Guérin's nature had for these subjects, I doubt whether, in treating them, he would have found the full and final employment of his talent. But the beauty of his " Centaur" is extraordinary; in its whole conception and expression this piece has in a wonderful degree that natural magic of which I have said so much, and the rhythm has a charm which bewitches even a foreigner. An old Centaur on his mountain, is supposed to relate to Melampus, a human questioner, the life of his youth. Untranslatable as the piece is, I shall conclude with some extracts from it : .

"THE CENTAUR.

" I had my birth in the caves of these mountains. Like the stream of this valley, whose first drops trickle from some weeping rock in a deep cavern, the first moment of my life fell in the. darkness of a remote abode, and without breaking the silence. When our mothers draw near to the time of their delivery, they withdraw to the caverns, and in the depth of the loneliest of them, in the thickest of its gloom, bring forth, without uttering a plaint, a fruit silent as themselves. Their puissant milk makes us surmount, without weakness or dubious struggle, the first difficulties of life; and yet we leave our caverns later than you your cradles. The reason is that we have a doctrine that the early days of existence should be kept apart and enshrouded, as days filled with the presence of the gods. Nearly the whole term of my growth was passed in the darkness where I was born. The recesses of my dwelling ran so far under the mountain, that I should not have known on which side was the exit, had not the winds, when they sometimes made their way through the opening, sent fresh airs in, and a sudden trouble. Sometimes, too, my mother came back to me, having about her the odors of the valleys, or streaming from the waters which were her haunt. Her returning thus, without a word said of the valleys or the rivers, but with the emanations from them hanging about her, troubled my spirit, and I moved up and down restlessly in my darkness. 'What is it,' I cried, 'this outside world whither my mother is borne, and what reigns there in it so potent as to attract her so often?' At these moments my own force began to make me unquiet. I felt in it a power which could not remain idle; and betaking myself either to toss my arms or to gallop backwards and forwards in the spacious darkness of the cavern, I tried to make out, from the blows which I dealt in the empty space, or from the transport of my course through it, in what direction my arms were meant to reach, or my feet to bear me. Since that day, I have wound my arms round the bust of Centaurs, and round the body of heroes, and round the trunk of oaks; my hands have assayed the rocks, the waters, plants without number, and the subtlest impressions of the air—for I uplift them in the dark and still nights to catch the breaths of wind, and to draw signs whereby I may augur my road; my feet—look, O Melampus, how worn they are! And yet, all benumbed as I am in this extremity of age, there are days when, in broad ·sunlight, on the mountain-tops, I renew these gallopings of my youth in the cavern, and with the same object, brandishing my arms and employing all the fleetness which yet is left to me.

.   .   .   .

"O Melampus, thou who wouldst know the life of the Centaurs, wherefore have the gods willed that thy steps should lead thee to me, the oldest and most forlorn of them all? It is long since I have ceased to practise any part of their life. I quit no more this mountain summit, to which age has confined me. The point of my arrows now serves me only to uproot some tough-fibred plant; the tranquil lakes know me still, but the rivers have forgotten me. I will tell thee a little of my youth; but these recollections, issuing from a worn memory, come like the drops of a niggardly libation poured from a damaged urn.

"The course of my youth was rapid and full of agitation. Movement was my life, and my steps knew no bound. One day when I was following the course of a valley seldom entered by the Centaurs, I discovered a man making his way up the stream-side on the opposite bank. He was the first whom my eyes had lighted on. I despised him. 'Behold,' I cried, 'at the utmost but the half of what I am! How short are his steps! and his movement how full of labor! Doubtless he is a Centaur overthrown by the gods, and reduced by them to drag himself along thus.'

.   .   .   .

"Wandering along at my own will like the rivers, feeling wherever I went the presence of Cybele, whether in the bed of the valleys, or on the height of the mountains, I bounded whither I would, like a blind and chainless life. But when Night, filled with the charm of the gods, overtook me on the slopes of the mountain, she guided me to the mouth of the caverns, and there tranquillized me as she tranquillizes the billows of the sea. Stretched across the threshold of my retreat, my flanks hidden within the cave, and my head under the open sky, I watched the spectacle of the dark. The sea-gods, it is said, quit during the hours of darkness their palaces under the deep; they seat themselves on the promontories, and their eyes wander over the expanse of the waves. Even so I kept watch, having at my feet an expanse of life like the hushed sea. My regards had free range, and travelled to the most distant points. Like sea-beaches which never lose their wetness, the line of mountains to the west retained the imprint of gleams not perfectly wiped out by the shadows. In that quarter still survived, in pale clearness, mountain-summits naked and pure. There I beheld at one time the god Pan descend, ever solitary; at another, the choir of the mystic divinities; or I saw pass some mountain-nymph charm-struck by the night. Sometimes the eagles of Mount Olympus traversed the upper sky, and were lost to view among the far-off constellations, or in the shade of the dreaming forests.

"Thou pursuest after wisdom, O Melampus, which is the science of the will of the gods; and thou roamest from people to people like a mortal driven by the destinies. In the times when I kept my night-watches before the caverns, I have sometimes believed that I was about to surprise the thought of the sleeping Cybele, and that the mother of the gods, betrayed by her dreams, would let fall some of her secrets; but I have never made out more than sounds which faded away in the murmur of night, or words inarticulate as the bubbling of the rivers.

"'O Macareus,' one day said the great Chiron to me, whose old age I tended; 'we are, both of us, Centaurs of the mountain; but how different are our lives! Of my days all the study is (thou seest it) the search for plants; thou, thou art like those mortals who have picked up on the waters or in the woods, and carried to their lips, some pieces of the reed-pipe thrown away by the god Pan. From that hour these mortals, having caught from their relics of the god a passion for wild life, or perhaps smitten with some secret madness, enter into the wilderness, plunge among the forests, follow the course of the streams, bury themselves in the heart of the mountains, restless, and haunted by an unknown purpose. The mares, beloved of the winds in the farthest Scythia, are not wilder than thou, nor more cast down at nightfall, when the North Wind has departed. Seekest thou to know the gods, O Macareus, and from what source men, animals, and the elements of the universal fire have their origin? But the aged Ocean, the father of all things, keeps locked within his own breast these secrets; and the nymphs who stand around sing as they weave their eternal dance before him, to cover any sound which might escape from his lips half-opened by slumber. The mortals, dear to the gods for their virtue, have received from their hands lyres to give delight to man, or the seeds of new plants to make him rich; but from their inexorable lips, nothing!'

.   .   .   .

" Such were the lessons which the old Chiron gave me. Waned to the very extremity of life, the Centaur yet nourished in his spirit the most lofty discourse.

.   .   .   .

" For me, O Melampus, I decline unto my last days, calm as the setting of the constellations. I still retain enterprise enough to climb to the top of the rocks, and there

I linger late, either gazing on the wild and restless clouds, or to see come up from the horizon the rainy Hyades, the Pleiades, or the great Orion; but I feel myself perishing and passing quickly away, like a snow-wreath floating on the stream; and soon I shall be mingled with the waters which flow in the vast bosom of Earth."

DENIS DIDEROT.

(1713–1784.)

ONE of the most active and original of the famous group of men of letters in France in the middle of the eighteenth century. He was born at Langres in 1713. He was educated by the Jesuits, like most of those who afterwards became the bitterest enemies of Catholicism; and, when his education was at an end, he vexed his brave and worthy father's heart by turning away from respectable callings, like law or medicine, and throwing himself into the vagabond life of a bookseller's hack in Paris. An imprudent marriage (1743) did not better his position. His wife was a devout Catholic, but her piety did not restrain a narrow and fretful temper, and Diderot's domestic life was irregular and unhappy. He sought consolation for chagrins at home, in attachments abroad, first with a Madame Puisieux, a fifth-rate female scribbler, and then with Mdlle. Voland, to whom he was constant for the rest of her life. His letters to her are among the most graphic of all the pictures that we have of the daily life of the philosophic circle in Paris. An interesting contrast may be made between the Bohemianism of the famous literary set who supped at the Turk's Head with the Tory Johnson and the Conservative Burke for their oracles, and the Bohemianism of the set who about the same time dined once a week at the Baron

D'Holbach's, to listen to the wild sallies and the inspiring declamations of Diderot. For Diderot was not a great writer; he stands out as a fertile, suggestive, and daring thinker, and a prodigious and most eloquent talker.

Diderot's earliest writings were of as little importance as Goldsmith's "Enquiry into the State of Polite Learning," or Burke's "Abridgement of English History." He earned one hundred crowns by translating Stanyan's "History of Greece;" with two colleagues he produced a translation of James's "Dictionary of Medicine;" and about the same date (1745) he published a free rendering of Shaftesbury's "Inquiry Concerning Virtue and Merit," with some original notes of his own. With strange and characteristic versatility, he turned from ethical speculation to the composition of a volume of stories, which are gross without liveliness, and impure without wit. In later years he repented of this shameless work, just as Boccaccio is said, in the day of his gray hairs to have thought of the sprightliness of the "Decameron" with strong remorse. From tales Diderot went back to the more congenial region of philosophy. Between the morning of Good Friday and the evening of Easter Monday he wrote the "Philosophic Thoughts" (1746), and he presently added to this a short complementary essay, "On the Sufficiency of Natural Religion." The gist of these performances is to press the ordinary rationalistic objections to a supernatural revelation; but though Diderot did not at this time pass out into the wilderness beyond natural religion, yet there are signs that he accepted that less as a positive doctrine, resting on grounds of its own, than as a convenient point of attack against Christianity. In 1747 he wrote the "Sceptic's Walk," a rather poor allegory —pointing first to the extravagances of Catholicism; second, to the vanity of the pleasures of that world which is the rival of the church; and third, to the desperate and unfathomable uncertainty of the philosophy which professes to be so high above both church and world.

Diderot's next piece was what first introduced him to the world as an original thinker, his famous "Letter on the Blind" (1749). The immediate object of this short but pithy writing was to show the dependence of men's ideas on their five senses. It considers the case of the intellect deprived of the aid of one of the senses; and in a second piece, published afterwards, Diderot considered the case of a similar deprivation in the deaf and dumb. The "Letter on Deaf-Mutes," however, is substantially a digressive examination of some points in æsthetics. The philosophic significance of the two essays is in the advance they make towards the principle of relativity. But what interested the militant philosophers of that day was an episodic application of the principle of relativity to the master-conception of God. What makes the "Letter on the Blind" interesting at the present moment is its presentation, in a distinct though undigested form, of the modern theory of variability, and of survival by superior adaptation. It is worth noticing, too, as an illustration of the comprehensive freedom with which Diderot felt his way round any subject that he approached, that in this theoretic essay he suggests the possibility of teaching the blind to read through the sense of touch. If the "Letter on the Blind" introduced Diderot into the worshipful company of the philosophers, it also introduced him to the penalties of philosophy. His speculation was too hardy for the authorities, and he was thrown into the prison of Vincennes. Here he remained for three months; then he was released, to enter upon the gigantic undertaking of his life.

A certain bookseller had applied to him with a project for the translation into French of Ephraim Chambers's "Cyclopædia." Diderot accepted the proposal, but in his

busy and pregnant intelligence the scheme became transformed. Instead of a mere reproduction of Chambers, he
persuaded the bookseller to enter upon a new work, which
should collect under one roof all the active writers, all the
new ideas, all the new knowledge, that were then moving
the cultivated class to its depths, but still were comparatively
ineffectual by reason of their dispersion. His enthusiasm
infected the publishers; they collected a sufficient capital
for a vaster enterprise than they had at first planned;
D'Alembert was persuaded to become Diderot's colleague;
the requisite permission was procured from the Government; in 1750 an elaborate prospectus announced the project to a delighted public; and in 1751 the first volume
was given to the world. The last of the letterpress was
issued in 1765, but it was 1772 before the subscribers received the final volumes of the plates. These twenty years
were to Diderot years not merely of incessant drudgery,
but of harassing persecution, of sufferings from the cabals of
enemies, and of injury from the desertion of friends. The
ecclesiastical party detested the "Encyclopædia," in which
they saw a rising stronghold for their philosophic enemies.
By 1757 they could endure the sight no longer. The subscribers had grown from two thousand to four thousand, and
this was a right measure of the growth of the work in popular influence and power. To any one who turns over the
pages of these redoubtable volumes now, it seems surprising that their doctrines should have stirred such portentous
alarm. There is no atheism, no overt attack on any of the
cardinal mysteries of the faith, no direct denunciation even
of the notorious abuses of the church. Yet we feel that
the atmosphere of the book may well have been displeasing
to authorities who had not yet learned to encounter the
modern spirit on equal terms. The "Encyclopædia" takes
for granted the justice of religious tolerance and specu-

lative freedom. It asserts in distinct tones the democratic doctrine that it is the common people in a nation whose lot ought to be the main concern of the nation's government. From beginning to end it is one unbroken process of exaltation of scientific knowledge on the one hand, and pacific industry on the other. All these things were odious to the old governing classes of France; their spirit was absolutist, ecclesiastical, and military. Perhaps the most alarming thought of all was the current belief that the "Encyclopædia" was the work of an organized band of conspirators against society, and that a pestilent doctrine was now made truly formidable by the confederation of its preachers into an open league. When the seventh volume appeared, it contained an article on "Geneva," written by D'Alembert. The writer contrived a panegyric on the pastors of Geneva, of which every word was a stinging reproach to the abbés and prelates of Versailles. At the same moment Helvétius's book, "L'Esprit," appeared, and gave a still more profound and, let us add, a more reasonable shock to the ecclesiastical party. Authority could brook no more, and in 1759 the "Encyclopædia" was formally suppressed.

The decree, however, did not arrest the continuance of the work. The connivance of the authorities at the breach of their own official orders was common in those times of distracted government. The work went on, but its difficulties increased by the necessity of being clandestine. And a worse thing than troublesome interference by the police now befell Diderot. D'Alembert, wearied of shifts and indignities, withdrew from the enterprise. Other powerful colleagues, Turgot among them, declined to contribute further to a book which had acquired an evil fame. Diderot was left to bring the task to an end as he best could. For seven years he labored like a slave at the oar.

He wrote several hundred articles, some of them very slight, but many of them most laborious, comprehensive, and ample. He wore out his eyesight in correcting proofs, and he wearied his soul in bringing the manuscript of less competent contributors into decent shape. He spent his days in the workshops, mastering the processes of manufactures, and his nights in reproducing on paper what he had learned during the day. And he was incessantly harassed all the time by alarms of a descent from the police. At the last moment, when his immense work was just drawing to an end, he encountered one last and crowning mortification : he discovered that the bookseller, fearing the displeasure of the Government, had struck out from the proof-sheets, after they had left Diderot's hands, all passages that he chose to think too hardy. The monument to which Diderot had given the labor of twenty long and oppressive years was irreparably mutilated and defaced. It is calculated that the average annual salary received by Diderot for his share in the "Encyclopædia" was about £120 sterling. "And then to think," said Voltaire, "that an army contractor makes £800 in a day."

Although the "Encyclopædia" was Diderot's monumental work, he is the author of a shower of dispersed pieces that sowed nearly every field of intellectual interest with new and fruitful ideas. We find no masterpiece, but only thoughts for masterpieces ; no creation, but a criticism with the quality to inspire and direct creation. He wrote plays—"Le Fils Naturel" and "Le Père de Famille"— and they are very insipid performances in the sentimental vein. But he accompanied them by essays on dramatic poetry, including especially the "Paradoxe sur le Comédien," in which he announced the principles of a new drama—the serious, domestic, bourgeois drama of real life —in opposition to the stilted conventions of the classic

French stage. It was Diderot's lessons and example that gave a decisive bias to the dramatic taste of Lessing, whose plays, and his "Hamburgische Dramaturgie" (1768), mark so important an epoch in the history of the modern theatre. In the pictorial art, Diderot's criticisms are no less rich, fertile, and wide in their ideas. His article on "Beauty," in the "Encyclopædia," shows that he had mastered and passed beyond the metaphysical theories on the subject, and the "Essay on Painting" was justly described by Goethe, who thought it worth translating, as "a magnificent work, which speaks even more helpfully to the poet than to the painter, though to the painter too it is as a blazing torch." Diderot's most intimate friend was Grimm, one of the conspicuous figures of the philosophic body. Grimm wrote news-letters to various high personages in Germany, reporting what was going on in the world of art and literature in Paris, then without a rival as the capital of the intellectual activity of Europe. Diderot helped his friend at one time and another between 1759 and 1779, by writing for him an account of the annual exhibitions of paintings. These *Salons* are among the most readable of all pieces of art criticism. They have a freshness, a reality, a life, which took their readers into a different world from the dry and conceited pedantries of the ordinary virtuoso. As has been said by Sainte-Beuve, they initiated the French into a new sentiment, and introduced people to the mystery and purport of color by ideas. "Before Diderot," Madame Necker said, "I had never seen anything in pictures except dull and lifeless colors; it was his imagination that gave them relief and life, and it is almost a new sense for which I am indebted to his genius." Greuze was Diderot's favorite among contemporary artists, and it is easy to see why. Greuze's most characteristic pictures were the rendering in color of the same

14

sentiment of domestic virtue and the pathos of common life, which Diderot attempted with inferior success to represent upon the stage. For Diderot was above all things interested in the life of men—not the abstract life of the race, but the incidents of individual character, the fortunes of a particular family, the relations of real and concrete motives in this or that special case.

He delighted with the enthusiasm of a born casuist in curious puzzles of right and wrong, and in devising a conflict between the generalities of ethics and the conditions of an ingeniously contrived practical dilemma. Mostly his interest expressed itself in didactic and sympathetic form. In two, however, of the most remarkable of all his pieces, it is not sympathetic but ironical. "Jacques le Fataliste" (written in 1773, but not published until 1796) is in manner an imitation of "Tristram Shandy" and "The Sentimental Journey." Few modern readers will find in it any true diversion. In spite of some excellent criticisms dispersed here and there, and in spite of one or two stories that are not without a certain effective realism, it must as a whole be pronounced savorless, forced, and as leaving unmoved those springs of laughter and of tears which are the common fountain of humor. "Rameau's Nephew" is a far superior performance. If there were any inevitable compulsion to name a masterpiece for Diderot, one must select this singular "farce-tragedy." Its intention has been matter of dispute; whether it was designed to be merely a satire on contemporary manners, or a reduction of the theory of self-interest to an absurdity, or the application of an ironical clencher to the ethics of ordinary convention, or a mere setting for a discussion about music, or a vigorous dramatic sketch of a parasite and a human original. There is no dispute as to its curious literary flavor, its mixed qualities of pungency, bitterness, pity, and, in places, unflinching shamelessness. Goethe's translation (1805) was the first introduction of "Rameau's Nephew" to the European public. After executing it, he gave back the original French manuscript to Schiller, from whom he had it. No authentic French copy of it appeared until the writer had been nearly forty years in his grave (1823).

It would take several pages merely to contain the list of Diderot's miscellaneous pieces, from an infinitely graceful trifle like the "Regrets on My Old Dressing Gown," up to "D'Alembert's Dream," where he plunges into the depths of the controversy as to the ultimate constitution of matter and the meaning of life. It is a mistake to set down Diderot for a coherent and systematic materialist. We ought to look upon him "as a philosopher in whom all the contradictions of the time struggle with one another" (Rosenkranz). That is to say, he is critical and not dogmatic. There is no unity in Diderot, as there was in Voltaire or in Rousseau. Just as in cases of conduct, he loves to make new ethical assumptions and argue them out as a professional sophist might have done; so, in the speculative problems as to the organization of matter, the origin of life, the compatibility between physiological machinery and free-will, he takes a certain standpoint, and follows it out more or less digressively to its consequences. He seizes an hypothesis and works it to its end, and this made him the inspirer in others of materialist doctrines which they held more definitely than he did. Just as Diderot could not attain to the concentration, the positiveness, the finality of aim needed for a masterpiece of literature, so he could not attain to those qualities in the way of dogma and system. Yet he drew at last to the conclusions of materialism, and contributed many of its most declamatory pages to the "Système de la Nature" of his friend D'Holbach—the very Bible of atheism, as some one styled it. All that he saw, if we reduce his opinions to formulas, was motion in space: "attraction and repulsion, the only truth." If matter produces life by spontaneous generation, and if man has no alternative but to obey the compulsion of nature, what remains for God to do?

In proportion as these conclusions deepened in him, the more did Diderot turn for the hope of the race to virtue; in other words, to such a regulation of conduct and motive as shall make us tender, pitiful, simple, contented. Hence his one great literary passion, his enthusiasm for Richardson, our English novelist. Hence, also, his deepening aversion for the political system of France, which made the realization of a natural and contented domestic life so hard. Diderot had almost as much to say against society as even Rousseau himself. The difference between them was that Rousseau was a fervent theist. The atheism of the Holbachians, as he called Diderot's group, was intolerable to him; and this feeling, aided by certain private perversities of humor, led to a breach of what had once been an intimate friendship between Rousseau and Diderot (1757). Diderot was still alive when the "Confessions" appeared, and he was so exasperated by Rousseau's stories about Grimm, then and always Diderot's intimate, that in 1782 he transformed a life of Seneca, that he had written four years earlier, into an "Essay on the Reigns of Claudius and Nero," which is much less an account of Seneca than a vindication of Diderot and Grimm, and is one of the most rambling and inept productions in litera-ture. As for the merits of the old quarrel between Rousseau and Diderot, we may agree with the latter, that too many sensible people would be in the wrong if Jean Jacques was in the right.

Varied and incessant as was Diderot's mental activity, it was not of a kind to bring him riches. He secured none of the posts that were occasionally given to needy men of letters; he could not even obtain that bare official recognition of merit which was implied by being chosen a member of the Academy.

The time came for him to provide a dower for his daughter, and he saw no other alternative than to sell his library. When the Empress Catharine of Russia heard of his straits, she commissioned an agent in Paris to buy the library at a price equal to about £1,000 of our money, and then she handsomely requested the philosopher to retain the books in Paris until she required them, and to constitute himself her librarian, with a yearly salary. · In 1773 Diderot started on an expedition to thank his imperial benefactress in person, and he passed some months at St. Petersburg. The empress received him cordially. The strange pair passed their afternoons in disputes on a thousand points of high philosophy, and they debated with a vivacity and freedom not usual in courts. "*Fi, donc,*" said Catherine, one day, when Diderot hinted that he argued with her at a disadvantage, "*is there any difference among men ?*" Diderot returned home in 1774. Ten years remained to him, and he spent them in the industrious acquisition of new knowledge, in the composition of a host of fragmentary pieces, some of them mentioned above, and in luminous declamations with his friends. All accounts agree that Diderot was seen at his best in. conversation. "He who only knows Diderot in his writings," says Marmontel, "does not know him at all. When he grew animated in talk, and allowed his thoughts to flow in all their. abundance, then he became truly ravishing. In his writings he had not the art of ensemble; the first operation which orders and places everything was too slow and too painful to him." Diderot himself was conscious of the want of literary merit in his pieces. In truth he set no high value on what he had done.   It is doubtful whether he was ever alive to the waste that circumstances and temperament together made of an intelligence from which, if it had been free to work systematically, the world of thought had so much to hope. He was one of those simple, disinterested, and intellectually sterling workers to whom their own personality is as nothing in presence of the vast subjects that engage the thoughts of their lives.   He wrote what he found to write, and left the piece, as Carlyle has said, "on the waste of accident, with an ostrich-like indifference."   When he heard one day that a collected edition of his works was in the press at Amsterdam, he greeted the news with "peals of laughter," so well did he know the haste and the little heed with which those works had been dashed off.

Diderot died in the month of July, 1784, six years after Voltaire and Rousseau, one year after his old colleague, D'Alembert, and five years before D'Holbach, his host and intimate for a lifetime.   Notwithstanding Diderot's peals of laughter at the thought, there is now just completed—nearly a hundred years since his death—an elaborate and exhaustive collection of his writings, in twenty stout vloumes, edited by MM. Assézat and Tourneaux.

JEAN DE LA FONTAINE.

(1621.)

JEAN DE LA FONTAINE, the celebrated French fabulist, and one of the greatest of French poets, was born in 1621 at Château-Thierry, in Champagne. His father was Maître des Eaux et des Forêts in that town, and had little time to bestow on the education of his son, who did not exhibit a spark of intelligence till he had reached his twenty-second year. At Rheims, where he got all the education he ever received, he devoted himself more to pleasure than to study, and, in after days, described in flowing melodious verse the gallantries of which he had then been guilty. In 1641 he entered the monastery of the Oratoire, but finding the monkish way of life extremely distasteful, he left it and returned home. Soon after this he married, and succeeded his father in his office, performed his duties extremely ill, and finally abandoned his wife (with whom he had lived on very indifferent terms) to go to Paris in the train of the Duchesse de Bouillon, niece of Cardinal Mazarin. Before this time, however, his mind had begun to awaken to a consciousness of its strength. An ode of Malherbe, which was once read in his hearing, is said to have elicited from him the expression, "I, too, am a poet," and to have first stimulated him to literary enterprise. He began a systematic study of the writers of his own country and of the ancient classics, and the first fruits of his labors was a translation of the "Eunuchus" of Terence. This work had very poor success, and was in many respects so unsatisfactory as not to deserve much. In the French metropolis La Fontaine was kindly received, and spent much of his time and far more money than he could afford in the pursuit of those pleasures for which that city affords unrivalled facilities; but none of the reverses of fortune by which he was overtaken ever altered his disposition in the least.

His indifference to his worldly affairs compelled him to sell, year by year, a portion of his patrimonial estate, and it is not known to what straits he might have been reduced, had not a charitable lady, Mme. de La Sablière, received him into her house and taken care of him for twenty years. When driven by her own necessities to reduce her establishment, this lady used to talk to her friends of having retained only her three animals—her dog, her cat, and La Fontaine. In 1684 La Fontaine was admitted into the French Academy; but Louis XIV., indignant that he should have been preferred to Boileau, refused to sanction his appointment. Another vacancy occurring soon after, gave an opportunity for Boileau's election, and both candidates were admitted without any opposition from the king. On the death of Mme. de La Sablière, La Fontaine was reduced to great extremities, and had seriously bethought himself of going to England on the invitation of St. Evremond. Luckily, the kind intervention of the Duke of Burgundy in his behalf enabled him to remain at home. His health at this time became very bad, and was not much improved by his squabbles with the clergy, who, believing him to be dying, threatened him with the terrors of the Church unless he made a public apology for his licentious tales, and burned a comedy which he was preparing for the stage. After a good deal of hesitation, he complied with both these demands. In 1693 his health became rapidly worse, and he spent the most of his time in translating hymns for the Church and in other literary exercises, chiefly of a religious character. His last days were cared for by the kindness of his friend D'Hervart, who received him into his house and tended him with almost filial care till his death in 1695.

The character of La Fontaine is a curious medley of strength and weakness. His acute perception of what was right, and his inability to practise it, remind us of Richard Steele. His invincible laziness and good humor are only to be paralleled by the similar qualities in the author of "The Seasons." His shrewd yet childlike simplicity, his vanity, his tenderness of heart, his awkwardness, and his absence of mind, are all qualities which he had in common with our own Goldsmith; and, indeed, the epithet of "inspired idiot," unjustly applied to that author, might with much propriety have been given to the French fabulist. His weaknesses were all of a kind that made him at once the pet and the laughing-stock of his friends. With Racine, Molière, and Boileau he lived on terms of the most intimate friendship. They often rallied him, and sometimes with good reason, on his many failings; but, as Molière said on one of these occasions, "Ils ont beau se trémousser, ils n'effaceront pas le bonhomme." The sobriquet of "Le Bonhomme" was so pat that it stuck to him through life, and has been confirmed by posterity. He often exhibited the strangest want of interest in matters of the deepest concern, and a dreamy absorption in trifles, such as seemed to argue some unaccountable intellectual weakness. Possessed, as he undoubtedly was, of rare and remarkable literary powers, his range both of sympathy and knowledge in literary affairs was astonishingly limited. On one occa-

14*

sion, hearing Racine read some extracts from Plato, he suddenly broke out into a rhapsody of admiration for the Greek philosopher, whom he praised as one of the most amusing of writers. At another time, being present at a theological debate that was carried on with much spirit, he fell asleep, and, on awakening, asked the company whether they thought that St. Augustine was as witty a writer as Rabelais. Racine once took him to the "Tenebræ," and seeing that he was wearied by the length of the performance, put a Bible into his hands. La Fontaine opened it at the book of Baruch, and was so much struck with what he there read, that he could not help crying out to his companion : " This Baruch is a very fine writer ; do you know anything of him ?" And for several days after, he asked everybody that he met: " Have you ever read Baruch ? He's a man of first-rate genius. Do you know who he was ?" One day he met his own son, whom he did not recognize, and remarked to him that he was a lad of parts and spirit. Being told that the youth was his own son, he merely observed that "he was very glad to hear it." In 1693, when he was believed to be dying, Poujet, vicar of St. Roch, brought him the New Testament. He read it, and assured his friends : " Je vous assure que c'est un fort bon livre ; oui, par ma foi, c'est un fort bon livre."

As an author, La Fontaine will be best known to posterity by his Fables. He published other works, of which the best known are his " Contes," or Tales, the first volume of which appeared in 1664, the second in 1671. These abound in fine touches of his genius, but are polluted with such a taint of gross license and indecency, that they are now seldom read even by his own countrymen. As a fabulist, however, La Fontaine has never had his equal, either in ancient or modern times. He has, indeed, little or no originality of invention, for most of his tales are taken from Boccaccio, Ariosto, Machiavelli, and others, and Æsop has suggested the idea of the great majority of his fables. His reflections are not remarkable either for depth or novelty, and he displays an almost total incapacity for continuous thinking; but his manner of telling his stories is quite inimitable, and in that lies the principal charm of his writings. "His narrative," as has been remarked by Laharpe, "is distinguished by that ease and grace which are to be perceived, not described; for if, after a profound philosophical investigation, we arrived at the ultimate causes of excellence, and referred the matter to La Fontaine himself, the 'bonhomme' would say, 'I know nothing about all this; I wrote as my humor dictated, and that was all.'" The rapidity of his transitions from the most sparkling wit to the most touching pathos, his occasional gleams of the finest humor and fancy, and his delicate touches of observation, are all enhanced by a diction simple and refined, and presenting in almost every line some happy turn of expression or some graceful naiveté of sentiment.

THE END.